He scanned her face with a dark intensity, "Is that the way you feel about me?" She shook her head, and seeing his hand rise she instinctively moved, only to see him run his hand through his hair as was his habit when frustrated. "Please Rosie, tell me the truth. Am I wasting my time here?"

If she answered 'I don't know' David would find that as maddening as 'It not being that simple'. "I...It's..." Desperate to bring a truthful answer, she looked beyond him towards the baize door, praying for inspiration.

David turned to follow her gaze, and then asked in an exasperated voice, "What are you waiting for? Your stage prompter?" Before she could reply, David marched to the door, wrenched it open and in his loud, booming voice declared, "Do join us Hawkins, Miss Rosemary needs your help, even if it is only to see me out."

With a shriek, Cathy, who must have been leaning against the door to peer at him, stumbled forward into the hall. Rosie's hand leapt to her mouth.

David let out a "What the..." but his words and breath were cut off as he caught Cathy before she hit the stone floor. He groaned under Cathy's weight and grunted heavily as he attempted to draw her upright.

That fright barely over, Rosie jumped as Hawkins arrived to proclaim in a sonorous voice, "You called Sir!" In seeing the scene before him, he added tightly but with underlying amusement, "Excuse me Sir, but that's *my* wife."

A kind of hysteria uncurled within Rosie as she watched first David's astonishment, then embarrassment as he had steadied and righted the well-endowed Cathy back on her feet. Cathy with a naughty grin leant against him, "But Jack love, it's thirty years since I've fallen into a man's arms. And this one is young, agile, rugged and strong.

RUTH JOHNSON

ROSIE
The Heart's Desire Series

BOOK 4

EMANUEL PUBLISHING

First published in Great Britain in June 2019
Copyright © Ruth Johnson 2019

The right of Ruth M. Johnson to be identified as the author
of this work has been asserted by her in accordance with
the Copyright, Designs and Patents Act 1988

This novel is entirely a work of fiction.
The names, characters and incidents portrayed in it are the work of the
author's imagination.
Any resemblance to actual persons living or dead, events or localities is
entirely coincidental.

ISBN: 978-0-9554898-3-9

A catalogue for this book is available in the British Library
from July 2019

Biblical quotes are taken from:
NIV, RSV & AMP

Quotes from song lyrics
'Can't Live if Living is Without You' by Harry Nilsson
'Love Grows by Edison Lighthouse

Printed and bound by:
CPI Group (UK), Croydon, CR0 4YY

Published by Emanuel Publishing
www.emanuel-publishing.com
36 Kenmore Crescent, Bristol BS7 0TL

Copies of this series can be purchased from:
www.heartsdesireseries.com

DEDICATION

On 16th December, 2018
aged only 68

Paul Harding

went to be with the Lord
He had loved and served.

For many years he was a firemen risking his life for others. He didn't just talk about his faith, but walked in it, sharing his time and energy to bring inspiration, encouragement and comfort to all those who met him.

Unfortunately, he didn't live to see his name in print and discover he had been nicknamed 'Hardy' due to the series having another Paul involved in the same scene.

ACKNOWLEDGEMENTS

BRINGING THE BOOK TO BIRTH

Each book wouldn't be completed without Brian, my beloved, a man in a million who deserves a million thanks! He faithfully resolves my technical issues and deals with my melt downs when all seems lost. He converts the text into Kindle and prepares the book for the printer. And if that weren't enough he organises the database, prepares the websites and deals with the sales.

++++++

MY 'THANKS' FOR YOUR CONTRIBUTION:

RESEARCH:
Gillian Adams who shared her memories of living in India before World War II.

Paul Harding who from the description of the scene advised on the fire brigade's actions.

PROOF READING:
The hours they spent with each draft:
Laure Fabre
Chris Galliott
Graham & Lynne Weakley

ENCOURAGEMENTS:
From those who have read the series as it has evolved and been continually asking when the fourth novel would be written and released.

AND TO THE ONE AND ONLY LORD:
Who has inspired the series, creates the plots
And proves over and over the truth of His Word.

Trust in the Lord and do good;
Dwell in the land and enjoy safe pasture;
Delight yourself in the Lord and he will give you
the desires of your heart.
Commit your way to the Lord and
Trust in him and he will do it...
Psalm 37: 3-5

THE REINHARDT FAMILY

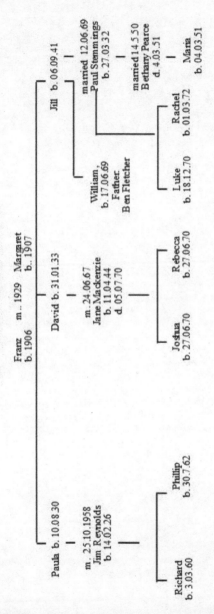

Franz b. 1906   m .. 1929   Margaret b.. 1907

Paula b. 10.08.30

m.. 25.10.1958
Jim Reynolds
b. 14.02.26

Richard b. 3.03.60

Phillip b. 30.7.62

David b. 31.01.33

m. 24.06.67
Jane Mackenzie
b. 11.04.44
d. 05.07.70

Joshua b. 27.06.70

Rebecca b. 27.06.70

Jill b. 06.09.41

married 12.06.69
Paul Stemmings
b. 27.03.32

William,
b. 17.06.69
Father
Ben Fletcher

Luke b. 18.12.70

Rachel b. 01.03.72

married 14.5.50
Bethany Pearce
d. 4.03.51

Maria b. 04.03.51

CHAPTER 1

Rosemary Doughty-Dawes stepped back into the house, closed the heavy wooden front door and leant back against it. She took a deep breath and tried to calm a plethora of emotions. Was she pleased or dismayed that David Reinhardt, the highly respected and austere Director of International Trade Promotions (ITP) had sought and found her?

A sudden shaft of sun pierced through the high circular glass dome above the dusty chandelier, causing colours of the rainbow to dance on the stone staircase and paved hall. Rainbows reminded Rosie of promises, in her experience spoken, broken and totally forgotten.

Life, like the many closed-up rooms in this dilapidated family mansion, proved to be less trouble if kept under wraps. There had been brief times of hope and opportunities but, as if on elastic, she found herself thrust back, shocked, bruised or badly hurt into this house with its painful childhood memories.

Nine years ago she had been grateful for the secretarial position working for Colonel Mike Reed, ITP's Public Relations Officer and for two years shared an office with him. Although ITP had rapidly expanded employing many young people, nothing had disturbed her uneventful life until Mike needed an assistant. Hope sparked to carve out a new career until Mike kindly explained it wasn't a woman's job, and added she would be sharing an office with his new assistant's secretary. In an attempt to cheer her, he had announced she would now be a Head of Department secretary which came with a salary rise and four weeks holiday a year. That news destroyed her excuse to her parents that she couldn't get time off to visit them in India.

Jane's arrival in the following March, her zest for life, cheeky confidence and religious zeal was so galling that she had tried to dampen Jane's enthusiasm with negative and spiteful remarks. To that strategy Jane appeared oblivious and her popularity increased which funnelled her loathing into malicious gossip.

Remembering that, Rosemary shuddered against the front door. One morning Mr Reinhardt, as she knew him then, had unexpectedly arrived in her office. His eyes with a cold assessing glint had steadily regarded her before succinctly warning her that besmirching another employee's character was a sackable offence. Stunned, she had stared at him but he had left as swiftly as he had arrived.

Attending the canteen Christmas Lunch, she had been scornful of David Reinhardt's entertaining speech and his being persuaded to kiss Jane. Later she had been publicly humiliated by him singling her out for the same treatment. Her instinct had been to run but surrounded, her whole body stiffened and she had snarled, "Don't touch me". But his playing to his audience meant she had no alternative than to take his outstretched hand. Led from the choir, fear began to eclipse her fury but before his mouth reached her lips he had murmured, "Forgive me" before succumbing her to an extended, but not unpleasant kiss. As their spectators clapped and cheered he had then taken her by the elbow and steered her into the annexe corridor towards her office. Fury then overcame fear which she vented telling him exactly the type of man she thought he was. Looking stunned he had swiftly departed.

Her dislike of Jane deepened when she was chosen over her to temporarily work for the Finance Director, and intensified when not long after Jane appeared to have inveigled herself into a permanent position in Mr Reinhardt's office. Again, despite her own qualifications, she had been overlooked and her antagonism was exacerbated at being left to work for both Mike and Paul until Jane's replacement was found.

Months later when it became known that Mr Reinhardt was engaged, she had commented "That'll put paid to any ambitions Jane had in that direction". That remark would have put paid to her ambitions of a promising career at ITP if Jane hadn't intervened. Summoned to Mr Reinhardt's office he introduced Jane as his fiancée, and with icy contempt informed her that ITP was terminating her employment. Unbidden tears had rolled down her face and she had sobbed her apologies to Jane, insisting that they talk alone. Tearfully she'd given her a brief insight into her life. Jane had explained her zest and joy came from her understanding that Jesus had died to take away man's sin. Seeing her puzzled expression, Jane described how she had asked Jesus to forgive her and then invited Him into her life as Lord and Saviour and every day experienced His love and peace.

14

It had been a straw of hope which she had grabbed. She kept her job, Jane befriended her and helped her believe that, as a Christian, the cyclical pattern of her life would change. When David needed a new personal assistant Jane had recommended her. Surprisingly he had agreed. This brought her to see that beyond the formidable stern authoritative figure, there was a generous fair-minded man. And during that time she had gained his respect by often doing more than asked in her efficient and quiet way.

Rosemary pushed away from the front door. Head down she considered the last hour. Today, no longer an employee, on her own territory, she had been invigorated rather than intimidated by her conversation with him. She stepped out of the vestibule into the hall and nearly collided with Hawkins carrying aloft the large silver tea tray. He came to an abrupt halt causing the clinking of china as he declared in the sonorous tone he adopted as a butler, "Ah, Miss Rosemary! It would seem our unexpected visitor came with a proposal."

Rosemary took a deep breath and stated, "You were listening at the door!"

At her pursed lips Hawkins gave a solemn nod, "I thought you might need my protection." Failing to disguise a wry smile he added, "I watched him leave."

Rosemary's hand touched the cheek David had kissed. In a soft childlike voice she asked, "Oh Hawkeye, what am I going to do?"

"I sense he's a man you could rely on." Hawkins' eyes glistened with emotion before he turned towards the table in the middle of the hall.

"Can I? Can I? My life has been woven in a fabric of lies. Any stitching together of people and happiness have either disintegrated or torn me apart." The pain in her voice turned to despair. "My father said he cursed the day I was born. My life reflects that."

The tray placed so firmly on the table caused the contents to rattle as Hawkins whipped around to scold, "Now Rosie, stop that." But perhaps guessing that life changing incidents were flashing through her mind his face filled with sadness. "Come here, my little love." How many times had his outstretched arms hugged and brought her comfort? She may no longer be little, but Jack and Cathy's unconditional love still brought her strength to carry on.

In November 1946, Jack and Cathy Hawkins had accompanied her and her mother from India to England. Although her mother, born in India, had returned for the obligatory English education, she had not known the Uncle who had made her the sole beneficiary of his estate. Harold had lost his wife to illness before the war, both his unmarried boys were killed during the war, and on returning to his conscripted property after the war it bore little resemblance to its former grandeur. The village solicitor reported his death certificate should have recorded 'heartbroken' rather than pneumonia.

In the freezing winter of 1947, with post war shortages and food rationing, she and her mother might have succumbed to pneumonia if the Hawkins hadn't stayed with them. Jack chopped down trees for firewood, they lived in the kitchen, stoking the ancient Aga for heat and cooking. They applied and received ration books but still had to eke out what the shops and the land provided. At six she didn't recognise the hardships but loved the Hawkins and remembered it as a happy time, before her father joined them eighteen months later.

Death duties and essential roof repairs claimed much of the money Uncle Harold had left, but it had been her father's extravagant lifestyle that had caused her mother to beg and then cry that he had made them paupers. Angry at the disgraceful state in which the house had been left, her father decreed the government should be forced to compensate them. When that money didn't materialise, he had sold the Home Farm to present a façade of wealth which he and invited guests enjoyed. To the Hawkins he had commanded, "Children should be seen and not heard. Keep her with you". How happy she had been with that edict and during her formative years, when not at school, she had been left in their care. The brighter West Wing needed greater refurbishment so she was given the large cold bedroom overlooking the front courtyard, while her parents and their friends slept in the less faded grandeur of the East Wing.

Years later, she had discovered how little the Hawkins were paid and asked why they stayed. Their answer was simple, Jack - as a motor engineer - could supplement their income with the occasional job and unable to have their own children, they had taken the opportunity to be 'adopted' as parents.

Now at thirty-one, too tall to bury her head into Hawkeye's

hard chest, she rested her head against his neck. In an age-old gesture Hawkins' hand stroked her hair. "Oh Rosie, my love, it'll take a while to get used to this short haircut." Rosemary drew back to see his beloved face haloed by white hair and lined by years of hard work in all weathers. "Your long hair did curtain and shadow your classical beauty." The skin around his warm brown eyes crinkled as he remarked, "That man was very taken with you!"

Rosemary stepped back, her voice firm. "David Reinhardt is not a man to be taken in by anything!"

Unperturbed, Hawkins grinned, "He certainly showed an interest in you and wasn't deterred to learn that you are the daughter of titled parents, and appeared entertained at you acting as lady of the manor. I would say he is a man who relishes a challenge."

Rosemary gave the enigmatic smile for which she was renowned. "And I'm a woman who has learnt to meet intimidation with silence and stopped unwanted attention with a haughty look or attitude, but when angry I will speak my mind."

Hawkins gave a derisive 'hum' before adding, "None of the former is recommended if you want to make friends and influence people."

"Unlike my father influencing people isn't something I desire to do."

Hawkins raised his eyebrows as he countered, "Whether you like it or not, young lady, you've interested and influenced David Reinhardt." Rosie gave him a sceptical look. "Although in thinking your parents were driving your great uncle's treasured but aged Bentley, he didn't seem keen to meet them."

Unable to hide her glee she exclaimed, "Really! David unsure of himself! That would be a first."

In his sonorous tone Hawkins pointed out, "Of course, I could be mistaken. His worry might not have been who was in the car, but that such a valuable vehicle might sustain damage from the potholes in the drive."

Ignoring the irony, she confessed, "A worry I shared." Her brow creased, "Why did I agree to drive it?"

Amused, Hawkins replied, "You wanted to please me!" At the increase of her frown he conceded, "Perhaps we did overdo your entrance." Returning to the table and tray he observed, "He couldn't miss the outer and inner decline of this place, but I didn't

17

want him thinking you were a failure." Rosie sent him a loving look. "I suspect having been left in the cold, damp and unheated library for forty-five minutes he felt this might come in useful." Her stiletto heels clattered across the stone floor to retrieve the cheque from his hand. He chortled, "Due to the thickness of the door it wasn't possible to catch every word." He mimicked her tone to repeat, "There's no reason for you to feel sorry for me. I don't want your money. I don't need a Reinhardt payoff."

Behind them, a slightly slurred voice repeated, "A payoff." Rosemary spun around. Helen, in scruffy nightclothes, had just emerged from the same corridor David had so recently walked. "The Reinhardts think giving money is showing they care. Take it, he can afford it."

Rosemary's voice rose sharply in David's defence, "They cared that Ben was worried how you and the baby would manage without him. They wanted to help you, but you neither thanked them nor used the money wisely." A snapshot of her London cottage after Helen had left it caused her to add, "And, when I was worried about you, David cared enough to help me clean up your mess and suggested we pack and store your things in his loft."

Helen hummed, as Hawkins declared, "Did he indeed?"

Rosemary glanced at the cheque in her hand and gasped, "Good heavens! Even considering the times I was up day and night looking after the twins, this is more than generous. I can't accept it."

"Don't be daft, you earnt it."

Hawkins ignoring Helen observed, "The Reinhardt family obviously values you. It's their way, as they did for Helen, to help you start a new life."

"That man is after something. Why didn't he post the cheque? Jill always wanted to know where and what you called 'home' was. It was a good excuse to find out."

Crossly Rosie retorted, "If they were that curious, they would have found out years ago."

"Jane instigated you living in the flat with us. I bet she told the Reinhardts to mind their own business."

There was truth in that but Rosie challenged, "David was concerned about you and concerned enough about me to want to talk about my abrupt departure."

Helen aimlessly ran a finger along the dust in the filigree of the iron balustrade of the stairs. "I liked Jane. I didn't think it would matter when Jill said her brother David owned the house and lived in the upstairs flat. He's strange! From the top of the basement stairs he would call in that pompous boom of his, 'I'm here, I'm coming down....' If no-one protested he would arrive, like today, uninvited."

Hawkins' obvious interest in Helen's observations encouraged her to continue. "Of course, it was Jane he came to see and once she'd married him he rarely visited. Jill would harp on that the women at ITP compared David to Jane Austin's Mr Darcy. Apparently when he smiles his grim features are so transformed they go weak at the knees. Have you experienced that Rosemary?" To hide her amusement Helen bent to write in the dust on the central table.

Irritated, Rosie spat out, "No I haven't."

Helen looked up to comment, "Rosie calls you Hawkeye but that's more fitting of David Reinhardt. Like you he pokes his nose into things that aren't his business." Oblivious to the narrowing of Hawkins' eyes, Helen rambled on. "He's got this way of lifting his square jaw and peering down his prominent nose before speaking to you. His cold, dark eyes seem to probe your soul." Her voice took an ominous tone, "And with that thick black hair he looks positively satanic."

Fiercely, Rosemary countered, "Oh, now you are being ridiculous."

Helen laughed, "Well he certainly cast his spell on Jane" and as she doodled in the table's dust she added, "She found him amusing." With a supercilious smile she glanced between them to observe, "But I guess she wasn't that besotted for she did get angry at his lack of thought or action, at that he always seemed dumbfounded. Just as I was dumbfounded, Rosie, when knowing about your spiteful comments about Jane you suddenly became her best friend, and bridesmaid at her wedding."

Hawkins raised a questioning eyebrow. Rosie grimaced. Helen continued, "Jane said you'd become a Christian. I couldn't see why that changed anything, so she then gave me her 'had the need to be 'born again' of God's Spirit sermon." Helen shrugged, "That's quite beyond me." Jill said Jane didn't like you living alone and insisted when Tania was told to go, that you should take her place in the flat." Rosie's eyes widened as she recalled Jane almost begging her to live there, believing she would be a steadying influence on Jill and Helen.

"This is Spode" Helen proclaimed waving a tea cup. "Have you got a whole set? It's valuable. And that silverware would fetch a bit." Hawkins visibly stiffened. Glancing around she remarked, "There must be other valuable stuff in this house you could sell to bolster the pittance you get paid as caretaker" and then as if realising his disapproval, she added, "Or make repairs to this place."

In a sonorous voice Hawkins pointed out, "We made the decision to live here. Sir Leonard and Lady Daphne have entrusted these things into our care and they are used when they have guests."

Immediately Helen challenged, "David Reinhardt wasn't one of their guests!" She gave a sardonic laugh, "But, of course, in wanting Rosemary to make a good impression, David Reinhardt might provide a way for you to feather your nest?"

Rosie opened her mouth to rebuke Helen but Hawkins with a contemptuous expression was already responding. "Young lady, let me inform you that whatever our circumstances we would never use people or things, to 'feather our nest'. And I would remind you, it is out of the goodness of Rosie's heart that you receive free board and lodging." Helen made a face, returned the cup to the tray and continued her dust etching. "This place might be dilapidated and Rosie's parents not here but as their representative if a guest arrives, we treat her as lady of the manor and their standards are to be kept." His stern face slipped into a grin, "I confess, Rosie, in introducing myself as the butler I forgot to ask who he was, as I burbled on about my being a Jack of all…."

"So this is where you are!" They turned as Cathy appeared from the green baize door under the second flight of stairs. Pointing to the tray she demanded, "Just who and what has been going on here?" Before Jack could answer Cathy declared, "Good heavens Rosie you look fabulous in that apricot suit. The colour brings a glow to your skin. With your figure and those high heels you could be a model. Very different to the dark clothes you've favoured all these years." Rosie opened her mouth to answer but Cathy had turned to admonish Helen. "You're still in your night clothes. Before I left I told you to get dressed." Helen looked vague and returned to draw in the dust. Tiredly, Cathy - nearly as broad as she was tall – sighed. Her short salt and pepper hair swayed as she nodded towards Helen, "We don't seem to be making much progress there."

Quietly Rosemary observed, "But she's better here than sleeping under the Hammersmith Flyover and stealing for her next fix."

Cathy with a sad expression slipped her arm through Helen's. "Come on luv. Let's have a nice cup of tea." Turning to them she decreed, "And the pair of you can tell me why, during my absence, you've seen fit to use the silver tea service and best crockery." Cathy's hand flew to her mouth, furtively she looked around and then whispered, "The Bentley is out. Don't tell me Rosie's parents have returned?"

Hawkins' mouth twitched with amusement as he answered, "Then I won't!"

Seeing Cathy's puzzled expression Rosie reassured her, "I had a visitor. I'll tell you once we're back in the warm."

Cathy's eyes narrowed, her finger wagged at Jack, "I'll deal with you later my man."

"Promises, promises" Hawkins muttered as she headed with Helen towards the baize door. Rosie grinned, she loved them and their banter. She proceeded to follow them into the corridor which formed the centre part of the 'H' shape of the house. A cold draft revealed the open door into the East Wing, beyond which she could see the formal dining room with its heavy dark Chippendale furniture. Behind her Hawkins confessed, "I was in a hurry and left it open. When I've washed and put back the china and silverware, I'll ensure that door is closed and the dining room secure." Did Hawkins think Helen might steal and sell the family heirlooms? Her father had tried that and failed.

Seven years ago her parents had exchanged life in this decrepit mansion, built on a plateau at the top of a hill with high and cold winds, for the 'high and comfortable life' of India. There, with the upsurge in tea drinking, their plantation was flourishing.

Rosie shivered but unlike the open aspect of the West Wing, the East one did have protection against the bitter winds from the tall evergreen trees lining the perimeter of the property. The East Wing looked over a formal rose garden which long ago had overgrown its paths because Jack's priority was the walled garden beyond the back courtyard. There Cathy diligently seeded, grew and produced fruit and vegetables which fed them throughout the year. In summer, in the original large old-fashioned kitchen, they would sort, clean, cook and bottle the crops in Kilner jars and store them on the shelves in the cold larder.

They had just passed that door when she stopped to ask Hawkins, "Do you think David wondered, as others have done, why we continue to live in this bleak, cold and damp twenty-two bedroom mansion?"

"You can double that if you count the large bedrooms the army partitioned off into smaller ones."

"Except, Jack, these days the majority of bedrooms on the second and attic floors should only be entered with extreme caution. It's not surprising with eighty people billeted here in the war that the fabric of the building became so damaged."

"The twenty-five years of neglect since we've been here certainly hasn't helped." Rosie nodded, as Hawkins still balancing the tray on one hand continued, "Despite the butler and housekeeper having the foresight in 1939 to ensure the valuable furniture, silverware and china were packed and stored in the basement, it's sad that Lord Dawes didn't live long enough after the war to restore and enjoy his home."

"And there is still the mystery of his art collection."

Hawkins shrugged, "With no monetary evidence of the paintings being sold, it's been accepted that they were stolen."

"And long before my father arrived so we can't blame him." Hawkins nodded and indicated she should move on. She stepped aside so he could pass and remarked, "My father hasn't had any luck selling this place but should that day come, or living here becomes untenable, I am still determined to sell my London cottage and find a reasonable size property where we can live together."

Hawkins turned to speak over his shoulder, "And David Reinhardt's proposal?"

Rosie shrugged, "Who knows! But whatever my decision it won't change me providing for you."

"When he knows how you've spent money to make the heart of this house warm, dry and cosy for us who live here, he's going to love you all the more."

"We may get to the 'when' but believe me, his 'loving' me doesn't enter into it any more than I him. It's his twins who love and need me."

Hawkins, with the tray still held aloft turned, "Believe me, any man seeing your love for his children would find his own heart responding toward you. You are one to give, not take, and in that it's hard to believe that you are your father's daughter."

"That's because I've grown up under the influence of you and Cathy."

Tears formed in Hawkins' eyes, "I heard your man saying his desire is to see you 'to blossom into all you were meant to be'."

His repeating David's words earned him a hard look before she declared, "He's not my man and that's not love."

"Isn't it?" Hawkins moved forward.

To his back she stated, "You and Cathy have always given me the courage to face the future, and today the confidence to behave as the lady of the manor. But working with David and living in his house has shown me life with him would be a constant challenge." Hawkins bent to turn the handle of the door at the end of the corridor while she added, "You and Cathy don't always agree but you are able to discuss, banter and laugh together. That's the kind of peaceful and loving relationship I would like."

Clearly embarrassed he protested, "Oh, get on with you!" as he entered the room and headed toward the line of modern kitchen units along the far wall of the refurbished servants' hall.

Cathy eyed them with suspicion, "You two have taken your time." Distracted by the boiling kettle whistle, she turned away as Hawkins lowered the tray by the double-stainless steel sink which was part of the 'L' shape unit under the window.

Surveying the scene Rosie observed, "David would have been more comfortable in here than in the fusty, dusty library."

Cathy, having poured the water into the teapot, whirled around. "David! David who? Is that why you are dressed up? You invited a man to take tea and didn't tell me?"

Rosie heard the underlying laughter in Hawkins voice as he stated, "It wasn't right on his first visit that he should be treated as a servant, and what he came to say was private."

"Except, it appears not so private since you were listening at the door."

Cathy glanced at them both. Arms akimbo, feet apart, she declared, "Would someone please tell me what's been going on?"

"Only if I deem it necessary!" Hawkins comment was aimed at Rosie but Cathy scowled at him.

Helen piped up from her seat at the table, "He came, as usual, uninvited!" Cathy glanced first at Helen, then Rosie before directing a frustrated gaze at Jack's back. As the sink filled with hot water, his eyes were focused on the window overlooking a similar sized courtyard to the one at the front of the house.

"Okay you three, you've had your fun." Cathy declared.

Hawkins appeared not to have heard Cathy's frustrated comment for wiping the silver tray he remarked, "It's fortunate the library is dark because despite my efforts there are still tarnished areas on this silverware."

"Right! They'll be no dinner tonight unless someone tells me what has been going on." With that Cathy gave a heavy sigh, picked up her cup of tea and moved towards the large overstuffed chair near the French window. Helen, at the far end of the room, muttered something she didn't catch.

Rosie poured herself a cup of tea and informed her, "David Reinhardt came to visit."

"No! Cathy's tea slurped down her jumper as she sat up to question, "How did he find you? What did he want?"

From her jacket pocket Rosie drew out the folded cheque and handed it to Cathy, "To give me this." Not wanting to cause more tea spillage she quickly added, "You'll see it's a substantial amount which I hope David decided upon before visiting."

In unbelief Cathy stared at the cheque, "This is more than we get in a year".

"Which highlights the pittance my father pays you for all you do here. And Jack, I doubt that David noticed the tarnished silverware, but considering the time he waited for a cup of tea, he probably thought we were still boiling water over an open fire!"

Jack chortled, picked up the cup of tea Rosie had poured him and joined her warming herself by the wood burner. "You forget I had to cajole you into wearing that suit, back the Bentley out of the garage, boil the kettle, retrieve the crockery and silverware from the dining room before I could make the tea. But I entered the library in perfect timing to see you driving the Bentley toward the house."

More tea slurped down Cathy's jumper as she exclaimed, "What! Rosie drove that valuable car up that potholed drive?"

At Cathy's horrified expression Rosie acknowledged, "I can barely believe it myself. I didn't have time to consider what would have happened if I'd damaged it."

Cathy fretting and mopping her tea spillages said fervently, "I suppose I should better thank God that you didn't."

Rosie smiled, "A good place to start."

Cathy grimaced as Hawkins admitted, "Any damage, I would have taken the blame, but it was a relief to see you and the car arrive safely."

Tears filled Rosie's eyes. "Oh Hawkeye!"

Helen added, "And thanks to me and the suit you look stunning."

"I was surprised how well it fitted considering, Helen, that you are shorter and thinner than me."

"Oh it wasn't mine. Ginger hair with apricot, ugh! It was left behind after a fashion show. I thought to sell it. Then the office made a big hue and cry about its disappearance…"

Rosie only just avoided slurping her tea over the pencil slim skirt as she exclaimed, "I'm wearing stolen clothing?"

Unperturbed, Helen replied, "It was five years ago. Still, it's a designer outfit, so wouldn't advise wearing it in London."

"Rosie is good at copying designer outfits. She could have made it."

Rosie ignored Cathy's remark to berate Helen and then questioned, "Have you stolen other things?"

Helen's head drooped, her voice childish as she confessed, "Only things no-one else wanted." bringing Rosie to consider if helping Helen had been a wise decision.

Hawkins scowled and murmured to Cathy, "Better check the house."

"I heard that." Helen challenged, "You don't like me, do you?"

Hawkins stiffened to declare, "I don't like or dislike you, but your behaviour needs improvement."

Crossly, Cathy exhorted, "Oh don't get into that! Jack what was your impression of David Reinhardt?"

Helen scowled. Jack refocused, "A professional man in his late thirties, tall, well built, heavy featured, well spoken with a pleasant attitude. I would say astute and with a sense of humour. He thought I was Rosie's father and tried to disguise his surprise at hearing Rosie had titled parents. I'd say a man able to rise to any occasion, and one you could trust in a crisis."

"Wouldn't be my description," Helen said tartly.

Hawkins replied stiffly, "Your opinion hasn't been called for."

"Jack's right! When you were attacked and lay unconscious David stepped in, didn't ask questions, did what was necessary, and removed Jane and I from the scene."

"When you told us about that, I don't remember you mentioning David's intervention."

"I suppose Cathy, I didn't think it important. But I did tell you when he intervened in my work crisis, Mavis, his secretary said the way he dealt with Robert was awesome. And he did apologise to me for not dealing with it earlier."

Cathy frowned, "He also apologised for wrongly accusing you over the twins' accident, yet you didn't feel able to stay after that."

Blinking back the tears Rosie explained, "After relaxing with him and his family at Christmas, I was devastated by his anger and lack of consideration for how I might feel."

"It would seem though since you left he's been considering how you might feel. It surely took tenacity to find you and courage to express how he felt about you. This gift surely shows how much he and his family regard you?"

Rosie grunted. Jack informed Cathy, "Rosie's reaction on seeing his car coming up the drive was to tell him she was out. I told her if I say that then she should better be out."

Grimly Rosie interjected, "And thanks to Helen pointing out David might ask if he could await my return, Jack thought to suggest that he could!"

"As butler it's my job to appear hospitable." Through pursed lips Rosie gave a negative 'hum'. "I didn't know he would accept. And it wasn't until he was installed in the library, it occurred to me that Rosie would have to leave to arrive. So she might as well do so in style by driving the Bentley from the back of the house to the front."

"Were you out of your mind?"

Helen informed her, "Jack told Rosie if David Reinhardt had taken the trouble to find her, the least she could do was to listen to what he had to say. It was then that I discovered he'd been snooping through my things." All eyes went to Jack who looked unusually sheepish. "He said he'd seen an apricot suit in one of my boxes and asked if Rosie could try it on."

"Not Jack's idea, mine. When Rosie had your boxes delivered I asked him to check for…"

Rosie interjected, "Jack just gawped when he saw me in that

suit. He told me I looked like the lady of the manor and that I should act as such and take command of the situation. I didn't feel in command by being frogged marched to the car and was near to tears when I kept stalling the engine."

"Good grief Jack!"

Tears again filled Rosie's eyes. "If you, my beloved Hawkeye, hadn't kept telling me how much you loved me, that I could do it and to do it for you, I would have given up."

"And my little love you drove the Bentley and brought it safely home."

"True, I prayed, drove slowly, waited until the road was clear for both the right turn onto the main road and into the drive. It would have been so easy to scrape the paint between those two gateposts. My worst fear was a wheel falling into one of the drive's potholes. Thank God it didn't."

"Your father may see that rare vintage car as his pension fund, but I'd say smoking and drink will kill him before he sells it." Hawkins continued, "David appeared anxious as the Bentley slowly approached. He either thought Rosie's parents were arriving or knew the Bentley's value and the danger of the potholed drive. When Rosie stepped out of the car his eyes widened." Jack chortled, "Fortunately he didn't turn when asking if you had a twin sister. I had such an urge to laugh I left without answering."

Cathy looked across at Rosie, "We noticed how happy you seemed after spending Christmas with the Reinhardt family. I can understand that being the only mother the twins have known, it would be difficult for you and the twins if and when David married again. If David is astute as you say, he must realise that. So why did he come all this way to give you a cheque?"

Helen muttered, "I've already asked that question."

"Ask Jack, his ear was to the door most of the time."

Unrepentant, Hawkins grinned and Cathy sent him an amused look. "I would rather you told me."

"The cheque was a gift from the family. And as I'm no longer employed by him, he felt it simplified things."

Cathy frowned and Helen remarked, "Use that money to get decent heating in for your bedroom, it's as cold in there at night as on the street."

Hawkins murmured, "And she would know!"

Both Rose and Cathy exclaimed, "Jack!"

Helen shrugged, "It's alright, because I love that little room you turned out for me. It's quickly warmed and very cosy." Rosie stifled a grin for Hawkins didn't like Helen sleeping in her room. He wanted to keep an eye on her in a small servant's bedroom closer to them at the back of the house.

Jack gave Helen a brief nod and cautioned, "Rosie, when your father finds a purchaser for this place, he'll not consider us. So don't buy anything that you can't take with you."

Frustrated Cathy interrupted, "What did David mean, 'simplify things'?"

"It left him able to speak his mind!"

Rosie drank her tea as Cathy prompted, "And…"

Guessing Cathy's reaction, she said slowly, "He wants me to be the only mother the twins will ever know. He asked me to marry him." Cathy gave a loud squeal of delight and leapt up to hug her.

At that Helen scoffed, "You! He wants to marry you!" Rosie flinched, causing Helen to clarify her derogatory tone, "Oh, I don't mean that unkindly, but you are very different to Jane."

"True. 'I'm not Jane and I'm not in love with David. I love the twins but marriage is for life…"

Helen interjected, "You've more in common with him than Jane."

Cathy asked, "Could you love him? Does he love you?"

"I asked him that. His answer: 'love takes many forms.' In seeing my reticence to accept he…"

"Your what?" Incensed, Helen said, "If you love his kids, grab the opportunity."

"He suggested a six month courtship."

"Good grief, you've worked at ITP for years. At least two of those working as his personal assistant and the last two looking after his babies. And, in sharing his basement flat, for all intents and purposes you have been living with him!" Rosie cringed and considered that it was exactly the connotation she had wish to avoid.

Helen now on a roll, informed the Hawkins about David, buying a bombed-out property off High Street Kensington and over the years extending and restoring it. "It's huge, selling that now he'd make a handsome profit. Rosie didn't you say Jill, her husband and three kids were planning to leave the basement flat and live in Kent." Rosie nodded. "So if you married him you could all leave this place and live there."

Cathy's questioning gaze at Jack caused Rosie to realise that despite her promises, they did worry about their future.

"David would easily find you two employment and by renting his basement flat, you could leave this place to rot."

"Oh Helen, you make it sound so simple." Not wanting to discuss it further Rosie stood. "I'm going to change. Cathy, I'll prepare the vegetables later. And Hawkeye, I'll leave you to tell Cathy the details of David's proposal, and consider if marriage was made for love of a man, or for what he was offering?" At the door Rosie turned, "Helen, your parents, after your troubles, disowned you as have mine. I'll not disown Jack and Cathy whatever choices I make in the future. I brought you here to benefit from their love and care, but you need to get dressed each day and help around the place."

For once Helen didn't scowl, and as Rosie reached the top step of the back stairs Helen called, and ran up towards her. "I know you've had your troubles. Oh, don't look so worried! Jack and Cathy's lips are firmly sealed where you're concerned. But when you offered me comfort and support about the baby… well… I'd an inkling that something similar happened to you." Rosie didn't comment. "I've always seen David as a rich toft with an arrogant and standoffish manner. As Jane would say, 'He's not in my league'. But David didn't see Jane that way and she came to adore him. You are definitely in his league. I might not like him but he is a good man. Give him a chance. Jane didn't have a sister, she thought of you as one, I know she would approve."

"Thank you." Tears pricked the back of Rosemary's eyes. In an uncharacteristic gesture she hugged Helen, who once released, scuttled away to her room at the back of the house.

CHAPTER 2

Slowly strolling along the corridor, Rosie considered the extraordinary events of the last two hours. Stepping into her bedroom she had to agree with Helen, as even in April it was bitterly cold despite being flanked by the two wings of the house. Her electric fire barely took off the chill. She pulled the eiderdown from her four-poster canopied bed and wrapped it around her before surveying the incredible view from the window.

From her elevated position, the trees that bordered the East Wing of the house gave way to fields, in which an envisaged bypass around Petersfield might one day cut through. In the distance was Home Farm where her father had evicted the tenant farmer and his family, and made what he termed a 'killing' profit. Rosie sighed heavily. He had no concern that such an act had 'killed' off the goodwill and friendship of the local people. With the town's expansion that was long forgotten, but then, as a child at school, she had borne the brunt of it. Her classmates either ignored her or called her names. The only exception was Johnny who became her 'special' friend. At eight, her father had despatched her to boarding school with no opportunity to say 'goodbye' to Johnny. She thought her heart would break and cried herself to sleep for weeks. When old enough to seek him out, he had left the neighbourhood.

On her left, the tree lined drive gradually inclined towards the house. It then turned towards the West Wing, passing the library windows, into the courtyard and up to the front door below her window. It wasn't obvious - but possible - to drive around the East Wing to the large garage where the converted stables adjoined the end of the 'H' shape of the house. Beyond the courtyard with its central fountain, a wide grassy bank ending with a ha-ha separated the house from the fields rented by the farmer for his sheep to roam. The drive followed the base of a hill which blocked her view of the lake beyond. As the north wind whistled through the window frames, she considered the two flats in David's house. They were both luxuriously appointed and with central heating. The Hawkins were used to space, David's basement flat could be either considered cosy or claustrophobic, and his walled garden was smaller than Cathy's strawberry patch.

It was nine years since she had returned here, jobless, friendless and ill. She took a deep breath as she remembered the disdain on her father's face and the way he had tweaked the ends of his handlebar moustache while telling her she had brought disgrace to the family name. He then announced they were returning to India to avoid further embarrassment. Jack - probably by listening at doors - later informed her that the tea plantation her father had acquired before the partition of India in 1947, was again producing tea. In fact, it was the prime reason for her parents to leave behind their British responsibilities and return to their comfortable lifestyle, surrounded by old colonial friends and servants. Why did her father always find a reason to blame her to bring about his wishes? He often called her 'a selfish brat' and she guessed that his parents must have referred to him as that.

Her parents had briefly returned in 1965 to take further items back to India, surprising her with an invitation to visit them at Christmas. After her visit she had not seen them until four years ago when, having determined never to return, they arrived to pack tea chests for despatch to India. It was then she had felt to challenge her father about the frugality of the Hawkins' lives. He looked just like Lord Kitchener on his war poster as he stiffened and pointed his finger saying 'We don't need them!' Angry, she reminded him of what they did, to which he retorted 'They chose to stay. They have a free roof over their heads and can live off the land'. With that he had spun around and marched off, leaving her mother to clatter after him in her high heels, calling 'Leo, Rosemary didn't mean any harm'. Within days Leo callously announced to the Hawkins that he had put the house up for sale and arranged for experts to come in to value and sell the contents. He added that he was keeping the Bentley as collateral. For what, they had no idea!

Jack had cautioned her not to spend her 'hard earned money' on refurbishing the servants' quarters. But she had! She had a log burner put in and extended its heating to their bedroom above and nearby bathroom which backed onto the one she used, opposite her bedroom. That was the extent of the burner capacity and her savings.

Now shivering, she jumped up and pulled open the door of the enormous wardrobe which she had never felt inclined to fill. She took out a well-worn pair of thick trousers and her old fur lined boot slippers. From the large drawer beneath, she selected one of the warm jumpers Cathy had knitted her. As she began to undress, memories of the Hawkins' love and encouragement flooded in.

Seven years ago, they had nursed her back to health and out of the slough of despair into which she had fallen. Jack cut up wood to burn in her bedroom fireplace and Cathy tempted her to eat by bringing her tasty morsels of food. Together they had tried to interest her back in life. It was Cathy's suggestion to refurbish her bedroom that finally stirred her into walking a little further each day to choose furniture from the other rooms, to replace the battered pieces she had been given.

In the early days, it was Jack who had persuaded her father to house his guests in the less worn East Wing bedrooms. So when her father had thought to commandeer her four-poster bed, Jack declared he did not have the skills to dismantle and move it. She had gloated over that small victory. It was also Jack who, having seen the need to protect them against drunken marauders, organised several able-bodied men to move a very heavy combination wardrobe across the upper stairs and entrance to the West Wing.

The Hawkins were a treasure her father didn't appreciate. Be it cloth, wool, gardening or cooking, Cathy could make much out of little, while Jack would find and refurbish useful items that cost next to nothing. The most useful was perhaps the table that opened up to reveal a sewing machine. When her legs were long and strong enough to rock the foot pedal to turn the big wheel that made the needle go up and down, she started to make all kinds of things. Later, while refurbishing her room, she used the fading and thin fabric from the chairs as a pattern to cut out the new material. That's when she got the idea of copying designer clothes.

She smiled, remembering Jack's homemade scaffolding that had enabled them to paint the high ceiling and walls of her bedroom. Transforming the dark, dingy green paint and wallpaper into this warm yellow had been hard work, but well worth it, and the exercise was the final stage of her recuperation. Once she was earning money, she replaced the faded threadbare brocade curtains around her bed, making them double-sided dark green velvet. As a child she loved pulling the curtains to make her bed like an exotic tent. It didn't just keep out drafts but was her place of refuge, to run, hide and weep.

These past days, she had done much of that. But despite the void and ache that was so difficult to assuage, it had been right to leave the two toddlers Jane had birthed nearly two years ago. It would have been far worse for them to lose her once older.

The moment she had set eyes on them, her heart defences were shaken then demolished. First, by their need and dependence, then by their cute ways and adoring love. Their acceptance - and that of the Reinhardt family - had begun to remove the barriers she erected around her life. But just as she began finding a new freedom and happiness, history repeated itself. This time, not her father's false accusations, but David Reinhardt's angry words. They ripped through her, tearing apart her growing sense of trust and contentment. When he calmed down and learned the truth, he apologised profusely for his unreasonable behaviour and tried to make amends. Nevertheless, she felt irrevocable damage had been done and her role as nanny was now untenable.

David's unexpected appearance today had not only been unsettling, but his marriage proposal disconcerting. The only reason to take up his offer of a 'marriage of convenience' would be because she would be the twins' official mother. Was that enough? She didn't dislike David and enjoyed being with his wider family, but could she live with him? More importantly, was this God's plan for her?

While considering these things, she hung Helen's suit in the wardrobe, absentmindedly tiding and dusting the room. With a grunt she realised one thing she and David had in common was the belief everything had a place and should be kept in it! Unlike Jill - his sister - who David quoted his father as saying, 'Without Rosie they were reverting into chaos'.

She thought back to Valentine's Day. David had sent her two dozen red roses with a card expressing his and the twins' appreciation. That evening, he gave her a record that had just topped the charts. She hummed it considering again the words, '*I can't forget this evening, your face as you were leaving.... but in your eyes your sorrow shows... I can't live if living is without you. I can't give any more.*' She didn't doubt their need and there was truth in David's words. In offering marriage, he skirted around love by saying it came in different forms.

Similar to her father, David had a booming voice and verged on being pedantic. Yet, marriage to Jane had changed him, as the twins' birth and Jane's untimely death. He handled the twins so gently, his voice always quiet and kind. On the occasions when he had spoken to her in a similar tone, it had brought on an onslaught of anxiety which she disguised by becoming distant. From an early age, when feeling afraid, she had learnt to shut down any comment or opinion in the hope of becoming invisible. Yet she knew in making succinct answers people often thought she was aloof.

On the nights when she had helped with the twins' bottle feeding, she had at first been embarrassed at seeing David in his pyjamas, hair ruffled, tired and vulnerable, but that had been quickly replaced by compassion. Maybe this is why last Christmas, staying with his family, she had agreed to David's plea to perform a parody of togetherness to ward off Felicity, his ex-fiancée. She had enjoyed the novelty of flirting, but her mind vied between that and the worry that like Doug Bradford he would take it further.

When David arrived at ITP, despite being often away travelling around the world's exhibition centres, he had quickly become a person of interest. Men spoke of his business acumen, women talked of his sex appeal. She had been incensed when he barely acknowledged her but addressed Jane by name and winked at her. No-one then could have foreseen that she, Rosemary Dawes, would be asked by David Reinhardt to be his wife. And he seemed to have concluded Jane would have wished her to be the mother of their children. There were plenty of single women at church who obviously desired to gain his and the twins' attention.

Rosie, crossing her hands across her chest, rubbed her upper arms. If she agreed to a courtship with David, she would have to tell him about her past. Could she face his rejection? Jane hadn't rejected her, she had befriended her, and even when she failed to be that steadying influence on Jill and Helen, Jane hadn't seen it that way. Despite both Helen's and Jill's foolish behaviour and shattered dreams, she had tried to help them as Jane had done for her.

Jane's sudden death was a bitter blow, and added weight to her belief that those she loved, she lost, one way or another.

A gust of wind rattled the window shutter. She shivered and cringed, for living in the flat below Jane and David she had heard their arguments. However, when it went quiet she guessed love and sexual compatibility cemented them back together. A 'marriage of convenience' wouldn't have those elements.

Gazing up at the sky, she wondered if Jane was still rooting for her in heaven. Missing her long thick hair, she drew the rolled sweater neck around her ears and almost heard Jane saying, 'Oh Rosie, let go, let life and God direct your steps'. With a hum, she closed the wooden shutters over the nearest window and murmured upwards, "Well, God, it's over to You" and moved to the second window. On reaching for the shutters she glanced out, her eyes widened, her hands as if in prayer flew around her nose and mouth. She gasped "Oh no!" In alarm she slammed the shutters shut and dashed downstairs to Jack and Cathy.

Bursting through the kitchen door she proclaimed, "David's coming."

"We've 'done' that today." Jack chortled.

"No! Now! Up the drive!" Dread clawed at her stomach. Agitated, she questioned, "What shall we do?"

Calmly Hawkeye answered, "When the bell rings I usually open the door."

Exasperated, Rosemary clicked her tongue, "David said every step would be taken at my pace, so why is he back so soon? Jack, I'm not going to see him."

Cathy pushed the large casserole dish back into the oven, shut the door and chided, "It's unlike you to panic." And then she jumped as the doorbell clanged like a belfry clock on the hour. Folding her arms against her amble bosom she decreed, "Jack, open the door before he deafens us."

As Jack hurried along the servants' corridor, Cathy hustled her out after him and from behind confessed, "Jack reported David felt his children had opened his eyes to see the real Rosie. He hoped in giving you the family you so deserve, he might become the desire of your heart." Rosie turned to scowl at her. Cathy chivvied, "Hurry up I want to take a look at this man."

"Surely you don't intend to spy on him."

"Why not?" Cathy giggled like a young girl.

Rosie groaned and proclaimed, "You can, I'm not. She stopped short of the baize door leading into the hall.

Cathy pushed past her as Hawkins shot back the bolts on the front door. The hinges creaked loudly as he slowly opened it.

"Oh Sir! I didn't expect you to be back so soon." Hawkins sonorous butler voice had an unmistakable smile. "Are these flowers for Miss Rosemary."

Cathy, standing by the open baize door, smiled at her. Rosie responded with a cynical grunt.

"Did you wish Sir, to give them to her yourself, or shall I take them from you?" At Hawkins temerity Rosemary seethed, and when he added, "In which case Sir, I'd advise with the cold wind you come in," she felt like throttling him. Rosie grabbed Cathy and pulled her back behind the baize door. It shut just as Hawkins announced, "If you'd like to wait here Sir, I'll see if Miss Rosemary is able to receive you."

David's voice boomed around the stone walls to broadcast "I don't wish to intrude. The shop in Petersfield said I was too late for today's delivery. As I had to pass here on my way back to

35

London, I decided to drop them in."

"Well Sir, I'm sure Miss Rosemary will appreciate them. I'll see if I can locate her." Rosie, worried Hawkins would expose them by opening the baize door, indicated Cathy to move away from it. When he didn't appear Cathy crept forward, bent over and looked through the peephole Rosie, as a child, had gouged in order to spy on her parents and their friends. Today at 5ft 8ins she would have to kneel to peer through it! It reminded her that earlier she was wearing five-inch stiletto heels. Her eyes then on a level with David's had given her confidence to address him as equals. Now, her feet encased in flat sheepskin slipper boots and sloppily dressed, she felt at a distinct disadvantage.

With an eye fixed to the spy hole, Cathy spoke in a loud whisper. "Your man is coming into view. My, even in slacks and jacket he's a smart dresser." Rosemary shushed her. Cathy grinned up at her, "He can't hear me." She continued commentating, "He's pacing up and down. Could be nerves! I wish he'd stop moving about, I want a better view. That's better he's come closer! He's standing by the table. I'd say more eagle than hawk, and attractive in a rugged and sexual way." Cathy glanced at her, and undeterred by her peeved expression reported, "He's taking an interest in the table, and bending around the huge bouquet he's carrying, it looks as if he's reading something."

Rosie whispered, "Helen doodled something in the dust."

"Whatever it is, he is not amused! He's scowling and looking around. My, when crossed he looks intimidating. I'd guess he's weighing up whether to leave."

Rosie jumped as Hawkins lightly touched her arm. Despite the closed baize door deadening the sound on both sides, Hawkins put a finger to his lips before beckoning her to follow him. In recounting Cathy's most recent observation Hawkins determined, "You must speak to him. You can't have him walking out annoyed."

"I'm not dressed to…"

"Whatever Helen wrote on that table, don't let it or her, mess up your life. She's right to say, 'Grab this man. He's offering you so much more than the twins."

"I know, but Hawkeye, I'm scared… I don't know… you know what happens when…"

Hawkins, putting his arm through hers, drew her across the servants' hall to the far door. Leading her past the back stairs he said quietly but firmly, "If you can't trust me, believe in God and let Him guide you." With a gentle push in the direction of the library he instructed, "Go!" Surprised at Hawkins words she obeyed, but without her long hair to hide behind, or clothes to boost her confidence, apprehension churned her stomach. Along the corridor to the hall she reminded herself that despite David's challenging nature, he could be pleasant and he had a sense of humour, but that didn't stop her steeling herself to remain aloof.

Her first glance took in the hall table on which lay a large bouquet of flowers. Her second went to the vestibule where David appeared to be contemplating the bolts on the front door. She stopped, told herself to lift up her head, and speak with confident surprise. "David? Are you leaving? Hawkins told me you wanted to see me." He turned towards her and with his mouth set in a grim line looked her up and down, but he seemed more upset than angry. With a glance towards the central table where the flowers rested, she asked, "Are those for me?" At his curt nod, she gave a small smile, and hoped her 'thank you' sounded sincere. He followed her as she walked over to pick them up. "Roses, how lovely!" Her eyes scanned the table to see what he read, but the flowers laying on it had dispersed the dust. She straightened up, faced him and apologised, "I wasn't expecting you. Forgive me for not being dressed to receive visitors." The cool assessing glint in his eyes made her feel uncomfortable. She bent her head into the bouquet to sniff the roses scent. She could feel his contemplative stare as she desperately tried to think of something to say. With a shy smile she looked up to say quietly, "I thought by now you would be on your way back to London."

"Rosie, I know the genuine from the play acting. I can stand just so much, but I won't be taken for a fool?"

What had Helen written on that table? Her brow creased as she cautiously asked, "Why would you say that?"

"You put up a façade and now this charade. When people ask questions you deflect them. When they try to get close, you become evasive. And now it seems you are reinventing yourself. What are you hiding from? You can change your hair, your clothes, your demeanour, but believe me, if you don't let go of the past it will remain your future." Anxious at what his investigations might have uncovered, she determined to look puzzled and asked, "I don't know what you mean."

"I'm talking about secrecy and silence."

With a sideways glance toward where Cathy lurked behind the door, she nervously clasped the roses and confessed, "It's not that simple." At his irritated expression she felt annoyed, straightened her back and determined to speak her mind : "A few hours ago you asked to marry me. I replied, 'you don't know me'. You appeared unconcerned by that. I thought it unwise. You suggested a six month courtship. I agreed to consider it. Any play acting was done at Christmas, at your request for Felicity's benefit. My having to adjust to life's problems isn't. I'm frugal with the truth because silence is safer." She stared into his dark, penetrating gaze, and hoped he would hear the sincerity in her voice. "It's never been my intention to deceive, or make a fool out of you."

In a brusque tone he accused, "What about leading us to believe you couldn't drive, when you so obviously can?"

"I didn't say I couldn't drive, I just didn't want to." She made a sad grimace and gave her attention to the flowers. When he said nothing, she lifted her chin, met his cynical expression and explained. "One evening in London my car wouldn't start, what appeared to be a passer-by offered to help. I was attacked and..." she hesitated, looking for the right words, "they robbed me of something precious."

Anger blazed in David's eyes as he boomed, "When was this? What did the police say? Were you able to identify the person?" She tried not to take the sharp enquiry as distrust, but concern. She swallowed hard trying to stop the tears prickling at the back of her eyes. When she failed to answer, he added with less vehemence, "You can't live life in fear."

On a sigh she stated, "David, it's not that simple."

The grim line of his mouth tightened before in a flinty tone he observed, "That sounds evasive to me."

"David, I thought this courtship was to be at my pace. Is this the way it's going to be? You coming here and haranguing me?" She raised her eyebrows and stated, "If you want my trust, the present prognosis isn't good!" With a brief grimace and a glance towards the baize door, she directed at him a questioning gaze.

David's grim expression relaxed. He stepped forward, she stepped backward. He gave a heavy sigh. "I'm sorry! I didn't return with the intention to pressurize or accuse you. I left believing you were considering my proposal. Afterwards I realized either by oversight, or design, you hadn't given me your telephone number. When the florist wasn't able to deliver the flowers, it was a good excuse to find out". David stared into her eyes as though to fathom the depths of her mind.

As the words 'It's not that simple' were unacceptable, she was at a loss as how to answer. After a quiet sigh he continued, "My proposal isn't just only about a mother for the twins, but because we all care about you. Please, read the card with the flowers."

Carefully drawing the card out, Rosie's mind flew back five years, when Jane received a huge bouquet from an anonymous sender. How jealous and rude she had been at the simple rhyme on the card! David seemed to feel flowers were a good precursor to saying 'sorry'! Rosie, having extracted the card, laid the large and colourful selection of tight and full roses on the table. She glanced up and caught the tension in his face before she read, "*Roses come in many shapes, colours and sizes, but you are the only Rosie for me. Sincerely David.*"

She looked towards the baize door knowing Jack and Cathy desired her to accept that. Could it be that simple? Or would it be a path fraught with disagreements and misunderstandings affecting more lives than hers?

It was impossible to deny the desolation in his eyes as he said, "I lost Jane, and wanted to believe that one day you might open up your heart to me, as you have to the twins." This wasn't David Reinhardt the hard-nosed business man, or the confident father of two, but a man who had loved and lost, revealing his helplessness and desperation for that not to happen again. Not knowing how to respond to such unexpected vulnerability she said nothing. With a sad smile of self-depreciation, he continued, "I'd hoped... but your silence and my reading 'David, Darcy, Devil' written in the dust of that table, I guess I have my answer."

At the pain in his voice, she briefly closed her eyes. On opening them, she discovered he had stepped closer. This time she resisted the urge to step back. He scanned her face with a dark intensity, "Is that the way you feel about me?" She shook her head, and seeing his hand rise she instinctively moved, only to see him run his hand through his hair as was his habit when frustrated. "Please Rosie, tell me the truth. Am I wasting my time here?"

If she answered, 'I don't know' David would find that as maddening as 'It not being that simple'. "I...It's..." Desperate, to bring a truthful answer, she looked beyond him towards the baize door, praying for inspiration.

David turned to follow her gaze, and then asked in an exasperated voice, "What are you waiting for? Your stage prompter?" Before she could reply, David marched to the door, wrenched it open and in his loud, booming voice declared, "Do join us Hawkins, Miss Rosemary needs your help, even if it is only

39

to see me out."

With a shriek, Cathy, who must have been leaning against the door to peer at him, stumbled forward into the hall.

Rosie's hand leapt to her mouth.

David let out a "What the…" but his words and breath were cut off as he caught Cathy before she hit the stone floor. He groaned under Cathy's weight and grunted heavily as he attempted to draw her upright.

That fright barely over, Rosie jumped as Hawkins arrived to proclaim in a sonorous voice, "You called Sir!" In seeing the scene before him, he added tightly but with underlying amusement, "Excuse me Sir, but that's *my* wife."

A kind of hysteria uncurled within Rosie as she watched first David's astonishment, then embarrassment as he had steadied and righted the well-endowed Cathy back on her feet. Cathy with a naughty grin leant against him. "But Jack love, it's thirty years since I've fallen into a man's arms. And this one is young, agile, rugged and strong."

Hawkins having stepped further into the arena, retorted fondly, "That maybe so my dear, but as this man has chosen Rosie for his wife, I rather think it should be she in his arms, not you!"

At the bizarre scene Rosie didn't know what to think, let alone do, but laughter was bubbling up. Cathy, unintentionally had turned a tense situation into a farce, and was now so creased up that she was holding on to David's arm for support. Bemused, David looked down on the plump, middle-aged, irrepressible, hysterically giggling Cathy.

Hawkins, in an attempt to keep equilibrium, returned to the sonorous voice of butler to suggest, "Now Sir, as it seems you and my wife have become acquainted, perhaps you would care to join us for dinner?"

Rosie's rising mirth was immediately squashed by Hawkins' presumption. With questioning eyes, she stared at him. It was surely too soon… it would mean… had he not thought? To deflect the invitation, she turned as if amused, "I'm sorry David, it seems the servants have taken leave of their senses."

To which Hawkins intoned, "Believe me Sir, with so rarely having the need to stand on ceremony please forgive us if, in our roles, we have become somewhat tardy about our station in life."

Bewildered, David glanced between them as Hawkins moved toward him his hand outstretched. "As I said, on your earlier visit, I'm Jack and…" David's eyes rounded, Jack stopped speaking and turned to see what he was seeing.

Dressed in tight, multi-coloured flowered trousers, a bright yellow jumper that appeared to be unravelling from the neck, and red curls overflowing from a lime green bandanna with yellow sequins, a thin pale waif demanded, "What's going on?" Her eyes were focussed on David, and contempt was evident in her voice. "Oh, it's you!"

Astonished David murmured. "Helen?"

Gleefully she agreed, "Yep, it's me. I ain't a ghost, though you probably thought me dead. Just as I'd have never thought to see you at fusty, dusty, musty, Munster Manor."

Rosie managed to say, 'Helen' in a reproving tone.

At five years old she had never heard of ghosts but had been terrified at entering such a large house with such a morbid façade and unkept exterior. And had cried out when the thick wooden door closed behind them and the sound had reverberated around the stone walls and floor. And once inside, the faded wallpaper, scuffed paintwork, worn out carpets and big old fashioned furniture had seemed imbedded with echoes of past voices, ready to transmit disappointment, pain and grief into the lives of those who lived here.

In the midst of her recollections, Hawkins had grabbed a chair for Cathy who in throes of laughter was sagging against David. As David lowered Cathy on to it Hawkins informed him with obvious amusement, "Fortunately Sir, I don't need a bolt to keep my head on my shoulders. Though I'm glad you didn't arrive after dark when I need an oil lamp to light the way to the front door. I'm afraid vermin in the roof have chewed through the electricity cable."

Straightening, David looked around. "It must be difficult to look after such a large place." With a wry smile he added, "It was kind of you to invite me for dinner, but I need to be back in London by nine o'clock. Jane's parents are looking after the twins and need to get a train home. With traffic it took me two hours to reach here."

Hawkins glanced up beyond the chandelier to the glass dome at the sky before assuring David, "Oh, you'll have time to eat Sir. The catch of the day has long since been prepared and is in the oven." David's eyes had followed Jack's thoughtful gaze, causing Rosie to think he might be wondering about the 'catch of the day'! She glanced across at Hawkins, by his amused expression she could see he had the same thought. Suddenly an unbidden snort of laughter erupted from her. Dismayed, she clapped her hand over her mouth. David and Helen sent her a puzzled look, and Cathy still wiping her eyes from the previous hilarity informed them, "Jack shot it this morning."

It was a rare occasion that she felt out of control, but a silent bone shaking laughter was beginning to overcome her. There was a pregnant pause before Hawkins, his voice a pitch higher than usual said, "We're talking of a rabbit, Sir."

"And I admit Hawkins… Jack, to be somewhat relieved to hear that".

Behind him Rosie leant against the table convulsed into not so silent laughter. David turned, raised his eyebrows at her unusual behaviour, but his mouth twisted into a wry smile before addressing Hawkins to admit, "Rabbit is a great favourite of mine. I would be sorry to pass that up."

Helen muttered. "Oh no!"

"But I don't want to intrude…"

With a hiccup, Cathy stood and stretched out her hand. "I'm Cathy, pleased to meet you." As David smiled broadly at her, she responded by saying, "You are most welcome and definitely not intruding."

Bending almost double, David spoke quietly by Cathy's ear, yet audible to all, "I'm not quite sure everyone here agrees with you!" Patting her shoulder as he straightened to his full 6ft 1inch height he bantered, "Thank you Cathy, for the invitation and the ability to now fulfil the rumours that I have had at least one woman falling at my feet." With that he slapped his thigh, a sign of his delight, and let out his booming laugh at which they all jumped and Cathy chuckling said, "Oh my, oh my…"

This was the side of David Reinhardt rarely seen outside his family, and she felt strangely warmed that he felt so relaxed with those she loved.

"Hawkins… sorry Jack, how do you keep such a straight face when you are so obviously amused?"

"Years of training, Sir. As a butler you have to act as if nothing untoward is happening." Hawkins serious face crinkled with pleasure as he added, "But I confess, right now, to being near the limit of my capacity."

"Is that so?" David's eyes twinkled, his mouth twitched, and he nodded toward Rosie and Cathy. "Should you have succumbed to laughter as they have, I believe I too would have been quite undone."

And then, casting decorum to the wind, Hawkins spluttered, "I like you, Sir. I like you a lot. Cathy and I are so pleased by the changes you and your family have wrought in our lovely Rosie. It seems you've put laughter back into her soul."

It was difficult to be cross with Jack in the midst of such a friendly exchange, but that comment seemed tantamount to his agreeing she should marry David.

David winked at her and advised, "Hawkins, I don't think I can take the credit for that, but let's shake hands on agreeing we would like to see more of it." Inwardly Rosie sighed. Her beloved Hawkeye had taken so readily to David that it could now seriously undermine her arguments or weaken her resistance about a courtship with him. In shaking Hawkins' hand, David observed, "This has to be the most bizarre situation I have ever encountered."

Hawkins tried, not very successfully, to look austere and surprised, "Oh surely not, Sir."

David, his voice strained with suppressed laughter, commented, "I guess you don't get many visitors?" before laughter boomed from him. A deep chuckle from Hawkins rumbled to the surface, but he managed to splutter, "These days we only attract the bad, sad or mad!"

To that Helen piped up, "I'm the bad, Rosie is the sad, and the mad, well he's just ..."

Cathy cut across her, "We're glad you came. It's been a long time since this place has resounded to laughter."

David responded with a chuckle, "Cathy I'm very glad I came, and must have been 'mad' to negotiate that pot hole ridden drive three times today."

In his sonorous tone Hawkins stated, "Potholes in an invasion would be an advantage."

David raised an eyebrow to enquire, "Are you expecting one?"

"No Sir, not in the foreseeable future." Hawkins gave a wicked grin, "Unless you and Miss Rosemary decide to have your wedding reception here."

"Now there's a thought!"

"And that is all it will remain." Rosie said sharply before adding vehemently, "Jack, who you invite to your dinner table is your business, but do not make assumptions on who I may or may not marry." Helen looked amused, Cathy was cringing, David had the whisper of a wry smile, and Hawkins taken aback suddenly looked embarrassed. David sent his new friend a sympathetic look before his dark, penetrating eyes rested on her. His expression was unfathomable, but his tone that of a barrister summoning up his case. "Rosie, your refusal to get engaged to me this afternoon was based on my not really knowing you. There is truth in that." Rosie gave a brief satisfied smile. "But the evidence before me, what I already know, and maybe about to discover, won't change my opinion or my mind about marrying you. Just seeing you here, dressed beautifully and then so casually, you have become even more fascinating and desirable."

"Oh good grief!" Helen's disgust was further confirmed by her putting two fingers in her mouth indicating the need to be sick. Rosie glared at her, but seeing Jack and Cathy brightening at David's words, she felt equally annoyed at them.

Ignoring Rosie's expression, David proceeded to release one of his broad 'knee weakening' smiles before proclaiming, "My belief is you are a treasure trove just waiting to be unlocked. It's not if, but when you marry me, and the wedding reception can be wherever you like."

Incensed at such a presumption she pursued her lips, took a deep breath and with a hard stare said sharply, "Don't count on it." David, unlike her father was not going to predetermine her future. Knowing the words about finding a treasure trove had come from Jane's last letter to him, she said in a quiet but equally fervent tone, "David, your treasure is your children, don't presume that includes me."

His knowing smile caused her to click her tongue in aggravation and he changed the subject. "Jack, I've not seen much of this place, but agree with Helen that the loud clanging bell, the sound of bolts drawn back, and the way that heavy door slowly creaks open does bring an expectation of meeting Herman Munster."

Hawkins reverting to his butler role responded, "I confess Sir, when we get unexpected or unwanted visitors, I have considered dressing in such manner as to appear alarming."

It was impossible to conjure up Jack looking alarming, but Rosie remarked "Unlike David whose manner is alarming without the need to dress up."

Shocked at her rudeness, Jack and Cathy chorused, "Rosie!"

But David let out a loud guffaw before exclaiming, "Oh, this is all so wonderfully entertaining. Whatever next!" Bemused, Helen studied him as he shook with laughter and sank on the nearest dusty chair to wipe his eyes and blow his nose. Then, in the distance, a high pitched and thin sounding wail could be heard.

Rosie tensed. Hawkins sobered. Cathy exchanged a worried glance with them. David's forehead puckered and his hand stilled. Helen sounding frightened cried out "The house is haunted!" Hawkins scowled. The wail drew nearer and grew loud enough to be identified as tuneless singing. They were immobilised by a variety of emotions. Rosie saw David glance around, his expression grew apprehensive as a slow, rhythmic thud accompanied the singing. When that ceased, the thud was more pronounced and alternated with a dragging sound. Enough - Rosie thought - to make your hair stand on end. Maybe David's use of Brylcreem stopped his rising. That thought, and nervous tension drew from her a snort of laughter which she turned to a cough. David shot her a questioning look, she ignored it, for the inevitable apparition was about to appear.

CHAPTER 3

The suspense was palpable. David stood, his fists clenched at his side, his face stern ready to fend off an unknown foe. Jack and Cathy exchanged a look of trepidation. Helen looked amused. Rosie felt anxious. There hadn't been a time or opportunity to prepare David, but then she had neither expected him nor invited him in. The house was about to divulge one of its secrets, would David be up to the challenge?

The thud became a tap, the dragging became a scuffing sound against the stone floor and Bertie emerged into the hall. A walking stick helped his movement as he dragged along his foot formed at a wrong angle. His smile at the gathered group was distorted by the slant of his head which almost met his risen malformed shoulder from which an arm, seemingly shorter than normal, ended in a gnarled fist. At twenty-three Bertie, a fan of Val Doonegan, copied his clothes and today wore a brown and cream V-necked Fair Isle jumper lovingly knitted by Cathy. Spotting a stranger in their midst Bertie headed toward David. Jack stepped forward. David appearing unphased by Bertie's deformities sent him a warm smile, and looked around expecting to be introduced.

Despite the Hawkins' pleas to her father, Bertie had been kept within the house and grounds from birth, except for the rare visit to a dentist in Southampton. Her father ignored Bertie's existence, and her mother believed the servants should take care of the children. For Bertie's fifteenth birthday, Rosie had a TV installed in his bedroom and during broadcasting hours he immersed himself in that black and white world. They had been astounded how the TV had accelerated his mental development and desire to learn which revealed he was an intelligent young man. However, his copying words and attitudes portrayed in programmes had brought times of amusement and correction.

Before anyone recovered enough to introduce Bertie, he spoke. For the untrained ear it took time to understand. "I'm Bertie. Who are you?"

David caught the gist of it and introduced himself. "I'm David, a friend of Rosemary."

Bertie looked around repeating several times, "Friend of Rosemary."

Helen sidled up, put her arm through his and declared brightly, "Bertie is Rosie's brother." Rosie frowned at Helen's unexpected familiarity with her brother and his obvious pleasure at her attention.

To David's credit he quickly responded, "In which case Bertie I'm even more pleased to meet you."

Bertie asked, "You stay for dinner?"

Cathy answered for David, "We hope so."

But before David could speak, Helen confessed, "We saw you earlier". And with a smirk added, "We watched you leave, didn't we Bertie?" Bertie hummed his agreement bringing Rosie to realise that Helen must have been in Bertie's bedroom over the library. Had Helen been given permission to visit him there? Rosie's questioning glance at Cathy was met with a puckered brow.

Bertie made a guffaw before indistinctly saying, "We said good riddance to bad ..."

Jack's muttered exclamation was drowned out by Cathy's horrified gasp and Rosie's sharp, "Bertie no!" Bertie frowned at her before twisting his body to look at Helen beside him. David met Rosie's dismayed expression with a raised eyebrow. Bertie glanced around trying to fathom out what was wrong, as an unrepentant Helen slid out her hand to clap and decree, "Oh Bertie, you're priceless!" Bertie grinned in delight.

Embarrassed, Hawkins explained, "Bertie repeats what he hears. Those are not our sentiments."

Helen admitted to David, "I never liked you, but Jane did. I was sorry to hear she died. I popped into her funeral, the church was packed. She loved people and they obviously loved her. I'm sure as Jane adopted Rosie as a sister she'd be pleased if Rosie, loving your children, were to accept your marriage offer."

Bertie swung his body around to Rosie to ask jerkily, "He want to marry you?" At her nod, he swung back to look David up and down, and as a dribble ran from his mouth he spluttered, "That's good."

Everyone, except Rosie smiled. David said delightedly, "Thank you Bertie. I hope Rosie will one day agree with you."

Cathy, placed a handkerchief in Bertie's gnarled hand and suggested, "Let's not stand here talking, but move into the warm." And with that she headed Bertie towards the baize door.

As Rosie waited to follow she was startled at David's sudden proximity. By her ear he said quietly, "It seems I have an unexpected advocate in Helen. Your extended family approves of me, all I need now is your agreement to a courtship." Irritated, Rosie felt it fortunate that Hawkins bringing up the rear took David's attention, "I hasten to assure you Sir, the servants' quarters are warm and cosy. A far cry from the cold and draughty library." Rosie stepped away to retrieved the flowers as Hawkins leading the way continued, "Dinner should be served in about half an hour."

David having obviously seen her vexed expression turned to ask, "Rosie, do I have your approval to stay?"

What could she say? What choice did she have? She would have wished to consider the future before drawing him into the bosom of those she called family, but common politeness decreed her affirmation, "Jack has invited you. Cathy is quite taken with you, so stay and enjoy your meal." From David's pleased expression and the way he strode forward to join Jack, she guessed he hadn't realised how carefully she had couched her agreement.

"If I'm to call you Jack, could you drop the 'Sir' and call me David."

"If that is your wish Sir." came Hawkins' sonorous reply before the tone changed to amusement, "They stopped to shake hands and Jack added, I'm surprised rabbit stew is a favourite of yours."

Behind them Rosie listened as David informed Jack, "During the war my sister Paula and I, with our parents, lived at my grandparents' farm. Rabbit stew was part of our staple diet. My mother ate it, but refused to be involved in its sourcing and preparation. She vowed when meat was off ration, never to cook or eat it again. Rabbit today is a rare treat."

"Not here. The estate is overrun with them. Like your mother, Cathy and Rosie are squeamish about killing such delightful little creatures, but once prepared, will cook and even enjoy the finished product."

"You'll have to excuse me rushing off after dinner. I can't risk that drive in the dark."

"No need, stay as long as you like because you can use the tradesman entrance."

Rosie groaned, tomorrow she would talk with Jack about stepping over his boundaries. Although she had no jurisdiction over who the Hawkins invited into their quarters. Inadvertently her grip tightened on the roses and as several thorns dug into her hands she exclaimed, "Ouch!"

David turned, gave her a meaningful stare and remarked, "Roses can be very sharp when put under pressure!"

To his back she quietly warned, "Don't let Jack's enthusiasm lull you into wrong expectations. It would be advisable if you don't get comfortable with those I call family."

David squared his shoulders and brought back his attention on Hawkins who, unaware of their dialogue, had continued talking, "…It could have been a dungeon, but it's an ideal temperature for a wine cellar." Suddenly she felt mean at having pricked his illusion of her complicity in his dinner invitation, after all David's family had always welcomed her. "It seems to me that tonight is a perfect opportunity to enjoy a bottle with our dinner. Do you favour red or white?"

"I'm not sure …" David turned, his eyes questioned her.

Rosie answered, "You choose, for a glass or two won't heed your driving home in the next couple of hours."

David's punctilious nod revealed her point had registered, as Jack enthused, "We so rarely have a visitor, and even rarer to entertain such an interesting one."

As they entered the servants' hall David proclaimed, "Jack, it is I who is being entertained. As an afternoon goes, it'll not be easily forgotten. It certainly has contained all the emotional elements to push me to the edge of reality."

Rosie crossing the room to get a vase from the cupboard commented in a quiet intense voice, "Except this life is our reality."

David ignoring her addressed Cathy. "I have to say when you fell into my arms, I thought I'd been set up for 'Candid Camera' and waited for Jeremy Beadle to appear. And Helen, your entrance, looking like a waif and stray, was priceless." Helen, obviously not thrilled by his description scowled.

Hawkins added, "Amusing as those experiences were, I confess they aren't part of our usual reality."

"I understand, but laughter is good for the soul" and with that David patted him on the back.

To ease the tension Hawkins suggested, "I'll give you a quick tour of the ground floor."

It was thirty minutes before they reappeared and Rosie could only hope Jack had been as tight-lipped about her past to David, as he had to Helen. She put the vegetables on the table and saw David's sad gaze at Bertie, sitting with a napkin tied around his neck and a fork in his good hand. During dinner, Bertie's aim to his mouth was distracted by his observation of David. Throughout Bertie's life the Hawkins rarely had visitors, invited or not. Cathy only offered tea and cake when Jack made sure Bertie would stay in his room. Cathy went to the WI in the village and Hawkins to the local pub. They could only go out together when Rosie was home. Yet despite their circumstances they were amazingly content with life.

David, as she knew he would be, was the perfect dinner guest. He included Bertie in the conversation, acknowledged his grunts and when Bertie spoke he listened. He ignored the spitting and splattering of food down his napkin which happened despite Cathy instructing, 'Eat now, mouth closed, talk later.' The stew and the dumplings were apparently the best David had ever tasted. And, to Rosie's surprise, he had knowledge of culling rabbits, shooting pheasants and fishing for trout and salmon. He was also keen to draw on Jack's opinions and experiences.

By the time they finished the first course, Jack obviously felt comfortable with him and asked about his family. It felt he was prying but it didn't stop Rosie listening. "The German side of the Reinhardt family, one way or another, died during the war." As if not wanting to dwell on that he hurried on, "Several generations of my mother's family were land owning farmers in Bristol. My grandfather insisted that my father moved to England with my mother several years before the war broke out. My father followed in his father's footsteps by dedicating his life to the research and development of drugs. When my mother's parents retired to a residential home, neither my father nor I wanted to take the farm on. They sold it, ending the family tradition." At the Hawkins' curiosity, Rosie realised how little interest she had had about David's background. "My father's business is based between Bristol and Bath so my parents bought a house on the outskirts of Bath. Paula, my older sister, is married with two boys and lives in Berkshire. I left home to do a law degree in London. During that time I bought a bombed out house in Kensington and took years to renovate it. By that time my younger sister Jill wanted to rent the basement flat, Rosie being one of her tenants. You've probably hear of Jill's exploits."

Cathy glanced at Helen who obviously had told her how Jill had entangled her in one of those, but Rosie stated, "It's Jill's story, not mine to tell." David sent her an appreciative look.

"Well suffice to say Jill married a couple of years ago and is spawning babies at an incredible rate. Obviously, Rosie has been an amazing asset to us all. She doesn't just cope with the twins, but also helps Jill with her three children under four. She's a natural mother."

What could have been an awkward moment was diverted by

Cathy declaring, "There's still stew in the pot, anyone interested in another helping?" She laughed as David enthusiastically lifted his plate, smiled when he eagerly consumed his second portion and declared, "You must come again."

"I'd like that." He glanced towards Rosie for her approval which he didn't receive. He turned his attention to the Hawkins by asking, "Tell me about yourselves?"

It occurred to Rosie as Jack talked of joining the British Army and being sent to India how little they spoke of their life before arriving at 'The Grange'. David's brow creased as Jack spoke of Cathy being part of the 'fishing fleet' from England and bemused he interrupted to question, "Women go to India to fish?"

"An understandable assumption! Jack chuckled. "That's the name given to young women who arrive in India with the intention of finding a husband from those serving in the British Army. It's a good life. With so many of us, it was rare a girl didn't find a handsome fellow to her liking." Jack preened and looked towards Cathy gathering up their plates.

"You were lucky, my man. I fell into your arms. Rather like the way I did into David's today."

Amused, Jack retorted, "Except it was off a horse, not due to being caught spying through a peephole!"

David chortled, "Really! Cathy... spying!" Cathy looked suitably penitent and headed with the plates toward the sink while David added, "And you Hawkins, I would suggest that earlier when I was talking to Rosie, you were listening at the library door."

"I'm afraid living here it became a necessary evil."

"Jack" called Cathy, "Let's not get into that." She turned to open the oven door.

David sniffed the air and asked, "Crumble, if apricot another favourite of mine." After his first mouthful he gave an appreciative murmur. "Now I know where Rosie's delicious recipe comes from." Lifting his hand, he rounded his thumb and finger to indicate 'perfect' and they all laughed when Bertie copied him. "Now Cathy, tell me why did you, an attractive woman and good cook..." Helen gave an audible groan, David ignored it to finish, "... felt the need to join a 'fishing party'?"

Cathy giggled like a school girl, "Oh, you flatterer! Attractive isn't how I'd describe myself, because as you see, I like my food, and I have always been on the chubby side."

Jack contradicted her, "You are attractive because you are

cuddly, fun and friendly."

David grinned. "I've a rotund friend, Sam, he works at ITP. Rosie knows him. He has this line, 'I'm not fat, I'm just not tall enough'." There was a general chuckle before attention was given to the crumble. Once consumed David said, "Seriously Cathy, it is what is in the heart that makes people attractive, but let's not understate physical attributes and splendid cooking abilities."

Laughing, Cathy batted her eyelids and mocked, "My, my, young man, you have a way with words." Good grief, thought Rosie, Cathy was flirting with David Reinhardt!

"It's not just words Cathy, it's the truth. As I see it, you've spent years caring for Rosie and Bertie, and more recently Helen. I'd say you too were born to be a mother."

Fortunately, Bertie at that moment took their attention by vigorously nodding his head, and with crumble spattering from his mouth to the table said in his indistinct manner "Cathy, mother, I love her"

Tears filled Cathy's eyes and she responded, "Oh Bertie, I love you too. I see you both as my adopted children." As Cathy moved forward to wipe Bertie's face and remove his napkin, she added, "I've always like caring for people. When I left school at 15, I cleaned at a local hospital and seeing how I liked to chat and comfort patients the nurses encouraged me to become an auxiliary. I'd opportunity then to work nights and that's when I met Gillian, a frail, well spoken, middle-aged lady who'd returned from India to have a major operation. She was lonely and frightened, and it helped her to talk about her wonderful life, married to a British Army officer in India. She told me that years before, she'd joined the 'fishing trip' to India. She gave me her address in India and said to me to look her up if I were to go.

It seemed a chance of a lifetime. I found out that an all-inclusive passage to Bombay with Ellerman's Shipping was fifty pounds and living at home I'd manage to save seventy-five. My decision was made when Ellerman's had a bunk available in a cabin for six on their next sailing, but my parents were distraught fearing they'd never see me again." Cathy gave a sad sigh. "I reassured them I'd be back. When I left, war was looming on the horizon, but I couldn't have anticipated our street would be bombed, and my parents in a nearby air raid shelter would have the breath blasted from their bodies." David gasped in horror, the vivid picture brought them to silence until Bertie fidgeted, a sure sign he wanted to leave, drew Cathy, hands on the table, to haul herself to her feet.

Helen jumped up. "Cathy, I'll go with Bertie." Addressing Bertie she offered, "We could watch TV or you could teach me how to play chess." Bertie's head nodded wildly, so with her arm under his she helped him to his feet. Unsure about Helen's influence on Bertie, Rosie sent Cathy a questioning look to which Helen reacted sharply, "I can look after him, remember. I've brothers of my own!"

Bertie passing David's chair patted his shoulder in the way David had done earlier to Jack, and in his own inimitable way said, "I like you. You marry Rosie."

David smiled up at him, took a second or two to understand, and then called after him, "Bertie, that's my hope" causing Bertie to turn and waggle his stick.

Rosie pursed her lips, took a deep breath and annoyed, she pushed back her chair and began to clear the table. Jack, washing dishes in the sink suggested, "Cathy, why don't you sit by the fire and tell the rest of your story."

David settled in the nearest armchair and Cathy put her feet up on the settee. "The girls in the cabin were a similar age to me, better educated, but kind. They helped prepare me for the social life needed to find a fellah. So when the sea wasn't rough, ship life was fun." She giggled, "They were quick to see I wouldn't cut a dash at sporting activities, but taught me to dance and play bridge. I didn't know then about the social snobbery, and how hard it would be to be accepted. When asked by Jeffrey to go riding, despite never having been on a horse, I didn't want to refuse. He and his friend helped me into the saddle, ignored my fears and made me the butt of their jokes before jumping on their trusty steeds. I guess my fear communicated to the horse as it whinnied, shook its head, reared up and I fell off. Apparently, he and his friend had a wager I'd do that before we'd left the stable yard. They found it highly amusing." Appalled, Rosie saw David felt the same but Cathy stated, "Don't be upset. Jack having overheard their conversation had been hovering and he rushed forward to break my fall. So Jeffrey did me a favour because, with the exception of this afternoon, I've never been in another man's arms."

David chuckled and sang in his baritone voice, "When the girl in your arms, is the girl in your heart, then you have everything."

Cathy laughed, and Jack handing him a mug of coffee commented, "That's true, but I'm surprised at you knowing a Cliff

Richard's song."

"Jane liked him. I was persuaded to see the film 'The Young Ones'. I was eleven years older than her, it wasn't to my taste but she enjoyed it and the tunes were catchy."

"We were sorry to hear about Jane, a lovely girl by all accounts."

"Yes Jack, she was." Cathy gave David a sympathetic grimace. Rosie having sat in the chair opposite David saw sadness filling his eyes. Momentarily David focussed inwardly before saying, "But life goes on. As Helen pointed out, Jane and Rosie became like sisters, so I do believe she would be delighted if Rosie took her place."

Rosie frowned and Cathy seeing it asked, "Now where was I? Oh yes meeting Jack. War had been declared by that time, and although raging in Europe, hadn't taken hold of Britain so letters were still arriving regularly. My parents were sad not to be at our wedding, but relieved that I was happy and safe when the bombing began. They reported homes being demolished, people killed and when rationing took hold, they assured us the British bulldog spirit would not be beaten."

"And was life in India all you'd been led to believe?" David asked.

"It hadn't been at first. It was a shock arriving in Bombay…" Cathy paused as if refocussing on the scene. "Our first impression from the ship was to see below a seething mass of people looking like a bright tapestry of moving colour from which came a cacophony of sounds. Once we were in the midst of the throng, the noise didn't just come from shouted conversations or enthusiastic merchants haggling over their wares, but calls of despair from beggars in doorways and corners, some with hideous deformities."

In her mind's eye Rosie visualised the scene, it felt so real that her heart started to beat faster.

"Intimidated, and I'll admit scared, we huddled together around our suitcases, our handkerchiefs over our noses. I felt sick and thought I made a big mistake. You can imagine our relief when an English voice hailed us, and a burly Sergeant Major arrived to escort us through the crowds to several waiting rickshaws. In those, we passed through streets where the stench of sewage fought with the tang of wood smoke and the smell of cooking."

Nausea was rising with the steady pounding of her heart. Rosie tried to ignore it by concentrating on Cathy's story.

"I was relieved when we came into wide avenues where

different colonial influences could be seen from victorian houses to grand mansions, and the only scent was from the prolific flowers and bushes surrounding them. We spent several days exploring Bombay with its unusual mixture of architecture of towers, spires, turrets, domes, statues, porticoes, much of it with an English…"

Cathy's voice had faded as pictures of women's bright saris, men's hairy legs and the feeling of being in a jostling crowd began to overwhelm Rosie. Vile smells, beggars' faces, their bodies in dirty rags were reaching out to touch her. She tried to hide in her mother's billowing skirt, but in sudden panic… she cried out, "She let go of my hand." The instant Rosie realised the vivid recollection had caused her to speak the words aloud, she clapped a shaking hand over her mouth and saw three pairs of eyes staring at her. Embarrassed she stammered, "It's… I've… I'm…" in despair she looked across at Jack and Cathy and as tears overflowed down her cheeks, she saw them exchange a perceptive look.

David, legs out in front of him and his hands steepled together, had been absorbed in Cathy's tale, but at her outburst he sat upright and scanning her face demanded, "Rosie, who let go of your hand?" Despite the sense of drowning in lost memories, she surfaced at his brusque tone to respond with asperity, "My mother."

At his shocked expression, Jack with a sorrowful grimace reported, "It's hard to believe that we've never talked with Rosie about that day twenty-five years ago when she was lost on Bombay dock."

"Well Jack love, with my suspicions founded, we best do so now."

Rosie, knowing it was David's penchant to ask questions with a tenacity to get answers, felt it was time to escape, to hide, to be alone and to recover. Feeling fragile she eased herself to the edge of the chair to announce, "You'll have to excuse me."

Jack stood to block her way, "Rosie, now the memory has surfaced I'd like to know what happened. That incident is etched on my mind."

David advised, "When you face a situation, it overcomes its effect."

Rosie's retort was sharp, "Not in my experience!"

"Perhaps I should leave?" David made to rise.

Upset Rosie turned on him, "You came here and opened up this can of worms. You want to know about me and my life, then it appears you've made a good start! The least you can do is hear this out."

Jack's arm came around her shoulders, but her eyes remained fixed on David as Jack said quietly, but firmly, "Rosie, it's not David's fault, any more than yours. My little love, much of what you have suffered has been done to you, not by you."

David's eyes were filled with compassion, "Believe me Rosie, it wasn't my intention to uncover bad memories, I would like to stay if nothing else to pray you would find peace in this. You may find it helpful to close your eyes and speak out the memories."

Jack gave her a gentle squeeze and Cathy nodded. She knew they loved and wanted the best for her so she sat between them and followed David's advice. A glance at David revealed his eyes closed, hands clasped with his forefingers steepled against his mouth. She knew he was praying so took courage from that and allowed the memories to return, "I...I... felt small. So many legs... So many people pushing by."

Jack murmured. "You were only five."

"I see undernourished nearly naked children with big rounded eyes, horribly deformed people sitting by rickety stalls, mothers with babies sitting on the ground, trying to swat the swarms of flies from around their mouths. Mummy's hand is swatting me as I keep pulling on her skirt trying to hide in it. It's so hot. My dress keeps sticking to my legs. I'm tired, my feet hurt. Mummy stops, I bump into her. She grabs my shoulders, shakes me and screams, "This is all your fault, you've caused me to lose Jack and Cathy". Frightened, I begin to cry. She looks angry, grabs my wrist and pulls me along. I try to keep up. I jerk Mummy's hand when people nearly fall over me. A little girl, smaller than me is in front of me, I avoid her, but fall over. Mummy shouts, drags me to my feet, my leg hurts I don't want to go on. She asks if I want a smack. Crying I shake my head and wipe my face with my free hand."

Rosie realised she was doing that now and opened her eyes. David looking grim dropped his handkerchief in her lap. Tears were also rolling down Cathy's face, her voice quivered as she asked, "Was that... when she let go...of your hand?"

Rosie shook her head, wiped her eyes and composing herself stated, "That probably explains why I don't like being in crowds. It's odd because I clearly remember you Jack, hoisting me up on your shoulders so the train wouldn't seem so big and scary. And on that long, slow, hot journey to Bombay you both playing with me. But I've no recollection of my mother, on that journey or on the ship. I can recall your cabin and Cathy giving me Monty the monkey." She informed David, "I still have Monty, bald and patched, so thin I made him a set of clothes. Where I go, he goes, always as a reminder of the Hawkins' love."

Cathy smiled, "Jack bought Monty for our little girl, but Rosie had a greater need that night."

"And Jack later you began calling me 'your little monkey.'"

Jack grinned, as Cathy explained for David's benefit, "In India white children have an Ayah, basically a nursemaid. And like the very rich here, beyond a daily visit, a mother doesn't look after the children. Daphne, or Dee-Dee as she liked to be called, had no idea how to care for her. She was also seasick for most of the voyage so Rosie stayed with us."

"I've only seen my mother smile when dressed up and entertaining."

David shook his head in disbelief as Jack clarified the dock incident. "Rosie, it wasn't your fault we were split up. Dee-Dee knew we were heading for the ship, people would have directed her there. In the throng it was impossible for the four of us to stay together."

"Maybe that's why she kept shouting, 'Walk properly or I'll lose you'." David gave a negative grunt. "I did try to keep up. I didn't want to be lost." Rosie paused, "A low wooden board suddenly rolled between us. On it sat a mutilated skeleton with no legs, his hands wrapped in filthy rags were propelling him forward. Sickened, not wanting to fall on him, I tugged on Mummy's hand and she let go. I fell backwards and she disappeared into the crowd."

David let out a strangled "No!"

"Someone lifted me to my feet. I rushed after her. I couldn't find her." Panic resurfaced, deep sobs took her breath away.

Cathy instructed her to take slow deep breaths while David exclaimed, "Good God, what kind of mother does that to her five year old child?" And then advised, "You need to let that pain out."

Jack drew her into his arms. Even if she had wanted to, her pent up emotion couldn't be stopped. When it was eventually spent, David appeared deep in thought and Cathy handed her and Jack a cup of tea. Red-eyed but calm she told them, "My Ayah told me if I was ever lost, to stop where I could be seen and she would find me. Crying, I stood by a merchant's stall. A man in uniform stooped down and asked me in English, 'Are you lost?' I nodded. He asked my name and I said I'd lost my Mummy. He offered me his shoulders to sit on to look for her. When I saw and pointed out the ship, he headed toward it bellowing, "Rosemary's here."

Jack took up the story. "After an hour, we'd become desperate to find you and Dee-Dee. I was climbing up on what Cathy felt was a dangerous pile of crates when, with panic in her voice, she shouted, 'Dee-Dee's here, she's lost Rosemary.' I looked down to see Dee-Dee looking as if she was about to faint."

Cathy added, "I felt faint knowing you were alone and lost among the hordes of people. Dee-Dee lent against me complaining of a splitting headache and feeling sick. She seemed unaware of the danger you were in."

"From my vantage point I spotted a child in the distance sitting on a man's shoulders. I waited until I knew it was you and called down the news to Cathy. She then took Dee-Dee to the ship and I began frantically waving hoping Rosie would see me. Even now, it's hard to believe Dee-Dee was heartless enough to deliberately lose you."

In protest, Rosie's voice came out as a tight scream, "I tell you, it's the truth! Why am I always the accused and judged?" Incensed, she leapt up. Cathy put out her hand to stop her, Rosie thrust the teacup into it declaring, "Leave me alone" before heading towards the door.

Jack, more agile on his feet, caught hold of her and quietly commanded, "Rosie calm down! Look at me." She turned and glared at him. "I made an observation, one for years we'd hoped to be untrue. Now hear me out." He drew her to sit down and explained, "Cathy and I fell in love with a beautiful little girl with long dark hair. Her sad dark eyes bewitched us, her inquisitiveness engaged us, and despite her somewhat self-important demeanour she charmed us, and her response to our love delighted us." He smiled at Cathy and added, "Let me tell you this, young lady, if I hadn't found you that ship would have sailed without me." Rosie blanched, tears filled her eyes.

"The soldier who'd hoisted you on to his shoulders spoke three languages and heading toward the ship expected someone would have seen a distraught woman looking for her child, but no-one had."

Bewildered she asked, "You believe me?"

"Of course!" I'm Hawkins by name, but Hawkeye by nature. I've seen and heard many things. It isn't my place to repeat or judge, but I can confirm you were dealt a raw deal. You were a little monkey, haughty and naughty, but that's no excuse to abandon a child. That's why we chose to stay to take care of you, and then Bertie."

David who had remained silent intervened, "And, if I may say, you both should be commended for your love and care of Rosie. Rejection of that magnitude, remembered or not, can often have a devastating effect on a child."

Rosie retorted, "To be blamed or accused when it's not your fault can always have a devastating effect. Even if there is remorse and apology, it reveals the person's lack of trust and confidence in you."

David gazed steadily at her, "In extenuating circumstances, when emotions are involved people can act out of character." Rosie hummed, for they both knew to what they were referring. "We all make mistakes and that's why the basis of the Christian faith is to forgive and forget." For that she had no answer. David stood, "Now you'll have to forgive me because I must get back. Rosie, thank you for allowing me to stay. I have every confidence that the Lord loves you, and He wishes as His Word says, 'to restore to you the years the locusts have eaten away'". With one of his disarming smiles he added, "It would seem that unintentionally I'm being used by God as a catalyst to do that."

Crossly, Rosie admitted, "In seven hours, you've certainly shown more interest and discovered more about my life than in the seven years since you arrived at ITP!"

David gave a perfunctory nod, and turned to shake Jack's hand. "It's been good to meet you." Bending he kissed Cathy's cheek, "Thank you for the delicious rabbit stew, just like my Granny's." He subjected Cathy to a sexy grin as he added, "After today, the rumours have become true, a beautiful woman fell at my feet."

Blushing Cathy giggled, "Oh get away with you."

As David turned towards her, Rosie hid her exasperation by promptly thanking him for the roses and telling him, "I'll be in touch." As dark brooding eyes looked down into hers, she added, "Jack, will show you the way to the Tradesman's Entrance and give you directions to the main road."

"Believe me Rosie, I've no intention of pressurising or persuading you into anything. I've really enjoyed being here, but further invitations must be from you. Jack before you show me out, I do have one last question." Rosie took a deep breath, what now? "Why, when there is a back entrance, was Rosie driving that vintage Bentley along that dangerous pot holed drive?"

"Ah! That's a question I hoped you wouldn't ask." David raised his eyebrows and Hawkins reverted to butler. "I'm afraid Sir that was my idea. Rosie told me to announce she was out, and I decreed to do that Miss Rosemary had to go 'out'."

David eyebrows rose as he verified, "So Rosie wasn't 'out' when I arrived."

Unperturbed, Jack grinned, "Very astute."

"As a lawyer I'm trained to spot flaws in the evidence."

Jack bantered back, "In that case me laud, I'll plead guilty as charged and confess that having invited you in, it was I who determined Rosie should make a stunning entrance."

"She certainly did that." David sent Rosie an appreciative smile. "With new hairstyle and those clothes, you looked sensational." He chuckled, "What an extraordinary day this has been."

"It has indeed, Sir. And my hope is we shall see you again soon."

"Rosie is certainly blessed to have you as friends. Now Jack, I'd better go, so lead the way."

CHAPTER 4

Rosie snuggled up in the comfort of her curtained bed, letting the scenarios of the day tumble in. Unlike Jane who always prayed aloud, she began to talk to Jesus in her mind and awoke after what she termed a 'cat nap', thinking of her mother.

When young, her mother's pretty face had been surrounded by peroxide blonde curls and with a perfect figure she looked like a Barbie doll. Yet there was a naivety, an irresponsibility and a childishness that showed in an excited flutter of words, a clap of hands in delight, a tendency to sulk or withdraw and to sink into a deep, silent depression. Years of smoking and drinking had taken their toll: her hands shook, her body bone thin and her lined face made her look older than her years.

Talking to Jane about her mother's lack of parenting skills caused Jane to worry about the kind of mother she would make, and in discovering she was expecting twins her anxiety grew. Rosie had reassured her that she would help but no-one could have imagined Jane's motherhood would only last a week, and within two years David would offer her that role. She drifted back to sleep thinking of those adorable children.

Several hours later she awoke to think of her father. A tall, thin faced, mean-mouthed man with a vague similarity to Lord Kitchener, helped by the stupid moustache he so fondly tweaked. Was it a desire to be a 'somebody' or a need to be in authority that he took on that persona? At home he would strut about, giving his orders, brook no argument, wouldn't listen to reason, and was furious if his commands couldn't be met. In India, she presumed he had worked for the British government. She had no idea of his position, but knew he had basked in the polite servitude of the people. During Jill's debacle, she had been led to question the validity of his Lordship title. How long would it be before David did too?

Jesus words "forgive them they know not what they do" repeated in her mind. It was three years since she had 'given her life to Jesus', yet her dislike of her parents hadn't dissipated. Jesus words echoed in her mind, "If you forgive, your father in heaven will forgive you."

Rosie, considering that, drifted off into sleep and returned to consciousness remembering the scripture about praying and loving even those who despitefully use and curse you. It was always a struggle to forgive, and still difficult to maintain when thinking of

Doug Bradford, twenty years her senior, who acted as a father figure but had nearly destroyed her. Why had she been so naïve and weak when she knew she was doing wrong? Maybe she should forgive herself for having been led astray. Was David the right man for her? Was he God's choice for her? Could she love him? To be the twins' mother would fulfil the desires of her heart. Her eyes grew heavy, she murmured, "Your will Lord..." and drifted back to sleep.

Daylight filtered through the shutters. The bright sun rays permeated them, touching and awaking her. She felt light of heart, and as she slid from the bed the words of a hymn came to mind causing her to sing, "*My chains fell off, my heart was free, I rose, went forth and followed thee*". Opening the wardrobe door, she viewed the dark clothes she had for years favoured. Today, she drew out her brightest straight skirt which was mid-brown and mid-calf and from the drawer a matching green jumper and cardigan. To that she added the creamy pearls David had given her and contemplated the smart, but very staid and dull woman in the mirror. Maybe it was time to create something brighter, although maybe not in apricot.

In the midst of eating breakfast Jack informed her, "David said that before Jane died, they used to have a weekly Bible Study in their house. You used to go to that and every Sunday to church with them. Rosie chewing her toast nodded. Why don't you go to church here? Do you think we wouldn't approve?

Rosie replied, "When I started at ITP I often came home for weekends. In recent years my visits have been more infrequent so I felt I would rather spend the time with you, or give you respite from Bertie, than visit the local church. I know from your colonial days you saw Christianity as a religion and thought Christians were either pious or poisonous. For me Christianity is a lifestyle, a relationship with Jesus. I like the church we go to, but I don't have to go to.

Cathy and Jack nodded thoughtfully. Jack said, "We don't mind if you go. Bertie seem to be enjoying Helen's company."

Cathy piped up, "There's a young new curate at St Peters and by all accounts he's enlivening the place. The ladies at the WI were talking about him."

Rosie smiled at that and tried not to look surprised as Jack remarked, "David didn't strike me as a religious bigot. I think we've a warped perspective of Christianity.

An hour later, Rosie backed the Viva out of the garage while considering how rare it was to hear Jack impressed by a man. His enthusiasm was usually reserved for anything mechanical. She smiled, remembering how ecstatic he had been on discovering the Bentley, and having restored it to its former glory. Her mother had sanctioned his driving them to the shops for their 'rations' and her to school. The car had drawn attention to Jack's mechanical know-how, bringing opportunities to maintain and repair farm machinery. It brought them an extra income to buy and run their own car. If their love of her and Bertie hadn't stopped them leaving, he could have run a thriving motor repair shop.

Maybe knowing his capabilities was why Jack hadn't been afraid to tell her father in a disgusted tone, "No child should witness that!" when she had innocently told Cathy what she had seen while spying at her parents' guests through the peep hole in the baize door.

After that, her father would find any excuse to get rid of her and timed his entertainment season for when she would be at boarding school. At 17 she had completed her 'A' levels so school was over. Coming home in the midst of the term, the first words he barked at her across the servants' hall was, "Don't unpack your case. You are off to help Freddy with his Parliamentary campaign. I met him in India." With a sneer he added, "Let's see how you get on with him."

Brigadier Greenhaigh was the total opposite of her father: a friendly jolly man with whom she had an immediate rapport, and who appeared delighted with everything she did. She quickly learnt about his party's policies, talked to members and handled office tasks. She was thrilled to be invited with him and his family to 'the count' and celebrate his win on polling night. The Brigadier's praise of her abilities, and her care of the elderly lady with whom she stayed, hadn't pleased her father. Within days of her return she was banished to a 'finishing' school in Switzerland where she spent a year becoming fluent in several languages. Those skills, her experience, and reference from the Brigadier, had opened up the way for her employment in the Foreign Office where she met Doug Bradford.

She pushed Doug from her mind and remembered that the money the Brigadier had paid her during her 'work experience' had enabled her to invest in a beautifully tailored navy-blue suit. Just as Helen's apricot suit had given her confidence yesterday to appear as lady of the manor, this one had done the same, making her feel efficient and worthy to be employed by the Foreign Office. In those three years she was promoted several times.

Outside of work, she had gone with the fashion, the lifestyle, parties, drinking and nightclubs, but never fully embraced it. When Doug had asked if she would like to caretake his London mews cottage, she didn't hesitate. When that went so wrong, the Brigadier had recommended her to Joseph Plaidon, one of his ex-army friends, who had started International Trade Promotions. The Brigadier had left ITP in pursuit of his political career, and it was sad that the year she started there, he lost his seat to Labour in the General Election. In the interim years they had only exchanged Christmas cards, but she knew that some years ago he had returned to his family home nearby Langrish.

On arriving in town, Rosie discovered the road opposite the church was empty. She parked, crossed over to the church, read the board outside and saw the service didn't start until eleven. With forty minutes to spare she opted to stroll around the town. Down a side street she noticed a brightly painted shop and wandered towards it. When she realised the window was displaying clothes, she moved towards it hoping to glean ideas for her future creations.

Over the years she had copied her first suit several times. Latterly, she made several not to flatter but to disguise her hour-glass figure and long shapely legs. She had liked the way her long hair had shadowed her face, but in a rash moment last week wanting to change her image, she called into Vidal Sassoon for a consultation. She was surprised they had a free stylist and that she had allowed her to do something quite so dramatic! Her long dark hair had been put in plaits and cut off from the neck. Too late to have second thoughts! She consoled herself that it would grow again. Moreover, the cost of the cut would be offset by the value of selling her plaits to a wigmakers.

In the shop window, a long blue sheath dress was a reminder of the red one Jane persuaded her to buy because she looked 'stunning' in it. Unfortunately, wearing it had drawn the attention she most feared and if it hadn't been for Ben…

"Beautiful clothes for beautiful people!" A male voice commented behind her. Beyond the window reflecting her Mia Farrow hairstyle sporting a pink and grey hat, a smiling man stood, slightly taller than her, around her age and his face a similar shape to hers. In her usual defensive manner she moved to walk away but he stepped forward, blocked her path and exclaimed, "Oh my, you are far more beautiful than I…" he sent a wry look at her poker face, and finished, "… your reflection." Rosie looked him up and down, taking in the black trousers and white shirt under a dark grey V-necked jumper. In seeing his slightly portly figure she doubted his black leather bomber jacket would zip up.

"Do you like what you see?" He asked. She pursed her lips unsure if he was referring to the shop window or her eyes scanning him. His brown eyes were bright, cheeky, yet attentive. There was a familiarity about him that reminded her of Ben who, despite the disappointments of life, had managed to maintain a positive spirit and inner kindness. She had liked Ben, as did Helen, but his interest was only in Jill.

Maybe her happy thoughts of Ben reflected on her face, for this man in awaiting her reply added, "In a couple of weeks, the shop will have a sale."

Snootily she replied, "Should I wish to purchase an item I've no need to await a sale."

Undeterred, he grinned, "You might change your mind when you see my sister's prices." She sent him a derogatory look, but the man's interest didn't waver. "Tell me, what brings you to Petersfield on a Sunday?"

Her brow furrowed, her reply stiff, "I live here. Now if you'll excuse me, I'm on my way to church." With that she moved around him to head towards the High Street, believing it should convey she wasn't the type of woman to be chatted up on the street. If possible, his broad smile widened, and for a few seconds he walked beside her.

Rosie sent him a haughty look. His eyes filled with mirth before, tapping his forehead with a salute, he proclaimed, "See you there!" before jauntily taking off down the next side road. To that she murmured, "Oh ha ha!" but paused to see him cross the road further down towards the Church Square. As if he knew she was watching he looked back and waved. She ignored him and looked the other way.

Was he going to church? If so, she didn't want to sit next to him and timed her arrival a few minutes before eleven o'clock. There were a good number of people filling the rows, and she guessed, if he was there he would be looking out for her. She selected a nearly full pew near the back with the aim of slipping out down the side aisle at the end of the service. The organist struck up the first hymn and the congregation stood. As those around her sung with more gusto than flair, '*Immortal, Invisible, God only wise,*' she contemplated God's wisdom as it related to her life.

The Vicar led the congregation to sit, stand and pray. After the notices she was delighted to sing, '*My chains fell off, my heart was free, I rose, went forth, and followed Thee*'. At the end she felt quite emotional and delved into her handbag for a handkerchief to dab her eyes.

At the voice announcing, "Today's reading is from James 3" she instinctively lifted her head, and seeing the man in the pulpit her eyes widened and inwardly she groaned, 'Oh God' and quickly ducked her head. How was she to know the man she met earlier was today's preacher? Had he seen her? What were her options? To hide she positioned herself behind the man in front and sunk further into her seat. The woman next to her leant over to whisper, "Are you alright?" In looking up to give her a reassuring smile she allowed herself a glance at the pulpit. In that second, 'preacher' man gave a wide smile with a nod of recognition, causing heads to turn to see who he was acknowledging.

She almost buried her head in her handbag, supposedly looking for her Bible and then remained head down as 'preacher' man expounded how the tongue, such a small part of the body, could do untold damage to others. He spoke of the old adage, 'sticks and stones could break bones, but names will never hurt me' and continued, "Words are like invisible poison darts producing mental anguish that infects and affects lives. He talked about speaking negative words about ourselves or others. How words reveal our attitudes, affect our behaviour and the atmosphere around us. "Jesus always saw the best in people and was kind to strangers, so should we be." Had 'preacher' man deliberately aimed those words (not sermon) at her? She kept her head bowed until he finished in prayer, "Jesus, may the words I have spoken today be as seeds falling on fertile ground and take root in peoples' hearts. Amen." The organist struck the first chords of '*We plough the fields and scatter the good seed on the ground.*" The congregation stood, and with no desire to meet 'preacher' man, or chat to anyone, she gathered up her bag and headed towards the door.

Behind her a familiar voice called, "Rosemary!" Her first instinct was to pretend not to have heard Brigadier Greenhaigh, but when he called again politeness over-ruled. She turned with a smile to face the tall, white-haired, portly gentlemen whose aristocratic voice was real and not one refined at 'finishing' school! Over the singing his voice boomed, "Oh my dear, it's good to see you. How are you?"

She put out her hand to shake his. "Fine, thank you. How are you?"

Smiling broadly, he jovially answered, "We are very well. Now tell me, my dear, how did your talk go with that nice young man?" Rosie inwardly winced. He must have seen her talking to 'preacher' man.

Jennifer, the Brigadier's large, plump and motherly wife bustled up as the singing swelled in volume and indicated they go outside. She told Rosie, "Over the years Freddy and I have prayed for you. We are so pleased you have become a Christian." Rosie gave a shy smile. "I'm glad Freddy spotted you. I hope we are forgiven for passing on your address to him?"

Her frown that 'preacher' man might decide to visit caused Mrs Greenhaigh to look anxious and said, "We didn't think you would mind."

Taken aback at their assumption, Rosemary repeated slowly, "You didn't think I'd mind?"

Mrs Greenhaigh's anxiety turned to bewilderment. "Oh dear, he is such an interesting and personable young man. We thought him a wonderful answer to our prayers."

The Brigadier, keen to express his delight, said cheerily, "He arrived just before lunch. We fed him, sent him on his way, and prayed you would be at home to receive him."

Revelation and relief had her exclaim, "Oh, you mean David."

The Brigadier's eyes twinkled. "Oh goodness, are there other young men trying to find you?"

With a wry smile Rosie countered, "Not to my knowledge. I'm sorry I didn't know who you were talking about. David is thirty-eight, I don't think of him as being a young man. I didn't know he knew you."

"Oh, he didn't until yesterday." The Brigadier chuckled, "Traced me through that reference I gave you."

Mrs Greenhaigh, with a knowing smile said, "He probably didn't tell you because he had something far more important and pressing on his mind." Rosie hummed, unused to people knowing her business. People were now flowing around them and as a woman came to speak to them Rosie took the opportunity to step back, intending to say 'goodbye', but the Brigadier forestalled her by taking her arm and telling her of David's visit.

Rosie slowly guided him towards the church gate and tried not to look astonished at David telling people he barely knew about his personal life and intentions. The Greenhaighs were kind people, and may only have a tenuous connection to her father, but she had felt to keep them at a distance. Groups of people swirled around them as the Brigadier asked, "Did David tell you that his family were distressed at your leaving, and he felt desperate to find you." She suggested they cross the road into the square. "And whether or not you accept his proposal they see you as part of their family and will always offer you love and support."

Mrs Greenhaigh joined them. "That's right, and he said you were like a mother to his twins. He showed us a photo of them, nearly two, so cute. You know we were sorry about... well it happened years ago. We were pleased Freddy's reference and recommendation to Joseph Plaidon opened up a position at International Trade Promotions. David told us you did well there."

In a fervent voice Rosie said, "I was so grateful to you. It was a lifeline. It put me back on my feet. I took your advice, Mrs Greenhaigh, to drop my double-barrel surname."

"Oh please, call me Jennifer!"

Rosie nodded. "I don't talk about my past or personal life. That's why David had difficulty finding me."

"Oh heavens, would you have preferred us to contact you first?"

At Rosie's rueful grimace, the Brigadier blustered, "But he told us you gave up your career to look after his twins. And he seemed such a good man to us."

Jennifer reassured her, "We didn't speak of your past. We told him we prayed for you. Our hope you would find a good man."

The Brigadier's eyes twinkled, "The Lord has done that alright. Out of an ill wind he has given you a ready-made family to make your own." As he gave a deep chuckle of satisfaction, Jennifer admonished him for his lack of tact.

To clarify the situation Rosie stated, "I have no doubt David is a good man, but I'm not sure he is for me."

"I told him I knew your parents in India. Your mother was a Dawes before marriage, a sweet, pretty thing, if not perhaps naïve and vulnerable." The Brigadier frowned. "When I was posted back to India I met her again, she was married by then."

Jennifer, with an indulgent smile, interrupted, "The sun is quite warm, let's sit on that bench."

To Rosie that was a good idea, because it was unlikely 'preacher' man would spot her there. The Brigadier happily informed her, "It was 1940, seven months into the war, I flew out on a sea plane. In three days, I went from a bitterly cold March to a blazing hot April when most people had departed into the coolness of the mountains. Your mother was at the Club waiting for Leo's return. I arrived early, wanted to get out of the heat so persuaded her to let me accompany her." His eyes focused on a distant time. Jennifer patted his arm. In a wistful voice he said, "Simla, such a beautiful place. I've such fond memories of that time." He straightened up and said abruptly, "Leo arrived just as I was leaving. We didn't keep in touch. After the war my father mentioned Lord Dawes had died, and a distant relative had inherited the property. At the time I didn't connect that with Dee-Dee. It was years later on hearing Lord and Lady Doughty-Dawes lived at The Grange I made enquiries and then called up at the house."

A grimace changed his jolly countenance. "Hawkins showed me in, Leo was cold and strange, I said the usual friendly things and left. Several years later when visiting my father I met your mother with Cathy in Petersfield. She recognised me, but sadly, not I her. She was a shadow of the girl I had known. Concerned, I suggested with Cathy we catch up in a local café. At first, Dee-Dee nervously chain smoked, she told me about you, now at boarding school and Bertie being born disabled and needing constant care. On asking about Leo, your mother's worries spilled out."

Jennifer said briskly, "Freddy dear, after this morning sermon, suffice to say Leo has an odd way of going about things. We met Cathy selling produce at the WI. She told us your parents are now settled in India and unlikely to return due to the house being cold and damp and Dee-Dee's deteriorating health."

Perched on the edge of the seat overlooking the square, Rosie refrained from criticising her father's spending on frivolous parties while the majority of the house was in disrepair. How they were always immaculately dressed while during all her growing years she had to make do and mend. "I'm afraid my father believes my behaviour contributed to my mother's nervous disposition and ill health."

Aghast, Jennifer responded, "Oh my dear girl you mustn't believe that."

The Brigadier confided, "After I had met Dee-Dee and heard about Bertie, I thought to call again. As before, your father wasn't pleased to see me, and obviously angry that Dee-Dee had talked to me. He dismissed my advice to have Bertie's learning capabilities assessed so he could be educated accordingly.

Wide-eyed Rosie interrupted, "And that wouldn't have cost

him a penny as the money could have come from the Educational Trust Fund set up by the Dawes a few generations ago."

Looking puzzled the Brigadier frowned. "But he told me Bertie was badly deformed, had little brain, made unintelligible sounds, nothing could be done for him, and basically said, 'we know what is best, and I was to mind my own business'. I'm afraid I left it at that."

Rosie spluttered, "His view is to incarcerate Bertie, if not at 'The Grange' in an institution."

The Brigadier made a pained face. "I admit I was surprised to hear from your father a few years later saying you were bored at home and asking if you could help with my Parliamentary campaign."

Despite the morning's sermon Rosie couldn't contain her bitterness, "He had no interest in me. He was worried that being home my inquisitive nature might reveal what he was up to. From school I had to write a weekly letter, an answer was rare but full of his injunctions. He used my stupidity about Doug to excuse his swift departure to India. He worried I had slurred the family name, yet it now appears his real worry was the debt he was in. When he returned briefly four years ago, he announced he had put the 'The Grange' up for sale, and told me when the sale was complete, I should arrange for Bertie to be put in an institution."

The growing astonishment on the Greenhaighs faces made her suddenly feel uncomfortable. Anxious to leave she proclaimed more cheerfully, "But the house hasn't sold and when it does, I'll find a way to support Jack and Cathy so they can continue to care for Bertie. They have taught him what they can, and beyond his physical disabilities he's got a very active brain."

"Gosh, yes, well I admit I barely knew your father. In India I understood he worked for the government, cut quite a dash, although like most of us he was a bit of a rascal. When your mother married him, he was envied, but as beautiful and loveable as Dee-Dee was, she had no knowledge of hard work or responsibility. I was shocked at his attitude toward me when I spoke of Bertie, and am now appalled he has turned out to be such a bad egg." Rosie said nothing, the Brigadier hummed thoughtfully. "You know, of course, Dee-Dee was the unexpected child of a late marriage, and her mother died giving birth." Rosemary shook her head, the Brigadier looked surprised. "Your mother told me after she returned to India from the obligatory schooling in England, her father was seventy, quite frail and keen to see her married. Dee-Dee said Leo had charmed him and he had lived long enough to see her wed. My understanding was her father left her well provided for. Like us all, Leo knew the Partition was coming to India, and it was feared they would be a bloody massacre when the British troops withdrew. It was fortuitous Dee-Dee was left the house here for it gave them somewhere to go."

Puzzled, she asked, "My mother had money? When we arrived here, we had barely enough to eke out a living. We had to live in the kitchen as it was the only room in the house with any heat. Cathy told me inheritance tax and putting on a new roof took most of the money my uncle had left.

"But your grandfather lived his whole life in India, his money safely banked and growing with interest. I wonder why she didn't have it transferred to England."

Rosemary frowned, "I overheard rows about money, or lack of it. My assumption was it was my uncle's money they talked of." The square was growing quiet, feeling awkward she stood. "I'm sorry I shouldn't be telling you these things. I'd better go, please excuse me."

Jennifer halted her flight. "My dear girl, we all have 'skeletons' in our cupboards. And here comes one of ours."

Rosemary turned and fast approaching was the leather jacketed 'preacher' man. With laughter in his eyes, he took in her expression of dismay and confessed, "I didn't believe you were coming to church, any more than you did me."

Bemused, the Brigadier asked, "Have you two met?"

Amused, 'preacher' man answered, "I said, 'hello' when I saw her looking in Diana's shop window."

The Brigadier stood. 'Preacher' man gave a wry smile, his bright eyes stared into hers, as the Brigadier formerly introduced them. "Rosemary Doughty-Dawes meet the Reverend John Hall." Subconsciously, she mouthed his name as the Brigadier explained, "Johnny grew up in the village and recently returned to do his second term as a curate here before getting his own Parish." Johnny's cheeky smile grew broader as he stretched out his hand to shake hers.

Automatically, she took it. Emotion overwhelmed her. Hesitantly she said, "Johnny. The Johnny who sat next to me at school, listened to my woes and hugged me when I cried. At his nodding, she added, "Only yesterday I was wondering how life had treated you." The Greenhaighs astonishment was evident by their faces. His eyes filled with similar emotion as she spoke, and he held on to her hand. Her voice faltered, "You...you wrote me silly notes, made me giggle, gave me sweets. Oh I... I...can't believe I didn't recognise you earlier. I'm sorry I'm wary of talking to strangers."

Gently he drew her closer. "My Rosie! My lovely Rosie. I recognised you the moment I saw you."

"Why didn't you tell me?"

"I might have done except for the clear brush off and the 'going to church' line. The question was 'would you turn up?' That day when you didn't turn up for school and we were told you had left... well the light went out in my life."

Tears pricked her eyes as she stammered, "Oh Johnny."

"Why didn't you tell me you were leaving?"

"I didn't know. On the Saturday my father said I was going to boarding school and Jack took me on the Sunday night."

Johnny gazed into her eyes. "Mum said it was too far to cycle to your house, and I should stop acting like a silly, lovesick teenager."

With the evidence of her father's spite before them, the Greenhaighs looked at each other, bringing the Brigadier to shake his head and say, "Oh Rosemary."

Johnny gave him a curious look, before listening as she burbled on about the girls at boarding school being bitchy, bumptious, boisterous and very sporty. "They called me 'Zombie' because to protect myself I kept silent. You had befriended me, so I befriended Sylvia who wasn't strong enough to stand up to the bullies who taunted her inability to walk properly. I had no money for sweets but could read and play board games with her."

"That's my Rosie." His eyes filled with compassion looked deeply into hers. "You so needed to love and be loved." She sent him a fond smile and wondered how he found consolation. By his rounded body, perhaps he ate all the sweets he used to bring her. "As I said earlier, you are a very beautiful woman. Though, it sounds as if the intervening years have brought their troubles." He looked at her left hand, "You aren't married!" He sounded surprised. She shook her head and thought how different things would have been if she had stayed at the local school. Johnny advised, "Cheer up Rosie. I've no sweets, but am very happy to offer you the position of a Vicar's wife?"

"Oh Johnny," the Brigadier chortled affectionately, "What will you say next?"

Relieved the Brigadier considered that a joke, she responded in like manner with a small, shy smile. "Could we please begin with the sweets… "

Johnny's eyes seemed to twinkle as he responded, "I would rush out and buy them now if the shops were open." She giggled as she had as a child.

Johnny, a month older than her, had been a gangly bag of bones whose trousers were always too loose and his jacket arms too short. Because of his general dowdiness he was ostracised by the other kids, just as she was, but for coming from the big house and not the village. Through adversity they were drawn together, and he was happy to protect her. Within days he captured her lonely six year old heart and she loved him.

Johnny looked at his watch. "Sorry folks, it's nearly one o'clock and I've a lunch to go to. Suddenly they realised they all should be somewhere else. The 'goodbyes' were hurried, and as they separated in different directions the words were similar, "We'll be in touch."

CHAPTER 5

On Rosie's return Cathy was waiting to serve lunch. Bertie seemed unusually animated. Helen with loud laughter and constant chatter appeared to be on a 'high' which sent Jack scurrying to ensure he had locked the cellar door.

The meal over, Helen, arm in arm with Bertie, went for a stroll in the sunshine, giving Rosie opportunity to tell the Hawkins about the Greenhaighs and David's visit to them.

"I wondered how David found you." Jack put on the kettle and asked, "Did you see the new curate?"

In a nonchalant tone she replied, "Yes. Johnny Hall preached a good sermon."

"I know that name." Jack's brow creased. Rosie waited for him to recall why. "Wasn't that the boy who befriended you at school? I often talked to his mother at the school gate. She once asked me why a rich kid like you would hang around her poor boy. I told her appearances are deceptive. You were no more a rich kid, than he a poor one. His attraction came from what was within him."

"And in becoming a priest it seems Jack you were right.

"What did you think of the boy turned man?"

Before she answered Rosie advised with a grin, "Cathy had better drink her tea before I tell you!" As she regaled her two meetings with Johnny she ended, "It was odd as the moment I recognised Johnny something akin to love rose up in me. He felt it too for he said he hadn't any sweets, but could offer me the position of his wife."

Cathy's empty cup jumped on its saucer as she exclaimed, "Good grief, Rosie! Two marriage proposals in twenty four hours, neither expected, and I assume neither accepted."

Rosie nodded. Jack wisely counselled, "Children's friendships are simple. It's good to know Johnny has done well for himself, but the only real proposal on the table is David's. And his parents saw you as family. Do you like them? "

"Franz doesn't suffer fools gladly. He is like David in build, can be tough, gruff and intimidating with a similar booming voice. He has always been polite. I was encouraged when he said he would employ me if I ever needed a job. Margaret is petite, attractive with a gracious, gentle manner and a dry wit.

"He would employ you! What does he do?"

"He heads up a pharmaceutical company. Paul, Jill's husband, sometimes works for him. As a doctor, he's useful when organising and visiting the clinics they set up in third world countries and can deliver a supply of what we see as every day drugs."

Jack looked impressed. Cathy asked, "Why doesn't David work for his father?"

By living in close proximity to the Reinhardts she had been privy to their lives, and knew Franz didn't like to talk about Inharts success, or his personal wealth. "Franz believes his children should make their own way in life."

Jack commented, "It sounds as if David has 'made his own way in life'." Rosie nodded. When she didn't expand on that, Jack added, "It's interesting how the real gentry with money and status are comfortable with both top brass and the likes of us. But those who want to be seen as gentry need to feel superior and wouldn't dream of mixing with those they see as the lower classes." Rosie knew Jack was referring to her father. After all he had taken upon himself to inherit Lord Dawes title and add his surname to it. "I felt comfortable with David. Look how he engaged Bertie at dinner and he wasn't fazed by Rosie's revelation - only concerned for her."

Cathy couldn't hide her smirk as she added, "There's no doubt of his sexual attraction." Rosie made a disdainful grimace.

"Don't worry Rosie, I played the role of your father and told him to leave you to process his offer in your way and time, but empathy, care and love are the best ingredients to open up your heart."

Cathy grinned, "My my, Jack, what a wise man you have become. "

Looking pleased Jack reported, "David thanked us for having such a major influence in your life." As it appears, even as a girl, Rosie had a major influence on Johnny's life! It must be rare, but nevertheless flattering, that two unconnected men, with different personalities and lives would propose within hours of each other to the same girl. Tell us more about the other contender for your hand in marriage?"

"I only saw him for a few minutes, but could you see me as a Vicar's wife? It's been an extraordinary weekend. I'm tired. I need to do something mindless! Should you need me I'll be in my bedroom."

At her table by the window with her electric fire as near as safety would permit, she looked through her box of Butterick patterns, and those she made from designer outfits. Fashions changed, it wouldn't be easy to adapt them to the clothes that had caught her eye in the shop window. She recalled Johnny saying it was his sister's shop. If nothing else a visit would give her ideas to come out of her self-imposed mourning clothes. Jack knocked on her door to inform her David was on the telephone. When questioned he sheepishly revealed he had given him the number.

David, a man who always get to the point, asked, "Rosie, I'm just checking to see how you are. I'm sorry I had to leave last night, but I have been praying for you to have peace today."

Uncomfortable at his concern, unused to talking to him about personal matters, her reply was limited to "Thank you." After a brief silence she said, "I went to church today, met the Greenhaighs. They told me about your visit."

"Is that so!" and she heard the smile in his voice as he continued, "Freddy insisted I stayed for lunch. After two hours I felt I had been grilled more than the bacon they served!" His laughter vibrated down the phone causing her to hold the receiver at length. When he spoke again, he confirmed, "It seems I passed muster otherwise they wouldn't have given me your address."

To that Rosie hummed, considered telling him about Johnny, but decided against it. "I understand your urgency in needing my decision, but I need to think about the outcome if it doesn't work out.

"Rosie, I'm not calling to pressurize you. A six month courtship would entail time spent together, but nothing more than you wish. As to the end, with us both wanting the best outcome and causing the least disruption to our lives, I would quote the Beatles, "We can work it out!" Ring me to clarify anything, or talk further. I'll wait to hear from you." She had barely thanked him before the phone went dead.

The next morning seated by the telephone in the 'butler's pantry' she hesitated to ring Grace unsure if she was doing the right thing. Grace in her fifties had been David's PA until she married Wilhelm and went to live in Germany. On their return she hadn't told them she owned the mews cottage they paid rent on so they didn't know it was her who had given them a month's notice to leave. She hesitated. Could the Lord 'work it out'?

Grace however was true to her name in saying how pleased to hear from her, had guessed the cottage belonged to Rosie and happily explained that in knowing they had to leave, it had been the catalyst for them to invest in a property in London. "David showed us your note. He thought we might know the cottage's owner who could help to find you. We understood your reasoning. Wilhelm told David if he found you and you needed a job, he would recommend and furnish you with a glowing reference.

"How kind! David found me. He arrived on Saturday and proposed marriage."

"And your response?" Briefly Rosie explained the offer and her reservations.

"You have worked for David, you know he rarely makes rash decisions. Five years ago his offer to you would have been unthinkable, but today he respects and speaks of you in glowing terms. I'm confident you have more in common with him than just loving the twins. I assume courtship will include your returning to London to look after them."

"That's the reason I'm ringing. David suggested you might agree to my sleeping in the second bedroom at the cottage. You wouldn't have to leave quite so soon."

"That would certainly help us." Grace added, "Believe me, even if marriage to David isn't for you, he wouldn't be so small minded to stop you looking after the twins. They love you, whether as a nanny or mother. If David remarries, your friendship with him and his family need not change. You could be the twins' favourite auntie and they could stay with you when David and his wife would like time together. I know it's early days, but I gleaned that David's father is keen that as Jane's close friend, and in their confidence, you should run Jane's trust fund in the way she would have envisaged. Once the children go to school, you would have time to develop that maybe into a full time job."

"Oh Grace, what a rosy future you paint!"

Grace chuckled, "One that could be yours! I would say there's everything to gain and nothing to lose."

"Put like that, I would agree. But if David and I can't agree regarding the twins, then there is a risk of loving and losing everything."

"Friends argue, but in life we learn to give and take, forgive and be forgiven."

Rosie smiled. It seemed God was keen to imbed that principle! "David is trying hard. He came twice on Saturday, first with the proposal, the second time with flowers. He met Jack and Cathy, who are like my surrogate parents. They invited him to dinner, they think he's wonderful! Trouble is, I can't imagine relaxing with him, let alone being married to him."

"Give him a chance," Grace urged. "We were all shocked by

Jane's death, but the Lord can bring good from that. I believe Jane would be pleased that her legacy of life is in your capable hands."

"Helen is living here, she said much the same."

In repeating Grace's perspective to Jack and Cathy, Rosie pointed out, "So assuming Grace is right, even if I don't marry him, there is no reason why you can't enjoy David's friendship and be like grandparents to his twins!" Joy filled their eyes. That hymn '*And Can it Be*' did seem to be impacting her life. If the chains of the past had fallen off, maybe her heart was free to rise, go forth, to see how life could be.

However, when Jack left, Cathy cautioned, "Think hard before you dismiss marriage to David. Without it, you'll look after the twins without the authority of a mother. Their home won't be your home. David is a sexually attractive man and assuming he marries again, your attachment to the family could cause jealousy, if nothing else because of the twins' obvious love for you. "

Thoughtfully Rosie conceded, "I take your point about being their mother, but if we have a 'marriage of convenience' and if, as you say, David is a sexually attractive man, would it be fair to marry him when I have no intention or desire to engage in a sexual relationship?" Cathy made a sad grimace and might have commented except Bertie entered the room, stopped, rested on his stick and looked at them with a furrowed brow bringing Rosie to ask, "Bertie what's wrong?"

Before he could bring forth an answer Helen arrived, snuck her arm into his and leading him away gave uncalled for advice, "I've been telling Bertie that we should enjoy each day, take what comes, and not worry about tomorrow." Coming from Helen and seeing where she had ended up Rosie didn't find that particularly helpful.

Whatever the future may hold, it was time to glean ideas for making new outfits and where better than the village dress shop. On arriving she saw little similarity between Diana and Johnny. She was younger, shorter, thinner and with light blonde hair, not brown. Diana smiled and left her to browse through the designer clothes, all were at Knightsbridge prices. Once the lady she was advising disappeared into the changing room, she turned to ask, "Can I help you?"

Unhooking a hanger from the rack Rosie smiled, "This skirt design, cut in strips like patchwork on the bias, is quite lovely in the way it swirls around."

Diana suggested, "Why not try it on?"

Rosie lowered her voice, "I make my own clothes, and use the designs of others to produce them."

Diana's smile tightened. She looked her up and down. "Did you make the dress you're wearing?"

Rosie glanced in a nearby mirror at the plain, dark grey tailored dress, with its classic round neck, nipped in narrow waistband, straight but not tight skirt, slightly longer than the fashion. "I did, but with my new haircut I feel the need for something less formal."

Diana hummed thoughtfully, before her attention was drawn by the woman leaving the dressing room. Feeling awkward, and having gained ideas for her new wardrobe, she felt to leave, but at the door was stopped as Diana called, "Don't go, I'd like to talk to you?"

Surprised, she nodded, and hoped her honesty hadn't upset her.

The woman bought the outfit and when she left Diana sighed, "I so needed that sale. Thank you for waiting. People are attracted to the clothes I buy in, but not everyone can afford them." Taking the skirt from the rack she asked, "Could you make a copy of this?" Seeing Rosie's nod, she observed, "You must have tailoring skills for the design, and the cut of the dress you're wearing looks like a Harrods exclusive."

"That's because it is."

Bewildered, Diana retorted, "But you said…"

Cutting across her Rosie explained, "I live in London. I look, picture the item, examine how it's put together and then copy it. The secret is in the quality of the material and the cut, but I confess it's easier to buy the item, make a paper pattern and return it the next day."

"Really! That's amazing! I could use someone to do that for me. My prices have to cover my overheads and living expenses. I have regulars, but most people only flock here when I have a sale. I rent the shop and flat above, but it's getting harder and harder to make ends meet. Fortunately, my brother is staying and he helps with the rent." She smiled, "Two can eat as cheaply as one."

That same endearing quality in Johnny she recognised in Diana, and hoped Johnny wasn't telling everyone to await her sale. Not wanting to get embroiled further she decided against mentioning their childhood friendship. "To my knowledge there isn't a law stopping the copying and producing of the designs of others. Could I borrow this patchwork skirt and bring it back tomorrow?"

Understandably Diana looked sceptical. "I don't know you.

Buy it, make one for me and return the original undamaged in the next few days and I'll give you a refund."

Rosie agreed. She had saved most of the money David paid her, made a little profit in renting her cottage, and just sent David's cheque to the bank. She had more in her account than ever before. At the Coutts Bank cheque, Diana looked impressed and rang them to clarify Rosie had an account with them. Having directed her to a fabric shop several streets away she declared, "I'm interested in seeing the finished result."

Rosie chose a fabric of similar weight to the original, picked an emerald green material with a navy pattern she could reverse and cut without waste, and a plain navy to go between each panel. The shop assistant helped in working out the amount needed, and sold her the end of two rolls of material to experiment with. That, with the green lining, was twenty percent of the price of the finished garment she had had purchased! Feeling challenged and excited she returned to the car.

To have a project, one she enjoyed, not only soothed her mind, but brought clarity to her thoughts. She tried on the original red and black skirt and saw she had lost weight, but it still flowed down widening and swinging around just below the calf. After several hours pinning and cutting, she had both a pattern in tissue paper and a tacked skirt using the remnant material. After a few alterations it was ready for machining, causing Cathy to comment, "You have a talent with the needle."

With a wry look she retorted, "More a case of need, and practise makes perfect. I want to finish this before dinner, if I don't appear save it for me."

Later, as Rosie appeared wearing the skirt, Bertie clapped his hands as she twirled around in the kitchen. Helen, intent on the Monopoly game they were playing observed, "Looks nice, but not my style." Bertie loved Monopoly and had long since proved he had the ability to read, count, strategize and win. It was fortunate for Rosie that the gravy had almost dried out on her dinner as suddenly Bertie banged on the table causing her plate to dance. She exclaimed 'Bertie' as she looked up and saw him grinning with delight at having bagged Helen's 'Park Lane' due to her inability to pay the rent.

Jack looked over his newspaper at their friendly squabbling and smiled. Bertie's communication wasn't clearer, but he had certainly become more animated since Helen's arrival. To Rosie it appeared Helen, banished from her own family, had adopted hers.

Despite her tiredness, once in bed, old worries surfaced. If Helen made Bertie happy that was good, but why did she feel wary about her motives? How much longer would they be able to live here? Bertie needed the Hawkins' care, could she support them? Her mind filled with the pros and cons of marrying David. She must have fallen asleep for she awoke to the wooden shutters rattling. It felt as if the high wind and heavy rain beating on the windows had taken up the battle of her mind. Snuggling into her bed she considered God's plan and purpose for her life, and as the storm began to subside, so did her fears at giving 'courtship' a chance.

After breakfast she telephoned David. As he boomed "Reinhardt" into her ear she took a deep breath and said more confidently than she felt, "David, it's Rosie." In the pause, she could almost feel his tension as if bracing himself for bad news. "I spoke to Grace yesterday. She has agreed I could stay with them. But before making a final decision I would like to tell you what she said."

Had David been warned? He didn't interrupt, and hummed positively throughout. As she ended, he immediately declared, "Grace is absolutely right, my thoughts entirely. I thought you realised, I should have explained. I, and the family, value your friendship. If it doesn't work out between us there is no possibility of you being rejected."

Rosie said, "I thought if I only stayed six months the twins were still young enough to forget me."

"That was if you decided to leave us."

"Oh I see! Grace said I have got nothing to lose and everything to gain."

In her ear David chortled, "Well that's one way of putting it. Rosie, we'll take things slowly. If you have decided to return, would it be too soon if I came to collect you this evening?"

"Grace and Wilhelm won't expect me quite so soon."

Confidently, David stated, "They'll be fine. I'll let them know."

Rosie pushed aside feeling bulldozed to say lightly, "Well, Grace did say to aid our romance they would be happy to babysit."

"In which case, I'll take them up on that for this evening."

"If you can arrive in time for dinner, Cathy will be delighted to feed you."

She heard the smile in his voice, "That's an invitation I can't refuse. ITP can manage without me for a couple of hours. I'll aim to leave at three and should be with you by five." He chuckled, "You can give me a tour of your estate!"

"It's not mine, it never will be. Bertie is the son and heir. My father has made it clear I'll get nothing."

"I'm finding it hard to like your parents."

"That's something on which we agree David! But on Sunday I felt the Lord was telling me, "'Forgive them for they know not what they do'. I'm still working on that!"

"Oh Rosie!" Surprised, she heard a sympathetic catch in his voice, before he added, "I'm grateful you didn't keep me on tenterhooks and for your willingness to return so soon. The twins will be delighted to see you. Let me reiterate my desire that despite my failings I want to make you happy."

Not knowing how to respond she replied, "Thank you. I'll see you later" and put the phone down.

The decision made, her packing didn't take long. In the need to return the original skirt, and finish the navy and emerald one, she had left out the electric sewing machine the Reinhardts had given her for Christmas. By twelve-thirty it was ready, the sun had dried out the wet roads, but driving into town there was a light debris of broken twigs and mud on the road.

Diana greeted her at the shop door. "I'm just closing up for lunch. Come inside, I assume you've made the pattern?" Rosie handed her the original skirt and after checking it, Diana returned Rosie's cheque asking, "How long will it take you to make the skirt?" Rosie lifted it from her bag causing Diana to gasp, "You've made it already!" She carefully examined it. "It's impossible to tell the copy from the original. In fact your colour co-ordination is better than the original. Would you be willing to make more clothes for me?"

"I'm returning to London tonight, and doubt I'll have much time in the days ahead."

Diana looked genuinely upset. "I was hoping as we both share an eye for good clothes we could become friends. Your expertise would be a tremendous help to my business. I could sell that dress you were wearing yesterday a dozen times."

In truth she answered, "I would like that. I have connections in the area and will make fleeting visits. I enjoy dressmaking and creating material toys for the twins."

"You have twins. Oh, how lovely, they must keep you busy."

Rosie didn't acknowledge that, but suggested, "I'll see what time I have. I usually work in my size, it is a popular one, and I would happily sell anything I make on to you for the cost of materials."

"Oh I need to pay you for this and your time."

"A thought jumped into her head. Why not repay Johnny's generosity to her as a child by giving his sister the skirt? She pointed to it on the counter. "Now I have the pattern, I can easily make another. Please, accept this as a gift."

Taken aback, Diana exclaimed, "Why, why would you do that?"

With a smile Rosie said, "Sorry I have to go" and backing towards the door answered, "How about because I like you?"

Diana followed her out. "Please do come again." Rosie walked around the car as Diana called, "I don't even know your name. Rosie slipped into the driver's seat, pretended not to hear, closed the door and drove off. She would like a friendship with Diana and Johnny, but one thing at a time. She had first to embark on a courtship with David.

Back at the house, Cathy reported Bertie was restless and upset at hearing she was returning that night to London. She ran up to his bedroom over the library. With his difficulty to articulate his words, they had developed a personal sign language, which had convinced her Bertie didn't lack intelligence. And now, with the sun shining, he indicated he would like to talk to her while strolling down to the lake.

From birth, their father had insisted he be hidden away, seeing it as a personal disgrace to have fathered a child diagnosed with cerebral palsy and prone to fits. Only Jack and Cathy's persistent desire to care for Bertie had circumvented his being put in an asylum. In nursing him from a baby, Cathy knew he didn't deserve that, and later proved he could learn when she taught him basic arithmetic, reading and writing. He loved reading. He still spent hours in the library studying the Encyclopaedia Britannica. He could write with his good hand, and as he moved into teenage years drew diagrams and made complicated equations they couldn't fathom. Understandably, he became frustrated and angry when having imbibed so much he didn't have the ability to impart it easily to others. Over the years, when at home and knowing his eagerness to learn, Rosie found games and puzzles to amuse him, and knew she shouldn't begrudge Helen doing that, or taking her place in his life.

When small, Jack had made a simple metal frame on wheels that fitted under Bertie's arm pits, stretching him and giving him enough mobility to exercise his good leg. The frame had been extended many times, and when Bertie got stronger he had learnt to balance using a walking stick. As long as Bertie had support he could hobble, rather than drag his leg.

From the day she had first held Bertie in her arms Rosie loved him, and as he grew his eyes reflected his love of her. She would tell him her troubles, he liked the attention and as his understanding grew his response was reflected in his eyes. As his speech improved she realised the need to be careful about what she said, or he heard.

The slope down to the lake was fairly gentle, she talked and she listened carefully to his indistinct words as he asked, 'What is a 'marriage of convenience?' When she tried to avoid answering he became frustrated so she attempted to explain, "A man and woman marry because they share a common aim, in this case our caring for the twins."

At her answer he looked puzzled, and asked, "No love? No sexual intercourse?"

She blushed and remembered the time he had pulled her into the library and asked her to explain the explicit pictures he had found in an encyclopaedia. To her relief birds suddenly arose out of nearby bushes, causing them to stop and turn. Bertie stared, and muttered something. As she peered into the undergrowth where disturbed bushes were still moving, Bertie tapped her arm and signed with his good hand, 'Rabbit for dinner'.

Rosie winced at the thought of Jack killing and skinning a rabbit, "Not tonight. That could have been a poacher. I'll tell Jack." Bertie looked worriedly through the trees. "It's alright Bertie he's long gone" and drew him on to the shed they fondly termed 'the boat house'. Jack had repaired the shed, but the little boat she had found there had long since rotted away. Several centuries before, the river above the estate had been diverted to create a lake in the natural basin of the land. It was only six foot deep at its centre. A mechanical sluice gate could be raised or lowered to keep the water level, but years of neglect had caused the lake to silt up with weeds growing in profusion under the water.

Rosie opened the wide wooden doors on to the 'boat house' veranda which enclosed the platform, making it a cosy balcony over the lake. It was warm enough to put out deck chairs, but not enough to sit on the edge and dangle their feet in the water.

In talking about David courting her it was obvious from Bertie's hand signals and odd words he liked Helen and wanted to court her. In knowing Helen's proclivity to sexual activities, she felt to try stalling that development. "David and I have been friends for several years, courting isn't to be taken lightly." Bertie didn't look convinced, so she talked about the twins and their cute little ways and suggested, "I'll ask David to bring them to visit you." Bertie in his excitement jumped up, causing her to leap forward in fear that he would fall into the water. With his size and weight, she would not be able to rescue him single handed as she had once before.

A sudden squall of wind whistling around the boathouse brought her back from that memory, as did a dark cloud moving over the sun. "Look Bertie we better pack up and return to the house." But it wasn't until she closed the wide doors of the boathouse that she saw how ominous the sky looked.

They were about half way up the incline to the house when she felt the first drop of rain. Bertie stopped, pointed to her scarf, and then his disabled leg. Immediately she saw his point. When children, she tied that leg to her good one and with her arm across his back, they would walk a three-legged a rhythm which eventually enabled him to run.

As she whipped off her woollen scarf, she laughed, "We're going to get wet whether we succeed or fail." Swiftly bandaging his left leg against her right, they were ready to go. After a wobbly start, the old rhythm slipped into place, and although the rain was now falling heavily, they made good progress having the kind of childish fun she had forgotten existed.

Hearing a voice on the wind, she looked up to see two figures standing at the edge of the West Wing of the house. "Jack is with a man, but it's not David." Bertie strained his neck to see. They lost momentum, balanced, and toppled into a heap on the wet grass at the side of the narrow path. Bertie's heehaw laugh could be mistaken for crying, and as she was untangling herself from falling on top of him, a worried voice above enquired if they were hurt. Rosie, in a need to undo the scarf so they could separate, only managed, "We're fine!" before a breathless Jack arrived.

He chortled, "I guessed what you did. You were always an inventive child." But by then Rosie was staring into the amused face of a man who was the boy she had loved and lost.

Johnny's cheeky bright eyes laughing into hers made the years vanished, he was rescuing her again. Somehow it didn't matter if she was dripping wet and her clothes stained with grass, her hand went up to meet his. Memories flooded in. That same hand had pulled her up from the nettles she had been pushed in and he had offered her dock leaves to relieve her pain. That hand had picked her up when she had fallen in the playground. He had wet his grubby handkerchief to clean her graze and held it as a cold compress to stop the bruising. Often his hand would take her from the bullying children and give her sweets to help her forget their unkindness.

Johnny's brown hair was hidden under one of Jack's peaked caps, the rain dripping off on to his nose. His high cheek bones as a child had been hollow, but now in his fully rounded face, his lips stretched into an even wider permanent smile. His missing front teeth hadn't grown in perfect formation, which seemed to make him even more endearing.

Two short discreet coughs from Hawkins brought them back to reality. With a wry smile she gave Johnny a shy look and said winsomely, "A sweet always makes me feel better" and with that, they hugged, and released the laughter brewing up inside.

Bertie presumably hauled up by Jack watched them, his frown creased as he questioned in his indistinct way, "Who are you?"

With the rain beating down, Jack admonished, "Not now Bertie, let's get you inside."

Johnny grinned at Bertie and then suggested, "Jack, if you clasp your wrist and with your other hand mine we can form a seat for Bertie to sit on." Jack complied, and as they bent their knees Bertie didn't need further encouragement to use his human carriage, his heehaw laughter revealing his amusement.

Head bent against the wind and the lashing rain, Rosie led the way. She wondered why, after all these years, Johnny should reappear in her life and bring her instantly back to childhood, the innocence of first love, and her lack of embarrassment in looking like a drowned rat in need for rescuing.

At the front door Cathy awaited with towels. Bertie, due to his weak chest was quickly stripped of everything he could decently take off, wrapped in towels and rushed into a waiting hot bath. The men having donned sou'westers, coats and boots, were dry underneath, and as they headed to the kitchen for a nice hot cup of tea, she ran upstairs. Her short hair quickly towelled dried, she changed into the jumper and skirt she had put aside to wear back to London. On arriving in the kitchen, she discovered the two men huddled by the fire chatting like old friends. Breaking into their conversation she asked, "Have you two met before?"

Amused, Johnny turned to reply, "Not since Jack picked you

up from school, but we've made good inroads in the time I've been here." She bent over the tray before them and poured herself a cup of tea. "While waiting for you, Jack and I found we had something in common."

"And what would that be?"

Johnny chuckled, "From the moment we first saw you we've been in love with you."

For the second time that day she felt her face heat up, and embarrassed retorted, "Oh Johnny, you can't love someone you don't know. I'm not the same girl you knew at school."

"You are to me. There's still that barb of speech, which reveals your vulnerability, uncertainty and fear. You have a caring heart and a sense of fun." Unbidden tears filled her eyes, she bit her lower lip to stop it trembling. Johnny stood to put his arm around her shoulders and instructed, "Enough of that" and turned her towards the kitchen table to point out a dress box on which was Diana's logo, "No sweets, but something more adult to brighten your day." How could she accept a present from one man, when she had just agreed to a courtship with another? She looked at Jack, he shrugged.

"Rosie, I had to persuade you that eating my sweets wouldn't poison you. Believe me, receiving and wearing what's inside that box won't harm you either."

"Johnny, it's not that simple."

"It can be. I saw how wistfully that haughty girl I fell in love at school was looking in Diana's window, so I decided to surprise you." He reached out and grabbed her hand. "Come on, open the box." Again, she looked to Jack who sent her a wide-eyed non-committal look. Had he told Johnny of her pending courtship with David? With a deep breath she lifted the lid and gasped. Inside was the skirt she had completed a few hours earlier. "It's beautiful isn't it? On Sunday evening, I told my sister I met an old school friend admiring the clothes in her shop window and wanted to buy something for her. Her reply was, 'You must think she's special, for at cost, it would be a huge slice out of your stipend'. Then a miracle happened. At lunch today, she told me about a woman who had just left after giving her a skirt and if it fitted you I could have it. I liked that, similar to Cinderella and the glass slipper!" Johnny grinned at her. "Well don't just stare at it, take it out and try it on." As she lifted it out of the box she debated whether to tell Johnny she made it while Jack's expression went instantly from incredulity to inscrutability as she truthfully confirmed, "Oh I love it. It's just what I would have chosen myself."

"Then let's hope it fits. Go and put it on, and give us a twirl."

Before Rosie could respond, the door opened to reveal Helen. She was wearing a very short, tight black skirt and a red, low cut, breast hugging top that showed as much cleavage as her small breasts could reveal without being indecent. Inwardly Rosie groaned. Did she deliberately dress to embarrass David? No doubt if she had known of Johnny's visit and he being the local curate she would have selected even more bizarre clothing. As always, Helen had started speaking before she was through the doorway. "Bertie's having a hot bath. Cathy said you got caught in the rain. It's turning into one hell of a storm out there. Oh hello," her voice took on a sexy lilt, "And who may you be?" It seemed Helen seeing any eligible male would lit up like a Christmas tree. Pushing back her mop of tight red curls, she stuck out her chest and sashayed towards Johnny, her hand outstretched. "A visitor here is a rare treat. You're the second in a few days. I bet you weren't invited either? Tell me, have you come far?" Johnny shaking her hand looked decidedly uncomfortable under her seductive gaze.

Rosie, still holding the skirt against her, intervened. "Helen is staying with us" and to Helen she said pointedly, "Johnny is an old school friend. He has just returned to Petersfield."

"Oh right." A frown formed on Helen's brow "Why are you hugging that skirt?"

"It's a present from Johnny. I'm about to see if it fits. "

"Of course it will fit, you…"

Rosie grabbed Helen's hand, and spoke over her, "Yes I know what you're going to say" she manoeuvred her toward the door, "I can always alter it."

Helen gave her a puzzled look, then undeterred sent Johnny a provocative smile saying, "Don't go away, I'll be back." Rosie shut the door behind them as Helen queried, "I don't get it!"

Hurrying her away Rosie urged, "I'll tell you on the way to my bedroom." On entering her room the wind was whistling through the window frames, the rain lashing against them, bringing Rosie to comment, "It's so cold and dark in here, no-one would believe it's only half past three. Help me close the shutters."

Shivering, Helen moved to the nearest one. "So two men are after you! Awkward if David arrives before Johnny leaves. He won't be pleased to find he has a rival for your affections." Rosie frowned. She had been forced to shutter out her love for Johnny, but he appeared keen to restore their friendship, and even to progress it further.

Helen commented, "Don't look so worried, with this weather, David will probably be held up. Did you know Cathy is making a steak and mushroom pie in his honour?"

A knock and Cathy's head came around the door. "I thought I heard voices, Bertie is…" Her eyes widened seeing Rosie in the skirt she had reportedly given to Diana.

Rosie quickly explained for Bertie was calling down the hall, "El'n, 'E'ln."

Helen grinned. "Just tell David when he sees that skirt that you made it," she shrugged, "it is the truth. You entertain Johnny, I'll go and play Scrabble with Bertie." Cathy looked skyward as Helen skipped along the corridor. Rosie asked quietly, "Is that grimace for Helen's friendship with Bertie, or Johnny turning up to confess his undying love of me?"

"Helen! I don't want Bertie hurt, or compromised in any way. And Jack told Johnny you were returning to London tonight to look after David's twins with a view to marriage. Johnny's response was you weren't married yet, and all is fair in love and war. There'll be no pistols at dawn, but he has hope for a fair judgement."

"I just wish he turned up before David."

There was no doubt about Johnny's love and admiration when he fixed his attention on her entering the kitchen and declared, "Rosie, each time I see you, you look more beautiful, and that skirt looks as though it were made for you." Behind him Jack and Cathy exchanged glances.

"Johnny you've always had a generous heart, and the truth is this skirt was made for me. I love it and accept it. I know the bond at school is still there, but I also need to tell you I just committed myself to a six-month courtship with David whose children I love. I feel I should stick to that."

"Dear sweet Rosie, I understand. If you also love him, I wouldn't want to come between you, but would wish to become good friends. Over the years I've cherished every moment and memory of you." He turned to the Hawkins, "I would sit with Rosie at school dinners, and eat what she didn't." He rubbed his stomach, "See Rosie what you started."

She giggled, "I could say the same to you. You introduced me to chocolate. Now when I start eating it, I can't stop, so I don't buy it anymore." Her eyes narrowed, "That's called discipline."

"And that's my Rosie, sweets from my sweetheart" Johnny

teased.

"But I'm not for unwrapping."

Johnny chuckled, "It could change by Christmas."

Laughing she replied, "Oh Johnny this reminds me of school!" Their continuing bantering back and forth led Cathy to comment, "I bet your parishioners love you."

"Of course! I rescue them from storms, lighten atmospheres, but am careful never to outstay my welcome." He stood. "In the hope they'll want to see more of me, and may even be enticed to visit the church. Rosie, you will be impressed to know that to lose weight, I am disciplining myself to cycle everywhere, and grateful the way home from here is downhill."

"You cycled! I assumed you drove. It's quiet in here, but believe me there is gale force wind out there. You can't possibly cycle in that."

"What then, dear Rosie, would you suggest? I stay the night?" His wink gave her reason to suspect he knew David's arrival was imminent.

Eyebrows raised she informed him in a stately tone, "We have the bedrooms, but cold and damp, and not recommended." She turned to Jack, "Would Johnny's bike fit in the back of the Viva?"

Jack looking out of the window observed, "I hadn't realised the weather was that bad. Come on Johnny, with the car and your bike in the garage at least we won't get wet while trying."

Rosie peeled the vegetables, as Cathy made the pastry she reminisced, "It was obvious as a child you were fond of Johnny, always saying 'Johnny said this, Johnny did that'. And it's lovely to see you so at ease with him. He would bring you a quiet and easy life, very different to the one I suspect you would have with David." The men returned to report they wrapped the bike in tarpaulin and put it in the boot, but the lid wouldn't close so they had tied it down to make it safe. Jack went on, "After I take Johnny home, I'll go around the house and 'batten down the hatches'."

"I can drive Johnny home."

Jack gave a pointed look to the clock.

"Petersfield is only ten minutes each way. I can be back in half an hour."

CHAPTER 6

As Rosie backed out of the garage, a gust of wind buffeted the car bringing her to exclaim, "Johnny, you couldn't possibly ride your bike in this."

Dark, menacing clouds hung over them. Twigs and leaves swirled around and rain splattered against the windscreen. On reaching the end of the kitchen garden wall, she turned through the open five bar gate into the narrow road, where bramble hedges on both sides brought a measure of protection from the storm onslaught. At the main road and waiting to turn right into the traffic, she switched on her headlights. With the regular beat of the windscreen wipers, the engine noise and the beating rain on the car, she had to raise her voice to be heard. "The trees make this road dark, but this is more like night than day!" Seeing a gap in the traffic she put her foot down and turned out. A car came up behind her flashing its lights and seconds later when he overtook her, she said loudly, "I would say in these conditions I am doing a sensible speed, but there is always someone in a hurry."

"In these conditions, I'm beginning to think that a cold and damp bedroom might have been preferable."

Having strained to hear Johnny's words, she turned to smile and saw the tension on his face. "It might feel scary, but we'll soon be on the outskirts of town."

"But you have to drive back through this."

Rosie smiled, dear Johnny, thoughtful as ever. With her eyes on the road she declared, "I'll be safer against the hill side, without the trees and a virtual precipice to my left!"

The rain, perhaps due to the overhanging trees, seemed to lessen, and it looked like Johnny felt safer for he asked, "Tell me about the man who's going to romance you for the next six months?"

Glad of the need to concentrate on the road, she asked, "Were you hoping we might take up again from being childhood sweethearts?"

"I had a mind to. No-one else in the intervening years has touched my heart in the way the beautiful girl with the giggle did twenty-three years ago!"

"Oh Johnny, surely not?" After another quick smile in his direction, she said thoughtfully, "I have precious memories of you and could say much the same. Since you, I've only once met a man I have found easy to love, but he had only eyes for another. His eyes, like yours, reflected a 'positive' disposition, a man you felt would understand your deepest hurts and fears." She chuckled, "You are an ideal person for a vicar in waiting!"

A glance at Johnny revealed a creased brow, as he questioned, "Are you able to tell David about your deepest hurts and fears?"

"David cares about me, but he's a complex…!" A loud thud made her jump, and as she exclaimed, "What the..!" a large tree branch, having just hit the windscreen rolled off the bonnet. To avoid driving into, or over it, she swerved, slammed her foot on the brake and glimpsed Johnny being thrown forward. Alarmed, she cried out, "Johnny!" but was diverted as the back end of the car skidded round and the remainder of the windscreen became like jigsaw pieces distorting her vision. The force and impact of Johnny's head hitting the windscreen had punched a hole in it before propelling him back into his seat. The engine stalled, the car halted. Shaken, she turned to see Johnny sitting upright with a stunned expression. When he said nothing, she reached out and touched his arm. Behind them horns blared. It compelled them to lean forward and push out the cracked glass. The steering wheel hindered her efforts, bringing Johnny to stretch across and help push out the glass at her eye level. It was then she saw mingled blood and rain dripping off his chin. Dismayed, she cried out, "Johnny you're hurt."

Ignoring her, in a tight voice he instructed, "Move the car." Rosie turned the key in the ignition, and at the same time saw they were straddled across the road. Her legs shook as she drew her foot up on the clutch, the car kangarooed forward before the engine stalled. As Johnny pushed out more glass he directed, "Try again." Down the hill in the pervading gloom, she could see the lights of a large oncoming vehicle. Fighting a wave of panic, she cried inwardly, 'Oh God, help us'! Johnny's voice took on a quiet urgency. "Start the engine Rosie." In obedience she turned the key. Despite the oncoming lorry and the rain now in her face, she concentrated on putting the car in motion.

Johnny, in a calm voice observed, "Slowly does it, keep moving to the left." She heard the screeching of lorry brakes as he instructed, "Straighten up." Light burst in before the lorry levelled with them. She braced herself for the impact on the rear of the car, and prayed she had taken the right action to avoid being pushed over the side of the hill. Her rear view mirror revealed the headlights of cars behind them and in front, through rain and darkness, the road was clear. Trembling from head to foot she automatically brought the car to a standstill by the side of the road.

Concerned, she looked across at Johnny who, with his head back against the head rest, released a whistle as if he too had been holding his breath. He wiped his face with a folded handkerchief, held it to his head and stretched out his other hand to comfortingly rest on her thigh. Mindlessly, they stared ahead of them.

Her car door opened, cold air rushed in, and a loud, gruff voice verified their experience, "That was a close call mate." The face of a middle-aged stubble-bearded man peered into the car, his expression and tone changed. "Are you alright lass?" She nodded. "You did well not to panic. Are you hurt?" Rosie pointed to Johnny, "No, but he is."

The words were barely out of her mouth when Johnny's door was opened, the blast of air across the car caused it to rock. A man using his umbrella as a roof over the open door bent down to look in. "Phew, that was a nasty moment. Are you okay?" She saw his grimace at Johnny's wound, but he said cheerily, "Seems you've had a bit of a bump." Shakily she explained what she had seen. Mervin introduced himself, assured Johnny he had done a first aid course and asked, "Mind if I take a look?" Slowly Johnny peeled back his bloodied handkerchief, causing Mervin to say quickly, "Okay, keep that tight against it. Rest your head back. Looks as if you might need some stitches." She saw his grimace across the car to the man standing by her.

"Don't worry lass, I'm Arnie and have a first aid kit in my lorry." As Arnie closed her door, Rosie realised several people were congregating in the middle of the road between the cars which were now stopped behind his lorry.

Mervin glanced across at her. "What about you? Did you hit the steering wheel?" She shook her head and pointed to her safety belt. He nodded. "Stay there. We'll see what's best to do."

As he closed the car door, she saw Johnny's eyes were closed and foolishly asked, "Will you be alright?" His hand patted a positive response. Shaking inside, she mopped her wet face with her scarf and relived what had happened in the last few minutes.

Another man using his umbrella like a shield against the rain knocked on her window. She rolled it down. He bent in to speak, "I've just been told that a branch fell and hit your windscreen. If you hadn't swerved" he swallowed hard, "we could have all concertinaed into one another. Rosie, already considering divine intervention, confessed in a quavering voice, "I called upon the Lord. It's Him I have to thank."

The man hummed, but his voice was filled with emotion as he said, "I don't know how that lorry coming up the hill missed you. If we're shocked, you both must be. Can we help in any way?"

Rosie informed him, "Johnny's hurt. He hit his head. Someone is going to bandage it." With her wits returning she stated, "He'll need an ambulance. There's a phone box about a mile up the hill."

He nodded, and went to relay that message to those congregating in the road. Johnny, without moving, sounded strained as he assured her, "Don't worry! Heads are prone to bleeding." Anxious, she took his hand in hers. He added, "It's my fault I wasn't wearing my seat belt. It's only about two miles into town, if…" a knocking on her window interrupted him.

She wound her window down. Arnie, his oilskins running with water shouted against the force of the wind, "We need to get this car off the road. I'm told further down there's a layby. Driving with the rain in your face is going to be hazardous. Do you think you can do that?" Not wanting to cause further problems she nodded.

Johnny's door opened, the cold wind blew through the car as Mervin bent in to instruct, "Hold this pad on your head and I'll wrap a bandage around it. We thought about an ambulance, but the driver behind me says he can drop you both at the hospital, which means you will get there quicker, and we'll clear the road."

Johnny in a pained voice said slowly, "Okay! But Rosie needs to get home."

Arnie repeated 'home' as Mervin asked Johnny, "Have you got a nasty headache?"

Over his groan, she replied, "It's two miles up the hill."

"Arnie turned to yell at the gathered group, "Those going up the hill can you drop this lady home?" As Arnie went to move towards those who had stepped forward, she protested, "I'm not leaving Johnny in this state."

Squeezing her hand, he said in pained voice, "Nice thought,

kiddo, but I'll be okay."

The shock, his being injured and his words stirring her love of the past she protested through her tears, "You are not okay. I'm not leaving you."

Mervin now bandaging Johnny's head indicated she could pass the first aid kit back to Arnie. Johnny took the opportunity to tell him, "Rosie lives at 'The Grange' two miles up, turn left and a mile down a narrow road." Arnie nodded and headed to those standing by. She could hear the strain in Johnny's voice as he pleaded, "Please Rosie, I'd rather not worry about how you'll get home. What would David think?"

Tearfully she cried, "I don't care what David thinks. You're my friend. You're my priority right now." Johnny squeezed her hand.

A teenager jumped into the back seat behind Johnny. "What a day! I'm Luke. I'm going past the hospital. I doubt anyone in this weather will go out of their way to take you home, but if you can drive to the layby I'll take you both to the hospital."

Arnie back by her window commented, "I'm afraid I've no luck with a lift for you, and without much of a windscreen, this storm is going to soak you and the interior of the car when you leave it."

Mervin added, "It would seem sensible to transfer Johnny now to Luke's car."

"There's a tarpaulin wrapped around a bike in the boot, perhaps I could try and use it to lessen the damage."

Arnie nodded, "I'll take a look." Mervin nodded and moved to the back of the car. One man was making his way down the growing line of cars behind the lorry, obviously asking if someone could take her home.

Arnie spoke through the gap at the top of her window. "The good news is, lass, it's a good size tarpaulin. I'll put it on the back seat. It will easily stretch across the windscreen and if you open the car doors and shut the ends into them it will help anchor it in place." Luke sat forward to confirm he could manage that with her help. "The bad news is, so far, we haven't found anyone willing to take you home, but a lorry driver said he would keep trying to find someone while his mate continues to direct the traffic around you. I'm afraid it would be foolish to attempt to take our lorry down a country lane. He gave a deep chuckle, "So lass you may get your way after all. Now, I'm going to have to move off. I'm causing a blockage in both directions."

Rosie choked out her thanks.

"Aye well, if it weren't me, it would have been someone else. I've a good view from my high cab, I saw the problem. It's easier to slow going up a hill than down. The man down there talking to car drivers could still find you a lift home. I'd best be going. Good luck." A minute later the lorry engine started, he gave a 'toot toot' and began to pull away. The cars behind him started up their engines, and as they moved slowly forward, their occupants stared at them sitting in the car. Mervin and Luke, at Johnny's open door, were discussing Johnny's transfer to Luke's car. In the distance a horn blared, followed by others. Their heads turned, and through the deep gloom they saw headlights rapidly approaching on their side of the road. Surely nobody would be foolish to overtake the slow line of traffic coming up the hill. There was no time to get out. Mervin slammed shut Johnny's door, she screamed, "Johnny" and squeezing his hand, she closed her eyes and braced herself.

Eyes closed, and calling on the Lord she awaited the crash. She didn't hear the screech of brakes or feel the impact, instead a bright light pierced her eyelids. She opened and closed them against it. In the distance she heard a voice booming, "Oh God!" It registered, causing her to open her eyes and murmur questioningly, "David?" In the bright dazzling light, a silhouetted man ran across her vision. She had heard of people who dying looked down upon themselves, but she could still feel the rain on her face. Her car door was wrenched open and that familiar voice boomed, "Rosie, Rosie can you hear me?"

Quietly, with more than a degree of annoyance, she replied, "Yes David, I'm not deaf." And before he could say anything further, she pointed to the blazing lights coming in through the windscreen and asked, what she already knew, "Is that your car?"

David frowned, "Of course it is!"

"And it didn't occur to you when overtaking all those vehicles we would believe you were about to hit us?"

David ran his hand through his thick hair and puzzled said, "No it didn't. A man knocked on my car window, he told me there had been an accident further up the hill, and the young lady involved needed a lift to 'The Grange'. You surely didn't expect me to sit in a queue of traffic and wait to see if it was you?"

Weakly, she agreed, "I suppose not."

"Right! Well, you stay here. I'll get my waterproofs out of the boot, sort this mess out, and get you home." Then, as if noticing Johnny, he added in a grim voice, "And then you can tell me whose car this is, what you are doing in it, and why you are out on a night like this?"

As he marched away, Mervin who had heard the conversation through Johnny's open window sent her a cynical grimace and concluded, "It would seem you are being taken care of. Are you happy with that?"

Rosie grunted. "He means well."

Mervin didn't look convinced, and seeing David approaching him declared, "I need to be on my way." Rosie was profusely thanking him, as David arrived and drew him away to gain information. Johnny, with closed eyes, said slowly, "It really is best if I go alone. I don't want to cause trouble." The carefully controlled turn of his head revealed his pain, but he managed a small, sad smile. "It's been so good to see you. If you ever need me...."

She cut him off to insist, "Ring me when you get home from the hospital. Don't worry about David. Once he knows who you are, it will be fine." Johnny didn't appear swayed by her assurance.   David reappeared dressed in a bright yellow sou'wester and standing in the middle of the road, he stopped the upcoming slow traffic to allow cars behind her to go around them.   Mervin went by with a toot and wave as Luke pulled up behind them. Determined to reassure Johnny, she declared fiercely, "No-one is going to stop us being friends." Johnny's eyes widened indicating someone behind her. David, having stepped back from his traffic management, was now standing by her half open window, his back to her. Not caring if he heard she added for his benefit, "And David will have to accept that." Johnny was a hurdle she had not anticipated in her courtship with David, but it was probably one of the many to come. Driving rain and ferocious winds didn't seem to lessen the boom of David's voice, as he strode to Johnny's door while saying to Luke 'I gather you are taking him to the hospital. I'll deal with the car and take my fiancée home. At that Rosie scowled and Johnny opened the car door. It quickly became apparent he was having difficulty, which brought David to his side. As he bent in to haul Johnny to his feet she cried, "Johnny I'll be in touch."

Over Johnny's head, David sent her an unfathomable look

and then speaking in a quieter voice he introduced himself and added, "Any friend of Rosie is a friend of mine" causing her to review her estimation of him. "Now don't worry about your car, I'll drive it to the Grange. Rosie can drive mine." Johnny murmured something causing David to say, "She'll be fine, I'll look after her." With that he stepped back, expecting Johnny would walk on, but almost immediately he swayed and bumped against the back door of the car causing her to give an anguished cry. As if knowing she would jump out, David bent in to growl, "Stay there, I'll help him." Undoing her seat belt, she knelt up on the seat to watch as he and Luke helped Johnny walk to the car, but before he got in, he was violently sick in the road.

Again David, knowingly, uplifted his palm to indicate she stay there, and although annoyed at his directive she realised there wasn't anything she could do. Once Johnny was settled in the car, Luke produced a dog's bowl from the boot, no doubt in case he was sick again. After a brief discussion with Luke in the driving seat, David looking grim headed towards her. Cars were now easily manoeuvring past them, and as Johnny went by, his head was turned in her direction, his face nearly as white as the bandage around it. He managed a small smile and a feeble wave, bringing tears to overflow and roll down her cheeks.

Infuriated by David, she sat and stared out of the damaged windscreen as again he wrenched open her door to state, "At least you had the sense to wear your seat belt, it'll be a good thing when that becomes law." And then commanded, "Right, you drive my car and I'll drive your friend's." Lifting up his arm he decreed, "Come in under this, no point in getting any wetter."

In order that David wouldn't see tears mingling with rain, she wiped her face with her scarf and as he lifted up his sou'wester, she slipped out and ducked beneath it. Her legs felt weak, it was disorientating being in a tent and only seeing the rain bouncing off the road at her feet. She stumbled, David gave a loud exclamation and his arm shot out around her waist to support her in the final few yards to the driver side of his car.

It was deliciously warm inside and felt secure against the raging storm. Taking off her wet hat and scarf, she watched David covering the two front seats of Jack's car with the tarpaulin before he sat inside and knocked out a larger hole in the windscreen to give him better vision. Her anger at his barging in and taking over began to fade for he was a man to know in a crisis, but wished she had stood up to him and suggested they take Johnny to the hospital. Immersed in her thoughts, she didn't notice his return until he tapped at the driver's window. She rolled it down enough to hear him boom, "Right, we're ready to go. Windscreen wipers on the right, indicators on the left, the lights are fine as they are. It will be easier with you facing uphill to go first. I'll do a 'U' turn and come up behind you." She opened her mouth to speak, but David was still issuing instructions. "Turn into the main entrance of The Grange. I'll secure the car there, but I'm not risking my car up that drive, so we'll go from there to the Tradesman's Entrance. Now I don't have to ask you if you can drive this car, because if you can drive a Bentley, you can drive this." With that he marched back to the Viva and her eyes bore her exasperation into his back. A reaction, and action, she often used at her father's forceful attitude. A commanding tone from David as an employer was difficult to ignore, but she had to do as he asked and say nothing. In the future, she was determined she wouldn't be that malleable.

In seeing the deep dent in the Viva bonnet, it was fortunate the engine had restarted - if it hadn't…! Tentatively, she turned the key in the Rover and determined not to kangaroo forward or stall the engine. David backed up to give her easier access up the hill. A quick glance showed nothing coming up, or down, so with a resolute breath she put the car into gear, did a perfect hill start and glided across then up the road. As she drove her confidence grew.

The Rover was bigger than the Viva, it was easy to drive. It wasn't buffeted by the wind, and despite the torrential rain the ride was smooth, comfortable and warm. David came up behind, and within minutes she slowed and indicated the left turn. At that angle, with this car, it wouldn't be easy to get between the gateposts. David realising that stayed out on the road, so cars had to overtake him, giving her more room to manoeuvre. Although he was watching, she took her time and only headed between the posts when she knew the car was perfectly lined up. The gates had been taken in the war effort and melted down to make munitions, replacing them had never been a priority. With such a narrow gap they ought to knock the posts down.

The drive, similar to the road, was lined with trees which blocked out the light, and from the darkened sky the storm wasn't showing any sign of abating. Having taken the left fork at the derelict cottage, she reversed into the right one in readiness for driving out. David appeared as she slid into the passenger seat and she indicated to him to take the left fork. The stone walls of the cottage and the thick trees would afford the Viva some protection. He was gone so long, she was just wondering if he had decided to risk the potholed drive. The yellow sou'wester came into view and she could see David drenched from head to foot, his prominent nose and square chin dripping with rain. She opened her window just enough to hear the whistling wind, above it he boomed, "I've parked the car by the wall and fixed the tarpaulin, it should stay dry, but in weather like this…" He looked dubious. "What shall I do with the bike in the boot?"

"No-one would venture down here to steal it, but it would be better to close the car boot,"

"Point taken. I'll put it in mine." He began to move away.

"David," he turned, with her head she indicated, "Put it in that 'lean to'." She called after him, "You could leave your wet gear there, save wetting your car seat." David gave her a 'thumbs up' as she added, "Jack will have locked the door, but break in." At his questioning frown Rosie shouted, "We'll blame it on the wind." But she couldn't blame the wind for Johnny's injury, it had been her fault. She had panicked and braked too hard. David, now at the 'lean to' door, drew her attention by pointing out a missing pane of glass. She frowned, Jack, keen on security must have missed that. Inside David put the bike against the wall and wiped his face on a towel that had probably been there decades! He divested himself of his sou'wester and in finding a piece of string, created a line on which to hang it.

Watching him, she considered the twins, courting David and how she was drawn to Johnny, just as she had as a child. David entered the car and she, feeling guilty on thinking about Johnny, ridiculously commented, "Here is superman!" Not being known for making frivolous remarks, David gave her a hard look. "Oh, I didn't mean that rudely. It was your quick change from man working on the road to businessman in a Saville Row suit."

"Superman! That's fine by me. Jane saw me as her guardian angel, but on both counts I'm a counterfeit, as are the Saville Row suits made by a Jewish tailor in Victoria." At his booming laugh she winced, and remembered Jane saying, 'David laughs loudest at his own jokes. I don't always get them so just smile sweetly'!

In this instance Rosie felt to confide, "I make clothes I copy from designers', but it's not our outer appearance that counts is it? But what's in the heart."

David turned in his seat towards her. "I shall then pray you will see my heart for you." Rosie gave the enigmatic smile she always hid behind and fixed her eyes on the drive. David concentrating on trying to turn into the main road observed, "My family holds you in high esteem. Dad is impressed with your business acumen, my Mum talks of your ability to bring calm to chaos." She sent him a sceptical look. He chuckled back at her, "It doesn't end there. Jill thinks your innovative creations for the children are nothing short of incredible, Paul and I are thankful for the way you organise the house and the meals you produce. We all appreciate the care, love and influence you have on our children."

He had made similar comments over the past year, but with the events and tangled emotions in the last couple of weeks and past hour, silent tears again welled up and began to spill over. At the main road, in waiting to turn left, David pointed out, "If there had been this much traffic earlier, you could have been killed. I sensed you were upset by my taking command of the situation, but I needed, as quickly as possible, to get you both to safety. When she didn't speak, he glanced toward her. In a soft voice he stated, "My intention is to take you from the past and give you a hope and a future, not to make you cry." He patted her knee.

Over the years, she had learnt to reject tactile gestures and flowery praise from men, believing them to be a precursor of their desire for a sexual encounter. She told herself that David's quiet voice held only concern and knew if she was to give him a chance, she had to reconcile that David's and Doug's motives were entirely different. David was a man of his word, he would not take advantage of her. He removed his handkerchief from his pocket, apologised for it not being best clean and dropped it in her lap. She gave a small smile and mopped her face. "Right, let's get you home, out of this storm." and with that he turned into a gap in the traffic. After a brief pause he said cheerily, "In that 'lean to' my anticipation of Cathy's cooking was such that I could smell her rabbit stew."

"Then you will be disappointed, for tonight she is treating you to her steak and mushroom pie! David, I need to tell you…"

"About Johnny! We weren't introduced, but I gather you are

rather fond of him."

"It's not that simple." David sighed heavily causing her to apologise, "Sorry, but nothing in my life has ever been simple."

At his grunt she determined to make it clear. "You need to know the Viva is Jack's car, not Johnny's." In seeing David concentrating on the road, she waited until they had turned left into the lane before telling him, "Johnny was my best friend at school and I've not seen him in twenty-three years! On Sunday I went to the local church and found he has recently become the curate."

David glanced at her before questioning, "Why was Johnny in Jack's car?"

"He came to visit on his bike. In this weather I offered to drive him home."

"From my observation, you usually steer clear of both men and driving."

At David's interrogative manner she determined not to be intimidated. "As I have said, there is little in my life that can be termed 'simple'."

They drove on in silence, outside the wind howled and the rain beat the windscreen. Had he not liked her reply, or was he being attentive to the narrow lane and the debris flying around in his headlights? When a nest of twigs hit the windscreen, she let out a nervous shriek.

"This certainly…" he broke off, to peer out. Rosie saw what he saw. Water was draining out from under the hedges from the higher fields on their right and was running across the road, but not draining off. David slowed as the water began swishing up on both sides of the car.

Quietly, she voiced her fear. "I'm afraid, the road dips here. It isn't obvious until it rains heavily. Usually it's passable, but" she paused to look out, "there have been rare occasions when it became flooded." David glanced at her. "This route to the house can be cut off for several days."

"Then we better pray this isn't one of those occasions, for if the road dips further, this car won't go through it."

"Once we see the house, the road begins to rise towards it." Rosie partially rolled down the window and ignoring the slicing rain and the wind peered out. Bringing her head back in she reported, "The water is up to the front bumper." David frowned, "Can you see the house?"

"It's so dark and murky, but it can't be far."

David ploughed on as she observed the rising water level. About to tell him the water was now over the bumper, she spotted in the distance against the dark sky the house chimneys. With a yell of relief, she pointed, "Up there. We've done it. Oh thank goodness!"

Almost immediately the depth of water receded in the steady climb, but the water rushing down the hill towards them was like a fast-flowing stream. "I have never seen it like this. It's frightening. If I had gone into Petersfield the Viva wouldn't have come back through this."

"Don't even think about it! We will not being going to London tonight."

Driving parallel to the kitchen garden wall, David saw the gate. She guessed Jack had left it open for them. As they slowly negotiated through a rather large muddy pool of water at the entrance she observed, "The wall on this side affords some protection, but when I backed out from the garage, the strength of the wind hit the side of the car and rocked it. I expect Jack is worried and awaiting my return." True to form, in his wet weather gear, Jack stepped out from the garage as they came parallel to it. Seeing them together in David's car, he gave her a questioning look, and Rosie partially rolling down her window shouted, "The Viva is parked by the cottage." Jack nodded and indicated for them to drive straight into the garage. Once inside David leapt out to help him shut the heavy metal doors against the howling wind. Rosie got out of the car and caught the tail end of their conversation.

"…I agree. I'm afraid after so short an acquaintance, I am going to have to prevail myself of your hospitality by asking a bed for the night."

David looked across the shining Bentley at her and called, "Is that alright with you Rosie?" Given the number of beds in the house, the relationship they were about to enter and the raging storm outside, surely that was a rhetorical question?

Jack offered with a grin, "Let me see, Sir. Out of the eighteen bedrooms on the first floor you have a choice of fourteen, eight guest and six servant rooms." Jack, reaching the door from the garage into the boot room indicated to David to go before him and added, "We have a similar number of bedrooms on the second floor, but unfortunately abandoned due to rotting

103

floorboards, damp and growing mould!"

Rosie felt strange, she was struggling to put one foot in front of the other. David stepped back to wait for her. She exclaimed, "Jack there's…" she struggled to speak, "no need…to give…a…"

Jack's face wasn't quite in focus. David prompted, "Rosie?" He put his arm around her back to steady her. The words were in her head, but she was unable to speak them. This was like a migraine without the headache. As they entered the boot room, she saw David and Jack exchange a concerned look. Any desire to protest at David helping her out of her wet coat was squashed by her inability to do so. As was her response to his alien request that she put her arms around his neck and be carried into the warm. At her stare David cajoled, "Superman, I'm sure, would sweep you off your feet, but Rosie you need to help me out." As his arm drew her close, hers automatically went around his neck, and she clung on as he bent to put his arm under her knees. Grunting with the weight, he straightened and then strode purposefully forward as she, closing her eyes, let herself nestle against his warm, wide chest. Even before David deposited her gently on the settee, Rosie heard Cathy's gasp. She opened her eyes as Jack announced they had both arrived in David's car. Once assured that Rosie wasn't injured, Cathy ordered Jack to put the kettle on, Helen to get a blanket, Bertie to bring a towel and was slipping cushions behind her head while demanding David to tell her what had happened.

CHAPTER 7

On opening her eyes, coloured lights running like water distorted her vision. All she wished for was a warm bed and some darkness. She glimpsed David removing her wet shoes and closed her eyes as he explained, "I understand a large branch fell on your car. It dented the bonnet and shattered the windscreen." At Cathy's horrified response David declared, "It was fortunate I arrived on the scene and sorted it out. Rosie was obviously shocked and now seems disorientated."

Cathy asked, "Rosie, did you hit your head?" She mouthed 'no' and did the same to each of Cathy's diagnostic questions. "David, I'm not a fully qualified nurse, but tension can set off a migraine, which she and her mother suffer from. It may come to nothing once Rosie is warm and rested. Now why don't you dry off by the fire?" Puzzled, she added, "Although you don't seem that wet."

"I keep Wellington boots and a sou'wester cape in my car, which tonight came in useful."

Rosie opened her eyes and saw David had retreated. Bertie handed Cathy a towel and watched her gently rubbing Rosie's hair while observing, "That thick overcoat you made seems to have kept you dry."

Jack commented, "The front of it is almost soaked through, her scarf and hat are dripping wet. I've hung everything up in the boot room to dry."

Bertie squashed himself on the settee at her feet, his hand kept patting her. She expected Helen to be scowling, having been sent to get a blanket, but even she looked concerned and asked if Rosie needed painkillers, before settling on the rug by the fire and hugging her knees. Cathy drew up the easy chair beside her head and David sat in the other chair, taking up his usual thoughtful position. Jack having handed out mugs of tea drew up a kitchen chair beside him and asked, "Tell us exactly what happened?"

"I was heading up the hill from Petersfield and came to a long slow traffic queue." Rosie saw Jack turn to give him a puzzled look, bringing her realisation that from London he should have been coming down the hill not up it. Quickly David explained, "I add an appointment there. Unimportant, but it would seem fortunate. A man indicated I should stop. He explained that a lady had been involved in an accident and needed a lift to 'The Grange'. I didn't give him time to say anything further, I just declared, 'I'm on it' and headed up the hill guessing that in the car near the top was either Rosie or you Cathy."

The hot sweet tea had revived Rosie enough to speak so she informed them, "The branch falling on the car was frightening. It rolled off in front of me. I tried to avoid it, skidded on the muddy road and the cracked windscreen blurred my vision. I was across both sides of the road, and had to move the car before a large lorry hit its rear. But far worse was seeing a car overtaking the line of traffic on the wrong side of the road and speeding directly towards us."

At each scene Jack, Cathy and Helen had made varied exclamations, but their mouths opened in horror as she continued, "Car horns warned us, but we barely had time to brace ourselves against what seemed an inevitable impact." Appalled Jack's response was to immediately give vent of his feeling about irresponsible drivers.

David gave her a grim look before confessing, "Rosie is talking about me! Once I was on the scene, I assessed the situation and the best action to take. A car driver had bandaged Johnny's head," Ignoring their questions David continued, "and another had volunteered to take him to hospital. Once he was on his way, Rosie drove my car and I drove yours. I have left it by the cottage and used the tarpaulin in the back to cover what was left of the windscreen. The bike is now in the cottage 'lean to'. The glass in the door was already broken."

Rosie interjected, "Bertie and I felt we disturbed a poacher this afternoon."

Bertie made a worried sound as Jack said, "Once the storm is over I'll check it out."

Cathy with creased brow said, "Never mind that. David what happened to Johnny?"

Rosie intervened, her voice caught in emotion as she envisaged the scene. "I...I did an emergency stop...Johnny hit the windscreen." A sob arose, "I didn't see he was hurt until he leant over to help me push out the shattered glass. Oh Cathy, rain and blood were dripping off his face." Tears overflowed down her cheeks and upset, her words were jerky, "Lorry driver...first aid box. Mervin in car... bandaged his head...needed a few stitches." In her anxiety she tried to sit up, everything spun as she cried out, "Oh Cathy, his head hurt, he was awfully sick and very pale."

Cathy bent forward to reassure her, "Don't fret yourself! By now Johnny is being looked after."

Despite Cathy's reassurances, tears rolled down her face. "But it was my fault I panicked…"

"Don't be ridiculous!" Jack and Cathy turned toward David, and at their shocked faces David tempered his voice to comment, "It was a prime example of what happens when a safety belt isn't worn."

"I should have checked it."

David protested, "Oh for goodness sake, Rosie, he's a man not a child. The man… Mervin, said if you hadn't swerved to avoid the branch, the car would have either catapulted over the side of the hill, or caused a pile up, shunting you and others into the ravine below. Another commended your ability, in having seen the oncoming lorry you didn't panic, but carefully drove it back to your side of the road. He and his wife felt they had witnessed a miracle when the lorry didn't catch the back of the car, causing a similar terrifying scenario, and one I don't even want to consider."

David's rebuke and commendation were spoken in such a fierce voice, there was a tense silence. He ran his hand through his hair and apologised. "I'm sorry if I sound and appear unfeeling. It's my way of dealing with shock."

"That's true enough" Rosie acknowledged, remembering another occasion. "And it seems my sight is restored without a headache so I must ring and find out how Johnny is."

Cathy's hand restrained her, and Jack volunteered, "I'll do it."

Bertie in his indistinct way said, "Johie give skirt, in hospical, be alright"

Rosie didn't translate, despite David's questioning look.

Jack jumped in to explain. "Johnny came on a pastoral visit. Rosie and Bertie were down at the lake when the storm started so we went to help them. This is the second time today Rosie has been caught in this storm."

"Oh look at the time! I must put the pie in the oven."

"Cath luv, there's no hurry. David has to stop the night, they only just made it along the back lane before it flooded."

Cathy looked unusually flustered, "We only clean rooms and air bedding when needed."

"Please don't go to any trouble on my account." As Jack

opened the door with the intention of going to the butler's pantry to make the telephone call, David stated, "When you've made your call, I better ring home." Jack nodded and David explained, "Our friends, Grace and Wilhelm are babysitting so I need to inform them of the situation. I'm sure they'll work something out."

Helen, who had appeared to be bored, piped up, "I arrived unexpectedly and shared Rosie's bed until Jack cleared out, cleaned up and repainted a room for me."

Grimly, David retorted, "That's quite out of the question" and although Rosie agreed, she frowned at Helen who was now sporting a naughty smirk.

Crossly, Cathy instructed, "Helen go to the linen cupboard. I need a pair of sheets and pillowcases. I'll air them by the log burner."

As Helen flounced out of one door, Jack returned through the other. "I'm afraid…"

Anxiety caused Rosie's voice to sound like a tight scream, "It's bad news!"

Jack protested over her. "No! No! Not Johnny. It's the telephone. The line must have been brought down by the storm."

"Oh!" she wailed, "How am I going to find out how he is?"

David stood to question, "Where is the nearest telephone box?"

Jack replied, "About half a mile downhill from the main entrance. On a night like this, with torrential rain, the back lane flooded, a potholed drive, a high wind wrenching branches off trees, driving or walking to it wouldn't be wise."

"That's probably true, but at the same time as alleviating Rosie's concern, I need to call home." David looked across at her.

She mouthed her 'thank you' as Jack pondered aloud, "Well, if you are adamant, I better come with you. Two sets of eyes are better than one!"

Cathy putting up a wooden rack near the fire for the expected sheets turned, and with hands on her wide hips stated, "You'll do no such thing Jack Hawkins! And, in taking my advice, neither will you, David Reinhardt! No-one is leaving this house to risk life and limb to make a phone call." Seeing David about to protest, she added, "Do you want to risk a freak accident that could leave your twins fatherless? You've already said the people looking after them will work something out? And if our line is down, there's no guarantee the phone box will be working either!" Taken aback at her vehemence, both men stared at her. Helen reappeared with the sheets and taking them from her Cathy said more calmly, "By daybreak the storm will have blown itself out. Jack's car is at the main entrance. Even without windscreen you can drive, if necessary, into town to make your phone calls. Now, Helen, you do the vegetables, I'll find a suitable room for you David, and we'll eat in about half an hour."

There was a distinct whine in Helen's voice as she said, "But that will be time for Coronation Street."

Cathy sent Helen a hard look, "Eat or watch TV, you choose!"

Helen stomped to the sink to peel the potatoes and carrots Cathy was producing, while David listened to Bertie telling him about the afternoon events, which, at times Rosie needed to translate.

When it came to dinner, although the talk at the table was desultory, the food was quickly and appreciatively consumed. But her appetite was spoiled in her worry over Johnny. She pushed her food around her plate causing Cathy to 'tut' and insisted she had another cup of hot sweet tea. When she pushed her plate to one side, to her embarrassment Cathy picked it up saying, "In this house it's 'waste not, want not', who would like this?"

David said politely, "Cathy that was absolutely delicious."

Jack suggested, "David, why not share it between us and save the bread and butter pudding for later?" Without hesitation David agreed, and Helen and Bertie took the opportunity to escape to watch their TV programme. Cathy put the kettle on, and as the men finished their meal and talked of this and that, she contemplated her short time with Johnny.

The door burst open, and an extremely disgruntled Helen complained, "The blasted TV has gone off. We had just seen the adverts when there was a newsflash about the ferocity of this storm lashing the south of the country, and then the TV conked out. What are we meant to do now?"

Cathy pointed to the sheets, "They're aired. Make yourself useful and prepare David's bedroom."

"Not likely, we might get plunged into darkness." She shivered, "This place is spooky enough without the wind howling around. It's banging the shutters in Bertie's room. He thinks it's exciting. He would like the lights to go out. I came to get candles just in case they do."

"Thoughtful but unnecessary, we have our own generator that keeps the lights on" Jack stated.

David asked, "Helen, you said about a newsflash."

"Apparently, we are having a hurricane style storm. Warnings have been issued to avoid the area and stay off the roads as many are being blocked by flooding and fallen trees. Overhead power and telephone lines are down in some places."

"Then Jack, thank God for the generator."

"Yes indeed, for otherwise we might have to revert to boiling a kettle over an open fire." Jack chuckled, "You probably thought that was what I was doing in the time you waited for that cup of tea on Saturday."

David gave a wide smile, "I did consider it." He turned to Helen, "Thank you for telling us about the news. Hopefully someone at home will have heard it, tried ringing here, realised the line was down, and guessed I had to stay here. He stood, "Cathy if you point me to the chosen room, I'm quite able to make up my own bed."

"Helen's quite capable to do that. Helen, take a duster and polish with you, give the furniture a quick wipe. I'm afraid David we can't offer you any pyjamas."

Helen made a face, pulled the sheets off the airer, grabbed a duster from the cupboard and announced, "I won't bother coming down again. I'll suggest to Bertie we play a game." As she disappeared, Rosie noted the scowl on Cathy's face. What had Helen done to upset her? Just before the door closed, Cathy called, "I'll come up later with the bread and butter pudding." Rosie's brow creased, it was unusual for Cathy to wait on people unless they were ill.

David, carrying the dirty dishes towards the sink asked, "Can I help with the washing up?"

"Good heavens no, Jack and I can do it."

"You cooked the meal. Jack and I can wash."

Cathy grinned, tossed him a tea towel and declared, "You've just earned a 'brownie point'"

David's 'knee-weakening' smile appeared as he bantered, "Cathy, tell me how I might earn more?" Rosie frowned, Cathy giggled, and he added, "I would really be interested to hear more about your time in India."

Rosie, glad to have something to take her mind off Johnny, agreed. "I'd like that too, you rarely speak of that time, I'd like to know more."

Cathy seated herself in a comfy chair, took up her knitting and as the needles clicked she began, "On our journey we only saw the shadowy lands of Tunisia, Sicily and Malta. I would have liked to visit them."

David observed, while wiping a plate, "You could fly there for a holiday."

Jack grunted, "Nice thought but we've no money for that kind of extravagance."

Cathy, ignoring that, went on, "There were dolphins on the coast of Libya, or was it Egypt? At Port Said, little boats came alongside, trading goods, some well…." She blushed, and hurried on. "Our progress was slow through the Suez Canal, the camels surprisingly near the ship, they kept pace with us. As we came nearer to India, the heat became more penetrating and stickier, not something I had considered. You asked me if India had lived up to my expectations, I'm not sure what I expected, and it took a while to adjust to life there. Everywhere we lived was basic and clean, but I was constantly uncomfortable and irritated by the Indian culture of servitude. Their constant watching in their need to serve us, their gross exaggerations to please us, and their obsequious manner toward us made me cringe.

In Calcutta, we went sightseeing, sweated in downtown avenues and wished we could bathe in the cool, beautiful pools attached to holy temples. In search of sea and breeze, we went to Chowpatty Beach, but the sea was greasy, sluggish and uninviting. Around every corner there was filth and flies. Beggars or men with arms dripping with their goods constantly harangued us, and food vendors wanted to feed us. On our third and final day, an English couple directed us to a pool where sahibs and the well-fed natives swam. It was a welcome relief, and hard to believe that not far away, masses of desperate humanity were reaching out gnarled hands to passers-by."

Rosie knowing David's interest for ITP to expand to India commented, "Six years ago, I had an overnight stay in Calcutta before flying on to Assam. Admittedly, I didn't venture far, but it seemed a thriving metropolitan city. The old and new melded together into fascinating, noisy chaos, especially on the roads. I am pleased I didn't have that flash back of the port while there."

David having finished the drying, hung up the tea-towel and sat in the chair opposite Cathy and asked "Rosie was that your first visit back there?"

"My first and last, as far as I am concerned."

David eyebrows rose to question that, but Cathy was continuing "We 'fishing girls' were certainly relieved to leave the city and its drifting outskirts, but the leisurely pace of the train meant a long ride to Simla at 7,000 feet above sea level. That first day, we girls continually jostled each other for a turn at the window, for even the dust and soot-laden air from the steam engine was preferable to the stifling heat inside!"

"Brigadier Greenhaigh mentioned 'Simla' on Sunday." Rosie added, "Apparently he once accompanied Mum there and seemed to have fond memories of the place."

Jack joined them and commented, "Oh we were in a different social stratum to the Brigadier, Dee-Dee and Leo, but it's true Simla is a beautiful place with something to please everyone."

Cathy's eyes had a faraway expression, "The countryside was also cooler, peaceful and we rarely saw a soul as we chugged through green hills dotted with jungle, down into broad valleys, clattered along rusting bridges over wide rivers. Very different to when the train stopped. People appeared from nowhere to surround and shout at us to buy their wares. It was like the whole town's population had come to greet us."

Cathy stopped and before counting her stitches asked, "Rosie, do you remember being there the summer before we met you?"

"Vaguely, being in a pretty garden with a bungalow which had a view across a valley." Rosie grimaced, "I remember being frightened by the noise of many people and faces pressing themselves against a train window. Genta, my Ayah, my nursemaid, pulled down the blinds and cuddled me."

Cathy went on, "On the train, the Indian bearers would appear morning and evening to make the beds from the bedding we had to purchase before getting on the train. When we stopped they would bring tiffin boxes as food wasn't available on the train. I assume Rosie you sampled those?"

"If you are talking about those three stacked tins of food, I loved them."

Cathy chuckled, "All part of the Indian train experience. We girls awoke early, invented games, played cards, and with night coming quickly in India we went to bed early. Once at Simla, we saw why people made the journey. It's a long strip of green mountainous land with houses perched on the hillside, filled with flowers and fauna. The British influence in the town helped stave off my homesickness. Due to the summer heat in the cities, families and government offices move out there. The days are pleasantly hot and the nights cool. Girls who had previously done the 'fishing trip' offered hospitality to us. I stayed with Julie who had married Thomas, a government official. With the servants wanting to do everything, we enjoyed a leisurely lifestyle at the club house with fellow compatriots. There was tennis, bowls, cards, board games and a social programme that gave opportunities to catch the eyes of British Army personnel. I stayed with them when they returned to Rawalpindi and helped to teach her two children the three 'R's."

David commented, "It sounds you had a wonderful experience."

"Let's just say the way Gillian, the lady I met at the hospital, billed life in India left much unsaid, but I'll get to that. Rosie said about bungalows, "Did you know the British adopted that name for their one storey buildings?" David shook his head. They were in beautiful grounds, watered constantly by the servants. There was a good supply outside, but not inside. Bathrooms were a 'lean to' built on the side of the house."

Rosie added, "Earlier I told David to hang his wet sou'wester in the 'lean to' at the old cottage. That's another name adopted from India."

Cathy nodded and continued, "The washing and cooking was also in a separate building. The servants did that, and produced excellent meals and served them in the most opulent style. In the 'lean to' was a tin bath, which took servants several hours to fill, due to collecting the water and having to heat it on an outside fire. Another servant was dedicated to emptying the thunder box," Cathy chuckled, "otherwise known as the toilet." Most of the bungalows had three good sized rooms, a lounge and two bedrooms, and a smaller one known as the 'box room' which was a place to store the boxes and trunks needed when travelling."

David stretched out his legs as he repeated, "A 'box' room, another adopted name for the smallest bedroom in the house."

"Except it wasn't that small. Tom and Julie kindly cleared theirs as a bedroom for me, which was quite adequate until I met my 'fellah'. There, I learnt about checking that servants didn't inflate the shopping prices to line their pockets, counting and keeping under lock and key the cutlery and silverware, and to watch for petty theft. On the whole life was easy, and they just loved the children."

"Being white and unmarried wasn't a problem if you had support. Some girls volunteered at the local hospital and made themselves useful by arranging flowers, making tea, talking or reading to English patients. Once married you could still be involved in sporty things, but could now entertain with coffee mornings, card games and organise dinner parties. I had to find a way to support myself. Indian staff did the level of nursing I knew, and children were looked after by an Ayah, so Julie suggested I teach the little ones. Tom, Julie's husband, heard that a General wanted an English governess to teach the three 'R's' to his four children. They were three, five, six and seven years old, and they would leave at eight for the customary boarding school in England. On his recommendation I was instantly accepted and cycled there each day.

Life wasn't that pleasant. The heat was tiresome. The General's wife treated me like a servant. The snobbery was annoying, if not downright nasty, but socially I began to find my niche, and made a few friends. It was in accompanying the children to their pony rides that I made a date with a young officer, before falling into Jack's arms." Cathy grinned at Jack, and then at David whose expression had her blushing. "Once Jack and I were married we had our own bungalow. I started a little school with several young English children from 'lesser' families, before it became unpopular with the 'establishment'." David's brow creased, and Cathy explained, "I took in Indian children who were eager to learn. It was having the children around me that kept me focussed when I heard of my parents' death. I felt I'd lost everything, but Jack pointed out we had a good life and should be grateful to be away from the war and safe in India."

Jack interjected, "We were safe then, but there were constant rumours of scuffles between the Hindus and Muslims. By 1945, it was known the British Army would be pulling out of India, but that didn't come to a head until the end of January 1948 when Mahatma Gandhi was shot and killed. I was due to leave the Army in March 1945, but then we found out Cathy was pregnant again."

"How many children do you have?" David asked.

Cathy shook her head. Jack said quietly, "Cathy had several miscarriages before having Fern. So in needing to rest, travel wasn't an option, therefore I signed on for another three years. On September 7th Fern was born, and you can imagine we were ecstatic. She was a beautiful, healthy baby," Jack paused, "But at six weeks, she had what they termed a 'cot death'."

At that David boomed, "Oh no! How absolutely dreadful." Rosie saw his eyes grow moist. He asked, "Did they give a reason for it?"

With a sad grimace and shrug, Jack replied, "There was a post mortem, apparently the cause is often unknown. We were devastated, and well…it was difficult not to blame ourselves for perhaps missing something."

Although Rosie knew about Fern, hearing it again brought up the emotion of not just their sorrow, but at the loss of her own baby she had never seen or held. She delved into the sleeve of her cardigan to find her handkerchief.

David in a halting voice said, "I am so sorry…"

Sorrow reflected in Cathy's eyes as she spoke. "It was a long time ago, and you've had your own sadness."

"But I had my family around to support me."

Cathy nodded. "For a time I was slightly unhinged, almost mad in my desperation to get away from the place where I had conceived and lost three babies. The Army said Jack could have compassionate leave, but weren't disposed to release him, or ship us home. Most of our savings had gone on the birth and buying what Fern needed."

Jack took up the story, "My whole battalion knew of our loss, of Cathy's anguish and her desire to go home. Several weeks later Leonard Doughty-Dawes visited our bungalow and after introducing himself said he would organise my release from the army, if we would be willing to accompany his wife and child to England."

Cathy chipped in, "With a generous offer of a free passage to England, he also asked us if we would stay with his wife until she was settled in their house. To us that was a bonus for we had nowhere to go, and little money to set up a home. Leo seemed very personable and appreciated our need to leave as soon as possible. He went straight from us to book the ship before going back to Dee-Dee to tell her that in two weeks she would be sailing to England. For us it was marvellous. For Dee-Dee it was traumatic to find herself travelling with a couple she had never met, to a land she had only been to as a child at school, and to a house she had never seen."

In disbelief David shook his head, causing Rosie to burst out, "Now that scene is etched on my memory. The servants lined up wringing their hands and wailing. Genta hugging and crying over me, telling me to be a good girl before my mother pulled me from her. Instinctively I knew something was wrong and I didn't want to get in the waiting car. I turned screaming to Genta, but my mother pushed me inside and frightened, I protested even harder."

Cathy, seeing David's appalled expression, commented, "Jack and I were in the car. The way Rosie was being separated from everyone and everything she trusted and loved was just awful. I hugged her as she cried, while Dee-Dee lamented that Leo hadn't come to say 'goodbye'. It became obvious that her mother had little interest in her child and no idea how to comfort her, so I lifted Rosie onto my lap. Finally, Rosie nestled into me and fell asleep and Dee-Dee stopped recanting her woes to sink into a daze of depression."

Jack elaborated, "Leo explained he needed to go to Assam having recently acquired a tea plantation. With partition looming, he had no idea when he would be able to return and needed to make arrangements for it to run smoothly in his absence."

Jack's expression caused David to ask, "How long did that take?"

"We didn't see him for two years."

"Two years! Good heavens! Rosie did you recognise him when he arrived?"

"No. I came home from school to find Mum in more of a dither than usual. I wasn't sure whether she was excited or scared when she told me, "Your father is here." In India I rarely saw him, and if Jack and Cathy hadn't met him, I would have doubted his existence. When we met, I disliked him on-sight and he felt the same about me."

Astonished David queried, "Surely not?"

"Mum pushed me on ahead of her saying brightly, "Here she is, our little Rosie!" He was facing the window, his arms clasped behind his back. He turned to eye me with a steely gaze, in what I would call now, a derogatory manner. So in bravado, I stuck my nose in the air and did much the same to him."

"I bet that didn't go down well."

"He looked me up and down, and spoke to Mum over me. I noticed his thin grim mouth and watched his fingers tweaking at the end of a ridiculously large handlebar moustache. His look was disdainful, his voice cold, 'Just as your name is Daphne, not Dee-Dee, her name is Rosemary, not Rosie. You appear to have slipped into frivolous ways, and this child needs to be taken in hand.' I wondered what 'frivolous' ways were when he demanded, 'Come here Rosemary.' I looked at Mum. She nudged me forward, and he repeated in a harsh voice, 'Come here'. I think I sensed Mum's fear and determined not to be. I obeyed but drew myself up and stared at him, as he did to me. He bellowed, 'Do you know what dumb insolence is?' I shook my head, and noticed his hands by his side were clenching and unclenching as he explained it was allowing your face to show your feelings, without voicing them. When I didn't respond a thin, bony hand shot out, grabbed and squeezed my arm as he commanded, 'Look at me when I am speaking to you.' My response was to tell him he was hurting me and struggle to get out of his grip. Over my head he decreed, 'Stop whining! Your mother will teach you manners, and the behaviour expected of you. Failure to comply will bring punishment.' Puzzled, I wasn't sure if that was directed at me or my mother, and wondered why he was being so mean? Johnny, who you met today, told me I had the manners of a lady. My teachers liked me because I was helpful, did my homework, responded to their questions and always had good marks." Rosie sighed, "Although those attributes didn't make me popular with the other children! Anyway, my father barked, 'Have I made myself clear?' Before I could answer mum began placating him so he let me go, and she backed out of the room drawing me with her. Throughout, I felt he was enjoying lording it over us and being nasty. It became a frequent event when I was at home."

David commented, "Oh Rosie, he sounds like a headmaster, not a father." Maybe his father treated him like that. What kind of upbringing did he have?"

Jack chipped in, "We've no idea. His attitude toward Rosie, and later Bertie, has never been fatherly. It sounds absurd, but he acts as if he was brought up in either an orphanage or the workhouse."

117

Rosie frowned, "That's a thought! It would account for his revulsion of fathering Bertie, his being incarcerated here since birth, and the continual demand he remains hidden."

Grimly David questioned, "Hidden? "Incarcerated? What do you mean?"

"You tell him Jack."

Jack made a sad grimace. "It's true. Dee-Dee birthed him here with Cathy on hand. When Cathy saw Bertie she felt something was wrong. She had to insist Leo called in a doctor who diagnosed Cerebral Palsy and suggested an institution. We couldn't let that happen! Finally Leo agreed we could be responsible for him, look after his needs, keep him out of sight, provided we didn't tell anyone of his existence.

"But his health, schooling…?"

"Cathy and I have taught him what we know. The encyclopaedias in the library have educated him. He has physical disabilities, but mentally appears intelligent."

Rosie added, "The threat was, if we told anyone, drew attention to him, or anyone interfered in his life, he would be bundled off to a mental asylum."

Jack nodded, "And that threat still hangs over Bertie if this house is sold."

"I realise now my father was afraid that in my childish inquisitiveness and my love of Bertie, I would reveal he had fathered a disabled son. Once I went to work, it made me wonder why there wasn't any NHS or financial provision for Bertie's care, and then discovered his birth was never registered."

"What! The authorities don't know Bertie exists!" David's face was grim. He looked at the Hawkins, "And you colluded with this?"

Worried, Cathy admitted, "Until Rosie looked into it, we didn't know he hadn't a birth certificate, and that the Government gave financial provision for home care as an alternative to an asylum."

"Bertie surely must have been seen by doctors?"

Tears formed in Cathy's eyes, "Only when he was ill enough to need medication. Leo gave us a number to ring. The doctor is old, he visits when there is a need, never asks questions beyond the symptoms, provides the medicine and each time Bertie recovered."

David shook his head, "Your faithfulness is astounding.

118

However, Bertie is now a man in his own right and can choose the life he leads."

Rosie said sadly, "I know, and I've told him. He's happy here, but he doesn't know what he is missing."

Jack and Cathy looked so upset David smiled at them, "You've nothing to regret. You've both done a wonderful job loving and parenting Rosie and Bertie. But you must see he needs to know about life beyond what he sees on TV. Beyond the NHS and institutions, there are charities who would fund his care and needs. If you wished he could still live with you. Whether I marry Rosie or not, I want to help you and Bertie enjoy the good things life has to offer."

"But if we have to leave, where would we live?" queried Jack, giving Rosie insight that despite her offer, they were anxious about their future.

"I know of funds that are available for such situations."

Rosie guessed he meant the fund his father had set up in Jane's memory. She sent him a questioning look, his response was to nod. At the Hawkins' profuse response to his kindness, David looked embarrassed and changing the subject, asked, "You said your father was nasty to you when you were at home. Did he hurt you?"

"More mentally than physically. Afraid I would expose his guilty secret of fathering a disabled son, within a few months of Bertie's birth he organised boarding school for me. It's only years later that I realised he had set me up to drop Bertie so he could put the blame on me for his damaged leg and arm, or even death. I just wonder now if Bertie had died, if he had in mind to persuade the Hawkins to bury him in the garden, under the guise of protecting me!"

The Hawkins looked stunned. An incredulous David boomed, "Good grief! Tell me what happened?"

"I loved Bertie from the moment I set eyes on him. Mum was constantly tired. When I was not at school I would help her. In being so little, Bertie had difficulty swallowing, often falling asleep half way through his feed so I would help Cathy bottle feed him. My father's slightly more pleasant disposition during my Mum's pregnancy dissipated into his rage at her inability to cope. I avoided him, but that day he came into the nursery - next to their bedroom - to demand, "Take him out of here." I wrapped him up in his blanket and headed to my bedroom. Halfway across the landing, he came up behind me and shouted my name. I jumped and Bertie flew from my arms on to the stone floor." David gasped, his eyes narrowed, and his jaw clenched as she continued, "I screamed in terror, fell on my knees to pick him up, and my father's foot kicked me hard in the back. I don't know how in falling forward I managed to avoid pushing Bertie under the stairs balustrade into the hall below."

"Oh no!" David sat forward and buried his face in his hands. Jack and Cathy stared at him as she finished, "Two days later I was taken to a boarding school with no opportunity to say 'goodbye' to my friend, Johnny."

David looked up to exclaim, "Dear God..." His self-deprecating expression told her he'd recognised the similarity to Rebecca's fall through the stair bannisters. "Oh Rosie, I can understand now why you were so affected by Rebecca's accident. I was sorry afterwards for the way I reacted, but can see why you were devastated by it.

She acknowledged that with a rueful nod as Jack stated, "We've always felt Bertie's accident was contrived and reassured Rosie it wasn't her fault. And believe me Rosie, by then we'd seen enough to know he was quite capable of blaming a little girl for Bertie's disabilities, or his accidental death. When the doctor gave his diagnosis, Leo blamed Dee-Dee, and more than once over the years said it would have been better if Bertie had been born dead."

David boomed, "In shock people often do, and say things they don't mean."

In a firm voice Jack voiced his disagreement. "Granted David, but Leo in confining and denying Bertie a full life has surely meant it!"

Cathy piped up. "Not entirely, Jack, he has known our love. It was when Rosie discovered Bertie's birth hadn't been registered that I feared Leo might have thought to use Rosie to cause his death. I can believe he would have reasoned with us to protect her and said no-one needed to know about it and we could bury Bertie somewhere on the estate.

Incredulous, David boomed, "I can hardly believe what I'm hearing!"

"I thought Bertie was dead. I wailed like a banshee, picked him up, held him close and wished my own life into him. I love Rebecca and in the midst of your tirade at the hospital I was as

120

distraught as you." David blanched. "With Bertie I held him tight fearing my father would snatch him, drop him over the banister, and then blame me. If Jack hadn't shouted up the stairs 'Rosie, what's happening?' I believe he would have done that because he had grabbed by arm and before Jack reached us, he said quietly by my ear 'You will be punished'. Then he told Jack - and I loudly refuted - I wasn't to be trusted. He said I had snatched Bertie from the nursery and then dropped him. Only years later did I realise boarding school had been planned, the accident an excuse to banish me."

"That man is…" David, shook his head, at a loss for the right words.

Rosie gave a heavy sigh, "That's just one incident…"

Jack, looking uncomfortable suggested, "Cathy, time for pudding and talk of better days."

David interrupted, "Sorry Jack, but I must ask Rosie, "Was my behaviour at Rebecca's fall the catalyst to you deciding you couldn't look after the twins?"

"One of the reasons."

"I'll serve up the pudding and make hot chocolate." Cathy, gave Jack a hard stare while saying, "With the storm, it would be wise to do another quick check of the house. I'll take a tray up to Helen and Bertie in his room, and we might as well have an early night. Bemused Jack gave her a questioning look. "It'll be a busy day tomorrow clearing up after this. Rosie, we'll leave you to show David to his room, opposite Helen's."

Rosie helped prepare the trays, and once alone she quietly admitted, "David I've been aware of Jill's intentions. I've enjoyed times making up a foursome with you, and your family make me feel part of them. Rebecca's accident and your over-reaction were understandable, but the accusations you hurled at me were hurtful and upsetting. I need to be honest with you. Working for you and with you is one thing, living in close proximity is quite another." At David's puzzled expression she elucidated. "You see you have a similar characteristic to my father, a voice that booms, barks and commands." At his appalled expression she clarified, "The incident this evening is a prime example. You made decisions, demanded answers, took action involving me but without consulting me." Seeing David about to protest she raised the palm of her hand, "Let me finish. As an employee I was paid to cope and comply with your decisions. As your wife I would wish for discussion before a conclusion is reached and know of your willingness to compromise in order to find agreement." At his perplexed expression she added, "Admittedly I've seen your gentler side with the twins, and on occasion benefited from that myself. You can be appreciative, thoughtful, kind and without doubt very generous. You and Jane had your differences. She stood up to you and I can do that, but I don't want to spend my life having to constantly argue my point - or for a quiet life bowing to your will."

"Good God woman, you make me sound like a tyrant."

"Not at all. But to live in reasonable harmony we need to find a healthy balance."

David appeared dumbfounded. Pouring their hot chocolate she handed his to him. Obviously troubled he commented, "As your employer at ITP, or as nanny to the twins, I have not been aware…"

She interrupted, "That's the point. You were the boss! An employer doesn't have to explain his decisions, he just expects his wishes to be carried out. At times your demands, commands and reprimands were without consideration of circumstances, reasoning or exploring the other person's thoughts or feelings."

A deep frown had formed on David's brow, he swallowed hard before asking, "Did Jane find me difficult to live with?"

"Jane was fun and feisty. Her self-confidence was such she would stand up to you, even when employed by you." David nodded. "And when your flat door was open we could hear your stormy arguments." Feeling awkward she hurried on. "Jane loved you as you did her. She did admit you were two very different people, declared God had joined you together and that every marriage was a work in progress." Rosie looked down at her hands as she added, "And, she confidentially told me that the pleasure of your physical union counteracted those times of dissention."

When David said nothing, she glanced up to see his hand wiping away his tears. Embarrassed, she bowed her head and considered how much he loved Jane. It really was too soon for him to consider marrying again.

Startled her head shot up as he boomed, "My dad can be domineering and appear abrupt and unfeeling, but he isn't and neither am I. Men aren't very good at showing emotion and we don't always get it right. My Mum believes in respecting and honouring one another. Their love over the years has deepened, but she does have a certain look or voice that tells him he is walking on thin ice!"

"It's not that way with my parents. My mother, despite the gin and 'It' she favours, is constantly depressed, dithers and worries about everything in fear she'll get it wrong."

To that David challenged, "But you aren't your mother. And when you first came to my attention, I realise now you were very much your father's daughter!" Insulted, Rosie stiffened, but David's wide-eyed look reminded her of how Jane had been the brunt of her spiteful words and gossip. His expression gentled. "Surely we could be honest and respect each other. The past and our experiences do affect the way we act or react. None of us are perfect, and we will have both changed since Jesus came into our lives. And, although you were an employee, you did feel enough of a friend to challenge me on several occasions when you considered my behaviour unfair or unwarranted. I see no problem in that. We all make mistakes, and as Christians our desire should be to improve. We all need to learn and benefit from forgiving and being forgiven."

Rosie replied, "I agree. But the question remains, could we live in relative harmony? I wonder if your Mum and Dad's marriage has a similar sexual compatibility that you and Jane experienced, for it does seem that is the glue that keeps couples together. Our 'marriage of convenience' will lack that and marriage is for life which would be far longer than the years the twins will need care."

David hummed. With an unfathomable expression he asked, "You say you haven't seen Johnny since you were eight, yet you appeared very fond of him. Would you see him as a more suitable companion and only want a 'marriage of convenience' with him?"

The hurt and jealous tone in David's voice surprised her. "This afternoon I had my first conversation with Johnny in over twenty years. It was wonderful how we slipped back into our friendship. Obviously I'm concerned about him and his injuries, having affection, maybe love could…"

David cut her off by demanding, "So where does that leave me, us, the twins?"

Exasperation had her striving to reply calmly. "David, I have agreed to a six month courtship with you so we can explore and deepen our friendship. That hasn't changed. Tonight, you said 'any friend of mine is a friend of yours' and Johnny knowing my agreement with you was happy to be just a friend. He will not compromise that. However, before I leave for London I need to see how he is, and you are welcome to come with me."

"And you will still return with me tomorrow?"

"Of course. Nothing has changed. She sent him a rueful smile, "You are a complex man, but when relaxed you can be good company. I really liked being with your family at Christmas, and especially our camaraderie over Felicity."

There was silence as he considered her words. And then sounding over jovial he suggested, "Then Rosie let's take it from there! I want to see you blossom into the woman God intended you to be. I have no intention of controlling you and certainly don't want to be like your father. If I am truly concerned with your happiness then I have to embrace the risk that you may, in the end, choose Johnny over me."

Taken aback Rosie didn't reply, but David rose in her esteem. And when he finished his chocolate and came to sit beside her, Rosie resisted the temptation to pull away her hands when he took them in his. It felt awkward to see his hands holding hers. In a quiet voice he asked, "Rosie, please look at me." She raised her head to see his eyes filled with concern and longing to be trusted. "Thank you for your honesty. Honour and respect goes hand in hand with care and concern. I believe we can reach that place, and that it is possible for us to have a very successful and happy marriage."

Sadly she acknowledged, "The past has made it hard for me to trust any man." As she slid her hands from his she admitted, "Before your second visit on Saturday I was reminded of Jane saying, 'Let go, let life and God direct your steps'." David made a poignant smile. "I told the Lord I would. Within hours you asked Cathy about India, and memories in my past arose as if from the grave. Since then, I have a constant reminder of the hymn 'And Can it Be?' with the chorus about chains falling off. I want to believe the chains of the past will be broken. Within hours Johnny reappears and I seem to awake as if the interim years never happened.

David took up her hands again. "Rosie, God is not only directing your steps, but accelerating your pace. The graves were opened at the release of the Holy Spirit. When you asked Him into your life, He began a good work in you. His love wants to reveal and heal all of us from those deeply buried hurts and fears so we can grow to know Him. God's resurrection life flows through us when we spend time with Him. And when that is outworked through our lives, even Jane's death can be seen as part of His plan and purpose for our lives." David looked sad, and then glanced at his watch, "And right now I thank the Lord, that even an accident and a storm will work together to bring forth good things because we love the Lord."

He stood and drew her up in front of him. "I would like us to continue talking as we have tonight. I feel this is a valuable part of your healing process and my getting to know you." He gazed into her eyes as if he could see things she couldn't, and he quietly prophesied, "I have seen that your life has been hidden behind the walls of a castle. The twins' love, and your's for them, has helped you lower your drawbridge and I have been waiting for an opportunity to cross it. But in so doing, I appreciate that despite your reticence and qualms, you have let me in to what I would call your family 'keep' and opened up a few private rooms in your life. My hope is that this will continue. In the days ahead, in seeing the castle as your heart, I hope to be able to unlock further doors so you will be free to enter into all that is your destiny."

With an enigmatic smile she responded, "You have been reading too many fairy tales."

"More believing in the need to live my dreams! But Rosie, as it is nearly eleven o'clock, my bed calls. So please show me the way to my room."

Taking his hand, amused she said, "Come on" and leading him up the back stairs she whispered, "Sleep well and have good dreams. That's Helen's room, this one is yours." She opened the door. There was a brief scuttling sound causing her to think 'mouse'. David walking past her turned to state quietly, 'To find Jesus they followed the star, to find you I followed the dream." Rosie made an amused grimace, as he added, "One day I'll tell you more" and with a brief kiss on the tip of her nose he said 'goodnight', stepped back and shut the door.

CHAPTER 8

"Good morning Jack!" The words spoken by David directly below her window startled her into wakefulness. She drew her quilted dressing gown from across her bed, before pulling back the bed curtains and opening the window shutters. A clear blue sky and bright sun greeted her, but the rigours of the storm were in evidence everywhere she looked.

Jack and David, with their backs towards her, were standing at the edge of the courtyard area, surveying and obviously discussing the scene. From her vantage point she could see laying across the drive one of the spindly trees that lined it, twigs and branches from many others were scattered across the lawn and beyond. The small dykes on either side of the drive were overflowing with water which gave it the appearance of a bubbling stream. A sure indication that the road they used last night would still be flooded and beyond use. They were marooned! Her thoughts went to Johnny, the damaged car, her need and David's to communicate with the outside world.

The nip in the air caused her to shiver. A glance at the clock revealed it was only ten minutes past seven. David was obviously keen and eager to be up and about. And as he was casually dressed in slacks, shirt and thick jumper, she wondered if in the boot of his car he kept clothes for every eventuality! She watched as he left Jack to stroll across the grass, jumped the ha-ha and set off down the field towards the main entrance. In his desire to reach the telephone box, it appeared he had no qualms about walking down the hill on the slippery long grass, and believed that was safer than negotiating the potholes in the water-logged drive. Hopefully Jack would have given him Johnny's telephone number so he could check up on him. Feeling cold she slipped back into her warm bed to consider how her trust in David was growing. He had not been put off by her honesty and maybe she could consider a future with him, but then there was Johnny. In the midst of her musings came a brief tap at the door which opened to reveal Cathy.

"David's up. He's very chirpy despite the fact it's doubtful he'll get home today." Rosie patted the bed. Cathy sat and continued, "David said if we had a pair of size 12 gum boots, he would take a stroll to the main gate so he could collect his own along with his waterproofs from the cottage 'lean to'. From there he decided he would drive the Viva into town where he could make his phone calls, organise the fitting of a new windscreen and get an estimate for the damaged bonnet. He's a good man Rosie. Don't let him slip through your fingers."

"But what about Johnny?"

Cathy gave a rueful smile. "They are both good men, but David has a great deal more to offer.

"He certainly charmed you!"

"More stunned us with his offer of support for Bertie, regardless of how it works out between you." Slipping under the eiderdown Cathy grinned, "His stern features belie the inner man, but that's only part of his attraction." Rosie raised her eyebrows at the sexual innuendo in Cathy's voice. "Oh, come on Rosie, we left you alone last night. Anything to report?"

"David said he felt privileged to have been invited into our castle, although hoped one day to be invited deeper into the keep."

"Really! That's so romantic. You'd better be ready then to welcome your knight back in. I've always thought believing in God was a religious thing, but I feel we are witnessing His love, kindness and provision for you."

"The Bible does say, 'God is good all the time', and He wants to bless you too. Wouldn't it be wonderful to be free from the whims of Ma and Pa? You, Jack and Bertie could live a normal life."

"The only problem with 'leaving this place to rot' as Helen suggested, is that one day it will be Bertie's inheritance."

"And could be sold at any time." Puzzled, Rosie queried, "You seemed interested in David's offer of accommodation, but always appear reticent to my selling my mews cottage and buying you a house in the London suburbs?"

"Birds leave their nests and children should leave their homes. We don't want you tied down to us and Bertie. You've blossomed by living with people of your own age and there comes a time in every woman's life when she wants a home. Even if you don't want a husband, we shouldn't take that freedom from you." Cathy grinned, "David has barely crossed the drawbridge into our castle, and his invitation into the family 'keep' has already managed to uncover several skeletons in our cupboards. I'm amazed he's not fazed by that, or by the man who owns this place. There are still plenty of old bones to be dug up, but David appears robust and willing to embrace whatever is uncovered."

"My beloved Cathy you have such a heart for people, and God sees that. I sense there will be others like Bertie and Helen who will need your heart and help to mend their broken wings."

Cathy nodded. "Oh Rosie I really like that idea. Helen has been a trial, but with love and care she will fly again."

"Estranged from her own family she seems to be adopting ours. Bertie is becoming a substitute for one of her brothers."

"I only hope Bertie sees her that way." Cathy looked worried. "She could be a bad influence. Look how he repeated Helen's words about David."

"Helen never took to David."

"Probably because he's a very astute man and misses nothing."

"Like Hawkeye! He watches Helen, he weighs her up, but she is harmless."

"Her raving doesn't sound harmless, but the more she comes off the drugs, the more aware she is of her surroundings. I wonder if she is up to something."

"Miles from anywhere there's not much to get up to!"

"She didn't want to enjoy the fresh air and exercise the way the doctor recommended, but recently she has wandered down to the lake and was gone for a couple of hours."

"The improvement in the weather probably has something to do with it."

Cathy hummed, but her face showed her concern. "Is she pretending to enjoy Bertie's company, but with an ulterior motive? Should she be left alone in his room? You never know what she might entice Bertie to do."

"Oh Cathy, Bertie's communication skills are flawed and he has disabilities but he is an intelligent man. He is not going to be enticed into anything he doesn't want to do, but he is a man, with a man's desires."

Cathy tutted, "That's what I'm worried about."

Rosie added, "I'm not advocating it is right, but isn't he allowed, like every man to take what is offered? Helen would now be settled with a husband, baby and a home of her own if it hadn't gone so horribly wrong. She lost everything including the ability to have further children." Tears welled up in Cathy's eyes. "And due to my own wrong judgements, I'm not in a place to judge her, but for all her faults I don't see her as a schemer."

A heavy banging on the bedroom door and Bertie shouting unintelligible words had Cathy leaping out from under the eiderdown to open it. "Good heavens! What is the matter Bertie? Bertie in his pyjamas began frantically pulling at Cathy. In Bertie's desire to communicate, frustration made his words sound as if they rumbled up from his chest. As Cathy instructed him to stop and take a deep breath, Rosie gathered up her dressing gown and joined them. His words were now clearer as he urged, "bedroom – David help" and then letting go of Cathy he waved his stick in the direction of his room and started up the corridor.

Cathy and Rosie looked at each other, sudden panic flared between them. Did Bertie feel they needed David's help? She had no idea what was in Cathy's mind but 'fire' dropped into hers. Together they leapt forward, bypassed Bertie and rushed into his room, before stopping dead. Except for the unmade bed, everything was in its usual pristine order. Relieved, but puzzled, they looked at each other.

Bertie arriving after them didn't seem any less agitated and continued dragging his body towards the window, which drew them to hurry past him and look out. In the distance David was standing in the bottom field, looking up at the house and waving his yellow waterproofs. Below him was a flat extension of the drive, beyond him the bushes and large trunked trees that hid the road running parallel to the Estate. Rosie opened the window and waved to indicate they could see him. Questions rushed through her head. Why didn't David walk back up? Even with the incline of the field, or the water on the drive his stride was such he could return in less than five minutes. David's wave changed to beckoning. Cathy announced she would find Jack and left. It was doubtful David could see her thumbs up from that distance, but having got their attention, he turned and strode off. Bertie pulled on the sleeve of her dressing gown wanting an explanation. "I don't know Bertie. I'll get the binoculars from the study."

On her return, Bertie was leaning out of his window. Cathy in the front courtyard was shading her eyes against the sun and watching Jack going down the hill towards the main entrance. Bertie grabbed at the binoculars. "Hold on, I'll adjust them for you." Rosie homed in on the trees and bushes, but it took a few seconds before she spotted David crouched down where the drive curved from the house to the cottage. Frustrated, Bertie grabbed at the binoculars, and guiding him where to look, she wondered what David had found. With the tradesmen entrance out of use, had the postman or the milkman attempted to come up the main drive and had an accident?

Bertie, having not seen anything to interest him, handed back the binoculars, and she couldn't see beyond David's back until he stood on Jack's approach. There, on the ground beside him was a dark curled shape. Was it a body? Was it dead or alive? How long had it been there? At her gasp, Bertie tugged on the binoculars. She shivered and tried to get a better look, but it was too far away. Had someone in the storm come up the drive for help? Jack and David were again blocking her view so she gave the binoculars to Bertie. And then jumped as Cathy asked from behind her, "I've come up to get a better view? Can you see anything?"

With Bertie avidly searching with the binoculars to see the tiny figures in the distance, Rosie drew Cathy down the room to whisper, "David has found something. It looks like a body."

"A human one?" Rosie nodded. Cathy looked horrified, "Was it moving?" Rosie shook her head. Cathy lunged towards Bertie saying, "My turn." Bertie made unintelligible noises of complaint but handed them over. In the distance Rosie saw David pick up a bundle, if a person, not heavy and disappear towards the cottage.

Cathy handed the binoculars to Bertie, saying "You can be watchman" and then indicated to Rosie they leave the room, "The person moved and Jack seems to be talking to them."

"Should I go and join them?"

"Jack said we were to stay here. He would rather we didn't risk life or limb getting down there. I assume that one or both of them will return. I'll put the kettle on and cook up some bacon. Whatever has happened they will need sustenance."

"I'll do that, you assist Bertie. Once he is downstairs, I'll come up to wash and dress."

When ten minutes later Cathy arrived in the kitchen, her scowl diverted Rosie's musings about the body on the drive, "You know we were talking earlier about Bertie..." Rosie, having raised her eyebrows in query, turned back to flip over the bacon. "Well, I think Helen has been...you know, if not actually... let's just say, 'turning Bertie on'!"

Rosie gave Cathy a quick glance, said, "Oh!" and was unsure who felt the most embarrassed at that revelation.

"I suppose it proves as a man he's not disabled, but I don't like to think of Helen taking advantage of him."

"And she may not be. She's just Helen who wears tight clothes and shows a great deal of breast." Removing the frying pan from the cooker, Rosie turned off the gas. "I don't think she'd intentionally hurt Bertie, but she takes life as it comes, and seems unable to think things through. She's easily led and makes wrong friends. That's why seeing her thin, dirty and out of her mind on drugs, I dragged her here so she could have an opportunity to

130

rebuild her life. Bertie has seemed enlivened and quite animated since she has been here, so who are we…" She broke off as the kitchen door opened.

"Ah Bertie, there you are. Rosie has made tea. Would you like bacon and eggs for breakfast?"

Bertie's lopsided grin was the answer, and then he questioned, "Helen?

Cathy answer was abrupt. "The food is here if she wants it. It's her choice to either sleep or eat."

Bertie's expression was such that she and Cathy exchanged a glance with a silent message. If not love, he was very fond of her.

Rosie raced up the backstairs to the bathroom and realised with a rush of anxiety that with the situation on the drive, David wouldn't have made his phone calls. Worrying about Johnny, she stripped, washed, slipped on her dressing gown and drew it around her before stepping out into the hall. Startled, she gave a cry and would have fallen if arms hadn't encompassed her. In the seconds it took for her to recover, David in a soft voice, filled with sexual innuendo, commented, "Now this is an unexpected pleasure."

Annoyed, she pushed back from him. His releasing her had Rosie rapidly drawing her dressing gown back around her. Embarrassed, she bit out, "What are you doing up here?"

To give him his due, his eyes hadn't strayed from her face. "Believe it or not Rosie, I came in the front door with a need to use the nearest toilet."

Still put out, she said sharply, "In that case don't let me hold you up!" And turning on her heel she entered the sanctuary of her bedroom, but not before she saw the wry smile at her remark with its unintended observation.

The repulsion she felt about intimacy with a man had her shut the door with a bang. As she battled with her mind, she pulled out her old clothes. She didn't care what she looked like, after all there was work to be done today around the estate and house. She could change later if they were able to get to London tonight.

There was no sign of Cathy when she entered the kitchen, but Bertie was munching on a piece of toast, and David was making sandwiches with the remaining bacon. Abruptly she questioned, "What are you doing?"

"Making sandwiches."

Irritated, she retorted, "I can see that, but why?"

"Jack is still at the cottage, I'm taking him food, along with a flask of hot tea." He gestured toward the sandwiches, "Help

131

yourself and have a cup of coffee or tea because you will need to come with me."

David looked up when she didn't move. He made a rueful grimace. "Sorry, that wasn't meant to be an order!" At Rosie's questioning stare he explained, "As I carried her to the cottage I was subjected to a string of bad language, and we suspect she has a broken leg, I pray in moving her I didn't make it worse."

Rosie didn't answer, but pulled a plastic box out of the cupboard and began putting in the sandwiches. Worried, David added, "We had no alternative, she was soaking wet and icy cold, and we had only our jackets to keep her warm. I helped Jack collect firewood and left him to make a fire. Cathy is upstairs packing a change of warm clothes and the necessities for a hospital stay."

"Have you called an ambulance?"

He shook his head. "If the telephone box is also 'out of order' we'll have to take her by car. Anyway an ambulance could take a while to get through the storm damage. If only Paul were here, he is so used to emergency situations in third world countries, by now he would have her leg set, and a splint made out of a piece of tree bark!" He grinned at the thought.

Rosie couldn't resist a smile. Before biting into her bacon sandwich she added, "You've done all you can."

Cathy appeared with a knapsack and dumped it on the table, "What I want to know is why was she out so early and where was she going?"

David answered, "In time all will be revealed."

With a grunt Cathy stated, "In here are two large towels, one to dry her and the other to wrap her in. I've squeezed in a thin blanket, Helen's thick jumper and a cotton wrap around skirt which is easy to put on and take off. At the bottom of the bag is a night dress, wash bag and dressing gown that she'll need in hospital."

"Why use Helen's jumper when I've plenty to give you?" Rosie saw Cathy and David exchange a look. Already exasperated by David and worried about Johnny, she challenged, "Oh for heaven's sake! What now!"

David answered, "I'm sorry Rosie. I thought you knew. It's Helen who is injured."

Bertie let out a wail and Cathy went to comfort him as Rosie questioned, "Helen? It can't be. She didn't go out last night. And never gets up early!"

With a scowl, his irritation now thinly disguised, David replied,

"Well, Rosie, believe me, it is! Jack informs me you aren't fazed by the hazards of a soggy and muddy hill. I'm sure you'll understand that despite Helen's shocked and pain dazed state, she wouldn't want Jack and I stripping off her wet clothes."

Ashamed, Rosie muttered, "I'll get my boots and Jack's spare sou'wester. I'll meet you outside."

David informed her as they headed across the soggy grass towards the ha-ha, "Jack thinks someone has been living in the cottage."

"That would account for the broken window!"

"And Johnny's bike has disappeared."

With a wail she cried, "Oh no! I doubt he can afford a new one."

"Our little adventure yesterday might have caused the unknown guest to take fright and leave."

"Yesterday Bertie and I felt someone was hiding in the bushes down by the lake."

"But why would Helen be up and out so early?"

"Perhaps David, she knows who has been living there and would have heard Jack saying he would today investigate the broken window."

David gave Rosie a sweeping look as he advised, "Let's not speculate or jump to conclusions."

Cross, she grunted and turned her head to look at the drive running in enough water to paddle in.

In seeing the direction of her gaze David reported, "We think Helen walked down the drive, but caught her foot in an unseen pothole causing her to fall and break her leg.

At the ha-ha David stretched out his hand. Rosie ignored it, jumped the two-foot gap, and nearly lost her balance. David gave a loud sigh, "Rosie please, be careful, it's very slippery underfoot, and the incline makes it far worse. I don't want you getting hurt."

"I'm fine and quite used to walking on this hill."

With a shrug he continued but kept pace beside her. A few seconds later, his hand shot out when she nearly toppled over as her Wellington boot got stuck in a wet muddy patch, but at least he refrained from saying, 'I told you so'. Soon it wasn't mud to contend with, but the slickness of long wet grass and despite being careful both feet went from under her. She landed with a bump, and before she knew it was beginning to slid downward. She heard David's request to catch his hand, but the long waterproof top belonging to Jack was like a sledge and she barely had time to grab

133

the hem, haul it up between her legs before laying back to enjoy the ride. Except for the occasional bump it proved exhilarating as the wind whistled past her cheeks. However, hitting a muddy puddle near the bottom and it splattering up all over her wasn't the best of landings. She was wondering how to extract herself without slipping and being covered in more mud when a breathless David appeared. His yellow sou'wester grass stained and muddy indicated that in his haste to get to her, he had also fallen over. With mud on his hands, looking bedraggled and anxious, he was so out of character that she began to laugh. At first he appeared puzzled, then his eyes filled with amusement and his booming laugh filled the air.

Taking her filthy outstretched hands in his, he pulled her from the mire and mused, "This is the real Rosie, the one enjoying all life brings, including mud baths. And I like it!" Feeling now beyond the chains of decorum and with a childlike freedom, she held on to his hands and confessed, "That was such fun. Jack and I used to sledge down..." Trust and panic vied within her as David's steady gaze had shifted to her mouth, his intention clear.

She heard Jack calling, "Rosie, Rosie, are you alright?"

David's eyes gazed back into hers as he murmured, "We'll return to this when we haven't an audience."

Breathlessly, Jack came upon them. "I saw you sliding down the hill."

Suddenly feeling shaky, her voice trembled as she answered, "I... I think so."

David's arm came around her waist as he chortled, "Not the cleanest way to arrive, but certainly the simplest and quickest."

Jack - unlike his normal cheery self - complained, "You've been gone for ages. I've been so worried. Helen has been shivering with cold, moaning in pain and going in and out of consciousness. Is the telephone working?"

David shook his head and together they traipsed across to the final field towards the bottom of the drive, where it turned towards the cottage. Rosie commented, "I've never seen this area so waterlogged."

David took her hand and warned, "Be careful. The water is hiding the potholes.

Jack turned having waded through, looked at David's hand in hers and smiled. "The fire is now sending out warmth, I've covered Helen with the picnic blanket from the car boot, but she's still icy cold."

"Cathy said she would probably go into shock and would need to be kept warm. She's packed a rucksack of dry clothes, towels etc, and another with hot tea and bacon sandwiches, but only tea for Helen as if her leg needs setting under anaesthetic, it's best she has an empty stomach."

"Someone has been there because they brought down the old mattress from upstairs. We've put it in front of the fire so Helen could lay on it. In the grate, there are signs of a recent fire and an old trivet placed over it, probably to heat up food and water. The walls have maintained a degree of heat which means whoever was there hasn't been gone long."

Entering the cottage 'lean to' David remarked, "I thought last night I smelt Cathy's delicious rabbit stew, and thought it to be a figment of my anticipation!"

Rosie smiled, pulled off her bobble hat and caught sight of her mud splattered reflection in an old damaged mirror. Stepping in the little scullery she suggested, "I'll get cleaned up before joining you." She slipped off her rucksack, "In here, Jack, are the things Helen will need at the hospital. Towels and clean clothes are on the top."

As Jack took the rucksack into the main room, David recommended she put her arms up and he would peel the waterproof off. She complied and was glad to find - although damp - her overcoat hadn't got muddied. It didn't take long to find the washbag Cathy had packed, and she used the contents to clean up under the cold tap. Removing her boots she walked into the only downstairs room.

It had been years since she had entered the little stone cottage, and was surprised how Jack's fire had transformed the dark parlour, with its tiny windows and close proximity to the trees. Red and yellow flames cast out warmth and glow on the stone walls, making it feel cosy against the outside cold. As a young child the place was out of bounds, but as a teenager in summer holidays when her parents were away in Nice, she had spent many happy hours here playing Mummy to Mary, her doll and Monty, her monkey.

David, having unpacked his rucksack, was kneeling on the mattress trying to persuade Helen to sit up. She lay there with a halo of red afro styled curls around a very white face and pinched cold lips. Shivering, she moaned in a pain-dazed way.

Rosie beckoned the men into the scullery and in a whisper advised, "We have to get her out of those wet clothes and get a hot drink in her. In her condition, she can't go to hospital in a car without a windscreen and a damaged leg. I think we should give her aspirin, keep her warm and wait here for an ambulance. I suggest one of you drives to the telephone box, if that isn't working then go down to the hospital and alert them to the situation."

Jack agreed. "I'll do it but it could be a while, for we've no idea of the state of the roads."

"Then, have a cup of tea and the bacon sandwiches David made for you. It will be a cold journey."

"Don't worry about me little one, I'll turn the heater up full blast, but I won't refuse a cuppa and sandwich before I go."

Ten minutes later Jack had left them, and David had risen in her estimation. Not only he helped Helen to sit up, but instructed her on the art of breathing through pain - gained she guessed, when Jane birthed the twins. With David acting as a backrest, Helen managed to drink the hot cup of tea laced with sugar and take aspirins for the pain. And, to Rosie's surprise, Helen didn't object to David staying in that position or helping her remove her windcheater and soaking wet jumper. Wrapped in a large towel she was quickly dry, redressed and wrapped in the blanket. Rosie told Helen, "We need to remove your wet ski pants, but I've no scissors to cut them off. If David behind you kneels up, he can lift you from under your arms and I'll try very carefully to pull them away from your bottom, and put a towel there to dry you."

Still shivering, biting her lip, Helen nodded. In position Rosie nodded at David. He lifted, Helen swore profusely so he loudly instructed, "Breath in slowly 1, 2, 3 and out 1, 2, 3." Gently, Rosie rolled the ski pants down to Helen's knees. When that was done and she was once again sitting on the mattress, they wrapped her in everything they had to keep her warm. David cheerily commented, "You'll soon warm up" and helped her to lay back down, as Rosie curled up on the settee beside her. That done he walked around to comment, "With a proper kitchen and bathroom this could be a nice cosy home for someone."

Helen muttered, "Roof leaks."

David looked around, "It seems quite dry in here."

In a strained voice Helen added, "Declan… bucket… upstairs."

A man, Helen had a man here! Over her head Rosie looked at David and stated, "So that's why the mattress is down here."

Although upset Rosie nonchalantly asked, "Tell me, who is …?" She broke off at the sound of bells. "If that ambulance is for here, Jack was quick." David strode out the door, and in a tight voice she said to Helen, "You must think me stupid. Twice I've given you a roof over your head, and twice you've abused it. I've brought you into my family, and you've been harbouring a man here."

In a whine Helen protested, "No, that's not…"

As she groaned in pain Rosie responded, "Really? Then you didn't help this Declan break in and make himself at home. And you didn't go out this morning to warn him about Jack's visit and let him steal Johnny's bike. How unfortunate for you that having waved off your lover you came a cropper on the drive. If David hadn't been up early to go to the phone box, you could have lain there for days, even died from exposure." Rosie near to hysteria said with a sob, "Do you know what really upsets me in all this? While having assignations with Declan, you've befriended Bertie and I suspect used him to cover for you. I don't know how you live…"

The door swung open, David announced, "The ambulance is here. Jack's taking a sledgehammer to one of those gate posts making it easier for the ambulance to get through. Then sensing something was wrong, he questioned, "Rosie?" In two strides David stood by the mattress, glanced down at Helen before asking, "What's going on?" An ambulance man appeared in the doorway and Rosie took the opportunity to leave. In the scullery, she put back on her Wellington boots and was just shrugging into her coat when David joined her.

Closing the door he reported, "I don't know what you said to Helen, but she's upset and wants you to know 'you've got it all wrong'."

To Rosie, those words were like a red rag waved at a bull. Her voice was quiet, but laced with an angry fervour. "Oh really, she's upset. I'm accused. I've got it wrong! When I think of all the support I've given her…" Rosie took a deep breath and waved her hand, "And now this!"

Puzzled, David looked towards the sitting room as Helen cried out in pain, then drew on Rosie's elbow, "We'll continue this conversation outside." Once outside David questioned, "What do you think she has done?"

Angry, she burst out, "Not think, David, but what she has done! She's taken and abused our hospitality by hiding her lover here, and all the while been leading Bertie on! Will that do?"

"Are you sure you aren't jumping to conclusions!"

"Oh for goodness sake, what other conclusions are there? Cathy had reason to be worried, but it didn't occur to me that Helen would be so devious."

"Rosie that's enough!" The coldness of his tone drew her to realize his sympathetic expression had changed. Black eyes stared stonily into hers, his mouth a grim line. She had forgotten just how intimidating he could be, but emotionally charged and with no need to hold back she snapped, "I won't have you tell me what to do." And then, with her nose in the air, she walked up the drive to meet a red-faced Jack, hot and sweaty from his exertions!

"My, they built those posts to last. I never thought I'd be destroying your father's property, but the truth is I should have done it before."

With a deep breath she forced down her anger and asked, "How did the ambulance managed to get here so quickly?"

Jack grinned. "I'd tried the phone box without success, set off for Petersfield and saw one coming up the hill. I slowed, hit the horn, and indicated for them to pull over, to my surprise they stopped, the driver jumped out, crossed the road and grinning said, 'Hello Jack'. And explained, 'Your Missus called from The Grange, told us of your predicament, that you had a broken windscreen and could have an injured woman in your car."

"At least that problem is settled. I've just had a rant at Helen who told me a chap called Declan has been living in the cottage."

Jack tutted, and was about to speak when the ambulance man strode passed saying, "She's ready to be transported to hospital."

With a nod, Jack cautioned, "I've tried to clear all the rubble and told your colleague to take it slowly, but be careful it wouldn't do to have a flat tyre now."

They let the ambulance pass and walking along behind it, Rosie repeated her tirade of anger towards Helen. At the 'lean to' they watched as it reversed in preparation to carry Helen into it. Rosie concluded, "You were right Jack not to trust her."

Behind her, David spoke in a steely tone, "I would ask Rosemary, is she right to trust you?" Rosie spun around, "I thought you had overcome making assumptions, spiteful talk and judging others without knowing the facts." Taken aback by David's words, her mortification was exacerbated by Jack's open-mouth astonishment. To that David stated, "Suffice to say Jack, and for Rosemary to know, Helen told me Declan isn't her 'fancy man' but her younger brother whose run away from home."

Bleakly Rosie repeated, "Her brother!"

"Yes Rosemary, her brother!" David addressed Jack, "Helen will be out directly, so I suggest Jack we have a cup of tea and finish off those bacon sandwiches." David strode towards the cottage. Jack didn't follow but stared after him. She may have misjudged Helen, but eyes blazing, Rosie exclaimed, "It's at times like this that I can't see how we could have a successful relationship."

After a brief silence Jack concluded, "I would agree David isn't one to mince his words, but I was surprised at what he said. Yet he did have good reason to speak his mind and unlike your father, David's heart is for you, his desire is to see you blossom." At her sceptical expression Jack cautioned, "That doesn't mean everything will be rosy. We all make mistakes, say things we regret, the point is to learn from those."

To that Rosie hummed, her eyes fixed on the ambulance men negotiating Helen on a stretcher, out of the cottage. Jack observed, "This is your opportunity to show David you can be humble, apologise and reveal your good and generous heart." Jack patted her arm, "I'm off to get a bacon sandwich before David eats them all"

Placing Helen in the ambulance one man asked, "Are you coming with her?"

Rosie nodded, and to Helen in her analgesic haze, she gave a small apologetic smile and confirmed, "Of course, she's my friend."

The doors were about to close when David reappeared. He called to Helen that she was in good hands and informed Rosie, "I'll follow in Jack's car, see about getting the windscreen replaced and then come on to the hospital." His nod and appreciative smile brought Rosie to realise Jack was right. Unlike her father, David was quick to forgive and forget.

CHAPTER 9

Three hours later, sitting near the operating theatre, Rosie could hardly believe it was still morning! In the ambulance she had held Helen's hand, apologised at having got it wrong about Declan, and assured her they would help him, and explanations could come later. When asked to give Helen's details, she enquired at the same time about Johnny and was told no-one had been admitted under that name. Relieved she returned to Helen, waiting for doctors, x-rays and results.

At each waiting stage, unanswered questions ricocheted in her head. Why and how long had Declan been living at the cottage? Where was he now? How old is he? Had the backroad flood subsided? David would be anxious to get to London and the twins. Would she have time to visit Johnny before they left? Should she leave the burden of Helen and Declan to Jack and Cathy?

"I'll give a pound for the thoughts of the lady in the muddy Wellington boots?" Rosie looked up at David to admit, "I did try to clean them." She rubbed the tips of her fingers against her thumb, "Money first, thoughts after." He chuckled, withdrew a pound note from his wallet and waved it in front of her.

With a wry smile Rosie snatched it from him. "Now I have your money, I can tell you my thoughts weren't worth a penny, much less a pound. And you won't like them!"

Laughter filled his eyes as he bantered, "Money accepted on false pretences has consequences."

She knew, if she had been Jane, what those consequences would have been. Swiftly she reported, "Helen's leg is broken in two places. She is in surgery as we speak, and will be in plaster for a few weeks." David sat beside her. "And I've checked, Johnny hasn't been admitted, so I assume they stitched him up and sent him home."

"Good news for Johnny, but Helen won't like being tied to a hospital bed."

Amused, she retorted, "Oh, surely they won't go to those lengths to keep her in?"

"Not exactly, but I assume her leg will be in traction to help it mend."

"Oh dear, I hadn't thought of that. And, just before you arrived my thought was is it fair to leave the Hawkins with this extra burden?"

"While walking around Petersfield waiting for the windscreen

140

to be replaced, I had the same thought. I have to get back as soon as possible. Paul isn't working but he and Jill are run ragged with Rachel not sleeping, and William and Luke's attics. Wilhelm and Grace stayed last night, but left this morning when Joyce arrived. On hearing about the storm, they did try ringing me on your number, and finding the line dead could only hope I had arrived safely and was staying with you. They were very relieved to hear from me this morning, and to know Joyce should arrive around nine-thirty."

Rosie frowned, "When I left at Easter, your family was there to help out. I expected your father would insist on organising outside help."

"Oh he tried!" Fortunately Paul suggested Lorna, she's been coming three days, and Joyce two. As you know on her days she leaves at 4.00 pm so I've come home, made tea, where two tired and demanding children ask every night, 'When is Rosie coming back?' I confess my answer has been "soon."

Knowing how one child set off the other and the tantrums that could ensue Rosie nodded with a sympathetic expression, before asking, "How are you going to get home? The water level in the lane will take at least 24 hours to drain."

"The way you usually do, on the train, which door to door shouldn't take more than two hours."

"Do you want me to come with you?"

"That was the original idea, but with Helen needing you, and the thought of lugging your stuff across London, it seems sensible for me to go back alone." Rosie nodded thoughtfully. That would give her breathing space, and a chance to visit Johnny. "And provided you agree..." he paused, and although his face was in its stern repose, she detected an underlying amusement in his voice, "I was wondering, knowing the twins would love a train ride..." David chuckled, as her face lit up with pleasure. "I could bring them on Saturday and we would all drive back together."

"You would bring the twins here?"

"Why not? There's plenty of space for them to run around, and as they think you are on holiday, they will love to see where you have been staying."

"Oh David, I'll get Jack to get my tricycle, scooter and other toys out for them."

"Good, then that's settled. When I rang Cathy to bring her up to date, she suggested I take you out for lunch before I get the train home."

"Did she indeed? I'm hardly dressed for that. Did you mention to her about coming back with the children?"

"I ran the idea past her, she sounded almost as excited as you, but she did say it wasn't her place to agree to that." Rosie hummed in approval. "As to clothes, I found a dress shop in Petersfield that I know you would appreciate. They had a skirt in the window very similar to the one you were wearing yesterday."

"That would be Diana's, Johnny's sister. I bought, copied and returned that skirt to her yesterday."

David frowned, "Do you often buy something, and then take it back?"

"When I see something I like, but feel I can't afford, yes."

"That's a bit hard on a small business."

"Except in telling Diana I copied clothes, she was interested to see what I could do. She would like me to copy clothes for her to sell at reasonable prices." It suddenly occurred to her to ask, "Did you see Johnny? He lives with Diana?"

"If I had, I would have told you. Is it because Diana is his sister that you offered your help?

"You know sewing is my hobby. I enjoy it, and the benefit to me is to copy the clothes for myself, and on occasion I can make two things as quickly as one. But I like her, and having only seen Johnny briefly at church, I saw no reason in telling her that he had been my childhood sweetheart."

"Ah ha, sweetheart, was it? Something you didn't previously tell me." He gave his broad smile. "Diana is an excellent sales woman. She may not have made any money out of you, but she did with me!" Rosie's brow creased. "I took the liberty of buying you an outfit I think you will like."

"You did what?"

"And as Wellington boots aren't the usual footwear for the rather pleasant place I've found for lunch, I need to buy us both shoes. My aim is to be at the station just after 2pm, where before I board the train you can thank and kiss me 'goodbye'." Rosie sent him a wide-eyed looked. He chortled and suggested, "Come on, Helen is not going to miss you over the next few hours. I have my wallet and cheque book in my trouser pocket and with a wardrobe of clothes at home, I've no need to return to the house. I told Jack I would leave his car with you. He said to call him before you return to check if the back lane is still flooded."

"It seems you have everything planned out."

"My dear Rosie, the plan was to take you back, get you settled with Wilhelm and Grace and life tomorrow would return to some semblance of order! But that will have to wait."

"As David unlocked the car door, her eyes widened. On the back seat was a very large dress box which brought her to exclaim, "Oh David, I fear you've been very extravagant."

"You're worth it. You can change at the restaurant. And on that he closed the door. Taking his place in the driver's seat he added, "It's a classic style dress in royal blue. An outfit that could be worn anywhere, and Diana sold me a few accessories so you could dress it up according to need."

"I bet she loved you and said to come back soon." From David's expression, they may not have been the exact words, but Diana had obviously indicated he would be welcome, and probably not just because of his spending capacity!"

Yesterday she had felt awkward accepting the skirt from Johnny, but his joy at giving it had overridden that. David too had been thoughtful, so she leaned over and kissed his cheek and thanked him. As they stomped in their Wellington boots along the High Street to the shoe shop, she took his hand. Both gestures produced expressions of surprise and pleasure.

Half an hour later, she was wearing the most expensive and elegant pair of navy patent leather shoes she had ever owned. She had dithered because of the cost causing David to quietly say, "Rosie please, let me spoil you."

The restaurant was just perfect. Small, yet not too intimate. It appeared the proprietors had been pre-warned she would need to wash and change and had provided her with their spare bedroom. On her return, she had been subjected to both David and the restaurant owners' admiration. The dress was tailoring at its best, as was the matching jacket, and the variety of accessories included a suspender belt and stockings! Today, she had complemented the dress with a long pale grey silk scarf that had a delicate swirl of blue matching the outfit.

"Once seated, David poured the wine. Waiting for their meal, she thanked him again adding, "It's wonderful to receive such a generous gift without fearing an ulterior motive."

David admitted, "But I do have a request. Oh Rosie, don't look so worried! I'm only going to ask if I might hold your hand." After his generosity how could she refuse? Slowly, she slid her hand across the table to his, where he intertwined his fingers with hers. "Now that wasn't difficult was it?" To her, it was a gesture and image of intimacy. With his other hand he picked up his glass and indicated she should do the same. Tapping their glasses together he softly announced, "Our courtship begins" and as he drank, she gently withdrew her hand and instead placed it on top of his, before lifting her glass and sipping her wine.

At his long, studied look she explained, "I prefer a simple joining of two hands. A common bond of respect and honour, a sign of trust. I value your friendship and your ability to accept me, damaged as I am, to look after your children." Seeing he was about to speak, she raised her free hand. "You believe I'm a bud that can blossom, but I can be a very prickly Rosie. Your interaction with the Hawkins, your promise to help Bertie see his potential fulfilled warms my heart towards you..." Gratified, David smiled. "But intimacy..." She wanted to say 'repels me' and struggled to find a better word.

Maybe her facial expression spoke for her as David interjected, "Is it just me or any man?"

"I just want to be friends. Friends can still hug, kiss and hold hands without...."

"...any sexual connotations." Rosie blanched at David's wide-eyed gaze before he said, "You told me that the hymn, "*And Can it Be*" has been echoing through your mind. Anything, 'can be' if you trust the Lord. The proof is, He is uncovering and removing the chains of your past. His aim is to heal, renew minds and change us into His likeness. When we embrace His path we don't know where that will lead." A sudden bleakness filled his eyes, he took a deep breath, his voice husky with emotion, "When Jane befriended you, neither of us would have envisaged this day."

Rosie felt his pain, squeezed his hand, and felt to say, "I loved her too. We would talk and she would pray."

"I know. And I believe in knowing you loved her twins, she would want you to see what she saw in me, and vice-versa." He made a rueful grimace, "The Lord spoke to you through a hymn. I tried a song but it didn't work."

"It did! I thought it was lovely when you sang from 'Oliver' that I should consider myself as one of the family." David shook his head. "Oh you mean the record you gave me on Valentine's Day, '*I can't live, if living is without you*'. I played it many times. It did speak to me, but I interpreted it as talking about what I did, rather than me as a person."

"Oh Rosie, I value you in both respects but now, he sang quietly, '*I only want to hold your hand*'." His normal stern expression changed with his 'high-wattage' smile. He couldn't be

144

called good looking, but in trying to romance her it was possible to see why women were attracted to him. "I am glad we are having this time together. I truly believe we can find common interests which will allow our friendship to go from strength to strength. And, talking of strength, time to build up mine, here comes our food." A huge steak, a tiny salad and a pile of chips was placed before him to which he playfully grumbled, "I expect in friendship I shall find you, as Jane did, taking an interest in my diet and weight."

Rosie shrugged, "Overeating is never good for your health."

Cheerily David responded, "Quite right! I'll bear that in mind tomorrow."

While consuming her delicious poached salmon with hollandaise sauce and a selection of fresh vegetables, she considered David's words. The food eaten and her glass of wine nearly empty, she had such a sense of well-being that she slid her hand across the table to invite David to take hold of it. She saw David's pleasure at her instigating that and felt encouraged to divulge her thoughts. "This reminds me of our romantic pretence for Felicity's benefit last Christmas. I enjoyed that. So maybe if I keep practising…" she trailed off.

There was laughter in his eyes as he stated, "Anything is possible. Shall we try it?"

"The same rules apply!"

He smiled and nodded as the waitress arrived to remove their plates and ask if a sweet course was required. Rosie shook her head. David ordered them both a coffee and lifting his glass declared, "Here's to a six month courtship, rules agreed to process and make progress towards our future." They tapped and drained their glasses. David glanced at his watched. "I mustn't miss my…"

Rosie, pointing out of the window, cut across his words. "Look over there, in the church yard, it's the Greenhaighs. They appear to be looking for something." As she spoke, a police car drew up and a uniformed officer got out. He spoke to them before ushering them into the car and driving off. Puzzled Rosie commented, "The Brigadier is a pillar of society, surely that officer wasn't arresting them."

David rubbed his chin, "How strange!" Their thoughts were distracted by their coffee arriving and David returned to the previous conversation, "In deciding to go home by train, I have assumed last night's accident hasn't put you off driving."

"Earlier you told me not to assume anything!" She gave him a wide-eyed look and added, "But you assume correctly. After seeing Helen settled, I hope you've no objections to my visiting Diana to enquire after Johnny."

"Rosie, it's not my intention to control where you go, what you do and who you meet." He gave a boyish grin, "After all, God will ensure the best man wins your hand." Thoughtfully, they drank their coffee. "I'm not sure I can cope with the twins' excitement at a train journey and seeing you. I might wait until Saturday to tell them."

Excitement at seeing them bubbled up in Rosie, and without further thought she invited, "Why not stay for the weekend? We have plenty of bedrooms."

"Are you sure? It would make more work for Jack and Cathy?"

"They'll love it. We have a few days to prepare. And cooking for six or sixteen doesn't entail that much extra work."

"Good heavens, surely you don't expect me to eat for ten!"

Amused she retorted, "Perhaps if I'm more circumspect with my sums, maybe you can be less pedantic."

The boom of laughter that burst from David caused Rosie to jump. She was glad there were only three other people in the restaurant. She couldn't see their reaction but David, highly amused, fumbled in his pocket to retrieve a handkerchief. Blowing his nose he confessed, "Oh now that sounds like the true Rosie, the one the Hawkins know and love. By the way, should you bless me by becoming my wife, I would be delighted for the Hawkins to be seen as grandparents. Whatever happens, they can always be in the Uncle and Auntie brigade. Now drink up, we must go."

Standing on the platform waiting for the train, she felt they were married as she issued him with instructions about what to pack for the children. David's quirky smile as the train came in gave her to understand he felt much the same. "I'll ring you tonight or tomorrow, but I should be back around twelve on Saturday. My car insurance covers any driver, feel free to use it. You'll need to pick us up from the train because it has the children's car seats in it." He opened the carriage door and turned, "Rosie, this has been a very unexpected and pleasant interlude." Before she could consider anything further, the whistle blew. He hugged her, his lips brushed her mouth as any loving husband might, before he leapt up into the carriage, closed the door and smiling down on her waved as the train drew out of the station.

Transfixed, she watched until it was out of sight, before

crossing the track to where they had parked the car. The brief hug and kiss hadn't disguised David's rising desire, something she had no intention of exacerbating. She turned her thoughts to the twins visit, and then to seeing Johnny. Driving along she sang, "*Sweets for my sweet, sugar for my honey*" a song that ten years earlier had so reminded her of Johnny. At the time, she had taken the line '*til your dreams come true'* to heart and visited her infant school. The teacher remembered her and gave her Johnny's address. Her elation was quickly deflated when she discovered his family had 'long gone up north somewhere'.

At the hospital she was directed to a ward, and walked the line of beds looking for Helen. A passing nurse pointed to a curtained area, explained they were setting Helen's leg up in traction, which might take a while. She offered to take the flowers David had bought and the hospital bag Cathy had packed. In seeing her wavering in what to do, she added in a stage whisper, "There's a room at the end of the corridor. It has a green door and is usually kept for those who are upset or grieving. If you wait in there, I'll fetch you when Helen's ready."

Walking to the room, Rosie considered how some people thought a cup of tea solved every ill. David it seemed used flowers. Twirling Jack's car keys in her hand, she remembered the sweets Johnny would bring to heal her aching heart. She could buy Helen sweets, but was without handbag and money. The room was empty. She sat on the settee and considered her growing dilemma of going out with one man yet loving another. Did she love Johnny, or was it circumstances that had intensified her desire to see him? To take her mind off that, she headed to the toilet.

A glance in the mirror had her stop to consider her appearance. With the modern haircut, dress, jacket and matching scarf, she looked a sophisticated model. A far cry from the clothes she had worn this morning and the tormented child she had been. Remembering the 'pound for her thoughts' from David, she set off to the car to retrieve it from the pocket of her trousers and returned via the WRVS counter to buy Helen's favourite Newberry Fruits.

As she pocketed her change, a familiar voice drew her to realise Brigadier Greenhaigh was in the process of ordering two black coffees. Out of curiosity she greeted him and commented, "David and I saw you being taken away by the police. What have you been up to?"

"They brought us here." When he didn't elaborate further, Rosie informed him, "Helen, who is staying with us, broke her leg."

The Brigadier nodded, his eyes on the coffees being made. Rosie looked around to see Jennifer, eyes closed, sitting in the corner of the area. Was she praying? In seeing his hand shaking as he reached for the coffees, she tucked the box of sweets under her arm and offered, "Let me carry those for you." He nodded, and together they walked towards Jennifer, who opened her eyes, first to see her before turning to her husband with a silent question.

The Brigadier shook his head, "No news." For a jolly, portly fellow with twinkling eyes that revealed his enjoyment of life, he seemed to be full of anxiety, a shadow of his former self. He sat down, and as she handed him his drink he said, his voice high in emotion, "My son is in intensive care."

"Oh no, I'm so sorry." During his parliamentary campaign, she had barely seen his two sons, and had no interaction with them. But the youngest must now be eighteen, if not older.

When the Brigadier didn't expand, Jennifer signalled for her to sit down and declared, "He was coming to us for dinner, but with the storm raging we weren't surprised when he didn't arrive. The lines were down so we couldn't telephone him, or he us. His sister thought he was staying with us. And this morning, seeing his bike chained up in its usual place she assumed he was visiting someone in town. But when he didn't appear by lunch time she rang us, and that caused us to query where he had spent the night. We made phone calls, no-one had seen him and then Freddy insisted ringing the police.

The Brigadier chipped in, "They asked if I'd rung the hospital, I had, but they'd no record of him." Tears filled his eyes. He lent forward with his coffee cup in his hands between his knees.

Jennifer put a comforting hand on his arm. "Drink your coffee love. The police suggested we bring in a photo, we did that, and then walked around the church praying."

Speaking to his shoes the Brigadier added, "That's where the police found us and bought us here."

"I guessed you would be here." They all looked at the nurse standing before them. The Greenhaighs disappointment was palpable when she added, "Helen is ready for your visit."

"Thank you, I'll be along shortly." As the nurse left, Jennifer explained, "The police made enquiries. An unconscious man was admitted last night, but he had no identification…" Between his hands, the Brigadier whimpered.

"Now Freddy, you mustn't upset yourself. He is being cared

for." Turning back to Rosie she finished, "The police are getting in touch with those on duty here last night to find out more."

"I expect quite a few people were injured in last night's storm. I was driving Jack's car when part of a tree crashed through the windscreen." She paused. Johnny was the curate of their church and the Greenhaighs were friends, but it was doubtful he would want to share his private life with them. They were also privy to David's marriage offer, so best she said no more. She stood, "I'd better go, but I pray that all will be well with your son."

CHAPTER 10

Helen, her bright red curly hair accentuating the pallor of her face, was leaning back on banked up pillows, her leg lifted by wires and pulleys. On seeing Rosie she queried, "Where have you been?" Quickly followed by, "Good grief! How come you are dressed like some boring politician?"

Undeterred, Rosie said succinctly, "I was delayed. I bumped into the Greenhaighs. Their son is in intensive care."

"Who the hell are the Greenhaighs?" Before she could explain Helen complained, "I'm going to be strung up here for weeks. When I live with you I always end up in hospital?"

"On both occasions your injuries had nothing to do with me." She was obviously strung up mentally as well as physically so Rosie placated her, "I've bought your favourite sweets, and those flowers are from David."

"Oh yeah, last time he gave me money to compensate for my injuries, but flowers and sweets won't compensate for my broken leg. I should sue you over the dangerous potholes in your drive."

Irritated Rosie burst out, "Oh feel free! It's not my problem, but if you want a roof over your head when you get out of here, it's probably not advisable." There was silence. Rosie pulled the cellophane wrapper off the box of sweets, "Oh Helen, I understand your need to reject people before they reject you. Believe me, the Hawkins are concerned about you and Declan. Let's have a sweet and start again."

Helen let out a banshee wail and cried out, "I don't know why you put up with me" before bursting into tears and sobbing, "You even thought to pack a bag of my things."

When she entered, Rosie had sensed eyes watching her, but now both patients and visitors stared at them. Patting Helen's hand she said, "Oh don't take on so. Cathy packed the bag for you." To distract her she stood to ask, "David bought me these clothes from Diana's shop. What do you think of the new outfit?"

Helen wiped her tears, stared at her and stated, "Clothes of that quality don't come cheap. I guessed David bought them for you. You look incredible! I know you can tailor but your clothes have never shown off your figure, and your face has always been hidden by your long hair." More tears spilled over as she apologised, "I'm sorry for being nasty and the trouble I've caused. David is a good man. He said he would find Declan and help him."

"Good! Have another sweet." After sucking on one, Rosie

asked, "Tell me why and what was Declan doing in the gatekeeper's cottage? Is he on drugs?"

"Declan! Good heavens no. What makes you think that?"

"You were! Why else would he choose to live in a run-down place?"

"He'd nowhere else to go! Frightened by my stepdad, he packed a bag, grabbed the savings' tin from the mantelpiece and ran. Sheepishly Helen confessed, "I used to ring Mum at her neighbour's house, but couldn't until you rescued me. You remember my stepdad said he didn't want an ex-convict's moll in his house." Rosie nodded. "I told Mum where I was now living and how good you'd all been to me. She updated me that my stepdad had thrown out their eldest two boys in an alcoholic temper, and it was now Declan's turn to have his life made hell."

Rosie observed, "Men want sexual favours, but not the responsibility of the children they create."

"Ben did! David does!" Rosie patted her hand. "Mum told me Declan had my address. Declan had rang to tell her he would come to see me, but overawed by the house and estate, he'd seen an empty cottage and was staying there. He might only be twelve…"

"Twelve! Oh Helen, he's only a child. You should have told us."

"He's very sensible, loves camping and thought the cottage was great. I couldn't be sure the Hawkins wouldn't insist calling the authorities or police. He doesn't want to be put in care like his step-father. He thinks he would have to become a bully in order to survive."

Rosie thought her upbringing was difficult, but this… She refocused on Helen as she continued. "When I rang Mum she told me about Declan. I asked Bertie and he said there was a cottage beyond the lake near the main entrance. So I ventured out, found Declan and Bertie helped me gather things that wouldn't be missed, including food."

"Hmm…thus Bertie's improved appetite?" Helen grinned. "So I assume this morning you set off to warn Declan that Jack would be coming to mend the broken pane."

Helen gave a heavy sigh, "Oh Rosie, I didn't know what to do. He packed up his things, I hid the stuff I'd borrowed, and Rosie I'm sorry I took money from your purse and suggested he take the bike in the porch and find somewhere to stay for a few days."

"I'm more concerned about Declan than my money."

"Mum reported that Dad is more concerned about the stolen holiday money than Declan's welfare. So you see he has good reason to be frightened to return home."

Deep in thought Rosie remarked, "At twelve his options aren't great."

In a whisper Helen said, "I'm going to be sick" before she slammed her hand across her mouth.

Leaping up Rosie called the nurse, the curtains were drawn and as Helen made a horrible retching noise she called out "I'll just take a walk, I'll be back." In the depth of considering Declan's plight, she headed for the quiet room and reached the green door at the same time as a middle-aged man. He gave her a sad smile, introduced himself as DCI Fulterer and opened the door. He waved her through stating, "You must be the Greenhaighs' daughter." The Brigadier arose from his seat across the room as she declared, "Sorry officer, mistaken identity!" Disconcerted by the Brigadier's hard stare, she apologised, "I'm sorry, I didn't mean to intrude. I thought the room was empty."

Before she could retreat, Diana's voice behind her declared, "I thought I recognised your voice. Did the storm stop you going back to London? Oh, my God, your clothes!" All eyes focussed on Rosie as Diana exclaimed, "You are the woman that gorgeously sexy man wanted to treat to a whole new outfit. He explained you had slipped in a muddy pool, and in his desire to take you out for lunch, this was the quickest way to provide you with clean clothes."

Jennifer gave the outfit an approving look. "It appears Rosemary that David has good taste."

Diana's brow creased, "You know him?" Jennifer nodded and Diana's puzzlement increased as she turned to ask, "And your name is Rosemary?"

Her reply was a nod as the DCI who had perched on the table, cleared his throat and apologised, "Sorry folks, but I need to press on. We now know Brigadier that your son arrived in Casualty last night, and was termed, 'walking wounded'. As yet we haven't ascertained how he got there, because he collapsed before he had spoken to anyone. We've ruled out foul play because he had nearly three pounds in his pocket." Diana dabbed her eyes, bringing Rosie to conclude she knew and was fond of the Brigadier's son. The DCI looked apologetic, "I'm afraid with no identification, we could only wait until someone reported him missing."

The Brigadier said fretfully, "What's the point of speculating who, how or why? We've already been told my boy is in a critical condition. I want to be with him."

The DCI nodded in agreement, "And so you shall. I gather he's just back from the operating theatre and is being made comfortable." With that he shook the Brigadier's hand, "If there are any further developments, I'll let you know."

Jennifer put her arm through her husband's. "Let's stroll towards his room."

Diana blew her nose and waited until they exited, before saying with an underlying edge in her voice, "My brother Johnny was besotted with a Rosemary at school. The Brigadier told him she was courting a very well to do man, who intends to make her his wife. Is that you?"

"David's intentions are not necessary mine."

Diana harrumphed before stating, "He and Johnny are very different. The man I met this morning is wealthy, has an air of authority and oozes sexual ..."

Rosie interrupted. "Something I'm often told! In the years I've known him, I still find him more disconcerting than attractive."

"Really!" Diana looked thoughtful. "A man only spends that kind of money on a woman when he's serious about her, and my God, I can understand why, you look incredible." Rosie gave her a shy smile, but perplexed Diana continued, "Johnny was willing to spend all his savings on 'a present for a friend' and I gave him that skirt you copied." Rosie's rueful smile was enough for Diana's eyes to widened, "Oh my God! Have you seen him? Did he give it to you?" Rosie nodded. Diana grinned. "What on earth did you say?"

"I didn't have the heart to tell him the truth. I thanked him and said it was exactly what I would have chosen."

"Is Johnny now a catalyst to your decision making?"

"We spent a wonderful afternoon reminiscing. He's easy to be with. David is very different. His wife died two years ago after birthing twins. I've looked after them. I'm the only mother they've known and I love them. I don't dislike him but I don't love him. He wants to marry me and I've just agreed to a six month courtship." She shrugged, "Did Johnny tell you he met David in the midst of chaos? At Diana's shake of head she added, "I intended to call into the shop to see you both, once I knew Helen..." Rosie paused at Diana's frowning expression, "You

153

know, the mud puddle, I went to help my friend. She has broken her leg."

Diana's frown didn't dissipate as hesitantly she queried, "You…you were going to call into the shop?" Bemused Rosie nodded, as Diana added, "To, to see…" her tone changed to disbelief, "You're not here because…?" Wide-eyed she stopped. Rosie now bewildered stared at her. Diana clearly disconcerted queried, "Do you know the name of the injured Greenhaighs' son?"

Embarrassed, Rosie apologised, "Sorry, I didn't think to ask. It has been years since I met their two boys and I can't remember…"

Diana clearly upset said, "You… oh… oh God… I must go," which only added to Rosie's confusion. Diana pulled open the door, "Meet me back here in half an hour." She watched Diana's rapidly retreating figure and rather than fathom out what just happened, she walked back to the Ward. Helen watching for her was quick to demand, "Where have you been?"

"I've just met and had the weirdest conversation with Diana from the dress shop." Helen didn't interrupt as she repeated it, but looked thoughtful. Rosie believing she was thinking about Declan stated, "It's far more important that we find Declan and find a way he can be looked after."

Helen put a hand on her arm, "You have all been good to me. Declan didn't steal Johnny's bike. I told him to leave it out of sight by the church so he would find it this morning. With your money, he could buy a train…" Rosie didn't hear the rest as she processed scraps of recent conversations. Jennifer said their son rode his bike everywhere. Diana said his bike was in the usual place. Their son entered the hospital as walking wounded. They thought he had sought refuge with those he was visiting, but didn't know who that might be. They had seen the Greenhaighs at the church… "Rosie, Rosie, are you listening to me?"

"Sorry Helen, I was grappling with Declan and Johnny's bike." Helen grunted. "Earlier I asked at Reception if Johnny Hall had been admitted, they said not. The Greenhaighs asked about their son and had the same reply. It wasn't until the police had a photo they identified him as the man undergoing an operation."

Helen sniffed, "Typical inefficiency."

"No, the staff notified the police that a man had come to the hospital in what they termed 'walking wounded', but collapsed before they got his name."

"Surely you don't think the Greenhaighs' son and Johnny are the same person?"

"I don't know. Diana asked me if I knew their injured son's name. Johnny's father was one of the first invalided out in the war. Johnny's birthday is 19th December 1940. And I know the Brigadier went to India in March 1940."

Helen counted with her fingers, "Time then for Brigadier to have 'knocked up' Johnny's mother before he left."

"Helen, you are awful!" Helen grinned, Rosie tutted before saying, "Despite her haggard face, scatty hair and cheap ill-fitting clothes, Johnny's Mum was still pretty. She used to meet Johnny from school with Diana in the push-chair. She shrugged, "Many people had fallen on hard times after the ravages of war."

Helen laughed, "The question is, did she marry an injured soldier to cover up her sins? Was Diana upset…"

Rosie finished her sentence, "…because she's Johnny's sister and he's the Brigadier's son." She leapt up, "Sorry Helen I have to find out" and headed off to find the Intensive Care Ward. With no-one to stop her, minutes later she was peering through a half glass partition, having spotted the Brigadier on one side of the bed and Jennifer with closed eyes praying on the other. Diana standing at the bottom of the bed blocked her view of who was in it.

What other explanation could there be? Shaking with nerves Rosie took a deep breath, turned the door handle and walked in. Diana sent her a sad look, the Brigadier's expression was sheepish, and Jennifer with a sympathetic smile beckoned her to the bed. She had hoped she would be wrong, but one look at the face swathed in bandages brought forth tears. She choked out, "Oh God! Johnny! Oh no!" Machines were linked up to Johnny. She turned to Diana to gasp, "Why didn't you tell me?"

Diana grimaced, "You said you'd spent time with Johnny. I assumed you knew he was The Brigadier's son, and hearing he was in hospital had come to visit him."

The Brigadier confessed, "Five years ago it was a shock to receive a letter from Patty, saying her husband had died and informing me Johnny was, without doubt, our child. I should have told you on Sunday, especially seeing you were old friends."

Jennifer added, "I'm sorry I called him a 'skeleton in our cupboard' but didn't explain why. Please, come and sit by him."

"But you don't understand. I am the cause of Johnny being hurt." She wailed, "I was taking him home. I should have ensured he was wearing his safety belt. A branch hit the car, I swerved, did an emergency stop, Johnny hit the windscreen." Tears rolled down her face, "I should have insisted I came to the hospital with him."

Jennifer indicated she take her seat and in shock she sat with a bump, before holding and sobbing her sorrow over his hand. The only other sound in the room was the regular pound and hiss of the breathing machine. When eventually her anguish was spent she looked up to see the Brigadier's unfathomable gaze across the bed, and cried out, "I'm so sorry." Jennifer rested a hand on her shoulder.

In a tone of disbelief Diana uttered, "Johnny was concussed yet you left him with a stranger to dump him at the door of the hospital."

Quietly she admitted, "When the young man assured me he would drop him off at the hospital I didn't expect him to leave Johnny to walk in on his own. It's no excuse but shocked I just went along with people's advice and David's suggestions."

"Ah ha! David was more important than Johnny who was injured."

Rosie sighed, "It wasn't like that."

"Diana! Stop it!" Jennifer ordered before acknowledging, "What's done is done! Even if Rosie had stayed with Johnny, the outcome would be the same."

"Which is...?" Anxiously Rosie stared at them, and the tubes and equipment in and around Johnny.

Jennifer answered, "Not knowing how he got the gash on his head, made it more difficult to assess the problem. He was concussed, and they've taken measures to avoid the swelling in the brain. We're waiting to hear from the doctor." And, as if she had bid him to come, the door opened and an elderly man entered. Jennifer gave her shoulder a comforting squeeze.

Diana urgently informed the doctor, "Johnny's injury was caused by hitting the windscreen of a car."

"That would account for the pressure on the brain. We've done what we could to relieve that. We'll keep him sedated for the next 48 hours. Mr Henshaw, a brain surgeon, will come to ascertain his condition and decide if he needs moving to Southampton. The brain is soft, the skull hard, and hitting a car windscreen would accelerate the brain forwards, and then backwards inside his skull causing tiny lesions in the brain tissue. These began to bleed and gradually built up pressure within his skull. The symptoms are a bad headache, dizziness, nausea and sleepiness which can bring on a coma."

Dismayed Rosie cried out, "If only I'd known that! He had all of those." Looking down at Johnny's head wrapped in bandages, eyes closed, his face nearly hidden by the ventilator mask she wept, "I'm so, so sorry Johnny."

Jennifer again squeezed her shoulder, "Rosemary please, don't upset yourself."

"Were you the car driver?" Dr Lewis asked. Rosie nodded. "Was Johnny wearing his seat belt?" She shook her head, and he repeated much as what David had said about safety belts and the law. "However, let me reassure you, the storm would have delayed the ambulance. Johnny being dropped off meant he was here quickly and had immediate treatment. So Rosemary, you have no reason to blame yourself for thinking he only needed a few stitches. Now, you'll have to excuse me…"

Rosie pulled herself together to ask, "Will he be alright?"

Dr Lewis sighed, "It's impossible to tell at this stage. There could be physical, cognitive, social, emotional or behavioural effects. In being treated quickly he could make a complete recovery, but the next few hours will be crucial to his life."

In the tense silence in the room, Rosie voiced what the others must be thinking. "Are you saying he could die?" Dr Lewis' face was grave as he nodded, and in their anguished silence, he left the room.

The curse of loving and losing entered Rosie's mind. Inwardly she determined not to subscribe to that, and that she had abandoned Johnny to his fate. She spoke her thoughts. "Luke, the teenager, didn't realise the extent of his injuries. I would bet Johnny told him to drop him outside, he could walk in."

The Brigadier remarked, "That sounds like my boy."

A high-pitched sound filled the room. Jennifer leapt toward the door. Over that Rosie cried out in panic, "Johnny, I love you. Hang on in there, don't go, I've only just found you, I don't want to lose you again."

People were filling the room, a nurse by her ear said, "You have to leave."

Jennifer insisted, "Rosie dear, let go of his hand."

"If I do, he'll be lost."

The nurse bent forward extracting her hand from his "Come now. We're here, we won't let that happen." She allowed herself to be pulled away, but turned at the door, "It's so frightening to be alone."

Another nurse assured her, "Don't worry, he's asleep."

A senior nurse entering commanded sternly, "Take her out of here and page Dr Lewis. He must still be in hailing distance."

The Brigadier came to her side. In a weary voice he chivvied her along, "Come my dear, this isn't helping."

Between them they drew her away. Frantic she burst out, "But I didn't help him. I should have seen he didn't have his safety belt on. I shouldn't have done an emergency stop." Guiltily she stated, "I've been enjoying life, while Johnny is fighting for it. Oh God help him, please don't let him die."

Jennifer, having opened the green door, drew her firmly inside. "Rosie, getting hysterical isn't going to help." Suddenly, she was encased in the fold of Jennifer's arms, bringing confinement and comfort against her amble bosom. It reminded her how she and David had clung together at the time of Jane's death. That same anguish had arisen, a fresh onslaught of wracking sobs and tears that made her insides feel they were being wrenched out. Wrenched out, her baby had been wrenched out, loss and death, death and loss.

Her behaviour must seem irrational, she fought to calm down. She could hear the Brigadier grunting as though in pain. It was a few minutes of Jennifer holding her before gradually peace trickled in. Giving her a consoling smile, Jennifer released her to reveal her cheeks were streaked with tears too, "Rosie we must believe in God for life, and I know you've had more than your share of sorrow." Rosie nodded and realised Diana was staring at her. In finding a seat, they all sat in silence awaiting news.

She had no idea of time, but was alert the moment the door opened with Dr Lewis saying, "Please, don't get up."

"Is he going to be alright?" The Brigadier asked in a faltering voice.

Dr Lewis drew up a chair. "In order for the brain to get the best chance of healing, we need to keep the patient in a stable environment. When patients become agitated we sedate them more heavily. We're going to do that for the next twenty-four hours and then begin to reduce the dosage in preparation to take him off the ventilator."

"Will he be able to breathe without the machine?" Jennifer questioned.

"We don't know. At present, we are trying to induce the blood vessels to constrict and limit the flow to the brain. The hope is that it will reduce the trauma and intracranial pressure. Although he may not recover consciousness straight away, the pressure should continue to recede and healing take place. If not, we might have to operate again to relieve that. But right now we're doing everything we can." He looked around the group. "The main thing is that you, his family, go home now and rest. And we'll contact you when we feel it is right to visit again." The doctor looked at Rosie, "I understand that it will be difficult for you, but you have no reason to feel guilty." Looking around he continued, "You will need to discipline yourselves in the days ahead to live your normal lives and not get entrenched in Johnny's situation. You will then be more able, and prepared, to support Johnny as he recuperates."

"What support will he need? How can we prepare for it?" Diana demanded.

"Until we know the extent of his injury, that's difficult to answer. It's early days, and at present rest is the most essential thing for him and you, the family. When he recovers consciousness, we'll see how he copes. Some patients accept constant visitors, others get tired quickly or become agitated because of them. We'll monitor that. It might be necessary if he remains in a coma to take turns to visit and stimulate him. Make a rota that fits your individual needs. I gather he is the local curate, if people offer, let them fill in the gaps. You will need to pace yourselves. It's easy to get tired out. Prepare meals in advance, or at least have a good stocked cupboard from which you can make a quick and easy meal."

Nervously, Rosie asked, "What's the average recovery time?"

The doctor gave her a sad smile. "Only when he's out of the coma will we be able to assess how this has affected him. It could take weeks or months."

The prognosis was met with silence and worried faces, but she saw it as positive and optimistically proclaimed, "But he will recover?"

She caught the gleam of appreciation in Dr Lewis' eyes. "My dear lady, the body is wonderfully made, and has extraordinary healing properties. I would say when a man has everything to live for, he has a resilience to fight and not give up." As his pager bleeped, he looked around and assured them, "If there's any change, we'll be in touch and notify you when we decide to take the next step. Now you'll have to excuse me - duty calls." And with white coat tails flying out behind him he strode off down the corridor.

For a few moments no-one spoke. Jennifer stood, brushed down her clothes, put her hand out to the Brigadier with a loving look, and as he joined her she announced, "Right, Freddy let's go home. I'll ring the church secretary and get her to inform the prayer chain and church members of the situation, and how they might best help."

"Diana, we'll need a lift back to our car, and as it is half day closing for your shop, you are welcome to come back with us, or make your own contingency plans. Obviously, your mother will need to know. I'm sure she'll want to be here. She may have thought we were stealing you both from her, but hopefully this will bond us together. I expect she would prefer to stay with you, but she's welcome to stay with us, and that includes any of your relatives."

The Brigadier put his arm around his wife drawing her toward him. "Well done Jen. A perfect battle plan, keep the troops active, fed and envisioned with victory, and we will get through this and come out stronger. We can convene at our house for dinner tomorrow night to put our thoughts and strategies together. Now let's go home for that cuppa."

Drained by emotion Rosie listened. It would be good to be part of that battle plan, and how wonderful to be part of a family pulling together in dire circumstances. As they stood Rosie offered, "Please, if I can help or there's news of Johnny, will you ring me?"

The Brigadier nodded, but Diana still distraught snapped, "How can you help? There's no point in giving Johnny false hope that you'll be here for him because you'll be off with David."

Jennifer jumped in, "Diana, please, that's hardly fair."

Sadly, Rosie acknowledged, "It's true. On Sunday I'm meant to go back to London with David and the twins. I don't know what to do."

"We'll keep in touch." Jennifer patted her arm, "I promise if there is any change in Johnny's condition I'll let you know. Before you go give us your London number?" Rosie watched them leave and made her way back to Johnny's room. No-one stopped her, the nurse smiled and slipped out. Standing by his bed, she intertwined her hand with his and spoke the same words she spoke earlier to David about their friendship, a bond that wouldn't be easily broken. Was it only twenty-four hours ago since they were laughing together? Was the depth of her emotion due to her own wretchedness at being the cause of his accident, or more than that? She pulled up the chair, sat holding his hand and talked to him until the nurse reappeared to advise her that being heavily sedated, he was unaware of her presence.

Helen, watching for her was eager to hear her news having guessed from the time she had been away the patient was Johnny.

160

After reporting everything, Rosie felt so drained that she listened without comprehension to Helen rambling on, first about Johnny, and then Declan. Tiredly she apologised and added, "I'm sorry Helen, I need to go."

"But you won't go back to London? I mean with Johnny in a coma, and me strung up like this!" With a winsome expression she pleaded, "Please stay? Let David find Declan."

"Helen, I don't know what I'm going to do? Life seemed so simple a few days ago. I'll visit tomorrow, but be assured Jack and Cathy won't abandon you. Now I have to go."

It was good after the storm to see the sun, but the way it flashed between the trees as she drove home was painful on the eyes. As her vision became impaired she knew a migraine was imminent. She needed to get home and rest. Jack had advised she ring before risking the Viva on the flooded back lane. At the phone box, she was grateful there had been change from the pound David had given her. The Grange telephone rang and rang. Where were they? She guessed the back lane would still be flooded and realised she would soon be beyond walking up the drive to the house. Where could she go? The Greenhaighs and Diana had enough troubles without her landing on their doorstep. She sniffed, tried to find a handkerchief and inwardly asked, 'Please God help me? I don't know what to do?' Now feeling sick, she breathed slowly, deeply, and rested back against the telephone box. Where was her handkerchief? She had one earlier. There were several in her muddy clothes in the car boot. Rummaging in the bag containing them she remembered David's back pack containing the tea, milk, mugs and painkillers. It wasn't in the boot so must still be at the cottage. She could go there, take a couple of painkillers and rest in the dark room. She made one last attempt to ring the Hawkins, but to no avail.

With her vision returning came the heavy drum beat inside her head, making it harder to co-ordinate her limbs. It was a relief to see the demolished pillar at the entrance and so much easier to drive in. After the rollercoaster ride of emotions this week, and today, she wasn't surprised her body was rebelling. Unfair as it may seem, she realised that in the last few years the person often at the root of her migraines was David! She sighed and parked the car outside the cottage. Hopefully in a couple of hours she would feel able to walk up to the house, or drive back to the telephone box to ask for Jack's help.

The pane of glass in the 'lean to' hadn't been replaced. The dark scullery was cold and bleak. On the draining board were three rinsed cups, the vacuum flask and Tupperware container of milk, but no sign of the painkillers. It occurred to her she would be warmer in her jumper and trousers. Fighting the pain and nausea she forced herself to the car to get them. On her return she filled a cup with water, entered the main room to find to her surprise that the fire put out hours before was still warm and the thick walls had retained the warmth. Seeing matches on the mantelpiece and the logs by the grate, she threw them in place and with some newspaper thrust between them, the fire quickly reignited.

Removing her tailored jacket, she put on her thick jumper and over her stockings added her still muddied but dry warm trousers. Having made a bed of sorts out of two rather tatty cushions she was about to lay down, when she spotted the backpack under the table. Groaning in pain she pulled it out. Inside was a large thick towel, useful as a blanket and having heard a rattle as she put the bag on the table, she realised in the front pocket was the small bottle containing aspirin. Eagerly she reached out for the cup of water, drank two of them down, and made herself comfortable on the old mattress in front of the fire. Wrapping the towel and then the blanket around her feet, she put her overcoat on the top, and lying down tried to consider through the thumping pain how the future might pan out.

CHAPTER 11

Sounds and voices permeated Rosie's sleep. It took her a few seconds to remember where she was. When she opened her eyes, the room was pitch dark. The fire must have gone out. She slowly lifted her head, winced at the pain and rested it back into the warmth of her pillow. The door opening sent a flow of cold air across the room. A young woman's voice reported, "It feels warm, someone has recently been here." Bright torch light flashed from the door around the room. In a nervous voice she pointed out, "There's a pile of old clothes on that mattress. Geoff you go and take a look."

Without moving and eyes closed Rosie spoke in a pained voice, "I've a migraine. No light." The woman's startled gasp and the light hitting the ceiling were simultaneous. A second later Geoff crouched down beside her to ask, "Are you Rosemary Doughty-Dawes?"

Although mystified at his knowing her name, Rosie didn't move but succinctly answered, "I am" before closing her eyes.

Geoff stood to instruct, "Babs, put your torch on that table. I'll radio in we have found her."

The young woman took his place. "Hi, I'm Constable Taylor, Babs for short. We were alerted to look out for a Vauxhall Viva. The car and it's driver hadn't returned home."

Lifting her head, Rosie caught a glimpse of Babs before the onslaught of pain caused her to close her eyes and rest back on the pillow. When the pain diminished she asked, "What is the time?"

"Twenty to ten."

At the lapse of time she lamented from the pillow, "Oh no! Jack and Cathy will be worried sick."

"Along with your fiancée who has been very active in trying to find you."

"Fiancée?" she murmured in a questioning tone. She heard Babs turn the pages of a notebook.

"I believe a David Reinhardt?" Rosie gave a derisive hum as Babs added, "Apparently he contacted the hospital. The sister on the Orthopaedic Ward reported he was persuasive and very persistent in his need to talk to Helen Giles who had been admitted earlier with a broken leg. He rang twice thinking Miss Giles might not have been told she could reverse the charges. And she had found herself apologising at not believing to find the telephone trolley was a priority and agreeing to immediately and personally

163

organise it. Rosie grunted. David had a way of triggering that response! "We also spoke to Miss Giles. Apparently she told Mr Reinhardt that Johnny Hall was in a critical condition in ITU, and you had left a 4.30 pm to drive home."

What, thought Rosie, had David made of that news? Babs was still speaking, "I'm told Mr Reinhardt contacted Diana Hall. She later rang the Hawkins in the hope you had been found. By then the Hawkins and Mr Reinhardt had alerted us that you were missing."

Rosie from her prone position apologised for the trouble she had caused, "I didn't know the pills would knock me out for over four hours. It's dark now, I can't walk back to the house, the back lane is flooded…"

Babs offered, "We have a Land Rover, we can take you home."

A thought struck Rosie, "What made you look here?"

"Your fiancée. He rang the station about twenty minutes ago. He said if you had a migraine you would have been looking for painkillers and somewhere to lie down. And if that was the case, you may have come to this cottage without the opportunity to contact anyone. We were in the area, we looked in and saw the car."

Twelve hours later sitting by the wood burning stove in the kitchen, Rosie was having her second cup of coffee of the day. Cathy having been notified she had been found had been waiting to take her to a warmed bed, bring her tea and toast and further painkillers, as Jack updated David and others she had arrived home safely.

Only minutes ago Cathy had told her David was so concerned for her wellbeing that he had decided to arrive with the twins a day early! At her reaction Cathy had tried to placate her explaining David had insisted they get help from a domestic agency. And Jack had added, "He thought you would be worrying about Johnny in intensive care and that the twins would help take your mind off that." And as Jack happily explained with two Agency people to help they could accomplish much in a short time.

"How will they get here? The Land Rover made quite a splash through the back road last night."

"I walked down there this morning. It's low enough now for a car to drive through, and the council were clearing the debris this morning."

Rosie made her way to her bedroom. In loving the twins she

had no doubt they would be a distraction, but she would have liked time to adjust to so many changes! Her feelings vacillated between her irritation at David inviting himself a day earlier than agreed, his quickly growing intrusion in her life, and her appreciation of his thoughtfulness and generosity to those she loved.

During the afternoon in the midst of preparing a trifle, Jack arrived pushing her second-hand pram, their Christmas present to her the first year here. It still contained the bedding, doll and the two sets of clothes made by Cathy who commented, "I thought Rebecca might enjoy washing the doll and her clothes. I suspect she's too small to push it."

Rosie agreed as Jack added, "I'll bring up your tricycle for Joshua. At two I doubt - even with the seat at its lowest - his legs will reach the pedals, but we can push him around. There's also the little cart that fits on it, I'll get that too."

Rosie thought of Joshua, already very much his father's boy, dark hair, dark brown eyes, and big for his age. "I'm sure he will love that. He can be quite boisterous but watches out for Rebecca. They often play doctors and nurses with dolls and soft toys." She smiled, "Obviously Paul's influence." Her mind went to Rebecca. She had Jane's heart shaped face and hazel eyes. Her hair in golden bunches would bounce up and down as she jumped in delight. Being small and petite, she had Jill's two boys adoring her. Jane had always said that without her father's strict discipline she would have been a spoilt brat. Rebecca was already showing signs of being stubborn and petulant, wanting her own way and enjoying the limelight.

By the kitchen sink Jack left an assortment of other age appropriate toys, and humming somewhat tunelessly Cathy was happily washing them. Bertie having overseen Jack's rummaging in his old toy cupboard, had clearly wanted his train set, wooden garage and toy cars brought down for Joshua to play with. And reunited with things he hadn't seen in years, he sat on the rug in front of the fire and played with them, every now and then giving his heehaw laugh and saying, "Twins like this." At which she and Cathy would exchange a glance, for it was a good sign he had recovered from his distress at Helen's accident, and subsequent epileptic fit the previous afternoon.

Rather than intrude on the Greenhaighs, she and Cathy inquired about Johnny while visiting Helen, to be told 'no change, no visitors'. And if it hadn't been for the dark cloud that loomed over

Johnny's future and her feelings for him, she could have embraced more fully all the future could hold for her. Helen, already fed up with the captivity of hospital, was pleased to see them, but unsure about Cathy's offering of needles and wool to knit squares. Worried about Declan her voice was woeful, "Mum uses a neighbour's telephone, she can't ring me here, I can't ring her there. A message telling her Declan is missing would just worry her."

Cathy sat forward, "Would you like me to ring the neighbour and get your mother to ring me?"

"Would you? But please no police, Declan's frightened about being taken into care.

"Perhaps Rosie when found we can find a way for him to live with us?"

Rosie addressed Cathy, "I have no objections to that."

"Really!" Helen's eyes brightened, "I was afraid to ask. I told Mum when Declan left to tell anyone who asked that Declan was staying with me at your London cottage."

Rosie frowned. Helen cringed, "It was only to delay anyone looking for him."

The next day, as Rosie waited for the train barrier to lift at Petersfield Station, she thought again about how life could take unexpected turns. Last Friday, she couldn't have imagined that this Friday she would be driving David's car to meet him and the twins at Petersfield Station. She parked and with fifteen minutes to spare, strolled to the nearby tobacconist shop, purchased chocolate buttons and dolly mixtures, treats for the twins when they were good. Her back was towards the door when it opened, and a woman entered talking with a tinge of northern accent.

"When little he loved this shop. Mrs Roberts and I would sit in the back with a cuppa, and he'd happily spend an hour deciding how to spend his pocket money. Mrs Roberts told me her Tom would often weigh him out extra because, in all seriousness, he told him he always shared them with his girlfriend."

The voice, and then words, had Rosie turn. Diana was standing next to her mother. When younger and nicely dressed she would probably have been as attractive as Diana. Diana seeing Rosie commented, "You caused quite a stir yesterday in more ways than one!"

Rosie made a rueful grimace. "So I heard. I've had an eventful week which I guess caused my migraine."

Mrs Hall proffered her hand, "You must be Freddy's daughter, I'm Mrs Hall."

Diana said crossly, "Mum's not been here for many years. I've just met her off the train."

With her hand in Mrs Hall's Rosie introduced herself. "I'm not Freddy's daughter, I'm Rosemary. I was eight when I last saw you collecting Johnny from the school gate."

Mrs Hall's eyes widened, "You're Rosemary who lived at The Grange." Rosie smiled. "My goodness my boy was besotted with you. It was 'Rosie said this, Rosie said that', and never the same after you left." Mrs Hall looked her up and down, shook her head, and stated, "You were too good for him then, and by the sound and looks of you, you're too good for him now."

"Mum!" Diana gave Rosie an apologetic look then added, "Don't worry, Rosie has a rather gorgeous, sexy rich man interested in her.

"Have you heard about my Johnny's accident?"

About to answer Diana interrupted, "Rosie was driving the car." Her mother gasped, and Diana quickly added, "It wasn't her fault. Johnny wasn't wearing his seat belt." As Mrs Hall frowned, Diana added, " But I have to say Rosie you did rather go overboard in proclaiming your undying love of him."

"Yes, it must have looked that way. That childish bond when we met on Tuesday took me by surprise and to see him lying there... Rosie trailed off.

As if still in the previous conversation Mrs Hall grunted and divulged, "I once caught the eye of a handsome, rich young man. I was once pretty, but life and smoking has aged me. He might have married me if he'd known I was pregnant, but by the time I found out, he'd returned to his regiment in India. With the war, letters taking time back and forth, and the terrible disgrace of being an unmarried mother, I did the next best thing and married Ronald Hall my childhood sweetheart. He'd been one of the first to be invalided out due to losing his right leg. I looked after him, and he always said he couldn't believe his luck in getting me. I'm ashamed now to say I never told him Johnny wasn't his child. We lived hand to mouth, moved north believing there was work there, but it didn't last long. Our lives were blighted by his ill health, difficulty in getting a job, and lack of money. Still, he was a good man and father. He'd look after the kids while I did night shifts at the mental hospital."

Rosie looked at her watch, "I'm afraid you'll have to excuse me as the London train is due in and David is arriving with the twins. It's been good to see you and I am sorry about Johnny's accident."

"Twins, I assume yours, but not his?

Rosie gave Diana an enigmatic smile and said, "His, not mine. Jane, his wife and my friend, died a week after giving birth. I've been the only mother they have known and the reason David wants to marry me." Rosie clasped Mrs Hall's hand, "Believe me, Johnny has a very special place in my heart and is very good for me! And, despite your problems, both your children are a credit to you. I'm sure with Johnny in hospital we'll meet again. I am praying for his full recovery." With a wave, she dashed down the street, quickly purchased apples, bananas, oranges and grapes for the children to snacks between meals. When the road barrier came down to herald the imminent arrival of the train, she had just enough time to stash her shopping in the car boot and make her way on to the platform.

As the train roared in, she felt nervous, inadequate, awkward, not so much at seeing the twins, but with her role changing from nanny to prospective wife and mother. Doors opened and banged shut. She looked the length of the train watching for them. And then they were running towards her calling, "Oosie, Oosie." She crouched down and as the two little bodies rushed into her arms, they nearly knocked her over. A glance down the platform revealed David watching and waving, before he drew out a good size suitcase from the carriage. A woman, with her back toward her, appeared to be waiting for him holding the twins blue and white striped folded double buggy. Rosie's first thought was 'Who is she?' and her second, 'He has employed a nanny to join them'. She would deal with that later, but with the twins in her arms she asked, "Did you have fun?" They nodded animatedly, and between the gibberish she caught the words 'train' and 'picnic'. Joshua with a worried frown, a shadow of his father's scowl, brushed her short hair with his hand, before announcing, "Hair gone!"

Rebecca had no such qualms about the change. Her little arms had thrust themselves around her neck to tightly clasp her. With Rebecca fixed to her like a limpet, and her arm around Joshua, she was trying to extricate herself in order to stand when David arrived. Putting down the suitcase he offered, "Here, let me help you."

Arms outstretched Joshua demanded, "Me, me…" and David obeying extracted him first. Rebecca clinging and stroking her face was repeating "Oosie, Oosie" even as David put out his hand to help her up. As their eyes fleetingly met, Rosie saw the love David had for his child, and it brought an unexpected onslaught of sadness and emotion. She hid it by hugging the adorable little girl still in her arms.

David chuckled, "There's no doubt they are pleased to see you." It was only then in turning she realised the woman holding the buggy was standing beside them." "Rosie, meet Annie Davidson. She got on the train at Guildford and has helped keep these two amused."

Politely, she sent her a wintry smile, and in a ridiculous urge to stake her claim she added, "Thank you that was kind. Shall I relieve you of the buggy? David, the car is just outside."

Annie, it seemed, understood the brush off for she smiled at David, and put out her hand for him to shake. "It was good to meet you. I have your card. I'll be in touch." And with a nod at Rosie, she walked away.

David's eyes followed Annie, and then with a wry smile he turned to ask, "Can you manage the buggy and Rebecca?"

After her stilted "Of course," she steered the buggy wheels in front of her through the door, past the booking office and into the yard.

David followed with Joshua on one arm and the suitcase on the other. Spotting his car he strode ahead, stowed the case in the boot, and was opening the car doors as she drew near. "The fruits I presume are for nutritious snacks?"

Joshua was standing beside him so she murmured, "And there are a few sweeter rewards." It was a rare occasion for her and the children to be in David's car together, but it came naturally to put their charges in their respective seats. Yet despite Rosie's assurances that she wasn't leaving, Rebecca stubbornly refused to remove her arms from her neck. To placate her she explained, "If you want to see my house, you'll have to let go." With an indication of their loosening, Rosie removed them but in seeing the little face screwing up to cry she went on, "I've got my toys out for you to play with." The frown turned to interest, and as she stepped back to close the car door, David stepped forward leaving her no room to manoeuvre. "Rosie, coming here and being invited to stay means a lot to me, well to us."

Finding herself trapped Rosie said abruptly, "A day earlier than planned."

"I know, but I couldn't wait to see you again. Shall I prove that to Annie? Before she could reply his mouth met hers in a kiss she couldn't call sisterly yet not overtly passionate." He drew back, as Annie's car turned right on to the main road, and commented, "You agreed to extend the Felicity farce of Christmas."

"My remembrance of that was any kiss would be on my cheek not my mouth."

"True, but if I'm telling people I'm courting you, it would be odd if we didn't kiss at 'hello' and 'goodbye'."

Rosie gave a heavy sigh, realising that it would be a natural progression, "Well that's as far as it goes."

"Good, that's settled then" and at his chuckle she became irritated, realising how cleverly he had extended the parameters of their courtship. The man was exasperating! Taking his place at the wheel he sent her a broad smile, she pursed her lips. As he started the engine, two excited children - oblivious to the tension - expressed their excitement with gabbling chatter.

Once across the train track and heading up the hill, there was silence as the twins took in the scenery. After a few minutes she reluctantly said, "Thank you for thinking about my being at the cottage." David gave a dismissive shrug. "Your interfer…vening can sometimes prove useful." At that slip of the tongue David glanced across at her with raised eyebrows. She hastened to make amends. "You stopped people worrying. And the police gave me a lift home."

With his eyes on the road David declared, "I hoped Rosie by now that you would see my 'interference' is always born out of concern. I couldn't sit and do nothing. What kind of man do you take me for?"

To that she acknowledged quietly, "I'm sorry. I'm unused to outside interest in my welfare."

David's response was a grunt, "When I heard Johnny was in a coma and knowing your fondness for him, I guessed you would be upset. Diana told me you were distraught so it made me even more anxious to find you. I asked Paul and Jill to listen out for the twins with the intention of driving down here in my Morris Minor."

Astonished, she looked toward him, "You were going to do that?"

"Of course, but Paul's refusal took me aback. Quite valid of course, with a young baby and two other children to care for. Paul pointed out the sheer foolishness of it. It was then he mentioned after stress or tension you were susceptible to migraine and that the best remedy was to take painkillers and lay down in a dark room.

The Hawkins were expecting you to ring them…"

"I tried! No-one answered. I now know Bertie was having an epileptic fit. I only meant to stay until the painkillers kicked in, but the room was still warm, I easily relighted the fire, and then fell asleep."

"A sleeping beauty!" Amusement crept into David's voice, "And with no superman to carry you home, no knight in shining armour to whisk you up on his horse, or prince to kiss you awake, you were for a while lost to us all." To such a whimsical anecdote she clicked her tongue and commented, "I'm perfectly capable of looking after myself! It was you who worried the Hawkins into calling the police."

David gave a heavy sigh. "Rosie, you can't seem to understand I care about you. I want to court you so we can have a companionship where it is natural to hold hands, hug, kiss and look out for each other. And in the next six months, by exercising in that, we'll get a clearer idea of whether this could lead to a future sharing those two little lives…" He glanced up at his mirror, "… who are now fast asleep."

"It's already been an exciting day for them."

"Believe me, by the time we had been in the taxi, on the train and they had eaten the contents of their picnic boxes, I was feeling quite exhausted myself. It was a relief when Annie stepped into the carriage and showed an interest in them."

"Cathy was expecting to give them lunch."

"Don't fret they've got good appetites. I'm afraid with nearly two hours on the train, I had to think of something to keep them occupied after the initial excitement wore off. Fortunately, up to Guildford we had a compartment to ourselves. I would have felt rather foolish singing and doing the actions to 'the wheels on the bus go round and round' in front of strangers."

Rosie admitted, "I can't associate you with singing on the train, but if the people in the next compartment could hear, they would have thought you were a wonderful father."

David turned down the lane. "Thank you. That means a lot to me."

"And no doubt Annie thought you were wonderful as she is going to keep in touch."

"She was very good with the twins." David's face turned toward her with what she would call a 'knowing' expression. Did he think she was jealous of the woman? "She told me she was considering working in London". Rosie thought 'really?' as David added, "I spoke of opportunities at ITP, gave her my card, and told her to speak to Norah Baird who is now in charge of employment."

"Did you tell her you were coming to visit your fiancée?"

David frowned, "Should I have done?"

"I believe that's how you described me to the police."

"Oh Rosie, we're not going to row about that, are we?"

"Despite working and living in close proximity to you for the last four years, I realise how rare it is to see beyond the business man. You have integrity, but in finding ways to obtain what you want or need, they can sometimes have a controlling or intimidating element. Some women are attracted by that, I'm not." David didn't respond, had she been a bit too harsh? "At Christmas with your family, I began to see a lighter aspect of your character, but I'm not Jane. I enjoyed our lunch on Wednesday, but I don't want a life having to continually confront you, or being annoyed when you make a decision involving me without taking my opinion into account."

David pulled into the back gate and stated, "You want the quiet life, the kind you think you would have married to Johnny."

Jack stepped out from the garage to wave David in so Rosie didn't address that remark. The trouble with David was that he was too astute for his own good, and again tension had risen between them. Once parked in the garage she slipped out of the car to undo Rebecca's seat belt. Gently, she lifted the sleeping child and blinked away the tears. This little girl had shown how much she loved her and was afraid of losing her again. For the sake of the children, she needed to find a way of getting along with David. Emotion welled up, this time remembering how often she had craved her mother's attention and love, and the lack often sent her to bed crying as if her heart would break. As though David's mind read hers, he sent her a troubled look. "Jack you go on ahead to tell Cathy we're here transitioning the twins into wakefulness." But instead of taking Joshua out of the car he walked around to where she stood. "Rosie I'm so sorry, that remark was uncalled for. It's obvious to both of us that the twins love you, and you love them. It's early days, but I'm sure we can adjust to each other."

172

CHAPTER 12

Throughout lunch David continued to endear himself to the Hawkins and Bertie as did the twins with their cute little ways. Rebecca sat in the high chair she and Bertie had once used and Joshua was brought up to table height by several large cushions. As David had predicted, they ate everything put in front of them.

The twins didn't notice Bertie's disabilities, he was just someone to play with, his speech often on a level with theirs. They quickly developed their own language and understanding as they raced his toy cars across the kitchen table. All three of them excited and shrieking at whose car would win and calling for David to catch them before they flew over the edge. Bertie would have been constantly in demand if Jack and Cathy hadn't taken him to visit Helen. Bertie rarely left the house as he was scared of the outside world. Even taking him to the beach, or to see the ships at Southampton, he was quickly upset by people staring at his disabilities. Usually they had to cajole him into the car, but not today.

Vicky and Gordon, sent by the Agency had worked hard. The bedroom for David and the twins had the windows cleaned, the cobwebs removed from the four-poster bed and ceiling, and the antique furniture highly polished. Gordon had chopped a pile of logs now stacked in a basket and in the grate prepared a fire to air and take the chill off the room. The room a mirror image of hers next door wasn't as cosy, but had brushed up well.

Jack felt he and Gordon had risked life and limb to retrieve the cot from the upper floor and now cleaned was ready for Rebecca to sleep in. Joshua was going to share the large bed with David and they had pushed the cot against one side of the bed so Joshua couldn't roll out, David being on the other side. Rosie's worry was that the bedroom door opened on to the stone balcony of the grand staircase, but Jack knowing about Rebecca's accident had found black wiring and tied it through the wide gaps in the iron balustrade to make that impossible.

When Bertie left, Jack suggested to the twins they look for their bedroom and once up the backstairs they ran on ahead with Jack close behind. She and David followed and on indicating her bedroom door, David asked, "Am I allowed to get a glimpse of my lady's boudoir?"

With an enigmatic smile she opened the door wide, and quickly closing it said, "You've had your glimpse!"

His eyes widened and gave a wry smile. "I see, or perhaps I wasn't to see, that the competent and well-organised Rosemary Doughty-Dawes at work, is undisciplined and leaves her bedroom untidy and disorganised."

She shrugged, "Think what you like. It's my sanctuary and I prefer to keep it that way."

With Jack and the twins in their bedroom, David's hand caught hers and bringing it to his mouth he gently kissed her finger tips before declaring, "Oh do forgive me my lady, how unseemly of me to ask. In the era of this house Mr Darcy, even if courting the lady would neither enter, nor expect to be entertained in her bedroom." Rosie's inclination was to snatch her hand from his. He gave a knowing smile and instructed, "This, Rosie, is where you giggle delightedly saying, 'Oh Mr Darcy that you should be so bold to ask.'" At Rosie's disdainful expression he chortled, "I thought you liked playing a part" and then turning her hand over, he planted a kiss in its centre and with an amused expression suggested, "Keep that for later." With that he strode into the bedroom where the twins leapt out to shout 'boo' at him and expressed shouts of glee at his over played reaction.

As the twins had their afternoon nap she stayed in her bedroom to be near them, while Jack with chores to do in the kitchen garden took David with him. On their return, the twins having had a drink and half a banana were now squabbling over her doll. David instantly broke it up by whizzing Joshua through the air. After he had left him several feet away, David returned to Rebecca, took her by the hand and asked Joshua, "Shall we ask Uncle Jack if we can look around the house." At their delight Jack smiled and cautioned it was wise to stay on the ground floor.

As they were in the refurbished servants hall at one end of the 'H' shape linking the two wings of the house, they moved from there into the corridor which had doors on the left to the Butler's Pantry, Cellar and Housekeeper's Room. On the right they entered the original kitchen overlooking the back courtyard which for several minutes took their attention with its big square white sink and wooden draining board, its huge cupboards and the large Aga range. Once they had run around the huge wooden table in the centre, they were out the door and into the East Wing playing peekaboo in the doorways of the dining-room, ballroom and front lounge. Her father's study next to the library in the West Wing had the longest visit as David showed them on the huge globe the British Isles, places he had visited and India where Rosie was born.

The twins' interest span didn't extend to the library but seeing the music room, they pulled Rosie toward the grand piano and then sat cross legged waiting for her to play. From memory she played excerpts from Scheherazade by Rimsky-Korsakov which she knew they liked.

David stood by the window, his hands clasped behind his back, looking out at the lake below them. She guessed he was thinking of Jane, who was a far better pianist than she. He didn't turn as she finished, so with a finger to her mouth, she took the twins' hands and they crept out. Guessing the laundry, coal hole, boot room and the stables converted into a triple size garage would be of no interest, she led them back into the large room where Cathy and Bertie having returned were having tea and cake. David joined them as Cathy was saying "Helen asked if the twins could visit her?"

David looked hesitant. "I'm not sure that's a good idea."

Puzzled Rosie asked, "Why not?"

"I can't imagine Helen wanting them bouncing over her with her leg in traction, or the nurses chasing them in, around and under beds. We'll discuss it tomorrow."

"Out of respect for their elders, I think Cathy it would be good for the twins to call you and Jack Auntie and Uncle."

"Oh David we'd like that."

"Me too?" asked Bertie.

Rosie smiled as David replied, "Yes, if you would like that."

Bertie appeared so thrilled that Rosie warmed toward David for his easy acceptance of her brother. And she watched with delight as Bertie sitting on the rug with the twins, showed them the car lift in the garage Jack had made. It seemed to completely enthral them.

During dinner the squabbling and tears began, bringing David to decree, "It's been a long day. I'd better take these two to bed."

Cathy jumped up, Jack was despatched to check the fire in their room and Rebecca - obviously worried her "Oosie, Oosie" might leave her - stretched out her arms towards her. To which Rosie happily jumped up to be part of their preparing for bed. Washed and night nappies on, the children wanted the curtains around the bed pulled, but sadly she had to point out one pull and they would fall into shreds.

"If you get into bed, Daddy can read you a story from one of the books I had as a child."

But before Daddy could respond Joshua demanded, "Oosie to read, Oosie to read" to which Rebecca joined in.

With a wry grin David challenged, "I'm sure you won't refuse these two little rascals? Her answer was to hug and ticked them both, before clambering into the centre of the huge bed, She rested her back on the pillows while they nestled into her with thumbs in their mouths. David's suggestion to snuggle up with them was loudly welcomed, but she had barely begun the story when David murmured, "They're asleep." Carefully David slid from the bed to gently pick up Rebecca, as Rosie whispered, "Sleep well little one" and kissed her 'goodnight' before David placed her in the cot. She stirred slightly, muttered "Oosie" and slept on. Rosie clambered from the bed, covered Joshua up and kissed him saying, "Goodnight precious one". As she looked up, David seemed to swallow hard before saying abruptly, "I'll stay here with the twins."

She gave him a questioning look. "If I'm downstairs, I won't hear them if they awake in this strange and large place. I don't want Joshua climbing out of bed to find me. If we stay more often, I'll rig up that microphone similar to the one at home. There is a nice fire in here and that chair looks reasonably comfortable. I don't expect you to stay here with me, and guess if I get a cup of tea and a book from the library, I'll soon be ready to sleep."

"Bertie over the years has probably read all twenty-nine volumes of the Encyclopaedia Britannica, but hopefully you will find something to interest you."

"If Bertie has done that, he'll have a massive knowledge base. However, life in practice is often very different. I might know how to mend a burst pipe, change a car tyre and hang a new door, but I've never done any of those things, nor do I have an inclination to do so. What are Bertie's interests?"

Rosie shrugged and considered that while David selected several books and got his drink. "These should keep me going. If I don't like one, I'll start another."

He bent forward to kiss her cheek, "Thank you. I'll see you in the morning."

On her return the conversation revolved around the twins and David, bringing Cathy to point out, "You're very prickly around David. Obviously, he's keen for this courtship to work out. No one could fail to see how his children adore you. Their eyes follow you, they cling to you, they're afraid of losing you."

"I know! That's why I left. I didn't want to break their hearts. There are times when, like my father, David is overbearing, exasperating and sometimes very hard to like."

Cathy responded crossly, "Oh believe me Rosie, he is nothing like your father! Yes he has a loud voice, takes charge in situations, but he also listens, cares and is thoughtful. His desire is to please. He takes responsibility for his children, looks after his home, business, finances, and is open, generous and kind."

"Crumbs, you make him sound like a saint."

"In comparison to your father, he is!" Cathy glanced at Jack, "Sorry Jack, I know Leo is our employer, and I'm not saying anything against your father Rosie, just pointing out the differences."

Bertie was making signs as though to agree with Cathy. Astonished, Rosie glanced between her and Jack. In all these years, she had never heard them talk about their perception of her father. Jack looking distinctly uncomfortable remarked, "Enough said Cathy love!"

Cathy smiled at her. "We love you. I see this..." she looked at Jack, "...we see this as a real chance for you to have children who value and love you and a husband that appreciates you. Don't spoil it by nit picking at David's every word. In desiring the best for each other and the twins, you will cement and build something far better than you can imagine."

Rosie hummed, and as if Cathy followed her thoughts, she added, "And Johnny is a lovely man. You would certainly have a pleasant life with him. But you've been trained for challenge and I think as a vicar's wife you would soon be bored."

Bertie grunted, looked morose, squirmed around in his seat, and then stood banging his stick on the floor repeating the word, 'bored, bored, bored'. Rosie guessed he wasn't so much in agreement with Cathy, but he was 'bored'. Before Helen's arrival, Bertie would have happily amused himself watching TV. Now he wanted entertaining so she suggested a game of Scrabble.

An hour later Bertie had proved his word knowledge by winning the game. And knowing the twins awoke early she headed off to bed. From the bathroom opposite her room she looked across at David's door, with no light coming from under it she guessed he was probably asleep. In case he needed the toilet in the night, she left on the light. Once in bed, she considered the day, the various ups and downs and fell asleep thinking of Cathy's words.

A child was screaming in her dream. It pierced through her sleep to wakefulness. Her eyes opened and her mind jumped into gear. The illuminated dial of the clock read 2.53 am. In David's house the twins slept on the second floor and she in the basement.

She had never been disturbed by their crying in the night. When they were babies, she had occasionally help feed them during the night, but now she wondered if they awoke often. But Rebecca's hysterical screaming indicated more than a dirty nappy, teething or even pain. And now Joshua had begun crying. Everything within her wanted to comfort them, but she could hardly barge into David's bedroom. The screaming didn't stop, and as Joshua's crying increased in volume, she guessed David had opened his bedroom door. She saw that as her cue to jump out of bed, fling on her dressing gown, put slippers on and step out into the hall. David was standing in the bathroom doorway, patting Rebecca's back while trying to soothe her. Rebecca was sobbing uncontrollably, her face buried in his shoulder. Joshua was hugging his leg crying for attention. At the other end of the corridor Bertie emerged, and then she caught a glimpse of Jack urging Bertie back to bed, as Cathy headed towards them.

"What's the matter little one?" Rosie rubbed the little girl's back. She cringed away into her father, causing her to ask, "Is she hurt?"

David, shaking his head, boomed over the crying. "I don't know."

Moving closer, David opened up the way for her to bring comfort to Rebecca, but in this instance she just wanted her Daddy, for any loosening of his arms caused her to scream, "No. No!" and push even harder into him. Rosie picked up Joshua, and said to both of them, "There's nothing for you to be frightened of. Daddy's here, I'm here." Joshua stopped crying, he looked into her eyes, his little hand on her face tried to keep her attention as she turned to question, "What's wrong Rebecca? Are you in pain?" After a brief raising of her head revealing a puce face with tears rolling down it, Rebecca buried her head back into her father's neck and continued her inconsolable sobbing. Cathy tried to attract Rebecca's attention from the other side. Seeing Jack Joshua said "Unc Juk" and he happily allowed himself to be put into Jack's arms. Rebecca briefly looked up, put out her hand to draw Rosie closer, but refused to leave her father's arms. They stood together, Rosie uttered soothing words, and David apologised for disturbing them. Rosie had the disturbing revelation that in her undressed state and close proximity to David, she could feel the warmth of his body and he - no doubt - hers. Embarrassed she stated, "I'll get Rebecca's Patch bear."

She headed down the corridor, opened David's door and

clicking on the light, David called, "It's not working. That's why I had to bring the children out here."

Jack, shaking his head growled, "You'll be wishing you hadn't decided to stay. My guess is the rats have chewed beyond the wiring of the main chandelier in the entrance hall."

By now Rosie was delving through the room's darkness and having found the large canopied bed, used it as her guide to find her way to the cot and retrieve Patch the bear. Before they were born she had made them each a bear. Joshua's was made out of two black fur hats, one she had found in a charity shop in Kensington, the other her mother's cast off. He had a rotund body and adorable face so Jane felt his name should be 'Blackie'. The pattern for both bears was the same, but the other bear had been made from several different shades of brown furry materials, from which Patch got his name. He too was rotund, had a cheeky, loveable face, and Rebecca loved stroking the different furs. It was unusual in any trauma for Patch not to be with her, and perhaps why she was crying so hard. Rosie reached her hand into the cot to find his furry body when something warm brushed past her arm. The shock caused her to scream. She clutched the bear and speedily withdrew her arm. What was that? A rat? A squirrel? Appalled and desperate to leave the room, in the pitch dark she lost her bearings and didn't know which way she was facing.

In the darkness it was a relief to hear David saying, "Rosie, Rosie, are you alright?"

She tried to pinpoint the direction of his voice and still horrified, struggled to divulge what had just happened as David called, "Rosie, where are you, speak to me."

Weakly she managed, "I can't see" as she bumped into a chair.

David instructed, "Walk around the bed."

"I'm trying to find it." She stopped and tried to orientate herself with the furniture she knew to be in the room. Carefully, with arms outstretched, she moved forward. Either she had misjudged the distance, or direction, for she couldn't find the bed. Desperately she said, "This would be funny, if I wasn't so scared." Then she squealed in surprise as she bumped into David. He held her close and relieved she rested against him before declaring, "Let's get out of here."

At that moment Jack pushed open the door which gave enough light to indicate which direction to go in and with no further ado she strode out into the corridor. Jack's eyes scanned her face before he proclaimed, "You are spooked! What did you see?"

"I…I…didn't see, I felt…a rat, a squirrel, in Rebecca's cot?"

"Oh God! No!" Cathy peered around the door of Rosie's bedroom. "At your scream we brought the children in here. I've put them in your bed to keep them warm."

David caught her hand and gave her a sympathetic smile. As Cathy stepped back, Rosie turn to Jack to suggest, "Please, inspect…you know…if there is any evidence… in here." and prayed there wouldn't be. Rebecca had stopped crying, and she smiled at the still fearful little face, "Guess who I've got here?" She waggled Patch bear's arm. To her dismay Rebecca began to scream hysterically again. Dropping the bear on the floor she bent over to ask, "Oh my darling, whatever is the matter?" Rebecca clung to her, and on lifting her from the bed, it was her neck she buried her face into. Indicating David to pass the blanket folded at the bottom of the bed, she wrapped the child in it and carried her to the easy chair by the fireplace. Cathy attempted to distract Joshua, who at his sister's upset had started to cry again. Jack, having switched on the electric fire, had inspected that part of the room and gave her a reassuring smile. David drew up a chair to pat Rebecca and ask, "Is this house always so cold?"

In the midst of cooing and reassuring Rebecca she broke off to answer. "I'm used to it. I turned off the central heating in my bedroom at the flat, and felt Paul and Jill keep the lounge too hot. Put your chair closer to the fire. She moved around to allow him part of the blanket, and curious Rebecca stopped crying, but tears still ran down her face, as she cautiously looked around before announcing, "Patch bear bite me."

Appalled, Rosie didn't know whether to deny that or not, for she didn't want the child further frightened. Over Rebecca's head she looked at David before saying, "Patch bear wouldn't bite you. He loves you."

Upset, Rebecca bounced up and down, shouting, "He did, did! Daddy, he did." With that Rebecca tugged the sleeve of her nightie. To please her Rosie lifted it up and before she could say 'there now, there's nothing there' she saw to her dismay a small, triangular weal with pincer indentations that had bruised, but not broken the skin on her arm. To stop her gasp she bit down on her lip, and wide-eyed indicated for David to look.   Tears filled Rosie's eyes at this beloved little girl being bitten by a rat while staying with her. David reached out his hand to cover hers as in an emotional, husky whisper she called, "Cathy, you need to see this."

Cathy, seeing the mark, called on the Almighty and then Jack.

"You need to see this. Biting at the wiring is one thing, but a child's arm is quite another!" Then turning to them Cathy advised, "We need to give that a good wash" and with that she bustled out. Rebecca curled up, perhaps realising the tension she had caused, nestled into Rosie with her thumb in her mouth.

Jack, without his usual cheery disposition, stood there staring, seeming suddenly old, white and gaunt. David got to his feet and gently rested his hand on Jack's shoulder. "No-one could have known this would happen. How about we put on the kettle and make everyone a hot chocolate."

Jack nodded, "I'll do that. You stay here. There's no evidence in here."

Rosie involuntarily shivered, and David's hand moved to rest lightly on her shoulder. She looked up and gave him a small smile. "Jack, if you are going to the kitchen, could you bring up that special red tin where I put those treats for little girls and boys?" At the speaking of treats, Rebecca suddenly sat up and looked expectant, which made them smile.

David offered, "If I had a torch I could find a packet of their favourite biscuits from the suitcase."

Joshua, who seemed uninterested and had remained tucked up in bed, also sat up at the word 'biscuits' and repeated it as a question. This caused David to give his son a cold, tired smile, bringing Rosie to suggest, "You look so cold why not warm up and get into bed with Joshua?" He nodded and obeyed while she thought how ironic that within a week, he had found his way into her bed, and at her invitation!

Cathy arrived with a small bowl, sponge and towel, and behind her Bertie followed waving his torch. Jack proclaimed, "Good timing Bertie, the twins' favourite biscuits are next door, I'll need that to find them." Bertie made his heehaw laugh, handed it to him before dragging himself across the room to watch Cathy gently dabbing the area of Rebecca's marked skin, now turning blue from the bruising.

Bertie screwed his nose up at the antiseptic smell, "Ooh pooh!" then, seeing Rebecca wanting to withdraw her arm, added in a sympathetic tone, "There, there, better soon" causing Rebecca to smile up at him.

Cathy had just finished saying, "There, that's better," when Rosie's bedroom door burst open to reveal Jack, his face white, his hand shaking as he held up a half-eaten packet of biscuits. Before anyone could speak, Jack shut the door, leant back against it and exclaimed, "I've never seen anything like it." No one spoke waiting for him to elaborate, but it was a few seconds before he felt able to do so. "I found the suitcase on the chair where you said. I shone the torch into it and inside there was a dozen pairs of bright eyes." Rosie and Cathy both gasped, their hands leapt to cover their mouths. It didn't bear thinking about, but Jack was continuing, "In the centre of this brood sat the largest, fattest rat I've ever seen, and in its paws the packet of biscuits. I expected they would scatter as disturbed and frightened, instead the large rat's eyes glared at me as if daring me to take what he - or she - obviously considered theirs."

Bertie gave his heehaw laugh as David boomed, "Oh Jack, I'm so sorry! The biscuits must have encouraged the rats."

"Oh David, believe me, this rat didn't need encouragement, it wasn't starving, it's been eating something, somewhere. Anyway, I clobbered him over the head with the torch and I grabbed the biscuits."

Wide-eyed Cathy said bluntly, "Jack Hawkins, whatever for? You surely can't expect us to tuck into those with our hot chocolate?"

Rosie felt a giggle arising. Embarrassed Jack stuttered, "No, no, well I…". Then straightening up he predicted, "They won't be eating any more" at which Bertie sitting on an upright chair wailed into his hands in a similar way to a distraught child.

Cathy frowned, "Bertie what is it?" He didn't answer, and in despair she shook her head. "Up until now I'd have said we led a quiet life, but this last week it's been one thing after another. Bertie, I'm losing patience. Tell me what ails you?"

Between his hands he sobbed, "Billy… Billy."

Puzzled, Cathy looked around the room hoping someone might inform her who Billy was. Mystified they could only shrug. Cathy put her hand on Bertie to command, "Tell me, who is Billy?"

Bertie looked accusingly around the room, his eyes resting on Jack before saying, "Friend."

"We know Jack's your friend…"

Roused, Bertie shook off Cathy's hand so violently it hit the table. "No…not friend."

Cathy rubbed it, Jack stepped forward. "Come on old chap, we're all tired. Let's get you back to bed."

Bertie thrashed about so Jack couldn't help him, and cried out, "Hurt. Hurt."

Cathy, who Rosie had rarely seen frazzled, became impatient,

"Bertie, that's enough. Jack's not hurting you. We're all tired. Stop it!"

Upset, and obviously frustrated by his inability to make himself understood, Bertie leapt up, unbalanced he fell backwards, knocking over the chair causing it to fall within feet of where Rosie and Rebecca sat. Immediately Jack and Cathy were on each side of Bertie, picking him up and at the same time restraining him from further harming himself, or anyone else. Rosie drew Rebecca into her arms and brought the blanket across her head in order to hide what could rapidly turn into Bertie having an epileptic fit. Lifting her she crossed to the bed, laid her beside Joshua, conveying to David with her eyes, 'don't let the children see this' as she announced, "Daddy will cuddle down with you both, and keep you warm, and I can make my bed into a tent. With that she pulled the thick curtain across one side so they couldn't see Bertie as Jack and Cathy steered him towards the door. Unusually he seemed intent to lash out at Jack, but despite the wrangling Jack's voice remained calm as he tried to reason with him. Bertie's frenzy caused his words to be even more indistinguishable, but Rosie managed to decipher, "Hurt, Billy hurt."

Cathy sounding near to exhaustion said, "Is he, well he'll be better soon. Now, let's get you to your room."

Rosie stood at the bottom of the bed. They could hear Bertie as he continued ranting along the corridor. Joshua, his face screwed up into a deep scowl, asked loudly, "Daddy, why did Jack hurt Bertie's friend?"

Rebecca answered brightly, "Cause Billy wanting my biscuit bit me."

Aghast at that news, astonished at Rebecca's perception, Rosie stared at her, and David groaned. "The biscuit, of course! She awoke, wanted you, so to pacify her I gave her a biscuit. A piece must have dropped in the cot."

Slowly Rosie verified her understanding. "Bertie has a friend called Billy who is a rat, and he's upset because Jack hit him?"

"It would seem so!" David grimaced, "Out of the mouths of babes. Rosie, don't look so appalled. It's not unusual for boys to have tame rats for pets. It's just they don't usually roam about the house and bite little girls in the night!"

"I can hardly believe what I'm hearing. Tamed rats! Bertie has tamed the rats in the house!" Bertie's unintelligible shouting was still echoing against the stone floor and walls of the hall. Rosie rushed out and up to Jack and Cathy who were trying to haul Bertie into his room while he strove against them. Loudly she proclaimed, "Bertie, Jack didn't know that Billy the rat is your friend." Bertie stopped struggling and a shocked Jack and Cathy let him slide to the ground. For their benefit she added, "The twins worked it out."

Cathy stood opened mouthed, as Jack crouching beside Bertie questioned, "Is that true? You have been feeding that rat and its babies?" Bertie, sitting on the floor, managed 'yes' causing Jack to comment, "No wonder it didn't scarper when it saw me. Bertie, Billy bit Rebecca." Bertie made a face.

Cathy gasped, "Oh Bertie!"

Rosie intervened, "David gave Rebecca a biscuit. Our guess is a piece broke off near her arm and drew Billy to eat it."

Bertie having righted himself pulled on Jack's arm and asked, "I see Billy."

"No Bertie, you can't. I didn't hit him hard, he'll be alright. We'll see him tomorrow. Sorry old chap, but enough is enough." And Bertie, as if seeing as she did, that Jack was at the end of his tether, nodded and took the arm Rosie offered him. Slowly she headed into his room and called back to Jack and Cathy, "Forget the chocolate, just get some sleep. I'll leave David in my bed and sleep in Helen's."

On her return she peered around the curtains. David looked so snug in her bed with a child nearly asleep on either side of him. David put his hands behind his head, and with a knowing smile said quietly, "I apologise for accusing you of being untidy. I can see you are as neat at home as at work and have made this room very comfortable. This is a nice big bed, are you going to come in and join us?"

"Like you, I believe everything has a place and that's not in bed beside you. I'll sleep in Helen's bed. She turned off the fire, and returned to say, "Rebecca seems to have got over her trauma, and Patch bear has been reinstated."

"Why do you live here?"

"It's my home. Jack and Cathy are like parents and they look after my brother. We make the best of it as there's nowhere else to go. I'm sorry I had no idea about the lack of electricity, rats and the danger the twins would be in."

"Rosie, it's not your fault. Tomorrow, if you'll let me, we'll sort out the rat problem, and get someone in to look at the electricity, but I think it would be better not to stay another night."

"I can understand that."

"If we leave late evening, the twins can sleep in their car seats. That should give you time to see Helen and hopefully tomorrow, Johnny will be on the way to recovery. If you wish we can all come next Saturday."

"You want me to come back with you?"

David looked surprised, "Well, that was the original plan. I think you would agree that Rebecca is not going to be easily parted from you."

Rosie nodded. "It's only that I seem to be needed here."

She caught the underlying steel in David's voice as he said with outward calm, "I thought Rosie you had made your choice. I would appreciate it if you would consider carefully how they would feel to be parted from you again. He turned on his side, "Good night Rosie, turn the light off as you leave."

CHAPTER 13

For the remainder of the night Rosie tossed and turned worrying about to whom she felt the most obligated. Jack and Cathy would expect her to go with David and the twins, but to do so would be to leave them in this crumbling old mansion with dodgy electricity, the rats, and along with the responsibility of Bertie and Helen in hospital. And she wanted to be there for Johnny. By dawn, exhausted, she finally fell asleep.

Awakening in a strange room she wondered for a moment where she was. Little voices laughing and chattering in the inner courtyard below Helen's window reminded her of the events of the night, and her decision to return to her mews cottage in Kensington and take up life looking after the twins. But today she wanted to support Jack and Cathy with the variety of problems facing them.

She padded along the corridor to the bathroom opposite her bedroom, took a quick bath and, having viewed the corridor she ventured across the hall. In her bedroom, the curtains around the bed had been drawn and tied back, the bed made, and the only thing out of place were the toys scattered in front of the fireplace. Rosie closed the door, walked around the bed to her drawer of undies. In removing her dressing gown, she folded it ready to put in her suitcase and had just slipped off her nighty when the door opened, David walked in and headed towards the fireplace. Naked, and knowing he would turn and see her, Rosie bobbed down behind the bed and assumed having retrieved what he wanted he would leave. She shivered, waited and not hearing anything manoeuvred herself from all fours to her knees. Facing into the bed, she stretched up to peer over it with the intention of grabbing her dressing gown, when she heard David exclaim, "Good grief Rosie, what are you doing?"

Her eyes widened in shock, her head turned to where David was standing at the corner of the bed. Deeply embarrassed, she simultaneously closed her eyes, groaned inwardly and pressed her naked body into the side of the bed while blindly reaching out to find her dressing gown. His voice next to her offered, "Here, let me help you." Furious at his even being there, let alone helping her, she shot forward to snatch it before he did. As she retrieved it, the satin eiderdown came with it, unbalancing her. She collapsed on the floor, it fell on top of her and although she couldn't see David she could hear him roaring with laughter. For a second or two she lay under it stunned, then fluctuating between tears and anger, she pushed it off her head. David was sitting on her bed, shaking with mirth and wiping the tears from his face with his handkerchief.

And realising she was looking at him, he could barely ask, "Oh Rosie....whatever next?"

Far from amused she snapped, "Oh go away!" before wriggling under the eiderdown to find her dressing gown. In doing that, the eiderdown caught the bottom edge of the bed curtain, and suddenly - inches from her face - was the back of Billy rat's fat round body. With a yell and no thought for her nakedness, she leapt on to the bed. The sudden heavy bounce on the mattress tipped David backwards and she, landing on her stomach, found herself laying in the crook of David's arm and looking down into his astonished face. Immediately his astonishment changed, his eyes filled with laugher and his mouth curved into a very provocative smile as the precursor to his murmuring seductively, "My dear Rosie, in my wildest dreams I couldn't have imagined that I would arouse you to such a passion that you would throw yourself upon me."

Livid at his response, shaking from her close encounter with Billy, feeling extraordinarily vulnerable, she was about to vent her anger when Jack asked from the bedroom doorway, "Rosie are you alright?"

Dismayed she murmured, "Oh God" and buried her head into the bed, as if it would also hide her nakedness. David, his arm trapped under her neck rolled over her as Jack in a mortified voice fretted, "Oh! Oh! So sorry! And in his rushing away Rosie realised he believed he had interrupted a sexual tryst.

David's body retreated from hers, but he made no attempt to remove his trapped arm and lay on his side beside her. Without moving Rosie turned her head, "Now look what you've done."

"What I've done?" His fingers stroked enticingly down her back, causing her to flinch. "I used my body to cover yours in the belief you wouldn't want Jack to see your splendid display of nakedness."

Rosie glared at him and snapped, "What you have seen you don't have permission to touch."

The tantalising sensation stopped at the small of her back. He replaced that torment by stating in teasing voice, "Maybe Rosie, you should consider 'what you have done'". She buried her face again into the bed and wished him gone. "You yell like a banshee that draws Jack's concern, and then throw yourself into my arms." Outraged and red-faced she clenched her jaw. "You have to admit my response has been very restrained to such an unexpected, yet demonstrative invitation."

She lifted her head and was about to screech, 'Just go away!" when David gently withdrew his arm from under her neck and with underlying amusement remarked, "However, I am left wondering what suddenly possessed the reticent Rosie to dive on my unsuspecting person." Her response was a deep growl of anger, and despite being prostrate on the bed she banged her clenched fists into it. This brought David - in what she considered a pseudo solicitous tone - to recommend, "I expect lying naked before me you feel at a disadvantage, but when you are dressed, your reasoning behind it will change." With that he rolled off the bottom of the bed.

Her retort came out in a highly-strung voice, "I was dressing. You came in without knocking. What choice did I have? I had to duck behind the bed. And believe me, I only leapt onto the bed because I saw..." the words caught in her throat, she strained it to finish, "Billy...under the bed."

David frowned and marching around the bed proclaimed, "He's long gone." and as she remained prostrate on the bed she wished him 'long gone'. There came a flutter of cold air before the eiderdown floated over her with the command, "Wrap yourself up in that!"

Cold, she pulled it around her and turned over. David was nowhere to be seen. Cautiously, she sat up and said his name. A grunt of acknowledgement came from under the bed. Realising he was looking for Billy she directed his search. "He was sitting in the curtain at the head of the bed." The curtain moved. Her eyes widened. Expecting the rat to run up it and land near her, she let out a scream and holding the eiderdown tightly around her she backed down the bed as David let out a "ah ha". Anxiously she queried, "Have you got him?"

Like a puppet at a Punch and Judy show, 'Blackie the bear' showed his face and then body over the side of the bed, his paws waving at her. As he danced on the edge of the mattress David unseen sang, "I'm Blackie, just Blackie, a very little bear, made by you with a heart of care, I'm not a rat, I'm not fat, I'm just Blackie, Blackie the bear."

Ridiculous as the song was it broke something inside of her, and not knowing whether to laugh or cry she did both. David's head popped up beside Blackie. "Oh Rosie, Rosie, what an emotional week you've had." He came and sat beside her while she battled with feeling stupid, or allowing herself to be comforted by a man everyone felt cared for her. "You look like a beautiful wood nymph in that eiderdown. Green suits you. Would the nymph be open to a hug from a branch of what I hope fits God's description of an oak of righteousness?"

Grumpily, she bantered, "I don't feel a nymph! More a wiggly worm who has a big black bird desiring to swoop and gobble me up."

David chuckled, "Oh Rosie, Rosie, believe me you aren't a wiggly worm. Although seen and desired, you certainly aren't a woman to be gobbled up. You need to be carefully and considerately imbibed to obtain the full pleasure, delight and satisfaction that will be greater than the provision of an excellent meal."

The sexual innuendo and his amused expression had her tighten her grip on the eiderdown. Self-conscious she looked down and said nothing. David gave a deep sigh, "Oh Rosie, I am now a father who has learnt to comfort his children." He stood and despite her protests, put his arms around and carried her to the armchair. "This is how a father should warm and comfort his child" and sitting her on his lap, his arms remained around her and together they rocked back and forth.

The action reminded her of Hawkeye comforting her as a child. The memory of its innocence having been destroyed by Doug. Tears rolled silently down her face, causing David to say "Rosie?" as a question.

"Doug!" was her one word reply.

David grim hummed, but she heard the concern in his voice as he requested, "Tell me more." Nestled in the eiderdown and resting against him, she didn't have to look at him and that made it easier to elaborate. "When I worked in the Parliamentary Offices Doug was an important man in his late forties. He took an interest in me. I looked up to him and saw him as a father figure. One day he suggested I could live in his spare bedroom if I would be willing to caretake his Kensington cottage. Naively I accepted. Over the weeks and months the kiss on the cheek moved to my mouth, his hug to a fumble." She cringed, "It was horrible. I didn't know how to stop it. I didn't like it. It wasn't right. I didn't know what to do."

David observed, "Rebecca was bitten by a rat that caused her pain and the rejection of Patch bear. But it wasn't Patch bear's fault. When bad things happen it's easy to form a wrong perspective. Not all men are black birds out to forage what they can." David looked rueful, "Nor do rats eat with an intention to hurt. But painful experiences and judgements can only initiate God's healing process when you forgive Doug and yourself for what happened."

"Jane said that. I've tried many times but I can't forgive him."

David continued to rock her, "You've been blessed by the Hawkins' love, and the Father's love sent Jesus to die for men's sin. Remember the words of Jesus to His Father at his crucifixion about those who organised it, 'forgive them they know not what they do'!"

Rosie nodded, "I know but in Doug's case, he did know what he was doing. Last weekend while considering my father, I understood I had probably exacerbated his hatred in the way I behaved towards him, and the fault wasn't entirely his. I would move his things, he would rant and rave, and when they were found in an obvious place, I loved the way it made him look foolish. I knew then I had to forgive myself and felt then I was able to forgive him."

David hugged her, "The Lord's love is to bring fresh insights into the past which enable us to break those yokes that have bound us. I didn't realise how simple words I had spoken over my life could affect it." Rosie moved to rest against the arm of the chair so to look up at him. "I came to the end of my tether just after Jane birthed the twins. Years before I had made an inner vow to never cry again and it had hardened my heart. The Lord revealed that to Beatty, and as I let the memories of pain and hurt come to mind, I wept and wept in her arms. In the same way Rosie, you have burdens that aren't yours to carry. I suspect you have made inner vows, for instance…" his eyes widened to question, "… I'll never let a man touch me again."

Surprised by his confession, vulnerability and insight, she nodded and wanted to reciprocate his trust in her, "It would seem that like Beatty, you have been given keys to the locked rooms in my life so I can release the skeletons within."

David gave a rueful smile, "In that hope, I would wish you to believe that in allowing me to venture over the drawbridge into your castle, it is - and it will be - a good thing!"

Rosie tutted, "I'm being serious. Since you arrived you have been a catalyst to my past being unlocked which released the memories of a childhood trauma. Do you think I have broken that inner vow by giving you permission to hug and kiss me?"

"I believe so. Just as I believe the Lord healed and prepared me for a future without Jane. He helped me take courage and draw on His strength and peace. The Bible says, 'All things work together for good.' We must learn to trust His words and that He has a plan and a future for each one of us. And should you agree we can do that together."

"David, that inner vow may have been broken, but…" she cringed, "physical intimacy…" Embarrassed she rushed on, "The Bible doesn't speak to me as it did to Jane and you. Your faith has given you some incredible experiences. Jane assured me God hears and He will answer, but she also said His timing is often different to ours."

"Healing does take time and Jane was right." His smile was gentle, "God is speaking to you, leading you through that hymn, and through His word. Trust Him, read His Word, and give yourself time to process it. Talk to Him and talk to me, as you did with Jane."

"Thank you." She slid from his lap, "I should get dressed. Jack and Cathy are obviously looking after the twins." She cringed, "They think we're doing the very thing I have no intention of ever doing again."

"Is that so? Another inner vow you may one day wish to break." David stretched out his legs, rubbing them as if to renew circulation. "I'm sure Jack and Cathy would find your reaction thinking you'd seen Billy amusing. I believe their hearts are open enough to tell them that it isn't me or my family's influence that is changing you, but the power of forgiveness. I sense they aren't averse to hearing about the Lord and how He desires in His love to be part of our lives." Rosie wasn't so sure. David smiled, "As for the twins..." he chortled, "They are well occupied. I only came up to find Blackie the bear because Joshua wanted to introduce him to Billy's family."

Astounded she shot round, the eiderdown slipped, blushing she adjusted it while questioning, "Billy?"

David grinned, "Well, Bunty it turns out!"

"What? Billy is a girl? They are to be pets? Can rats be tame?" To each question David nodded so she finished, "I suppose they must be if you caught them."

"I didn't, Jack did."

"The only catching Jack has ever done is with traps, and they kill not preserve."

"Apparently when Jack hit Billy, I mean Bunty, and grabbed the biscuits, he also had the forethought to close the lid of the suitcase. This morning we told Bertie and he was keen to watch us carefully carry the suitcase downstairs. He was so excited! He encouraged the twins to finish their breakfast so they could meet his friends. They have been 'helping' Jack unearth an old kitchen cabinet from the storeroom then watched him as he took out the glass and covered the frame with chicken wire. Cathy took them to her greenhouse where she keeps straw to put between the strawberry plants and they happily filled a couple of bags with it. Then as the back of the cupboard would be the rats' floor, they dropped it there and spread it out. Jack suggested they break up the remaining biscuits with some milk in saucers and put them inside. Then taking our hutch outside and - with my careful opening of the suitcase - they all entered safely. They are now installed in what is a very good temporary accommodation."

"And Rebecca isn't frightened by Billy, I mean Bunty?"

"On the contrary, because Bertie is thrilled to have his rat friends living in the garden shed, Joshua is now enthralled and Rebecca - after a little reticence - understanding they didn't mean to hurt her, is interested."

"And all before 9.00 am!"

David stood, "Exactly! Although I wouldn't be too complacent, for I suspect there are other vermin not so tame still at large. But it's unlikely you'll see them, they prefer to run from people, and it seems sensible not to have any food in the bedrooms."

"Cathy has always been a stickler for all meals being taken downstairs."

"Don't tell the twins or Bertie, but Jack and I are off to the shops to buy rat poison and traps to ensure the house isn't breeding more Bunty and 'Billy' babies. Oh, and to purchase a new suitcase. It's amazing what little teeth can chew through. Cathy insisted on washing all the clothes in the case, so the twins are wearing what they had on yesterday, until I have bought them new outfits."

"Then I'd better get dressed and come with you."

"That sounds like a good idea. And as it's nearly ten o'clock and the sun is shining, I think when we've done our shopping it will be time for me to buy lunch out for my new friends."

"Oh David, that's kind. Jack and Cathy rarely have such a treat, but it might be harder to persuade Bertie."

"Just leave that to me." Rosie, having toddled in the eiderdown to the bed, realised that David had picked up from the floor her scanty pants and bra and placed them on the pillow, bringing again the embarrassment of their unexpected intimacy. David now in full flow of his plans didn't seem to notice her snatching them from the pillow. "After the hospital visits, if we leave about six o'clock we'll be home before Paul and Jill go to bed. They can listen out for the twins while I see you settled in with Wilhelm and Grace."

Rosie stiffened, "David you said, 'we' but I don't remember telling you of my decision and plans."

"Oh Rosie, please? We've both had a hair-raising week, and in London I think I can guarantee a quiet, but sociable Sunday before returning to work. And as I have already said, with Helen and Johnny in hospital, we'll come down for the day next Saturday."

"David, you are taking control and organising my life without consulting me." Seeing his exasperated scowl, she reasoned, "Think about it. I'm not saying your plans or intentions aren't good, but next time please discuss them, rather than telling me." His expression was as if she had just made an extraordinary and outrageous statement, but she waved him away saying dismissively, "Now away with you while I get dressed." And in case he didn't acquiesce, she pulled across the bed curtain to hide her.

The rest of the day his plans went like clockwork. They'd taken two cars, purchased everything needed, had a really tasty three-course meal with wine in a public house in a room set aside for children, and Bertie loved it. To Rosie's surprise David suggested the twins could visit Helen. And to David's surprise Helen excelled herself. She not only thanked David for the fruit basket, but hiding different fruits she had the twins guess which one had disappeared. Not only did the twins enjoy it, but they gained an audience from other patients nearby. David in sensing the twins tiring had drawn them away with lots of waves and promises to visit again. The twins already 'loving Unc 'ack' happily returned to the car where he read them a story so Cathy and Bertie could visit Helen and they Johnny.

They arrived just when Johnny's family exited the waiting room where they were told that the swelling on Johnny's brain hadn't reduced as much as they'd hoped. His sedation would therefore continue until Mr Henshaw the consultant from Southampton arrived on Monday. Despite the daunting news, Diana hadn't been able to take her eyes off David, as he assured her mother and the Greenhaighs they would be praying and expecting that by next Saturday Johnny would be on the road to recovery. And Rosie couldn't fault him for he had asked to be kept in touch and offered any assistance he could provide. Throughout, as if knowing she was struggling with emotion, he had held her hand and placed a supporting arm around her waist, specially when they looked through the glass partition at Johnny laying so still, his breathing assisted by a machine.

When Cathy and Bertie returned from the hospital, she occupied the twins while David and Jack finished laying rat poison and traps around the house. They were packed and ready to leave when the phone in the butler's pantry rang. Cathy rushed to answer it. On her return she beckoned Rosie to leave Bertie playing with the twins, causing her to close the door on them and ask, "What is it?"

In a theatrical whisper she explained, "That was Helen's Mum. She seems very cowed by her husband. He hits her if he doesn't get his way. Rosie, it's awful for the poor woman hasn't any money of her own, and none to spare to visit Helen. She really worried what Archie - Helen's step-dad - might do if she did. That confirms the things Helen has said about what would happen to Declan should he return home. She thanked me for getting in touch, said she would alert the neighbours to look out for him and ask them to tell him he would be welcome where Helen lives."

From the other side of the room Bertie piped up in his own way, "Like Declan, good boy, stay in cottage."

Cathy raised her eyebrows and murmured, "There's nothing wrong with Bertie's hearing!"

Rosie thought to ask him, "Have you met Declan?"

Bertie's hands became animated, he managed to say, "'eln" before signing, 'secret and near boat house."

Rosie put her thumb up to indicate she understood as Cathy drew her outside the door to divulge quietly, "Norah, Helen's Mother, told me about Helen's pregnancy. How the man she was to marry turned out to be an ex-convict and disappeared, and his prison mates beat her up. She also said you've been a good friend to her."

"Rosie sighed, "Ben was a good man, he 'served time' because he tried to help a friend. It was Jill's fault Helen was beaten up, not Ben's. If you are thinking of helping Declan then let me tell you Helen's story."

As she finished, Cathy asked, "How can peoples' lives go so terribly wrong? I would like to help Declan long term. Norah said he's never been a problem, he's quiet, a good lad, wants to learn. Archie is more brawn than brain, it's Declan's bookishness that causes friction. Norah said she didn't report him missing believing he was with Helen. When the school inspector called, she said he was with his sister and staying in your London cottage. If not already, you or your friends staying there will get a visit, but I've told Norah by the time they chase that up, I hope we will have found him. And as his sister is in hospital here, that he'll be allowed to stay and go to the local school. Helen said if that could happen, once back on her feet, she would get a job and pay for his keep. It appears Declan has given Helen the incentive to return to normal life, and having safely lived in the Gatekeeper's cottage for a couple of weeks it also appears he knows how to look after himself. You can pray he soon hears he's welcome here and returns."

"Why don't you try praying, it can be very rewarding."

Cathy looked thoughtful. Rosie moved towards the door as Cathy added, "I wanted to say earlier how relieved Jack was that he hadn't walked in on you and David… well you know. But also we felt it was lovely that you and David seemed so together when telling us what happened and had both seen the funny side, and those…."

She broke off at the sounds of contention in the living room. Rosie raised her eyebrows before walking in to bring clarity to whose turn it was to wind up the lift in the toy garage. Cathy having nodded her approval at Rosie's action, suggested, "Those two could do with letting off energy before you go back to London." When David and Jack reappeared, they all took a walk down to the lake. To the twins' disappointment there weren't ducks to feed but Rebecca loved her piggy-back on Jack's back as did Joshua on David's. And then, with tummies full of banana sandwiches and Cathy's scones, and assurances they could visit again, they were happy to wave 'goodbye' and promptly fell asleep in the car.

With quiet classical music playing on the radio and the sun beginning to set, they drove for half an hour in silent contemplation. "I can barely believe all that has happened, it's only been eight days since you proposed to me"

"And, if you had accepted and come back with me then, life would have been less complicated."

Rosie hummed at the truth and then challenged, "Did you expect me to say 'of course I'll marry you. I have been hopelessly in love with you for years'?"

David glanced in her direction. "Well I thought you might be reticent to confess that, but you will one day."

At such an egotistical remark, Rosie pursed her lips and tried to think of a suitable rejoinder when David chuckled. "Oh Rosie, one day you'll also know when I'm teasing."

To that she retorted, "Don't bank on it!"

He sent her a broad smile, "I would like to think we have taken down a few barriers between us, and uncovered things that have haunted your past. The things I've learnt about your parents haven't impressed me, but your surrogate ones are amazing, wonderful and resourceful people. I think Bertie has tremendous potential that needs to be tapped. I've seen you laugh uncontrollably, and from your 'mud bath' I know you can have fun. There is already a new freedom to talk of how you feel, and I so enjoyed sharing together the 'rat' story with the Hawkins. It revealed to me - and I think to them - we could be very good together."

"Assisted by an excellent meal and two glasses of wine."

David chortled, "Perhaps we should eat out and drink more

often. I could certainly dine out on the story of 'Rosie and the rat' for weeks."

It not being a story she would want bandied about. She was going to protest when David assured her, "Don't look so worried, I would never intentionally embarrass you."

"There were definitely incidents where Jane embarrassed you."

"True! But maybe I deserved it because I couldn't resist bantering and teasing her. It was fun, laughter is good for the soul, and I'd like more of those times."

"I admit and confess I couldn't envision us enjoying time together, but the way you have been with me - and my family – has helped me feel more comfortable with you. I love the twins, and for their sake, I would like it to work out between us."

With his eyes on the road he commented, "I suspect as they get older they will be quite a challenge." He patted her knee, "But believe me, you are the mother they need and the woman I desire to be my wife."

Rosie didn't reply but minutes later admitted, "It's going to be strange living with Grace and Wilhelm and, as I'm no longer in your employ, I will act differently. Previously, I've not strongly expressed my opinion or challenged your decisions, but as wives need to do that, this will be a time to see if we could live amicably together. We have talked about chains breaking off and a new freedom to be myself, but in my budding and blossoming you might decide I'm not the wifely material you thought you were getting. And should that be so, or I decline your marriage offer I hope you will still feel able to re-employ me."

With a glance across at her he replied, "I need you to mother my children, and if we have to revert to employment then so be it. Which brings me to say whichever role comes forth - although not getting paid - I have arranged for you to have a personal payment into your bank account to cover your needs, and a household account to manage as a wife and mother." As if knowing she would argue he rushed on, "This is the same arrangement I had with Jane. Along with that it would be good if you would consider driving my Morris Minor. I grant you this is a rather unusual courtship, but would you also be willing - in practising to be my wife - to be responsible for other household tasks like the washing, shopping and cooking."

Rosie had always helped out in those areas, but she could see that as a wife and a mother she would have little time for her own pursuits. Deciding not to commit herself she replied, "We'll see how it goes."

It seemed natural on arriving at David's house for her to carry in Rebecca, and for David to lead the way carrying Joshua. Their charges once in their cots just stretched and continued sleeping. David gave the thumbs up and switched on the microphone which would relay any disturbance to either his or the basement flat.

In the basement flat Rosie saw, in the two weeks of her absence, that Jill's face had become strained with exhaustion. Her hair was a straggly mess and the jumper stretching over her enormous bosom was stained with either a recent spillage, or overflow from Rachel who was nestling against her. Even Jill's voice sounded weary as she welcomed her back, and relayed the children's antics. While David sat, Rosie automatically began folding the tipped-up pile of clean nappies on the settee. Paul emerging from the kitchen gave her an enthusiastic welcome, offered a cup of tea, and apologised for the state of the flat. It was then David jumped up to help him clear the remains of their meal from the table. As they chatted in the kitchen, Rosie moved on to fold the piles of clean washing bringing Jill to observe, "It's good to have you back."

Paul bringing out the tea agreed, "Rachel is a demanding baby and the boys a handful. Jill tries to sleep when she can."

"I expect you know we've been employing Lorna. She's good with the boys, but unlike you she has to be asked to help out with other things."

Rosie felt to pointed out, "I'm back but won't be around as before." David, sipping his tea looked up, his brow furrowed. "I'll be living at my cottage and having frequent weekends away. And of course you will be moving in a couple of months to your own house."

Paul stroking his beard said worriedly, "I'm not sure how that's going to work out. We are definitely going to need a 'Rosie' person in Kent to organise us, for we so easily descend into near chaos."

"Paul you exaggerate!" Jill challenged, "And once in Kent we'll have your family around us to help. Bob and Lilian can't wait for us to arrive." Paul raised his eyebrows for it was obvious they would need far more help than Paul's large family could give. Beatty wasn't frail but had her limits, and Bob and Lilian both worked during the week.

Visiting the bathroom Rosie picked up the towels from the floor, the children's bath toys from the bath, cleaned the toothpaste spillage on the sink, and quickly gave the toilet a scrub. When the opportunity arose, she slipped into the kitchen where the chaos was worse than the living room. As David sat talking, she soaked the saucepans and casserole dishes in hot water, and having filled up the dishwasher she put it on. She had just put things away in cupboards, returned the food to the fridge, and was wiping down the counter surfaces when David appeared in the doorway to ask, "Are you ready to go? Paul and Jill can't get to bed until I return from taking you to the cottage."

Her wide-eyed expression seemed to cause him bewilderment so she informed him, "My keeping them from their beds means I've cleaned the bathroom and tidied the kitchen. And in their waiting for you to return, they can wash the pans and dishes I've put in to soak." With that she moved past David into the lounge.

Paul having heard her said, "Oh Rosie, Thank you. You have the ability to quickly restore order. I don't think we have ever appreciated just how much you did. She gave Paul a small smile and queried, "I know Mrs Perkins doesn't clean at the weekend, but surely you've not made all that mess today? The floor looks as if it hasn't been washed since I left."

She saw David, Jill and Paul exchange a glance. Paul answered. "I'm afraid Mrs P told us at Easter that she had been happy and able to clean the whole house over five days a week when there were no children around. And although she appreciated our friendship, and being part of life in the house, with two families living here - and getting older - she felt it was time to retire."

"Oh no!" Rosie wailed, "We can't manage without her. She does so much more than the cleaning. She's like a grandmother to the children."

David put his arm around her waist. She went to move away but his arm tightened slightly as he said cheerily, "When I said that to Mrs P she said much the same about you being a mother to the children. When I told her I had found you she was so pleased. I couldn't persuade her to clean the whole house, but she did agree to look after my half!"

Rosie moved from the circle of his arm, her voice sceptical, "Why am I not surprised? What did you offer her?" Paul grinned at Jill, knowing as an employee Rosie rarely had the audacity to question David's actions or motives.

David laughed and bantered, "Nothing. I just said she was my secret weapon and if anyone could, she would be the one to encourage you to marry me."

"And she fell for that?"

"Oh yes! I would even say she was delighted to oblige."

Raising her eyebrows Rosie declared, "But surely having told me that destroys her potential. For forewarned I'll be forearmed, and could use her as a double agent!"

Paul chucked, Jill grinned and David proclaimed, "Great isn't it, the real Rosie is beginning to emerge." He turned his eyes steadily regarding her. "Every day you become more interesting and my attraction grows."

As his focus moved towards her mouth she quickly sidestepped and headed for the stairs before turning to say, "David, these people are waiting to go to bed."

David with the palms of his hands outstretched shrugged and Paul observed, "This Rosie isn't going to be easily plucked."

Jill said balefully, "Men! What they haven't told you is Mrs P has a neighbour. Apparently she is used to heavy duty cleaning, but due to a new government act four years ago, her job dwindled away. I've invited Mrs Smith to come on Wednesday to clean down here. I wasn't getting into David's belief in application forms and references, look how Helen turned out!"."

David contradicted that saying, "And even less successful was the way - without prior knowledge - you foolishly invited Tania to share the flat."

Seeing a row brewing, Rosie decreed sternly from the first stair, "But Jill, not entirely her fault!" Paul stroked his beard and Jill looked sheepish. Moving upwards she called, "David, we need to go" and to her surprise he strode over to join her. As the stairs turned, Rosie looked down into the room to call 'goodnight' and saw Paul and Jill exchanging an amused wide-eyed expression giving her believe they liked her new combative confidence.

CHAPTER 14

It felt strange being in David's house but no longer living there. Equally, she felt awkward staying in her cottage with Wilhelm and Grace as she only knew them from working at ITP. Fortunately, their purchase of a vacant flat overlooking Eccleston Square was proceeding well and expected to be completed in a few weeks. As it needed refurbishment, they had decided the work could be done while they would visit the many members of Wilhelm's family who lived in Germany.

The first week began as it had since the twins' birth. Both families went to church on Sunday, and ate lunch in David's dining room with its large table. With Jill so fraught, she and David prepared and cooked the beef roast dinner. Throughout the meal, Rosie felt she was fielding Jill's continual questions about her home and those she lived with. Afterwards, Paul recommended that Jill rest and to aid that, Rosie proposed a walk down Church Street, across the park and returning via Notting Hill Gate. Paul pushed Rachel with Luke on the pram seat and she took turns with David to walk beside William riding his tricycle and to push the twins in the double buggy.

Once in the park with the children running free, Rosie had the opportunity to talk to Paul about Johnny's head injury. With his experience working in Casualty, he was quick to assure her that the body had a remarkable way of recovering from trauma.

The children squabbling heralded tea-time and the twins, having loved her Rupert the Bear book, begged Rosie to read a story to all of them before they were hustled off to bed. Then the adults had a companionable hour together to discuss how daily life would pan out. That ended with David coaxing her to use his Morris Minor to travel back and forth from the cottage and saying, "Come on Rosie, it's highly unlikely you'll be attacked again."

Jill gasped and started asking question. Paul stroking his beard gazed at her while she, glaring at David, responded, "Oh, that happened years ago!" before heading downstairs with the intention of leaving. David following had apologised for his thoughtless comment but in anger she had snatched the keys from his hand, and then had to wait for him to back the Rover off the drive so she could drive the Morris out of the garage. With the briefest wave she had driven off. Half an hour later, he rang the cottage to check she had arrived safely. He did ask her to forgive him for speaking of something she had told him in confidence, which she did somewhat grudgingly.

Life resumed much as before, except now she drove to start her motherly duties at eight-thirty. Each day it was decided she would arrive with the twins up, breakfast eaten and after a brief hand-over, David would leave for ITP. With the car, she realised she could now extend the children's weekly activities. On Monday, she didn't want to leave the house as she was anxious and expectant of hearing from Diana about Mr Henshaw's visit to Johnny, but needed to take the twins to the church toddler group. On arrival, she was surprised at her welcome and their belief that as a nanny she had been on a 'well deserved' holiday. And, due to her brown skirt and cream blouse, a new member of the group thought she was a Norland Nanny.

In the old routine her day had finished at six. To aid their new relationship she had agreed to stay on each evening, eat together and talk of their day, but after that the time would be hers to do as she wished. It was gone six when Diana rang to tell her Mr Henshaw had advised that Johnny should not be moved, and his sedation gradually be reduced. After assuring Diana that sounded positive, she booked a visiting slot on Saturday afternoon. At 6.30pm when David had still not arrived Rosie dispensed with the twins' bath, washed and prepared them for bed. She let them lay on the settee with their thumbs in their mouths listening to her playing the piano. Simultaneous with the clock chiming seven, the lounge door opened bringing the twins to jump and shout 'Daddy'. Over their heads David gave her a rueful smile. With a child on each arm, he moved over to where she stood to impart a quick kiss on her mouth before asking if she had a good day. When she just nodded, David apologised adding, "With you here I knew all would be well."

Cross she responded, "True! But I expected you home at least an hour ago." The children - now wide-awake - ran around him as he explained, "That was my intention, but after last week, I had so much to catch up on I didn't noticed the time until it was six o'clock. I tried ringing but the phone was engaged, probably Paul or Jill on the party-line. How's Johnny?"

"Put the twins to bed and I'll tell you as we eat. It's fortunate it's only cold beef, salad and jacket potatoes tonight!"

In Tesco's the following day, she smiled when several people commented on her little family and as she did the week's shopping she considered life if she were their mother. After lunch as they slept for nearly two hours, she hung up the washing to dry in the boiler room. She was thankful with David needing a clean shirt every day that Mrs P did all the ironing. The children were eating their tea, and she was preparing the dinner which the twins would eat for lunch the following day when the phone rang. Cathy, with a highly excited voice exclaimed, "Is David there? You'll never guess what he's done. He's paid for a colour television to be installed."

"He is not home yet." Perplexed Rosie asked, "Did you want one?"

"When David talked about the gardening and cooking programmes, we expressed an interest in them." Feeling miffed as David hadn't told her of his intentions, she had to inject enthusiasm into her response. "And then, oh Rosie, Bertie was just getting frustrated that there was only the 'test card' to see when we had another delivery." Rosie scowled, "This time it was a portable typewriter in a black zipped case. David must have realised Bertie types on a heavy old typewriter. This one is lightweight and the keys electric." Cathy chortled, "There'll be no end to his questions now."

In knowing Bertie's endless questions Rosie smiled, "That was thoughtful! David was late last night. Best you ring later and thank him yourself."

"I will. And, I asked the nurses about Johnny, it was their usual answer, "As well as can be expected." Helen however is anxious about Declan. Oh, I have to go! Bertie's pulling on my sleeve. Bye love."

David appeared just after six o'clock, said a brief 'hello' and quickly whisked the twins upstairs for their bath. She could hear their squeals and laughter. Once they were out of the bathroom she cleared up, and popped into their room to say 'goodnight'.

Rosie broached the subject of David's gifts after they finished eating, "I was wondering David when you were going to tell me about sending gifts to my family?"

"I wondered if they would arrive today."

"Cathy was ecstatic and is going to ring later to thank you." David looked as delighted as Cathy had sounded excited, but that didn't stop Rosie needing to voice her fears, "David, as much as I

202

appreciate your thoughtfulness, if I am to be your wife, I would appreciate discussion before you make decisions, especially those towards my family." At David's perplexed expression she added, "Your generosity worries me." Aware this was a delicate subject she carefully chose her words. "I've seen how money, in different ways, can be used to influence people!" David visibly stiffened. "For instance, Mrs P wanted to retire, you admitted to changing her mind. Now I don't begrudge her being paid for five days when she is only doing three, but generosity and extravagant gifts can change peoples' opinions, beliefs and persuade them to say and do things against their better judgement. A benefactor also has the ability to change peoples' loyalties or bring them to feel beholden to them." In the tense silence that followed she took their empty plates into the kitchen. On her return, she knew comprehension had dawned for in a steely edge he queried, "Let me get this right. You think generosity can be used as a subtle form of blackmail?" At her questioning look he appeared appalled, "Is that the kind of man you think I am?" He didn't give her time to answer before asking, "Do you really hold the Hawkins in such little esteem as to imagine their opinion of me - and my suitability as a husband to you - would be swayed because I have given them gifts to make their life more comfortable? My perception is that Jack and Cathy have had a very raw deal in life, yet have accepted that in order to look after you and Bertie. In Bertie's case, given up their lives for him. They are wonderful people, I enjoy their company, and if I can't do something to bless them without you thinking I have an ulterior motive, then I wonder what kind of heart you have?" David threw his napkin on the table, "I can't believe you even thought that, let alone said it."

Not to be put down she replied frostily, "And I had hoped you would be willing to hear, even if not understanding, my perspective. For me, gifts come with price tags."

"So what was the price tag on the sewing machine we bought you for Christmas?"

"It was extravagant! It was Christmas and I was thrilled you had all chipped in to buy it. I make things because I want to. But when Jill said my creative ability could become an enterprise and had - without my knowledge - approached a local shop to stock the toys I had made, the gift changed from enjoying creating things, to feeling as so much money had been spent on the machine, I was now obliged to use it to make toys and sell them."

"That's ridiculous!"

"To you David, maybe. When I accepted the expensive clothes and shoes from you, I had a need, and you insisted on spoiling me. But I have had to wrestle with the comments of how lucky I was to have a man so 'willing to spoil me', 'how wonderful that such a thoughtful sexy and generous man should be interested in me'. And, believe it or not, those clothes gave rise to the inference that I should 'stick to men in my own class' and, of course, the inevitable one 'when a man buys a woman expensive clothes, he usually has an ulterior motive'." At his horrified expression she commented, "You asked me to be honest. I've made you angry. I'll leave you to think about it."

With that she headed to the peg, retrieved her coat, hat and scarf, picked up her handbag, and seeing a bewildered David sitting at the table as she passed the door, she called, "See you in the morning" and was out the front door before he could respond.

At her cottage, to Grace and Wilhelm's cheery welcome, she was succinct, "The twins were very good, but excuse me as I am feeling rather cross" and headed upstairs to her room. Unable to concentrate on dressmaking, she attempted to read a novel.

To allow Mrs Smith more leeway to clean on Wednesday, and knowing Joyce was coming to spend time with her grandchildren, she volunteered to look after Jill's two boys. Unfortunately, Joyce didn't arrive and later rang to explain an elderly neighbour had fallen and she was at the hospital with her. Without doubt, William - nearly four with blond hair and bright blue eyes - was a handful. First, he knocked the water jar over Joshua's masterpiece before splashing paint on Rebecca's. Not convinced that the Biblical edict to 'spare the rod and spoil the child' was necessary, like a referee at a football match, she called him to 'time out'. But his refusal to go, then stay in the naughty corner, had her dragging him back and forth almost caging him on a chair in the corner with his back to the room. Luke's gleeful smile at William had her turn to see him climbing over it and it would have over balanced causing damage to him and the chair if she hadn't caught him. She suspected his naughtiness came from boredom in doing the things the twins and Luke enjoyed. Luke, six months younger than the twins, wasn't as big as Joshua. Rebecca being small and petite for twenty-two months was good at whining, usually about being left, or being 'in the wars' due to the boys' boisterous behaviour. The idea not to get in Mrs Smith's way meant they couldn't go downstairs to the back garden, and she wasn't risking taking four children to the park.

Rosie knew William's insolent mantra of 'No!' was his way of testing her, and at each incident she faced and spoke firmly to him. When she caught Joshua throwing a piece of sausage at Rebecca, William looked the picture of innocence, but she knew he had started and naively Luke told her. Rosie declared, "Food is to be eaten, not thrown. As you aren't hungry William, I'll take it from you."

William turned up his nose, tipped his plate up and declared, "Don't like it!"

Rebecca passionately observed, "I hate boys"

Joshua's face creased and believing she would take his plate he cried, "Sorry Oosie!"

Rosie said nothing and removed William's mess, but when she didn't give him the chocolate mousse, he banged his spoon on the table chanting, "Where's mine, where's mine?" Over his angry shouting, Rosie removed the spoon from his hand, explained in not eating his dinner he wouldn't get the mouse, and stood behind his chair to ensure he couldn't leave the table. It was a relief when Mrs P appeared for a cuppa and sandwich, kindly validating her stance.

While the younger ones had their sleep, Rosie read William a story and kept his attention for a short while by asking him to use Joshua's lettered bricks to make up the words she pointed out. Despite further attempts to engage him, he seemed intent on doing what he was told not to do, which included banging on the piano and running around the room as a plane, his arms outstretched.

Mrs P went to collect the children awoken by the noise. At the very moment the children appeared in the doorway, William swiped David's last photo of Jane off the sideboard, breaking the glass in the frame. Dismayed, Rosie ignored them, caught hold of William by his shoulders and crouching down looked him in the eye to reiterate when she said 'no' she meant it. At his shrug and belligerent look, she added, "Then this maybe will remind you, 'no means no!" and with that she slapped his bare leg. His face creased, tears formed in his eyes and a gasp went up from three wide-eyed children. Shocked that she had resorted to hitting him, she stood and moved past the children toward Mrs P who was in the dining room with a dustpan and brush in her hand. Upset, she whispered, "I've just hit William."

"'ave you indeed. Good! "That boy's been asking for it. Don't upset yerself ducky, take a break, I'll sweep up and keep an eye on 'em."

When Rosie returned from having a cry in the toilet, Mrs P was at the table making a biscuit mixture. The children were watching and waiting to make it into shapes. Mrs P said firmly, "William" before she nodded towards her. Immediately he jumped up, hugged her legs and looking repentant said, "Sorry Oosie," to which she crouched down, hugged him, but felt guilty seeing the mark her hand had left. For the rest of the afternoon William was a changed boy. He helped the others cutting out the biscuit shapes, played with them as they cooked, and looking at the finished products, he announced, "I'm giving one of mine to Daddy."

Luke unable to speak clearly said something like 'Mummy'.

Rebecca looking thoughtful declared, "Joshua you give one to our Daddy, I give one to Oosie, she's our Mummy." Tears pricked in Rosie's eyes.

When the biscuits cooled, William grabbed his six, smiled cheekily at her and then handed her one, and another to Mrs P."

As Rosie thanked him, Mrs P responded, "Would you like two of mine?"

William's response was immediate, "Yes please."

Mrs P observed, "He's not a bad un, just needs taking in 'and".

Using a finger to wipe her eyes, Rosie remarked, "Oh dear, I'm getting emotional over biscuits."

Mrs P gave her a kindly look, "Jane was lovely, but you are a natural mother. You'll be a wonderful wife to 'the master' and 'e knows it! She took Luke and William's hands, "Now I'll take these two kiddies back to their mother and see if me friend is ready to go."

On her return Mrs P confided, "She's keen, job's regular, the wages good. She said it was interesting seeing 'ow the rich lived" and chuckled, "I told 'er it weren't that different, births and deaths, problems and difficulties, money don't bring 'appiness." She liked Dr Paul, said 'e kept saying 'sorry about the mess' and tried to tidy so she could clean. I fear she called Jill 'a fat slut' but I put 'er right. Since this baby Jill's not been 'erself, but then they've never saw 'ow much you did. 'ow Jill will cope when…? There's me friend." Mrs P picked up her things and headed downstairs.

Curious to know Paul and Jill opinions, Rosie took the twins down to the basement. Jill had become fat, had no care about her appearance, or how spick and span the flat now looked. She answered, "She's not a woman I could take to."

Paul rubbed his beard, "That's because Mrs P didn't keep tutting at the mess. Don't scowl, you are untidy! Mrs Smith worked hard. She's done a good job. Rosie, how did it go looking after William and Luke?"

In a need to be positive and honest, Rosie reported, "The age difference makes it harder to keep them occupied without arguments, mess and calamity. As adorable as William is, Ben was persistent in chasing Jill, he didn't take 'no' for an answer, and William has similar traits." Jill's eyes filled with tears. Rosie rushed on, "With three children under four you've got your work cut out. It will be a few years before you can consider again going abroad for David's father."

"I agree. I waited a long time to find another wife. I missed Maria growing, and have every intention to be here for Jill and my family. William needs strong discipline. One day he'll be a fine young man, making both Ben and I proud. When we move, I'll need to keep up to date in medicine, but aim as to do shifts at the hospital and perhaps fill in as police surgeon near home. And you Rosie what are your thoughts on your changing role?" Rosie grimaced, Paul laughed. "We're pleased you are considering marriage to David. The twins love you, we all appreciate you, but I reiterate, you aren't expected to help us out." Rosie opened her mouth to speak but Paul continued, "You've told us a little about your home, the Hawkins, and Bertie's cerebral palsy. You said he was physically disabled, has difficulty with speech, but not mentally impaired. Medical science is constantly coming up with new techniques and surgical procedures that can bring physical improvement. I'd like to meet him."

Eagerly Jill suggested, "We could come and visit. Even as a run down and rat infested house, with the grounds and lake it still sounds impressive. How about next month? A picnic in the grounds and a swim in the lake?"

Paul looked as uncomfortable as Rosie felt, "I'm afraid the lake water is murky and so weedy it's dangerous for both swimming and boating. When younger, Bertie fell in and was caught in the long fronds. I had difficulty dragging…"

Jill gave a loud bellow as projectile vomit flowed over her and the carpet. Paul leapt up and took Rachel. Jill whined, "What's wrong with her? Why does she keep doing that?"

"Darling I don't know, but if she is allergic to something you eat, once on solids she'll get over it. Don't distress yourself. I'll run you a bath. You enjoy that with her, and I'll rinse everything out and put a wash on. "No Rosie, leave it, I'll clear it up."

Pulling herself up out of the chair Jill remarked, "Mrs Smith didn't even flinch when she was sick this morning." With Paul's support, she breathlessly took her cumbersome body up the stairs to their bedroom and bathroom on the ground floor. He followed carrying Rachel. William and Luke were engaged in their jigsaw puzzles, so she waited until Paul reappeared. She indicated they go in the kitchen and there she quietly confessed, "Paul I must tell you, I'm so sorry but this afternoon I smacked William." Paul's kind velvet brown eyes looked into hers. "He wouldn't take 'no' for an answer and cross I…" Tears filled her eyes.

"Rosie, I'm sure it was well-deserved. The children know you love them and naughtiness isn't to be tolerated. Believe me it's not the first smack William has had, and it won't be the last." Rosie moved to see the twins. They were now jumping on and off the bottom stair. Paul behind her commented, "I know you consider me 'a mild-mannered man'," she turned to see him rubbing his beard before he added, "The Bible tells us in sparing the rod we spoil the child. Don't be upset. I think we agree He knows best. And, if we don't heed His instructions, the next generation could become unruly with no respect of people, or their property! Rosie, I trust you." Paul gave her a reassuring hug as screams of 'Daddy' came from the twins.

As though guilty, they jumped apart. David sent them a wry smile. "Should I be asking Paul if I trust you?"

Paul grinned back, "You know you can. Rosie has had a difficult day."

Joshua reported, "William broke Mummy's picture. Rosie smacked him."

Rebecca insisted, "But Oosie is our real Mummy."

"Out of the mouths of babes" David commented with a meaningful look into Rosie's eyes.

Paul added, "Rosie looked after Luke and William, the latter rather naughty. I've told her she shouldn't feel obliged to help us out."

Puzzled David asked, "Didn't Joyce come today." Troubled, Rosie shook her head, which brought David to assured her. "The picture and frame are replaceable, now come upstairs and you can tell me about it." Noisily the twins obeyed.

"David?" He turned. Rosie did too, and saw Paul's wide-eyed look as he suggested, "Rosie needs an early night."

"In that case, let's eat our dinner as the twins have their tea. Then you can follow doctor's orders and go home. I'll put them to bed."

On her arrival next morning, David was waiting by the dining room door looking delighted and ready to leave. He announced, "I've managed to get tickets for the Mouse Trap." Amused he added, "Very apt I thought!" Before she could query he added, "I've arranged to collect Grace and Wilhelm on my way home. They've agreed to give the twins their tea and put them to bed. Please eat a main meal at lunch time, I'll use the canteen. We'll go to the theatre via the cottage so you can change. After the play, we'll head back here, and you can take Grace and Wilhelm home in the Morris."

Rosie took a deep breath, "It appears you have my evening planned. It's fortunate I'm free." David took in her expression, hummed, picked up his case and running down the stairs called, "I'll be back by five-thirty."

As they drove to the cottage for her to change, Rosie reminded him, "I'm happy to be courted but not controlled." At David's puzzled expression she explained, "You're meant to ask someone out, not organise their lives."

David sighed, "I thought it would be a pleasant surprise!" This time Rosie hummed. It was an opportunity to wear the outfit he had bought her. She could dress it up with his birthday present of a pearl necklace and the matching earrings Paul and Jill had given her. When she appeared, David leapt up to declare, "Rosie, you look amazing. It will be my pride and joy to have you on my arm tonight."

Graciously she replied, "Thank you." And then added, "After a twenty-year run in the West End it's fortunate I've not already seen it." David's eyebrow rose slightly as she moved towards the front door. With the unexpected twist and play's well-guarded ending, she and David had an animated conversation on the way home. Secretly she admitted David's arrangements had been perfect, pampered with the best seats, cocktails in the interval, and a taxi taking them door to door. Wilhelm and Grace were ensconced in the Morris Minor when she thanked him for the lovely evening, and so she felt safe to instigate a kiss which she allowed him briefly to extend.

The following day was forecast as being warm and sunny. So, making sandwiches and putting water in a flask, having the children each chose a fruit to eat, they set off for a picnic in the park by the Serpentine. The twins squealed in delight running around, sitting on the blanket to eat, and clapped their hands watching the ducks and swans eat the bread they threw into the water. While they slept in their double buggy, she watched the people passing by and considered her life. When they awoke, they were anxious to get to the slide, roundabout and swings. And while she cooked the dinner, they played quietly under the table with their Lego bricks. David arrived at five-thirty, suggested again they ate as a family, and later with the twins in their cots, she offered to read their bedtime story.

In joining David in the lounge, she felt perhaps she could adapt to marriage and 'motherhood' and smiled as he enquired, "Have we made progress this week?"

Feeling more comfortable to sit with him, she answered truthfully. "It's been tiring. I'm not back into a routine and certainly have less time to myself, but last night and today have been enjoyable."

"That's good to hear. Tomorrow I assume you still want to go to Petersfield?" Rosie nodded. "Shall I pick you up at nine o'clock?"

"I need to go home and finish the skirt I've made, but suggest - as we're only going for the day - can we leave at eight?

As they drove into the Tradesman's Entrance, Bertie came out to greet them, and practically flung himself into David's arms, while talking and thanking him in his own inimitable way for his gifts. Once the twins were out of the car, he was pulling on David's hand to show them to him. The twins each caught one of Jack's hands, chattered and skipped alongside him, pleased to go wherever he took them.

David expressed his surprise at the typed two-page 'rat' story Bertie had written for Rosie to read to the twins. Jack added that although he could only type with one hand, he hadn't grown tired. He had also typed many questions he wanted answered, which revealed his desire to learn. For David's benefit Rosie announced, "That was such a thoughtful gift," and received David's 'high wattage' smile.

Cathy pointed out to her that in Bertie's desire to see Helen, he was also gaining confidence at being out and about. Throughout the morning, David and Jack cleared branches and debris from the storm that still littered the kitchen garden. Joshua helped by picking up twigs and putting them in a sandcastle bucket, while Bertie lent on and pushed an old wooden cart where the smaller pieces could be transported to the bonfire.

Cathy engaged Rebecca in making the dinner. It included making shapes with the flour, water and suet mixture before finally rolling it into balls to drop in the stew pot.

With Rebecca engrossed at the table, Rosie and Cathy sat by the fire to talk quietly about her first week. Cathy agreed with Paul and David that it was important to discipline a child. She felt both men - in whatever way they felt to administer that - would balance it with love and acceptance. When Rosie related Paul's desire to meet Bertie and his belief his physical problems could be helped, Cathy remarked, "It's odd Rosie how things come together. Seeing the operations and the medical advances on Helen's ward, I've been thinking much the same. Bertie might be fearful of that but maybe Paul could persuade him. The subject reverted to Helen and her worry that Declan had been missing for ten days. She told me yesterday I'm more of a mother to her than her own! But I suspect that's down to Archie's influence."

"And still no change in Johnny's condition?"

"At least Rosie he is breathing on his own. As I said on the telephone, no-one knows when he'll come out of the coma, but I gather the pressure to his brain is reducing. I saw Diana yesterday. She said it was suggested the family talk to him, bring in a radio or something which might stimulate a response from him."

"What about music he liked when growing up? I've got a limited selection of records, but I can go and see what I have. Her collection of 78 rpm Bakelite records wasn't vast but "Young Love" by Tab Hunter brought memories of Johnny. She opened up her old Dansette and played it. *They say for every boy and girl there's just one love in this whole world, and I know*

211

I've found mine. Young love, first love, filled with true devotion, young love, first love we share with deep emotion." Memories and tears overflowed, and hearing the words, *"There will never be another love for you or me"* she wondered if that declaration was her problem. If nothing else, music had just proved it stimulated the brain, and may help Johnny regain consciousness.

When lunch was served Rosie grinned at the way the dumplings - after so much handling - had risen beautifully, and at the delight on Rebecca's face as she chanted, "I made them, I made them."

Joshua not to be outdone sat up to declare, "Bertie and I made bonfire." Bertie gave one of his heehaw laughs.

Once the washing up was finished David suggested, "Shall I read the story Bertie wrote?" Immediately the twins charged towards Bertie sitting on the settee, sat on either side of him, and with thumbs in their mouths, cuddled up against him as David began. But he had only read two paragraphs before he realised the three of them were asleep. Quietly he drew Rosie aside to ask, "Do you mind if I stay here to help Jack with the bonfire when you go to see Helen and Johnny? The twins can run around the kitchen garden, and when you get back, although I've baulked at the idea, I suppose we can create an area where Bertie can let his rat family out to play."

"Hmm, I can't say I'm keen on that idea, but as long as it is outside and away from the house. Talking of ideas, I thought I could use music to stimulate Johnny's brain, but I don't want to start lugging my record player about. I wondered about going into town to buy a cassette recorder."

"That's a good idea, but no need to buy one. You can use the one I bought when Jane had the twins. I have a packet of blank cassettes somewhere. You can use my stereo system to record on them."

"Oh, David thank you. That's kind." She placed a kiss on his mouth, only to turn and catch Cathy giving him a wry smile.

Her allotted time with Johnny was three o'clock which she hoped to combine with the hospital visiting hour and seeing Helen. In seeing him laying so still, his eyes closed and the endearing permanent smile in a face as white as the pillow on which his head rested, her heart went out to the boy she knew, and the man she wanted to know. The nurse had instructed 'Talk to him' but it was strange to do that to someone who wasn't able to respond. But as she had recently taken to praying aloud it wasn't as difficult as she expected. With Johnny's hand in hers, love flowed. She spoke of their school days, the teachers, their lessons, her trust in him and their 'special' friendship. She had just told him she had returned to London to look after David's twins when the nurse indicated her time was up, so she finished, "I promise I'll be back next Saturday with a surprise for you."

She went on to update Helen on her week, David and Jill's difficulties to cope with three children which according to Cathy was post-natal depression. When she told her of William's naughtiness, Helen sadly confided, "I often wonder what the child Ben and I conceived would have been like. With me as his Mum probably worse!" Rosie not knowing what to say changed the subject to Declan.

On their return, Jack and David's heads were deep in discussion over - it appeared - the house finances. The twins were playing at their feet with Bertie, his garage and cars. Unexpectedly, David looked up to ask, "Cathy, if you had all the money in the world, what would you want or do?

Cathy didn't hesitate, "Money can't buy me love! It couldn't buy the family I desired, but I've found love in giving love to Rosie and Bertie and getting to know Helen. You and the twins bring further opportunities."

In the silence, Rosie contemplated that before Cathy added, "Despite our difficulties with Helen, she's brought a new purpose, a goal to attain and has risen in my estimation by her concern for Declan. I'd like him to reappear so we could love and take care of him. You've been talking to Jack, you know how we eke out a living by planting, growing, picking, preparing and selling what we don't eat. We make do and mend, but I'm content in that and plodding through each day. I'm enjoying visiting a hospital. If Bertie wasn't so dependent, I'd consider nursing again. We couldn't afford a TV, let alone a colour one, but thanks to you our lives are opening up in seeing the news and learning from documentaries." At the mention of TV Bertie looked up excitedly, bringing Cathy to say, "Okay Bertie, put it on. There should be a children's programme for the twins to watch. Let's talk around the table while I make the sandwiches for tea."

David with a winning smile informed her, "Cathy, you are a home-maker with a mother's heart who shouldn't have to worry about finances. With Bertie, Helen, and maybe in the future Declan, it's possible to access funds to make the place more habitable."

"Where from?" Jack brow furrowed, "We work for his Lordship, in trying to maintain the house and looking after Bertie, we haven't the time for any other work."

"Jack, we now live in a welfare state. Declan is a child, at least in looking after him you would get the government child allowance, and fostering a child or even children, would bring you an income."

"Wouldn't we have to ask His Lordship's permission to do that? And let's face it, this place would be considered dangerous for children."

"Something Jack, I've become acutely aware of! But supposing that wasn't an issue, would you be interested in doing that?"

"I've been a bit iffy about Helen. I'm not sure how to take her, but children, we've enjoyed our involvement in Rosie and Bertie lives. I've enjoyed making and mending their toys. And Rebecca and Joshua are a delight to have around."

"If it were possible would you wish to stay here?"

"When we first arrived we saw the potential here. There was money then to put things right and bring in outside help. As it is, we're getting older and sometimes I feel it's getting too much for me. But with a few extra people living here, they could either share the work load, or with that welfare money I could pay people to do what I can't. Last time His Lordship was here, he vowed never to return. But if he did, he wouldn't take kindly to us having strangers living in his property. He doesn't know about Helen, and if Declan comes to stay we would have to treat that as a temporary arrangement." Jack shrugged, "And, if someone buys the house everything would change."

Cathy buttering the bread admitted, "When His Lordship first put it on the market, we were worried by the flurry of interest and felt we might quickly be turned out." She smiled, "Rosie always assured us she'll find somewhere for us to go."

Rosie kneeling on the rug with the twins turned to smile at Cathy, and David sent her a 'high wattage'. Jack informed him, "Last year there was renewed interest. A building company wanted to redevelop the site. They talked of leaving the façade and turning the house into six flats. The Estate Agent was kind enough to immediately inform us when the company decided that a smaller house and less land would prove a better investment and a quicker turnaround. They did warn us they might think again if that project went well. George, at the pub, told me that a prospective buyer had to consider sitting tenants, and we could cause a problem if we refused to move."

"Surely the Doughty-Dawes who have employed you for years to caretake the house would wish you to continue to look after Bertie and feel obliged to buy you somewhere to live.

Cathy and Jack exchanged a glance, but Rosie knowing they wouldn't want to be disloyal to her parents, slid Rebecca to one-side and stood to answer on their behalf, "Jack and Cathy have never been officially employed." David looked astounded. "When they arrived, Jack helped my Mum with the solicitors. They got their National Insurance numbers, but it took months before Mum received her inheritance money. She gave them a lump sum just before my father arrived, and she continued to support them until her money dried up. My father sold Home Farm to renovate part of the East Wing for his entertaining. When that money was spent, and unable to pay the Hawkins more than a few pounds a month, my father told them he paid them with free accommodation and they could live off the land."

David's jaw clenched. Jack took up the story, "My farmer friends in the pub had been furious when the Binghams who rented Home Farm had it sold over their heads. They suggested that I take up His Lordship's suggestion, and ask him to sign a short agreement and have it witnessed so it was official. It said something like: 'I permit Jack and Cathy Hawkins, for as long as they desire to remain caretaking The Grange, the Estate and our personal property, that they, in lieu of wages receive free accommodation with sole rights to whatever the land produces." David chuckled. "I went cap in hand to His Lordship, to tell him we wished to stay for as long as Bertie needed us, and to ensure we'd understood his terms we'd written them down and it would be good if he could sign them."

"Looking pleased he told me I was a 'good man', patted me on the back, and was happy to call Dee-Dee in to witness his signature."

David's booming voice reiterating, "Oh good man!" and his laughter caused even little heads to turn.

Jack grinned and waited to add, "When His Lordship didn't

receive the farmers' rents the following month, he made enquiries, and was furious to discover they were paying me. I explained I'd done nothing underhand, and advised he take his copy of our Agreement to a solicitor. His Lordship tried to change it. The farmers stood against him and I suspect, afraid his life would be exposed to further scrutiny, nothing more came of it."

"Jack, that's brilliant, and justice! Would I be right to think the rental of fields was greater than your wages?"

"Correct! They tripled overnight and have risen each year with inflation. The farmers' support spurred me on, because up until then we'd been grateful for him to pay our trip home, giving us a home, and the pittance he paid us. We'd buy our clothes from the charity shop, as well as gifts for the children's birthdays and Christmas. Neither parent was interested, or it seemed able to provide anything the children needed. The only thing His Lordship appeared keen on was Rosie's education."

Rosie felt to point out, "Which came from Lord Dawes' provision of an educational trust fund for his family and my mother was the only surviving member. This included my school clothes, as well as my board and lodging"

David nodded thoughtfully as he gained understanding.

Cathy added, "We did glean that Dee-Dee's father grieving for her mother, had ensured Dee-Dee was well cared for, but it was a sheltered life and although she received presents, she had never given any! And from my observation of His Lordship, didn't have much of a family life and no idea about managing money. When flushed he'd spend it on what was important to him, and if tight he would disappear and leave us to make ends meet."

Jack returned to his tale, "Eric, a close friend of the Binghams, prodded me to tell His Lordship that as we cared for Rosie - Bertie was a well-kept secret - they should provide money to clothe and feed her, along with petrol costs for shopping and school runs. His Lordship's response was that I was ungrateful after all he'd done for us. By then I'd done my sums and pointed out in lieu of five years proper wages, we'd more than covered his original monetary outlay. To that he said he would think about it. It took many prompts before he finally demanded that in telling him the children's needs, he would either want proof of the cost, or a receipt before he could release any money."

Grimly David stated, "That's ridiculous!"

Jack nodded, "We realised too the need to make a stand about the extra work when they entertained. In caring for Bertie, we rarely had a day off as he had to be invisible at all times."

Cathy chipped in. "Dee-Dee would help out, but His Lordship stopped that! Early on Jack told him there were regular meal times and we couldn't be at their beck and call. Oh my, he didn't like that, or my declaring we couldn't keep Bertie a secret and look after his guests. He was furious at having to pay for extra staff."

"The money from renting out the fields is still a bone of contention." Jack grinned. "When the electricity bill wasn't paid and the septic tank not emptied, he informed us the fields rent financed those. We replied we would contribute with a set sum each month, and here alone, obviously we pay those bills."

"Their contribution to Bertie's keep hasn't changed over the years, but fortunately the rent of fields has" stated Cathy cutting through a pile of sandwiches. "We manage. We're content and we don't need luxuries. Four years ago, Jack told them if they wished their bedroom cleaned, food cooked, and heating in the rooms they used, they needed to pay in advance. They left after two weeks, saying the house was cold and damp, but with outstanding estate costs and other debts his only option was to disappear back to India. When the house is sold, he will have to repay those."

Rosie summed up, "And when that happens, both Jack and Cathy's 'employment' and that Agreement will be terminated."

David with a rueful expression explained, "And I'm afraid Jack you can't claim to be 'sitting tenants' as without proof of paying rent, you have no right to stay. But surely as Bertie's parents they would provide for him?"

"I'm supposed to have him committed to a mental institution!" The contempt in Rosie's voice was as evident as David's expression of incredulity. "And it occurs to me that if the Hawkins were to approach the Welfare State for Declan's keep, it could highlight Bertie's existence, a disabled man with no formal education or medical assessments. The Hawkins could then be seen as colluding with my father."

"Good grief! It would be like Ben, helping someone and… " He trailed off, and then quickly added, "I'll put some consideration into how best to resolve that."

Cathy filled the kettle. Rosie gave David a wide-eyed look and Jack, looking worried, said, "If we involved the police to find Declan that too could have a knock-on effect. I was hoping he'd reappear at the cottage. I went down first thing and he's not back. Poor little chap. Helen says he can fend for himself, but it's a big ugly world out there."

"Rosie, how about asking Gerald Maysfield to help?" David asked with raised eyebrow.

"Gerald? I've not spoken to him in months!"

"I have. He helped me find you. Perhaps he could find Declan too?"

"Do it! The sooner the better. Ask him to lunch tomorrow."

David bent to kiss her cheek, "If it's alright with you Jack, I'll use your phone."

Rosie called after him, "Invite him to church. He enjoyed it when he came with me. He's good with the children, four adults and five children around the table, last week was bedlam.

Cathy enquired, "Is Gerald the policeman who discovered the man involved in what happened to you and wanted you to prosecute him?"

Rosie nodded, "But in knowing how Ben's mistakes destroyed his medical career, I couldn't ruin his. He was threatened and forced into it, and saved my life by following my taxi and dialling 999."

"But a life was lost, and you nearly died from blood loss, and then septicaemia." Cathy cringed, "Oh Rosie, it was a terrible time! We thought we might lose you."

"Which didn't concern my parents for they neither visited me in hospital, nor supported me once home. They were packed and ready to leave for India, in the belief I would bring disgrace upon them which was completely unfounded. But that aside, Gerald is a lonely man and he enjoys the family atmosphere. He has helped with odd jobs and is always happy to accept a meal. He's much older than me and although going out with him several times, there was nothing in it beyond friendship." Cathy said, "Well, friendship is always a good place to start any relationship and if you stop being so prickly and give David a chance, I think you could grow to love him as you do the twins".

CHAPTER 15

As predicted Gerald was delighted to accept an invitation to lunch and was pleased to hear she and David were courting. His enjoyment was always obvious by the way he took an interest in their lives and was eager to help in any way he could. With a photo obtained from Declan's mother, it didn't take Gerald long to discover that Declan had been caught stealing fruits in a market near his home. Due to his unkempt condition - and refusal to tell his real name - he had been detained in a children's home.

On Wednesday Cathy rang to report, "Gerald arrived half an hour ago. He felt the quickest way to get Declan here was to personally collect and deliver him."

"He's a good man, although we'd thought Declan might stay here for a few days."

"Oh Rosie wait until you see Declan! He's so small for twelve. He was so nervous and frightened that when I hugged him he went rigid in my arms. Gerald said David suggested Norah, Declan's Mum, write two letters. The first to Declan so he knew about Helen's accident and that she'd arranged for him to stay with us. The second to the children's home giving our address, explaining he would stay with us to be near his sister in hospital. Norah wrote a third one, thanking us for offering to look after Declan. Gerald reassured Norah he would deal with all the legalities and with those letters - Declan's offence being minor - Gerald obtained his released.

Gerald speaks highly of you, he's staying for dinner and Jack's giving him a tour. Bertie was anxious to welcome Declan, and although Declan was cautious at first, he did follow Bertie to see the colour television, and since he's been wide-eyed watching it."

The next evening Cathy reported, "Declan's eating like a starved horse, and after his first meal he flopped over like a dead one. Jack carried what he calls, 'the little lad' up to Helen's room where he slept for twelve hours. Jack feels Declan's afraid of him, so sent me up to wake him. He's very like Helen with bright red hair that tends to curl, and enjoys being with Bertie. When he saw Helen with her leg in traction he burst into tears! Helen cried in relief that he'd been found, and it was so sweet as Bertie tried to put his good arm around them both. I was afraid in their hugging they would disturb all Helen's balances and wires!"

On Friday morning, Rosie heard the panic in Cathy's voice as she informed her, "The Estate Agents are sending several men to assess and estimate the cost to restore the house with a view to making a suitable offer. Oh Rosie, what are we going to do? We've just given a home to Declan, and of course Helen."

Rosie felt to reassure her, "Their interested will fade when they know any restoration will cost a small fortune. And should they go for a deal, my father will milk out of them as much as he can, that could go on for months, and even fizzle out. Wilhelm and Grace will soon be heading back to Germany. They came last night to babysit so we could go to the cinema, and as I've said before, I can put my cottage up for sale and buy something suitable for all of us. Let's talk about it tomorrow."

Over dinner, it seemed David wasn't unduly concerned at the interest in The Grange, pointing out that buying property especially of those proportions wasn't done overnight. And then added, "When Jill and Paul move out in June, the basement flat will be free. Declan and Bertie could have the downstairs bedrooms and Jack and Cathy the double one with the ensuite on the ground floor. And, if you didn't have objections, Helen could share your cottage. It could work out very nicely for all of us and they would be ideal babysitters. You know Stan, the ITP's caretaker? Well he told me that the large mansion we use as offices needs constant attention, and he could always do with another pair of hands."

In endeavouring not to appear prickly, Rosie gave a small smile. "It's good of you to concern yourself on the Hawkins behalf. A home, and job for Jack, whatever next?" David gave her a searching look before continuing. "Paul says Mrs Smith's cleaning is excellent, but Jill thinks she is nosy."

Rosie hurried on, "Mrs P told me Mrs Smith was asking questions about us. And, knowing she wants to retire, she asked Mrs P on Wednesday to see over the rest of the house. She refused believing she should first ask you."

"If the Hawkins lived here, Cathy could look after both flats and do much as Mrs P does."

"David, I'm sure they would appreciate your thoughtfulness, but you may want to consider that after years of space, fields and fresh air, they and Bertie might feel the flat too confining."

"I take your point, but in London Bertie could easily be assessed mentally and physically. I told Paul about his foot, he says there is an operation to correct that, and Bertie would have other opportunities here to improve his life." Rosie hummed seeing he too had a point, "I'll talk to the Hawkins tomorrow to reassure them they won't be out of a home, and opportunities to help Bertie."

"Would you leave the flat empty for months on the basis they might use it?"

"After the decorators have been in, Jack and Cathy could move in and try it out. They may not want to go back."

Although seething inside at David planning their lives Rosie kept her expression thoughtful, but once they'd finished eating she stood to declare, "I'll leave you to clear up. I'll be ready to be picked up at eight tomorrow morning." He stood, she picked up her handbag, said 'Goodnight' and as a frown began to crease his brow, she headed down the stairs.

The drive down to Petersfield was uneventful. They listened to Radio 4, had a toilet stop and stretched their legs. Each twin asked several times the inevitable question 'Are we nearly there yet?'

At the Grange, Bertie and Declan appeared as the car drove in. Declan seemed shy but quickly perked up seeing the twins. Rosie noticed that when Jack came near Declan, he cowered as if expecting a cuff around the ear. While the twins slept on the settee after lunch, David spoke about his ideas for their future. Jack hummed thoughtfully. Cathy with a smile sent her a 'knowing' look to which Rosie responded with raised eyebrows. She knew David's intentions were good, as was his generosity to lend her the tape recorder. She took it later, with a cassette, into Johnny's room where he lay unconscious and drip fed.

Once she started to speak to Johnny her words seem to flow and like a DJ, she talked between songs to tell him why she had chosen each piece of music, "I bought this record 'Candy Kisses' by George Morgan second-hand. It reminded me of the sweets you would buy and share with me." Playing a 1962 Searchers rendering of "*Sweets for my sweet, sugar for my honey*" she spoke of their school days, the teacher's names, the subjects they learnt and the things he had said to make her giggle, "When I was sent to boarding school, I missed you and cried every night. As you befriended me, I befriended Sylvia who was small, skinny and with buck teeth. The girls called her horrid names. She wasn't beautiful on the outside, but gentle on the inside and funny. I've always remembered your birthday on 19th December, with mine a few weeks later. That first year away, I made you a card with a big '9' on it. I asked Cathy for your address and used my weekly stamp to send it to you. I put my address inside, but when you didn't reply, I wondered if you had received it. All post was censored by the head teacher, and I had a sense I was being constantly watched as though expected to be naughty." She went on to tell him about her friendship with Sylvia and explained, "A year later, in the January, I had just arrived back at school to celebrate my tenth birthday. Sylvia gave me a book called 'Black Beauty' which I loved. A month later, in the cold and wet weather she developed a cough. A few days later she was in the school infirmary, and a week later in hospital. I asked to visit her, but was told she was too ill, but the teacher took the card and the funny shaped cuddly toy I'd made for her. A few days later the Headmistress, a strict grim woman, called me into her office. I was afraid, but she gave me a sad smile, put her arm around me, sat me down and told me Sylvia had died. As I shuddered and wept, she took me in her arms and held me close. Through the weeping I told her how I loved Sylvia, how I'd loved and lost you, and that I loved my baby brother, but had dropped and injured him and been sent here. I can still remember the depth of that pain, and not being able to say 'goodbye' to either of them." Her voice caught "I didn't get to say 'goodbye' to Jane either. She was David's wife. She died a week after having the twins. You must push through this Johnny, I can't bear the thought of losing you a second time."

She pressed the play button and took Johnny's hand, "This next song '*Cry*' by Johnny Ray, became particularly poignant." Her eyes widened. Was it her imagination or had Johnny just given her hand a gentle squeeze? She didn't want to take her hand away, or turn the music off, so she asked loudly, "Johnny did you just squeeze my hand. If so, do it again." But there was no response.

When the song ended, with tears dripping off her face she felt spurred on to say, "Fight through, come back to me. The nurse is signalling my time is up. I'll come again next Saturday to play you more songs." She stood, the nurse entered and Rosie burst out, "I'm sure Johnny squeezed my hand. Do you think my music helped him?"

"That's possible. I'll make a note of what could be a good sign."

"Oh, thank you." Rosie made an instant decision, "I leave this cassette player. I've only played three songs, but there are more. If played, they too might stir memories, and help him to regain consciousness." The nurse smiled. Rosie bent, kissed Johnny's cheek and taking one last sad look at his prone figure walked away.

On the journey home as the children slept, she felt she owed it to David to tell him of Sylvia and the pain of losing people. "I think by speaking about those things, where Johnny wasn't in a position to judge or reject me, I came to realise I had imposed upon myself a silent captivity in fear of just that. It does seem that the Lord is on my case to give me confidence to allow me to be me!"

David, his eyes on the road, reached across and patted her knee. "I'm pleased, not at Johnny being unconscious, but the way the

Lord is using the situation to bring you healing. And I've no objections to you visiting him."

"And you didn't mind me leaving your tape recorder so the songs I had chosen could be played during the week."

"I wasn't using it and I am pleased if it helps his recovery."

The days were beginning to fall into a pattern. Toddler group and quiet activity on Monday, the shopping and playing/learning activity on Tuesday, Wednesday had always been Joyce's day to visit, and with the car they could now adventure further than the local park. For the first time Joyce had invited them to lunch at her house in Osterley and Rosie felt it was a sign that she too was considering her as a prospective mother to her grandchildren. David assured her she had Joyce's approval, but she still felt nervous, but needn't have been. When she drew up outside, Joyce rushed out to hug her, thanked her for coming while helping to release the twins from their car seats.

Seven years earlier Jane's father had died, and Joyce had just married Ted when David proposed to Jane. And Ted, once Bruce his son moved away, had sold his house to modernise Joyce's 1936 semi-detached home. With the twins happily playing with their toys, they sat drinking coffee when Joyce confided, "Jane told me she was praying you would find a good man with a ready-made family. She didn't tell me why, but is it because you can't have children?" Rosie nodded. Tears glistened in Joyce's eyes, "It would seem Rosie, she was the answer to her own prayers!"

"Oh Joyce, I would wish she was still here, I loved her too. I love her twins, and know David is a good man, but marriage, I'm not sure."

"Did she ever tell you that at first I wasn't sure about her friendship with David with his tailor-made suits, posh voice, booming laugh and big house, and did have serious doubts about their marriage? Despite their differences and disagreements, they were happy so I came to accept he adored Jane and she him. And since, have come to appreciate that underneath, David is as human as the rest of us. With the twins and all he's been through his faith has been genuine. He's a wonderful father, he seems more thoughtful, considerate, his approach to life has gentled and we've appreciated the way he still includes us in his family."

"And why not, you are the twins' grandparents!"

"The Reinharts never criticised Jane's outspoken fun and feisty nature, but at times she had me cringing at their family dinners. Were you there when she admitted to David she was taking the birth control pill? Do you remember the tension when it was revealed Franz owned a multi-million pound company? Rosie smiled. Joyce shook her head, "It worried me that Jane didn't seem to realise she embarrassed David, or undermined peoples' respect for him. I did have a rapport with David's mother, but always felt awkward because we weren't in their league. We know little of your background and education, but it's obvious to us you are far more suitable for a man like David. You will make him a wonderful wife and mother to the twins."

Unshed tears glistened in Rosie's eyes at Joyce's commendation. "That's kind, but working for someone is one thing, marrying them quite another! David sees me as the only mother the twins have known. Whether we marry or not, he wants me to remain in their lives. As their step-mother, I would have authority and influence in their upbringing and would value your advice and support as their grandmother. Should I decide to remain their nanny, it might be necessary together to find a way to express our opinions and ideas."

Joyce gave her a knowing smile, "Bless you dear. Without doubt the Reinhardts are, well… Ted calls them a 'class act'. We only knew you as Jane's friend until you stepped in so valiantly to help when the twins were born. When you gave up your job, and which later David described as a 'brilliant' career, we saw your devotion to the children. And, it was sad that you had to leave before we all realised how little we knew about you, and came to appreciate you. I don't want to pry, but it would be lovely to know more about you and your family."

Four weeks earlier Rosie would have used the twins' constant interruptions to divert the conversation. But in Joyce's sincerity, she realised she had found a friend and that enabled her to talk about the Hawkins and Bertie. When the dull day became sunny after lunch, they strolled to Osterley Park. With the twins occupied in throwing bread to the ducks, Rosie observed, "When I was their age our lake had ducks, but it has now become murky and weedy."

Joyce's eyes widened, "You have a lake! Just how big is your house?"

Embarrassed, she brushed it off. "It's not mine! It never will be." Joyce waited, so she felt obliged to elaborate. Built in the mid 1800's, it has an 'H' shape from a fifteenth century design. It has three storeys, plus attic and basement. In the war, it was commandeered from Lord Dawes and then he left it to his last surviving relative, my mother.

Joyce exclaimed, "You are related to a Lord! And the house

sounds enormous and very grand."

"Believe me, it isn't! We arrived from India in the winter of 1946. It was bitterly cold and damp, and still is, with much need of repair and renovation. When Cathy first saw its castellated roofing and darkish stone, she commented it looked like Dracula's castle." Afraid Joyce might feel she was out of their league, she quickly added, "Jill is eager to visit and wants to come in the summer for a picnic. If that happens I would like you and Ted to come."

Joyce's eyes lit up, "Oh Rosie, thank you." Encouraged Joyce asked, "Would you get married there?"

A realisation Joshua was no longer throwing bread, but pebbles at the ducks diverted the conversation, but later when Joyce asked again she answered, "We may have a few things in common, but once the twins are grown up, I'm not sure our faith would be enough to sustain a happy marriage." Joyce countered that by saying, "Jesus' love unites people. After Jane's father died, Ted worked his way into my heart by being constantly around and very supportive. I believe David's desire is to be there for you." David words echoed in Rosie's mind 'love comes in many forms'. She hummed and considered while driving back into London if that would be enough."

The front door opened, Mrs Smith and Mrs Perkins emerged as she drove on to the forecourt in front of the garage doors. They waited for her to step out of the car and she did that with an outstretched hand, while introducing herself to the thin faced Mrs Smith. A cold bony hand encompassed hers, steely blue eyes stared into hers as Mrs Perkins testified, "Rosie's like a mother to the children."

"Well good for you." Rosie detecting a sneer looked across at Mrs P as Mrs Smith said, "Nice place." Mrs P's embarrassment turned to bewilderment as Mrs Smith added, "Quite a success story."

Rosie used the twins' clamouring for release to say, "Excuse me, the children need me" and turning away, she saw Mrs P grabbing Mrs Smith arm and leading her away. With the twins tired and skittish from their outing, she had little time to consider what a strange woman and odd conversation.

By reading the twins a Rupert Bear story, she created a quiet lull destroyed when David bounded up the stairs to proclaim with outstretched arms, "Hello, I'm home!" With a shriek they leapt up, threw themselves at him and placing a child under each arm, David lent forward to kiss her and ask, "Did you have a good day?" Seated with the twins, they gave him a disjointed but animated report of their outing to the park with London Grandma. Amused David declared, "Rosie if you finish preparing our dinner, I'll tire them out. I've not fixed up a date this week, but thought we could have a bottle of wine and a quiet evening in together."

Rosie's grappling with his determining when she was free was halted as the telephone on the hall table rang. She answered it, David waited on the stairs with the twins and with her hand over the receiver she announced, "It's Diana." David nodded and was continuing upwards when she let out a squeal of delight. He turned, looked down on her and she called up, "Diana says they feel the music tape has initiated Johnny squeezing people's hands." David put his thumb up as Diana requested she make another.

When he reappeared it was to tell her, "The children are waiting for you to say 'goodnight'. I'll open the wine, and we'll celebrate the good news. Rosie turned, and seeing her wavering he asked, "What's the matter?"

"Grace and Wilhelm are out for the evening. I intended to use the lounge space for dressmaking, and it would be a good opportunity to record more music for Johnny."

"It's Wednesday, the night we have quality time together."

With pursed lips and a steady gaze, she sighed. "David, we've been out twice on a Wednesday night, so I've no reason to believe Wednesday was a regular 'date' night. Had you done so, I would have told you earlier of my plans for this evening." David scowled, and trying to be kind she offered, "Tonight we only have cottage pie. You haven't opened the wine, and tomorrow I could cook something to warrant that and stay later. At her suggestion he perked up, smiled broadly and said, "Done!"

The following evening, she prepared his favourites, a rabbit stew and an apricot crumble. He arrived with flowers, came up behind her hugging her as she put out the plates, confessed to seeing the benefit of warning her of his plans and told her of his appreciation of the effort she'd made to please him. They ate, and he showed interest in the songs she had recorded to provoke Johnny's memory. She told him of the story behind the songs, but felt it unwise to mention the Tab Hunter one, 'Young Love' with the words, *'There's just one love in this whole world, first love…'*
"As I left your tape recorder at the hospital, I have replaced it." Before he could protest she added, "It occurred to me we could use it in the car when travelling with the twins, so I also purchased a tape of nursery rhymes they could sing-a-long with. A little less embarrassing than you having to sing the 'wheels on the bus' on the train. He grinned and she chuckled, "As they also appreciate

classical music, I also purchased the Brahms Lullaby to send them to sleep!"

In the midst of enjoying her crumble David said, "Everything they need should come out of the housekeeping account and if there isn't enough you must let me know. When 'out and about' with the twins there are extra expenses like ice creams, petrol for the car and incidentals like cassette tapes." He gave her a broad smile.

To that she reasoned, "You give me a very generous allowance, and although happy for you to pay for the petrol, it's my pleasure to treat the twins. The way I see it, you pay for the food I eat, which is far more than the incidentals I buy. I probably owe you money."

He grinned, "I doubt it. And talking of food, you really do make the best crumble I've ever tasted. Marry me, and I guarantee you'll not want for anything for the rest of your life!"

At his 'high wattage' smile she raised her eyebrows, pursed her lips, but said without rancour, "When I marry, it will be 'for richer or poorer' until death do us part. Money is not a basis on which to build a relationship."

"I agree. But whoever said, 'the way to a man's heart is through his stomach' is right! I hope my asking for another helping of crumble will clarify that."

Rosie tutted, her expression didn't change as she pointed out, "Should I marry I will make an agreement before God to be with that man in sickness and in health. In a desire to keep him healthy I'll try and ensure he doesn't overindulge in food, which would include two helpings of crumble."

David gave a wry smile, lifted his dish and retorted, "In that case, right now I'll be grateful we're not married!" And with no further ado, Rosie filled his dish.

Relaxed by the wine, the banter and the classical music playing quietly in the background, she felt able to kick off her shoes, curled up in the corner of the settee to drink her coffee and give a contented sigh.

David, sitting opposite her gave her a thoughtful look before saying tentatively, "Am I right to believe this weekend you want to go to Petersfield?" Rosie nodded. "That's fine by me, but the following one Mum and Dad want us to stay with them."

Amused she pointed out, "Are you asking me to join you, rather than just telling me your plans? David's smile was rueful. "In fairness, you will have been to Petersfield four weeks in a row."

"True, but I can't help feeling responsible and feel a need to support the Hawkins. After all I introduced Helen to them, and now Declan. Added to which the worry of those men assessing the

Grange. Can we see how this weekend pans out before I decide?" David didn't look pleased but nodded. To engage his interest she asked, "As the façade of the Grange can't be changed, I wonder what could a prospective buyer do with it?"

Relaxing back in the chair he suggested, "It could be a luxury hotel run like a small, historical family home. Americans would love sleeping in a four-poster bed, sitting at a Hepplewhite table and eating from Spode china."

Rosie nodded, "But to make it 'a going concern' you would need visitors all year round. What is near Petersfield to attract people?"

"A view of fields, a quiet retreat, a lake filled with fish for anglers, an area to row boats, maybe a golf course, and an ideal wedding venue." His mouth twitched with a smile.

"A project of several years and a great deal of money! Maybe you should suggest it as a business venture to your father." David frowned. "With a heated pool, massage and treatment rooms, it could become a therapy centre and a showcase for Inhart's new range of beauty treatments."

With furrowed brow David sat forward to ask, "What new range of beauty treatments?"

Rosie endeavoured to keep a straight face, "Many drug companies are branching out into anti-wrinkle, anti-aging creams, tanning sunbeds, moisturising creams, mud baths and associated products."

"Suggest that to Dad next weekend."

"Oh David, I don't think so! His interest is in medicinal drugs, not products associated with what he would call 'the frivolities of life'!"

"With Dad, you never know. Look how having set up the Jane MacKenzie Trust, he was happy to match fund the monies the T-Dance dinner dance raised."

"Only because the vision is to attract young people in deprived areas off the streets. Teaching them to dance brings fun, friendship, a goal to aim for, a trophy to win, and creates a community around that." David sat back, stretched out his legs, and in thought, steepled his hands before his mouth as she continued, "I would suggest if your father were to invest in the house and estate, he would be more likely to support a care home for the disabled, disadvantaged or elderly, but I doubt if he even has the funds to accomplish that. As the exterior can't be changed, I'd like to see it split into rented flats, highly sought after, as a very pleasant place to live. Imagine Bertie's room over the library, that in itself could be a studio flat with marvellous views."

"Well there are few certainties in life, but one thing I know is I can beat you at Cribbage."

Rosie raised a querying eyebrow and mimicked his favourite phrase, "Is that so? At Christmas the game was new to me. You get the cards. I'll make more coffee."

By Saturday Declan seemed to be settling in. Cathy's mothering was bringing out a cheekiness that had her laughing, but wasn't rude. She saw he still cowered at Jack's overtures, but liked Bertie's company and helping him when needed. As he, Bertie and the twins played tents under the large kitchen table, Rosie and David listened to the Hawkins talk of the five men who had visited the previous day.

"They were here for hours. I felt obliged to offer them tea and cake."

Amused Jack said, "Oh Cathy, you don't need to feel guilty because you were hospitable."

Cathy lent across the table in a clandestine manner to say, "I had an ulterior motive. I wanted to find out about the prospective buyer." She sat back, "All I learnt was the Estate Agents had employed their varied expertise and suggested the interest was from someone living abroad."

"They did a thorough job!" Jack cringed, "And quite fearless in scouring the second floor and attic. I overheard the roof is in good order, but previous leaks undermined the plaster, damp, and woodworm has penetrated into much of the second floor. No surprises after twenty-five years of neglect! If Leo had used the money from Home Farm's sale, that wouldn't have taken hold. They discussed new plumbing, central heating, rewiring, replacement floors, and 'double glazed units', whatever they are. Restoring this place to today's standards sounds like a major undertaking!"

Rosie looked at David. When he didn't comment she did, "The prospective buyer must be keen to pay a sizeable sum for five experts to spend hours surveying the place."

Cathy added, "I did glean each would write a report and send an estimate of the cost to renovate the house to today's standards."

"That's something I'd like to see as the other evening David and I had an interesting discussion on the use of this place if money wasn't an issue." Rosie went on to repeat their ideas.

David didn't join in, but afterwards assured the Hawkins, "It could be months, if not years before a sale price is settled. Paul has

229

just asked me if he and Jill can stay on until September. My basement flat needs decorating but once done, you are welcome to live there." Seeing their hesitation he added, "Why not do your fruit and vegetable harvesting then come and spend the winter in London? There's room for Bertie and Declan." Rosie didn't want to dampen his enthusiasm, but however cosy his flat and pleasant patio garden were, in comparison to the space they were used to, they were tiny.

Lunch over and the twins asleep, she, Bertie, Cathy and Declan visited the hospital. The majority of time she spent with Johnny and with the poignancy of Elvis' songs, 'Heartbreak Hotel' and 'Return to Sender' she was sure his hand squeezed hers. When talking about the sweets they shared and asking which were his favourites, there had been a definite twitch at 'pear drops'. When Diana arrived to replace her they were both ecstatic when she confirmed that was true. They now had reason to believe he was hearing and understanding. So thrilled, she nearly forgot to give Diana the skirt she had finished.

That news had her nearly dancing to Helen, and she had no embarrassment when proclaiming, "Prayer works. Johnny's condition is improving. I'm believing for complete healing."

David and Jack were deep in discussion when later she burst into the kitchen to make a similar announcement. Jack response being, "That's one less worry." David looked up to smile, but with the twins pulling on her skirt and wanting her to see Bertie's train running under the chairs, she gave them her attention.

David, it seemed, was in the midst of trying to lessen Jack worries and was talking about his and Cathy's employment opportunities because people were willing to pay good money for hard working people. "I'm sorry to say this, but from my perspective the Doughty-Dawes have been using you to further their own ends."

"That's probably true, but having lived here for so many years, I've become a land girl. You talk of London, but I feel I'd be yearning for fields and the fresh vegetables from my kitchen garden."

David declared, "I was brought up on a farm but quickly readjusted. I've also been talking to Jack about funding Declan without involving social services. His mother has agreed to send you his child allowance and inform those who need to know that he is staying with friends to be near his sister in hospital. I've told Jack to organise that he attends the local school and can cover any extras incurred by his being here." David stood and stretched,

"Now I would like a breath of country air and a walk around that lake. Does anyone want to come with me?"

From behind the settee Rebecca shouted 'Me' as Joshua jumped up and grabbed his father's hand.

"I'll get the double buggy for when you get tired." Once coats and new Wellington boots were on, the twins were out of the front door and running past the library windows. Declan grabbed their hands before they headed off down the tarmac path to the lake, while Jack and David strolled behind.

A routine was beginning to develop with the normal children hitches, which Rosie was beginning to feel more comfortable in sharing with David. However, on Monday, as she chatted about the twins' activities over dinner, although David responded with a smile or nod, she sensed he wasn't really listening. Tuesday evening, he seemed equally pre-occupied, and didn't object when after the meal she quickly left. With Joyce visiting on Wednesday, they ate with the twins at lunch time. Joyce took a portion home to Ted and she put aside one for David. After welcoming him, she suggested he and the children eat together. With no mention of a 'date night' she informed him, "Grace and Wilhelm are visiting friends tonight." His lack of response had her suggest, "I thought if you haven't plans for tonight, I would go home and cut out a copy of the dress you bought me." At his rather abrupt 'fine' she braced herself to enquire, "Is something troubling you?"

David's reply 'Why would you think that?' contained an underlying tone of annoyance, and pointing out his lack of communication she was brushed off with, "Don't be ridiculous!"

Hurt by his attitude, and alone in the cottage, memories of Doug surfaced. Why hadn't she been suspicious when Doug told her not to speak about her caretaking his cottage? Why had he thought people would make wrong assumptions if they were seen together outside the work environment? She had been taken in by his fatherly attitude, concern, kindness, and flattered by his interest in her thoughts on Parliamentary matters. Why had she thought it natural for him to give her a hug or kiss?

Was she being blind, naïve and stupid again? David wanted to court her. So far it consisted in a bouquet of flowers now dead, an evening at the theatre, another at a cinema and one cosy night in. Like Doug when asked a personal question he had been put-out. A girl's dream was of marriage and family. Yet she felt on a bridge viewing motherhood, its responsibility and feeling alone in it. Jane's words came to mind, 'When David is wrapped up in his work, he seems to forget I exist. And when confronted he appears affronted. When I challenge him, he says I have to accept that it doesn't mean that I've upset him or that he doesn't love and value me'.

To change her maudlin thoughts she rang Diana who immediately said, "Johnny has opened his eyes. I've tried ringing, but the phone line this last hour has been constantly engaged." Rosie looked up at the clock. There were times with a houseful of children, someone would take the telephone off the hook, so it couldn't ring and disturb them. For future use, she gave Diana the cottage number before discussing Johnny's progress and Diana's business. In realising David had talked about going to his parents at the weekend, but not mentioned it since, she decided to arrive early and catch him before work encompassed his life.

The twins were eating their cereals and at her 'Good morning David, who was watching the toaster on the work surface between the hatch and kitchen, looked up pleased to see her and hear the news about Johnny. As he brought the toast to the table she stated, "I know your parents want to see you this weekend. We've not discussed it, but with Cathy's anxiety and Johnny's recovery, I'll go on the train tomorrow and stay the weekend."

"What!" David exclaimed with toast in mid-air between plate and mouth. "My parents are expecting you."

Her knife paused in buttering Rebecca's toast, "I understood they asked if I would like to join you."

"And, I am given to understand, you've decided to put Johnny before me and my family."

Rosie removed the spoon Joshua was banging on the table, and gave him half the toast while saying, "It's not that simple." David grunted. "I didn't cause Johnny's accident, but it is a pivotal time of his recovery and I want to be there."

"This is a pivotal time for me to have an important discussion with my father."

"I'm not stopping you going!" David gave a sharp intake of breath at her tone, picked up the cereal boxes and returned them to the kitchen cupboard.

Rosie gave the other half of the toast to Rebecca and poured herself a coffee. David reappeared through the arch adjoining the kitchen area and sitting beside spoke quietly, in the dangerously calm manner he used during negotiations, "Rosie, it may have escaped your notice, but driving to Bath on my own with the twins is not an option."

"The twins enjoyed the train to Petersfield. Bath isn't that much further."

With furrowed brow David asked, "Rosie, have I done something to upset you?"

Like the steam hissing free from a pressure cooker she said tightly, "It's not what you have done, it's what you haven't done."

David instructed, "Joshua stop playing with your toast, eat it! Rebecca finish your milk. I won't be a minute." Touching her elbow, he bent to say quietly, "Not in front of the children" and headed towards the lounge. She followed and in a quiet voice she said with no less zeal, "This week, I've no doubt you had important issues on your mind which you saw no necessity to share with me, but you've barely listened, or showed interest in the twins' activities or mine. If courting is a prelude to marriage you are not encouraging me to enter it."

David's frustration was evident by the way he ran his hand through his hair. "That's ridiculous."

"Is it? When I asked if you had a problem, I was made to feel I had a problem. Now, because I desire to put my friends' needs before yours, you are trying to make me feel guilty."

His response was terse, "I've things on my mind. You aren't the problem, but I am put out on hearing your decision about the weekend, but believe me I'd no intention to make you feel guilty. It might help you to understand that this week, despite heading to bed soon after you've left, I'm very tired due to disturbed nights with Joshua cutting teeth."

Determined not to feel sorry for him, she said pithily, "If you had told me that, and talked about the weekend, I wouldn't have had cause to be upset. And believe me, when you feel you have a valid complaint, it isn't conducive to any relationship to be told 'That's ridiculous'."

The running of his hand through his hair came with an apology. "Oh Rosie, I'm sorry. I forgot that you, like Jane, need to talk about your day, and with the twins your need is even greater than hers. Forgive me for what appears to be my lack of concern. You know my desire is to support you. However, there may be times when I may feel too exhausted to do so."

Now feeling wrong footed, Rosie said stiffly, "I don't mind my own company, but with the twins it's easy to feel 'used' rather than valued. I miss living downstairs and sharing in Jill and Paul's lives."

David gave her a rueful look. "Rosie, can we talk about you feeling 'used' another time. I need to go to work, but please can we make a bargain?" Sceptical at what that might be she frowned.

"You tell me when I appear not to listen, and I'll tell you where possible, what's on my mind." She nodded her agreement. "And it is on my mind to find a compromise about this weekend." Rosie was about to object when he added, "Not now! I'll ring you before lunch and, if necessary, we'll discuss it at dinner this evening."

Unsure what a compromise might be, she gave him the benefit of the doubt. With a gentle smile he put the palm of his hand against her cheek, "I knew how to express my appreciation to Jane, but for now this will have to suffice." Before she could consider what that might be, his head bent, his lips gently nuzzled hers and with a thumb stroking along her jaw line, the kiss was provokingly pleasant. When he stepped back with expectant eyes scanning hers, she determined to remain nonchalant telling him, "You'll be late for work." Returning to the dining room, she found Joshua stirring with his fingers a pile of crumbed toast on his high-chair tray and Rebecca, leaning across, tipping milk from her lidded cup onto them.

At Rosie's exclamation, "Oh no, honestly, you two!" David peered around the doorway.

"Now you two, be good today, and do as Rosie tells you" and as he headed downstairs they called out their 'goodbyes'.

An hour later he rang to suggest, "How about Bath on Friday and Saturday night, and Petersfield on Sunday for lunch and back late that evening?" To that she happily agreed.

CHAPTER 16

After David's phone call, Rosie turned to see Jill coming up the stairs with Rachel in her arms. Worried at Jill being so out of breath she asked, "Is everything alright? Come and sit down" and indicated with her hand the dining room where the twins were eating.

The cumbersome Jill exhaled on "fine" but didn't look it. Her voice took on a tone of complaint, "We've barely seen you since your return. You used to potter about in the garden. Bring the twins down, you won't be intruding. On a heavy sigh she declared, "How our lives have changed! It was good when you, I and Helen lived together!" Rosie smiled. Jill drank her tea then brightened up to say, "I miss you." And then asked, "How are you and David getting on?"

"It's early days. We have many adjustments to make. And you Jill? Three children! William is certainly a handful."

"Do you think Helen's child would have been too?"

"Ben was a lovely guy, but I remember when he made up his mind, he could be very persistent!" Rosie made a sad grimace at Jill's obvious inner turmoil.

There was a brief silence before Jill changed the subject. "David is very taken with your friends the Hawkins. When are we going to meet them?"

"It's early days." Rosie ticked Rachel's nose and received a smile, "David says you don't want to move with Rachel being so unsettled, although she seems more content today. You must be looking forward to living in your own house." At that Jill looked so bleak she didn't know what to say, so diverted her attention to the twins, and was relieved when Jill left.

It didn't seem long after that when the twins started shouting 'Daddy, Daddy' and as he appeared she commented, "You're home early" and with a child in each arm David's eyes scanned her face. Joshua demanded, "Fly Daddy" and gleefully shrieked. On request he repeated it for Rebecca. Next came the demand that he played 'hide and seek' and as they disappeared, she had a brief interval to tell him of Jill's visit.

"I suggested to her that together we could take all the children to the swings, but she made a variety of excuses."

"Paul is at his wits' end. He feels Jill has fallen into a slough of despair. She is not open to any of his suggestions and her mobility isn't helped by the excessive weight she is carrying. But she is interested in seeing where you live and I…"

Interrupting she said sharply, "No David! Not that, not yet!" And walked into the kitchen to prepare the twins' tea.

From the noise, she concluded he'd found them and was continuing the game. Ready to announce teatime she entered the lounge where eagerly Joshua exclaimed, "Oosie, we find treasure for you."

Rebecca pulling on her hand indicated she sit and as David sat beside her he declared, "Start… far, near, far… " until they discovered in the piano stool a box of chocolates whereupon David sang, "*Sweets for my sweet, sugar for my honey.*" Having heard her recorded that song for Johnny, she turned but could see no guile in his expression. As she thanked him, Joshua clambered up beside her while Rebecca with wide-eyed expectancy stood by her knees.

"Would you like one of these?" Little heads nodded enthusiastically. "Then when you have eaten all your tea, you can come back and choose one." At their sudden enthusiasm for macaroni cheese they both laughed.

Later, with Rebecca on his lap and Joshua squeezed in beside Rosie, David declared as little hands headed into the box, "Only one". Engrossed in choosing their chocolate from the shape rather than flavour, Rosie said obliquely, "Yours to give, mine to dispense".

Joshua's cheeks bulged as he popped the whole sweet into his small mouth and David replied, "Point taken!"

Rebecca tentatively bit into hers, bringing Rosie to ask, "Is that nice?" At her fierce nod she instructed, "Pop that last bit into your mouth before it melts. Then you can have another." She felt, rather than saw, David tensing beside her as Rebecca gobbled hers up and Joshua still sucking and dribbling with his first one reached for another.

In that second, David slid Rebecca off his knee to the floor, stood and lifted out Joshua from next to her announcing, "Bath time." Over the loud protests, he took their hands preventing them returning and at the same time he sent her a pointed look.

Outmanoeuvred, she closed the box but promised, "You can have another one tomorrow". She had just lost that battle of wills, but David's expression held no triumph as he mouthed, 'thank you' she assumed for not overriding his decision. As she ate a second one, she considered why she felt the need to challenge and contradict him. Had he been testing her to see if she would undermine his authority? Children needed the stability of parental unity and if she was to be their mother, she knew they must agree in front of the twins. With that thought she ventured upstairs. Her appearance in the bathroom doorway had the children chorusing 'Oosie, Oosie'. David was swishing the water into waves for the ducks and boats to bob up and down. She knelt beside him and murmured, "A united front is important."

"As was the integrity of your response". His next words were spoken quietly and interwoven with water play. "In your changing role, I need to respect your will as much as you mine. My hope is, if nothing else, we have a close friendship and we enjoy life together. With trust and respect, we can ensure neither of us ever feels used or abused."

Rosie nodded feeling enough had been said. She was gratified when Rebecca wanted her to wash her hair, which she accomplished without the usual screams of 'there is soap in my eyes'. Gently she splashed Rebecca, but when her retaliation was to fill and throw a cup of water at her she ducked behind David and laughed, as soaked he cried out. Rebecca - unsure if there would be retribution - quickly laid down in the bath, and Rosie guessed if she'd been Jane what his response would have been. As she stood so did he. There was a yell from Joshua and his dripping body was flying through the air towards her. With only a second to grab a towel before he landed in her arms, Rosie squealed in surprise. Under Joshua's delight at his unexpected flight David grunted, "That was quick" before turning to Rebecca and asking, "Come and cuddle your poor wet Daddy."

Rebecca wailed, "I want Oosie dry me."

Joshua, wrapped in the towel was now standing on the bath mat while David mournfully declared, "It appears I'm not wanted." Rosie pointed to Joshua who was happy for his father to take her place. Wrapped in a towel, Rosie placed her on the mat beside Joshua. In needing an extra towel for her hair she turned to get one and realised at eye level about two feet away David was removing his wet shirt by unzipping his trousers. Gasping his name, she shot to her feet, to first be faced with a wide, muscled and dark hairy chest, and then a mouth twitching with laughter and eyes filled with mirth. "As you initiated my soaking, I concluded you desired to see me in a state of undress?"

Cross, she retorted, "Then you concluded wrongly!" She grabbed the towel, wrapped it around Rebecca's head and carried her to their room. Once ready for bed, she took Rebecca to Joshua.

Each evening the twins would dispel the last of their energy by using David's bed as a trampoline, after which he read them a story before carrying them to their cots, and calling for her to say 'goodnight'. The bath night ritual had been that she cleared up the bathroom while he would read and once she had said 'goodnight', her day with them ended. To her surprise David decreed, "I'll clean up the bathroom, you read the story."

Immediately the children chanted, "Oosie, Oosie, story." She hesitated, not at the story but at sitting between the children in the centre of David's bed. Rosie looked at David, "This is their time with you. I don't mind clearing up."

David gestured towards the empty space, "It's not my name they are calling." And before she could further object he disappeared towards the bathroom. As they squabbled over which book to pick, she sat on the edge. In this bed Jane and David conceived these children. She didn't feel ready to take Jane's place in it, or on it! How long would it be before the twins asked questions about their Mummy, and why she didn't live with their Daddy?"

The twins, perhaps thinking her silence was to await their agreement, were now looking puzzled as Joshua waved their choice. Rosie took a deep breath and clambered across to the space in the pillows left for her. Perhaps the twins sensed her discomfort for they quickly snuggled into her and thumbs in mouths listened to how the ugly duckling didn't have anybody to play with. Entranced, the twins barely noticed David's return, but she did! Admittedly having been inveigled to join the Reinhardt family on holiday, she had seen him in his bathing trunks, but half naked in his bedroom was another matter.

Her slight hesitation in reading was enough to alert him to her discomfort, and although she didn't look up, he said, "Rest assured Rosie, I'm just here to get dry clothes."

Embarrassed, she ignored him. He left and she continued to the end, "Then one day the ugly duckling saw a beautiful swan swimming in the pond and bent his head in shame. But his reflection was no longer an ugly duckling for he had turned into a handsome swan."

Fully dressed and if on cue, David appeared in the doorway, his eyes and tender smile included her as he took in the scene. Crossing to the window, he bent to gather Joshua in his arms. Conscious of his proximity and embarrassed as his warm arm brushed against the side of her breast, Rosie turned her head towards Rebecca. She heard his faint sigh before he acknowledged, "There's a truth in that story?" Hugging the sleepy child in his arms, he explained, "Life can make us feel ugly, unwanted, afraid and ashamed of who we are or what we have done. But when we ask Jesus into our lives, He changes us from inside out. We don't always realise it, but we need to believe it." That said, he moved away to instruct over his shoulder, "Bring Rebecca when you're ready."

David was right, for years she had hated herself, hid her guilt and shame behind a mask, but life, and she, had changed. The sleepy child beside her murmuring, "Love Oosie" seemed to confirm it.

The twins' unconditional love and acceptance of her was like that of Jesus. She saw her heart had been an unattended open wound, her silence had caused the wound to fester, and the puss flowed out in jealousy and spiteful gossip. The children's love and David's respect had similarities to a poultice drawing and draining that out and it was now enabling healing to take place. Being open, vulnerable, talking to David, Johnny and others had been as applying antiseptic, painful at first, but ridding her of infected thinking. The pain of Jane's loss had given David insight and being accused of murder had shown him how easily wrong judgements can be made. If she was to speak of her terrible ordeal, she needed to trust he wouldn't be disgusted. Wounds come with scabs to protect while restoration takes place. Maybe it was time they fell off, for then even with scars they would only be visible to her, not as a reminder of the past, but how she had been healed.

In an ungainly fashion, she slid off David's bed thinking that given the right opportunity maybe she could tell David about her darkest hours, and why she had no desire to share this bed with him. Overwhelming love filled her as she picked up and carried the cute little girl with her heart-shaped face to her cot. She was so like Jane right down to her feisty ways. David, who had been sitting contemplatively in the rocking chair, looked up as she entered, his eyes crinkling with pleasure at the sight of his daughter. Placing Rebecca in her cot, she pulled up the covers and commented softly, "Jane would have loved them."

Unexpectedly David murmured by her ear, "As do you." She swallowed hard at the feel of David's hands lightly resting on her shoulders before drawing her to face him. Compassion seemed to fill his eyes as he queried, "Is that what is troubling you? Do you feel by stepping into Jane's place, you are ousting her?"

"Sometimes it's hard to believe she's gone. There are so many reminders… " She forced herself to add, "And I… in your bedroom… on the bed… you half dressed, well… it feels… " she trailed off.

"Not right?" With that he took hold of her hand and led her downstairs. Feeling awkward she said, "Dinner is ready."

Kindly, yet firmly, he declared, "That can wait. Come, sit down." Suddenly she felt nervous, she curled up in the corner of the settee, as David settled in his familiar contemplative position. With an encouraging smile he coaxed, "Tell me about your thinking?"

She hesitated, then explained how she felt God was healing her wounded heart, "I see how our hearts and our minds are affected by what we think. I read in Romans 12 that the Lord wants to transform us by the renewing of our minds so we can see ourselves as He sees us. But I have difficulty believing the verse that says, 'I am beautifully and wonderfully made'."

David's response was his 'knee weakening' smile along with his assurance, "Oh believe me Rosie, it's true." At her sceptical expression he added, "You are very attractive in body and mind, and your loving heavenly Father is restoring and renewing your mind. Let me tell you about my ongoing dream which began before Jane died." He sat forward, obviously keen to explain.

"David, I'd like to hear about it, but we really need to eat." He nodded, leapt up, took her hand and helped her to her feet. He laid the table while she retrieved the casserole and jacket potatoes. With food in front of him, it was several minutes before he wanted to talk beyond, "This is delicious. Yet another good reason to make you my wife." His hunger assuaged, he ate between each sentence, giving time for both the food and his dream to be digested, "It started with what appeared to be thousands of ants going one way. Then they all turned and headed in the opposite direction. When it came again, I felt I was one of those ants in the midst of an army. I was riding on horseback, leaving the dawn and going into darkness. I felt I was off to war. Each dream took the scene a little further. The darkness grew blacker. I could only hear the beat of hundreds of horses' hooves, but couldn't see them. Light emanated from the chests of the riders beside me and I realised I had that light too. It revealed the shadow of those in front and glancing back, those behind. It was imperative I held on for should I fall I would be trampled to death." David pushed his empty plate from him, "Each time I dreamt, I sensed the Lord was with me.

When Jane died, and everything which followed, the dream gave me the faith and strength to get through that terrible time."

Rosie acknowledged, "It certainly bears a resemblance to the way your life panned out."

"Months later the dream came again. I was alone in an oasis in the desert, resting from a battle which I hadn't fought. I began to sense it was time to start a new journey. Over weeks and months, I cantered over hills and down dales with no sense of a direction or resting place. And then on a high hill, I saw a distant castle which seemed a good place to go. My next set of dreams brought me through a forest, on to a grassy bank where a deep moat and high walls revealed I was at a castle. I walked around and could see no way in except by invitation, for the drawbridge had to be let down. Over a period of time, I saw that the drawbridge was regularly lowered to allow two children in and out. I watched carefully to see how I might cross with them. On occasions I did try to enter with them, but was rebuffed as an intruder. So I knew I had to wait to be welcomed. And when it came it was not as I expected, but it allowed me entry into the keep. And I'm still believing that one day I will be allowed into the very heart of the castle and enter into the fullness of all that is within."

Rosie observed, "Write it down. The twins would love the story. They say, 'every Englishman has his castle'. You may think the drawbridge, castle and twins are connected to me, but I could name several unmarried women at church who would love your children and whose heart you could win."

David took an apple from the fruit bowl, "God led Joseph to his destiny with dreams for himself and others. John in Revelation didn't know if what he saw was a dream or a vision. Jane didn't have dreams she talked about, but was envisioned with pictures given by the Lord often unfolding over weeks - if not months - and scripture would confirm what she saw. I often wonder if she had a premonition of her death that brought her to write these letters to me and the twins? I believe our heavenly Father will communicate with us, both in the natural and supernatural."

"My father didn't communicate with me, so I can't imagine God doing that."

"Oh Rosie, He has! Think about it. You have been asking and received answers! Just as we teach the twins right from wrong, He does the same for us and underpins our mistakes with His love, bringing us a greater desire to grow to know Him better. My Dad is gruff, strict and rarely hugged or played with me as a child. Yet I know deep within that he loves me, even if outwardly he finds it hard to show it. Your father's attitude towards his children is unusual. I'll make the coffee and let's sit in the lounge."

Curled up in the corner of the settee she opened up the chocolate box, indicated to David to help himself and took courage to say, "I thought Doug, twenty years older than me, was attractive and charming. He appeared to be the kind and thoughtful fatherly figure I had always yearned for?"

David raised an eyebrow, and at her corresponding questioning expression, he elucidated with a broad smile, "Obviously, my debonair presence and charisma aren't something you've ever desired."

"Jane Austin's rather aloof Mr Darcy never appealed to me."

David chuckled, "Don't tell me, you preferred Mr Collins?"

Hackles rising, she glared at him, "Is that a dig at Johnny?"

Hastily he contested, "Believe me, it's entirely coincidental that they share the same profession. The only time I've seen Johnny, he just received a nasty bang to his head. I was trying to lighten the atmosphere."

Rosie sipped her coffee, "I need to tell you about Doug." David gave her an encouraging nod. "He befriended me. In hearing I lived in a bedsit, he asked if I would like to caretake his two-bedroom cottage in South Kensington. His home and constituency were in Norfolk and he only stayed overnight if there was a late vote in Parliament. Despite Helen's mess you've seen how cosy, comfortable and central the cottage is."

David's nod acknowledged that. "In that first month Parliament wasn't in session. In the second, his overnight visits were spasmodic and he would kiss my cheek 'goodnight'. In the third month his overnight stays were more regular and the kiss developed into a hug."

Unable to look at David she focussed on her hands. "I said I would happily cook him a meal if he was staying. He bought wine, it became a weekly event and in his company I felt interesting and attractive. I enjoyed his intellect and wit so didn't complain when his kiss moved to my mouth, but did when the hugs became invasive. I explained I saw him as a father figure and preferred to keep it that way. He admitted he cared for me more than a father should and extolled my virtues. Flattered it added to my infatuation, but he agreed he would go no further than I allowed." She glanced up at David, knowing he would recognise those words!

"After another month, he said it was difficult because he so desired to make love to me. I stated I valued his company, but he had a wife and family. He said they were more interested in financial investments than him. He had the ability to make me feel sorry for him. That and the wine gradually weakened my resolve. What harm was there in a kiss and a fumble on the settee if it gave him pleasure, but finally he cajoled me into letting him 'make love' which I found a painful and degrading experience. I felt ashamed as his children were only a few years younger than me. He said it wouldn't be like that next time." Crying I said I didn't want a next time, I hated it and vowed I would never do it again. For over a month he barely spoke to me at work and didn't come to the cottage."

"I accepted several invitations for meals or drinks with men my own age, but they seemed frivolous and immature. I liked the cottage, valued my friendship with Doug, and then appointed to the Cabinet he began to stay regularly. At first it was fine, but gradually the kiss and fumble were reinstated. He kept assuring me, kept pushing me to go further, saying he and it wouldn't cause pain this time until finally I gave in. He proclaimed 'a romp in the hay' was great fun and so enjoyable."

"Is that how you felt?"

Tears pricked the back of her eyes as she shook her head, "He was busy, rarely home until late, he would tell me he adored me and our secret love nest. When I found courage to tell him I didn't like it and felt used, he became angry. He dismissed that by pointing out I lived without charge in his pied-a-terre and he had recently organised my promotion. I argued that I cooked and cleaned the house for him. My promotion came due to speaking, reading, writing and ability to do shorthand in four languages. Astonished at my standing up for myself he strode out, slamming the front door and didn't return that night. Nor, when I asked, did he deign to tell me where he had been."

The revisiting of those scenes caused her voice to falter, bringing David to comment, "From my perspective, his adoration only involved satisfying his sexual needs without any thought of yours."

"I don't have sexual needs, it's vile, messy and I hate it." David looked about to contradict her so she hurried on, "Doug avoided me for a week, either staying away or so late I would have gone to bed. Finally I waited up to talk to him. His immediate response was to blame me for being naive and stupid in not understanding that caretaking the cottage included taking care of his needs, and he had been very patient with me. I rushed into my bedroom and locked myself in. He banged on the door and told me to stop being childish. What he said was true. I had fallen for an age-old trick of a fatherly figure. He had used my vulnerability to fulfil his sexual desire. I buried my head in the pillow and cried."

Her throat tightened and she swallowed hard. David gently probed, "Doug was your first but since... "

Abruptly she sobbed, "And last!" She saw David's grimace, but was unsure if that was from her decree or the sharpness of her tone. She hurried on, "Next day Doug arrived with flowers, chocolates and wine wanting to make up. He said he enjoyed my company, and to prove his love he didn't need an intimate relationship."

At the long, sad look she directed at David he intuitively clarified, "But he didn't mean it. Let me assure you, I do! I admit I will try to tempt you, but you can set the pace, or halt the action."

"I want to believe that. Doug stayed at the cottage, we had several pleasant evenings. Until one evening, he arrived late and buoyed up with alcohol. I was in my nightclothes making a hot chocolate. He took one look at me and snarled, "You give me this 'don't touch me lark' and then appear before me practically naked."

"I replied I wasn't expecting him and my thick cotton nightie covered me from head to foot. I left making a drink, but as I walked past him... " she gave a sob, "... he pushed me over the back of the settee. Closing her eyes, she repeated the words he had growled at her 'You act like a child, so I'll treat you as one'. Unable to describe to David the pain and humiliation she had suffered, she curled into a tight defensive ball.

David's voice, husky with emotion, said, "Oh Rosie..." Astonished, she opened her eyes to see his brimming with unshed tears.

Hardening her heart she retorted, "He blamed me. He said that when a virile man loves a woman and is tempted and denied what he had come to enjoy, it wasn't surprising that he became overcome with anger."

"He blamed you for his lack of control?" David's derogatory tone was evident enough of his disgust.

"Next day I couldn't go to work so began packing up to leave, and penitent he assured me it wouldn't happen again. I felt the only reason it didn't was when he didn't want to take 'no' for an answer I always capitulated."

"Good grief! Rosie, married or not, every woman has a right to refuse a man." David's jaw clenched, "And when that refusal is ignored Rosie, it's called rape."

Rosie flinched and ridiculously defended Doug, "It was the drink that made him belligerent."

"Why did you stay?"

"I... I don't know. I enjoyed the times when he was charming, funny and appreciated of my ideas. He presented several to Parliament, and told me at Cabinet Meetings that he had received several accolades for his clear and innovative thinking." At David's derisive grunt she admitted, "Oh, I see now how manipulative he was. He used my mind on governmental issues which he also used as foreplay to 'making love'. Mentally, I saw myself being like the daughter he never had. Physically, to keep him happy I gave him what he wanted. I didn't like it, but he didn't appear to notice." David shook his head as though in disbelief. "He said he and his wife were estranged. She didn't understand him or his interest in politics."

With a heavy sigh David ran his hand through his hair, "I guess his wife knew more about his lifestyle than you did. When the Profumo affair hit the headlines, I had just started out as a barrister. I gathered from colleagues that - in lose terms – there was a 'gentleman's club' within governmental circles, which had the ability to hush up unseemly acts of its members. Bribery or intimidating people into silence weren't unknown."

Rosie hummed, "As I was later to discover. Doug said he couldn't live without me and would talk to his wife about divorce. Initially I was flattered, if I was to suffer marriage, why not to him. Then I thought of Jack and Cathy's reaction to my affair with a married man. Three months after that, Christine Keeler became famous for having an affair with a politician. My guess is that scandal later frightened Doug and his wife into giving me the cottage.

"Did Jack and Cathy know about Doug?"

"Yes, from the day it ended." David's eyebrow rose. Rosie paused, she wasn't ready and wasn't sure he was, to hear the rest. She looked down at her hands, "They knew I shared a mews cottage and assumed the friend in the Foreign Office was female. Doug and I couldn't go out anywhere together, but I gave Jack and Cathy the impression that the places I went to alone was with friends."

David's expression matched his words. "Oh Rosie, I'm so sorry that happened to you. He took hold of her hand. I really appreciate your trust in confiding in me.   Embarrassed, Rosie focussed on his tie, for the truth was last Saturday, she had told Johnny the whole story which had initiated a comforting squeeze of his hand. "I would like to hug and comfort you, but feel in the circumstances it would be inappropriate.   He lifted her chin, waited until her eyes met his, before saying sadly, "I sense there is more, but I have no intention of pressuring you. And as time is getting on, the need to pack for the weekend and to drive to Bath, I think it would be wise if we both have an early night."

Twenty-two hours later, having negotiated the traffic out of London and the goodies in the picnic boxes eaten, the twins were sleeping as the tape recorder played Braham's Lullaby.

Rosie considering the weekend observed, "You said you had important things to discuss with your father, would that be about Jill?

"What makes you ask that?"

"Your concern! You insisted on leaving the Rover so she and Paul could take the children out for the day. Even Mrs P mentioned Jill hasn't bounced back from the birth of Rachel nine weeks ago. I know Rachel is a difficult baby, but Jill sounded so bleak when she talked about the future. She has always been a bit scatty and untidy, but she seems depressed and her weight gain must be a problem."

"Rachel's early arrival, the trauma of the operation and the blood loss obviously exhausted her. Paul isn't sure that she'll cope in Kent, hence their delay in leaving, but his family seems keen to support her. Dad asked them to join us his weekend. He offered to lay on all they needed, but Jill said she was too exhausted to contemplate the packing and a long journey.

"She didn't tell me! I could have helped. She just moaned about the drudgery of life with children. You refused your father's offer of a Norland nanny, but could he get one for her?"

"I can suggest it. Is she happy with Mrs Smith's cleaning?"

"She is, and pleased she's not squeamish about sick! I've barely seen her, but she seems a strange woman. As Joyce was visiting, we looked after William and Luke for a couple of hours. I went to collect them. I've the feeling she doesn't like me, her words always seem underpinned with a sneer."

David glanced over at her, "Why? What did she say?"

Rosie frowned and repeated, "Mrs P thinks highly of 'the master'. Clever to use his family and children to ensnare him."

"Did you reply?"

"Baffled, I said nothing. When I told Mrs P I didn't think she like me, she just hummed and changed the subject. Odd I thought for Mrs P has always been polite, kind and helpful. The day she reported Rebecca's accident it wasn't to make trouble, but she believed you needed to know, and I needed support."

"Whereupon, I failed miserably! She's a good woman. A treasure I would be loath to lose." Rosie was reminded of Jane writing that David would find his treasure through the children. Maybe his seemingly being loath to lose her brought him to think marriage would be the solution.

"We're nearly at the Bath exit. This new part of the M4 Motorway certainly speeds up the journey. It has only taken two hours." Deep in thought, she hadn't realised how time had flown. Twenty minutes later, they were through Bath into Kelston and turning into the drive of his parent's house.

Franz always sounded gruff, his voice - like David's - tended to boom, be it in irritation or enthusiasm. Margaret immediately complimented her on the new hairstyle, and companionably slipped an arm through hers as the men released and carried in the sleeping children. "Rosie I'm so delighted that the charade you and David put on at Christmas to ward off Felicity is now a reality. I hope we can soon officially welcome you to our family."

"That's kind Margaret. But whether or not David and I marry, I would like to be able to count on you and your family as friends."

Despite looking taken aback Margaret responded, "But of course, dear."

With the twins safely transferred into cots, she and David took the rooms on either side of them. After a delicious meal of succulent roast lamb and two glasses of wine David coaxed her to talk about her family and home. And as they drank coffee in the lounge, she felt so relaxed she talked of meeting Johnny, the accident, David's rescue and her need to visit him in Petersfield on Sunday, "I can't help worry because in my experience when I find people to trust and love, I lose them."

Perplexed, David's parents glanced at him and she added, "Of course the most recent was Jane." To distract from what was an awkward silence, she told them of Sylvia's illness and death, causing Margaret to sympathise and Franz to leap up announcing gruffly, "It's time for News at Ten."

David drew closer to her and with his hand along the back of the settee, gently caressed her neck as he quietly confided, "Thank you for clarifying why you need constant news and want to visit Johnny." Not liking the sensation his fingers were creating she sat forward. Seeing his arched eyebrow, she whispered, "Arm around is allowed, nothing more" and then snuggled under his arm where tantalising fingers couldn't touch her.

Franz sent David an approving nod. After the news Franz announced they were off to bed, David agreed, "We'll follow you up."

Breakfast in the Reinhardt household was always eight o'clock sharp. You were expected to attend fully dressed and would receive Franz's look of disapproval if a minute late. There wasn't any fear of that because the twins were calling "Daddy, Daddy" just before seven. Passing the doorway as she ventured to the toilet, she realised it had been a while since she'd seen him in his pyjamas, hair tussled, and with a dark stubble of beard. It made him look surprisingly young and vulnerable. On her return she asked, "Do you need any help?"

Immediately two pairs of eyes, outstretched arms and voices chorused together, "Oosie, Oosie,"

David gave a heartfelt 'Yes please' before saying, "Good morning Rosie" and planted a quick kiss on her mouth, in much the same way as he had said, 'goodnight' outside her door the previous night. By the time Margaret arrived downstairs, David had delved into the fridge and decreed it would be a full English breakfast. The bacon was already sizzling in the pan. Sitting by the twins, Margaret commented, "This is a treat."

When Franz arrived at the designated time, the twins had already had their cereals. After his boom of 'good morning' he informed them, "Jenny is coming in late afternoon and agreed to stay the night." Rosie, cracking eggs into the pan, gave him a puzzled glance, wondering if she had missed something. "David, haven't you told her?" She turned to David who was intent on filling the toaster. Franz continued, "Inhart Pharmaceuticals are hosting a 'Jane Austin Ball' in the Bath Assembly Rooms tonight." Obviously, she wasn't expected to babysit, but she had bought nothing suitable to wear.

Margaret said perceptively, "Don't worry Rosie, we have hired costumes, even down to shoes. David gave us your size and said a dress in rich leaf green would suit you."

Rosie cracked the last egg into the pan remembering rich leaf green was the colour of her eiderdown! She frowned at David, "When did you intend telling me about this?"

His response was a wry smile, "It's a surprise and very special date." At Rosie's hum, David's smile became unusually self-deprecating as he confessed, "I was afraid that if I told you it was the Inharts Company ball, you would be reticent to go as people might speculate on you becoming my wife."

"And you would be right, as much for your sake as mine."

David looked genuinely upset, "I would rather that, than go on my own, but it's your decision." He turned to place the full toast rack on the table. Even over the twins' loud chattering she was certain his parents had heard their conversation.

Rosie slid the eggs on to the waiting plates. David's mother receiving her breakfast stated, "We would both be disappointed if you don't come tonight."

"Why would Rosie not come?" boomed Franz.

Margaret sent her a quirky and sympathetic smile at Franz's inability to comprehend such a preposterous idea. David turned to retrieve further slices of bread from the toaster and Rosie answered truthfully, "I have an aversion to decisions being made on my behalf" With that she picked up her breakfast plate, sat down opposite Franz and Margaret and clarified, "I'm sure I'll enjoy the ball, and have no wish to spoil your evening. However, please introduce me as a friend of the family, so should I not become David's wife, it will be far less embarrassing for him."

"Whatever reason could there be for you to refuse his proposal?" Franz challenged.

Margaret frowned at her husband, glanced at David with a small smile playing around her mouth. Rosie addressed Franz, "In business I admire tenacity but in private if someone tries to orchestrate my life, it brings me concern."

Margaret tried hard not to show her amusement, but Franz as if unable to comprehend her reason barked, "Are you still in love with this boy… Johnny?"

Before Rosie could respond Margaret said sharply, "Franz, please!"

"The truth is I fell in love with him when I was six. Sent to boarding school at eight, I thought my heart would break. When I was old enough to find him, I was dismayed to discovered he had moved 'up north'. I recently learnt he had once cycled to my house to leave his new address, but my father had informed him, 'She doesn't live here anymore' and shut the door in his face."

Margaret tutted, Franz barked, "It sounds as if your father didn't think he was suitable company for you."

Her retort was immediate, "And why I don't appreciate people making decision on my behalf." Franz's eyes took on a cold, assessing glint. "It could be that Johnny's accident and subsequent coma has exacerbated my feelings for him, but is it love? He still feels something for me, as I for him, and I need time to assess that before I make any decision about my future."

David and his father exchanged a look before Franz querulously asked, "And have you assessed all that David is offering you?"

Rosie glanced at David now intent on eating his breakfast. "Franz, your son is offering me far more than I could hope for or imagine, but for me love is the only consideration. I love the twins but they will grow up, so I have to ask myself do I have enough in common with their father to sustain a marriage until death do us part?"

Taken aback, Franz stern expression didn't change as he declared, "But you've worked for and with David. You have a quick brain and an eye for business. That alone should be enough?"

"I am sure Franz, you are aware that marriage is meant to be more than the melding of business minds. It's having a companion who will reciprocate your desire to listen, encourage and support them. That way you grow in understanding of each other and it brings a oneness of mind regarding the love and upbringing of children."

Margaret nodded, "I agree, but no marriage is perfect and with children it's full of ups and downs."

Franz frowned at Margaret. Rosie ate her breakfast. David unabashed at the discussion buttered his toast before adding, "And we'll take a step at a time. First we need to enjoy friendship. I suggest this evening we dress up, we go to a ball, and guess what, we might have fun." In the midst of a mouthful Rosie hummed.

Franz pushed back his chair, "If you have finished David, we have things to discuss." David winked at her, grabbed another slice of toast and followed him. Hopefully none of that would involve her.

CHAPTER 17

David was right, the ball was fun!

Dressed in a beautiful emerald green satin dress with short puffed sleeves, low neckline with built in bra and high waist, she knew she looked stunning even before David's wide-eyed appreciation. And tonight David did look the epitome of Mr Darcy dressed as a man of regency times. With his parents they made two very handsome couples welcoming the guests to the Ball.

The evening progressed with a delicious buffet and after dinner speeches. When the dancing resumed, David was engrossed in conversation, so she indicated she was slipping away to the Ladies. When she came out of the cubicle, she was surprised to see Felicity resting back against the wash basins. Unable to avoid her, she greeted her before moving to use the wash basin furthest from her. In a superior voice Felicity addressed her, "So you are still hanging around David in the hope by being nanny to his children he might decide to marry you." Rinsing her hands Rosie ignored her. "There has been much talk about you making up to him at Christmas." A sudden urge to laugh communicated itself in a small smile which obviously irritated Felicity, for with disdain she looked her up and down to comment spitefully, "Despite the new hairdo, mutton can't be dressed up to look like lamb."

Despite knowing it wasn't a Christian response but so disliking the woman, she eyed Felicity up and down and mocked, "In your case there is no lack of trying."

As Felicity processed her barb, her attractive features turned into a snarl before she claimed, "David's father rules the roost, he won't want someone like you in their family."

Drying her hands Rosie sent Felicity a sad look, "If that is how you see it, you really don't know David or his family."

"Oh yes I do! I've known David for years. I was his girlfriend for four, and when we were engaged I practically lived with him. We would have married if that Jane hadn't thrown herself at him."

Incensed, Rosie threw her paper towel into the bin and turned to contradict her. "Untrue!" At Felicity's scowl she added, "Oh, think about it! If David had really loved you, Jane wouldn't have changed his mind." She waved her hand. "Face the facts! David and his family have rejected you." Felicity glowered at her. "And for your information, David has asked me to marry him. Should I do so it won't be for money, but out of love for his two delightful children."

"Oh really, what are you after, another cottage?" Taken aback Rosie stared at Felicity who with a nasty smile scoffed, "And a marriage proposal, that's all it is. An empty promise and like Doug Bradford, once he has had you he'll soon tire of your frigidity."

Rosie did what she did best. Drawing herself up to her full height, she said haughtily, "I beg your pardon?"

"You heard, Doug wanted to dump you. He organised for his wife to meet and confront you." Rosie's eyes widened, bringing glee into Felicity's face as she informed her, "You thought your affair with Doug was a well-kept and now buried secret. Wrong! Even when he was with his 'uptight' Rosemary, he was still enjoying 'romps in the hay' with several of my friends." Practiced at wearing an unfathomable expression, Rosie drew on that ability, pulled out her lipstick and reapplied it while her heart thudded painfully, and her stomach sickened at hearing of Doug's duplicity.

Felicity's hard blue eyes fixed on her and in Rosie's lack of response she thrust from another angle, "You can't tell me that day I met David in the park and he told me of Jane's death that it was a coincidence you arrived on the scene."

"Then you don't want the truth." Rosie returned her a questioning stare.

Felicity frowned then made further insinuations, "You stepped into Jane's shoes as his secretary, moved into his house, next step the decision to become the twins' nanny. Very clever! In knowing that I decided to delve into your life. Oh my, that was fascinating!"

Years of practicing silence held Rosie in good stead, for she merely raised her eyebrows causing Felicity to respond, "I found out you were not Rosemary Dawes, but Doughty-Dawes, the very one Doug talked about." Not wanting to hear more, Rosie picked up her evening bag and headed towards the door as Felicity claimed, "You weren't the first of his 'living in' bits on the side, but the problems you caused made you the last one he shacked up with. I warned you at Christmas that once David knew about your past he won't, nor will his toffee-nosed family, want any connection to you."

Ignoring Felicity, and with others entering, Rosie moved passed them into the empty corridor. But Felicity wasn't to be brushed off that easily for coming up behind her she asked, "Does

252

David know that Doug was just one of a string of men you sought to influence and blackmail?"

Incensed Rosie stopped to face her, "I don't know where you get your information, but that's not true."

"Who do you think told me?" At her puzzled expression Felicity gave her silly, tinkly laugh, "Doug, of course! He told us he'd shacked up with a frigid bitch. And to get rid of you he'd set up his wife to find you at the cottage. How he laughed on hearing you'd told her that he wanted to marry you." Rosie closed her eyes against the echoes of misery, pain and depression, if only it had been as simple as Felicity related. "Silly you, didn't you know Roman Catholics don't divorce? If need be wives turn a blind eye, in this case to Doug's panache for naïve young women, who usually left before being thrown out. But you were different. Doug told us he'd been subjected to your 'man hating' revenge, you'd blackmailed them into giving you the cottage." Rosie bit back the truth for Doug and his wife had been scared into giving her the cottage, not by her but what an investigation might uncover. Felicity's pretty mouth curled into a malicious smile, "Nothing to say?" Her face hardened, "The whole family relocated to London with a view to furthering their banking interests which curbed Doug's philandering and he took to drink to maintain his 'happy go lucky' nature. You no doubt know he died of a heart attack a couple of years ago. You ruined his life."

Her instant reaction was to retort that Doug had ruined hers, but there came an inner restraint, and in that pause relief flooded in. Felicity didn't know the whole story! She drew on that knowledge to reply confidently, "David knows the truth. Doug was a selfish and weak man who lived for his own pleasure. You and he would seem to have a lot in common. Now excuse me, I have a ball to attend."

At her retreating figure Felicity shouted after her, "I bet David and that stingy father of his aren't aware of the way your father gained and spent your mother's fortune until all that was left was a seedy mansion no-one wants to buy?"

Rosie stopped and advancing toward Felicity decreed, "From my perspective it would seem you hang out with a seedy crowd so let me warn you, be careful who you slander."

Undeterred Felicity laughed in her face, "There's a difference between slander and truth. I know all about your father's gambling and how he upped and left the country because he owes thousands of pounds to the loan sharks." Not wanting to hear more

Rosie headed towards the ballroom, but determined to have her say Felicity was hot on her heels. "He won that tea plantation he owns in a card game." Rosie walked faster, a slightly breathless Felicity hurrying behind spat out, "After the deal was done, the loser was found shot and your father beat a hasty retreat to England to join your mother." Shocked to the core, Rosie stopped abruptly and turned to face her. Ignoring Rosie's outraged expression, she burbled on, "They say these things are in the genes. Your gambling is for subtler. Get David's kids liking you, play hard to get, marry him, and then like your father I've no doubt, you'll drain him of his inheritance and leave."

Unsure as she was about the truth of her father's activities, she knew the truth about herself, "Felicity, there are things in my past that, like you, made me a jealous, spiteful gossip. When Jane first came into my life I despised her as it seems you do me, but I'll tell you what she told me." Felicity's mocking countenance changed to curiosity. "It's quite simple, whatever my past or problems I face, I discovered Jesus loves me. And He wants to love you too." Felicity's curiosity turned to aversion. Now it was Rosie following her, talking of God's forgiveness for sin, and her voice only faded when Felicity pushed through the doors into the ballroom.

But Felicity's disturbing revelations were still reverberating through her mind. In trying to make sense of them, she wandered back down the corridor and leant against the wall to wonder why she didn't think Felicity was lying. Memories surfaced and raced across her mind. Her father leaving the house and sometimes not returning for days. Was he gambling or like Doug was with other women? In her turmoil, she flickered her fan against her face while trying to compose herself. When Jack brought her home from hospital, her father pinching the ends of his moustache accused her of disgracing the family and the stigma that would bring meant they had no alternative than retreat to his tea plantation in India. Ill and weak she had tried to speak to her Mother who - in those last days - was rushing aimlessly around like a frightened mouse, unable to hold a sensible conversation. But with tears in her eyes, she had come to say 'goodbye' and on the brink of telling her something, her father bawled 'DeeDee, taxi is waiting, get yourself down here.' And she had scurried away as her father's voice echoed up from the hall 'You, and this cold and dilapidated mansion, has brought nothing but trouble.' Trouble included her, a disabled son and unpaid household bills. But was it more than that?

She reflected on Jack receiving instructions to pack and ship to India tea chests of valuables from the house. The unexpected invitation to visit her parents to see their new home. Mike not promoting her, unused holiday and chance to go over the Christmas break, she'd accepted. She liked India, its friendly helpful people and the house's location, on stilts overlooking fields of tea plants. But she hadn't like Tom who had also been invited to stay. He was forty years old, fat and pot-bellied, thought he was amusing, knew everything about everything and, as he saw himself as God's gift to women, a 'touchy feely' man. After days of avoiding his advances, being cool but polite, her father informed her she would do well to marry Tom. He was very rich, knew about her past and didn't mind. Her expletive ridden reply shocked both her mother and father and she discovered she enjoyed being nasty, spiteful and rude to Tom. That came to a head just before New Year, embarrassing her mother, and causing her father to call her an ungrateful bitch and decreeing he never wanted to see her again. To this she retaliated by telling him that the feeling was mutual, but as her flight out of Assam wasn't booked until the 3rd January, he had no choice. The next morning he left in his vile, rich friend's car."

Startled by a hand touching her arm, Rosie jumped out of reverie and at the intensity of her expression David asked, "Rosie, what's wrong?" Concerned, his eyes anxiously scanned her face, "Mum told me she'd seen Felicity leave just after you, and had returned with a face like thunder. When you didn't reappear I felt I should come and look for you."

"Felicity believes I'm out to snare you and… "

Interrupting, David jovially exclaimed, "If you had let me I'd show everyone it's my intention to snare you."

Rosie lamented, "Believe me she has information to change your mind."

"Doubtful but pray tell me what that might be?"

Irritated she retorted, "This is serious."

David led her down the corridor to a quiet corner, "Tell me about it?" Briefly she repeated Felicity's allegations and saw his face filled first with suppressed anger, then puzzlement bringing him to question, "And why would that affect my marrying you?"

"Felicity suggested gambling was in my genes. That I would marry you and like my father one day lay claim to you, and your father's fortune." After a thoughtful hum David questioned, "Did she indeed. And what was your reply?"

"I told her I used to say spiteful things because I was hurt and unhappy, but that changed when Jane introduced me to Jesus."

A broad grin broke through the grimness of his face, "Ah! The reason she burst through those doors like a bullet from a gun." Rosie cringed. David responded, "Sorry Rosie, wrong phrase, but don't believe everything she said. There was much unrest in India at that time and the British were advised to leave the country due to the partition."

"She also said when hearing my surname was Doughty-Dawes that she realised I had been 'the frigid bitch' who had shacked up with Doug and then blackmailed him. Oh David, that just isn't true."

"Now don't get upset! I believe you. And so believe me, a woman could only be considered 'a frigid bitch' because the man hasn't taken time to bring her to the boil!" He laughed, "Don't look so incensed, think of gas and electricity." Puzzled, she stared at him. "A man like the gas quickly heats up and diminishes. A woman slowly heats up and takes time to cool. The trick, or experience, is to get the right balance. 'Making love' is not meant to be an act for man's sexual gratification. And I can assure you within marriage, mutual love and desire brings a depth of oneness and pleasure beyond any casual intimate relationship. You didn't enjoy it… I rest my case. And believe me, succumb to my charms, marry me and you'll know you're not 'frigid'." Rosie used her fan to hide her flushed face. "In your growing freedom to speak your mind, I see a very passionate woman. The only gambler here is Felicity and she's not a good loser. You aren't a gambler or a money grabber, just the opposite. You rented your cottage far below the market price, first to Helen and then to Wilhelm and Grace. Jack has told me you paid for the refurbished kitchen, bathrooms, and the support you give to him, Cathy and Bertie. You can add Helen and Declan to that list."

"They're adopted parents, my brother and friends." Still upset by what she'd heard Rosie continued, "There were times my father would disappear for days. If it hadn't been for Cathy's home-grown fruit and vegetables and abundance of rabbits, Mum, Bertie and I would have starved. The Hawkins scrimped and worked hard to feed us, and now I know my father was gambling away our livelihood."

David's eyes were full of compassion but his voice urged, "Rosie, calm down. People will think it is I upsetting you. Jack told me what it was like. They wanted to protect you from knowing about your father's gambling and debts."

With widened eyes she protested, "They knew and didn't tell me, yet they told you?"

"Shush! Don't be cross. I trained as a lawyer to extract information without actually asking questions." David reached for her hands, his expression rueful, "Let's not talk about this now. Don't let Felicity spoil our evening." He bowed gallantly, drew her right hand to his lips and kissed her fingers before looking along them into her eyes, "If I may speak as I am found, Mr Darcy would say be of good cheer Miss Dawes. I declare, should you take my hand in marriage, it will be my pleasure, and my family's, to look after you and yours."

Rosie didn't doubt his sincerity, but equally had no intention of that influencing her decision about marriage. The best way to counter it was to act in a similar playful fashion. Flicking open her fan she waved it gently, her expression coquettish, "Oh Mr Darcy, how noble and kind is your gesture. And although quite able to look after me and mine, I thank you and will bear your proposal in mind." With that she moved forward to slip her arm through his, "You're right. Felicity shouldn't spoil our evening, and… within reason… you can show her your intentions towards me."

"Does that mean I can kiss you in public?"

"Mr Darcy, I fear that would be far from circumspect."

With a grin David declared, "Damn!" But bent toward her to declare quietly, "I really like this Rosie, so smile…" And with that they entered the ballroom, where he murmured by her ear, "It will be noticed that I can't take my eyes off you."

The next morning as they drove towards Petersfield, she said in a serious voice tempered with amusement, "I hope you realise that in not taking your eyes off me last night, it created the illusion that you were in love with me, and I was a strong contender to be your next bride."

With a raised eyebrow he looked across at her, "Isn't it the case?" As she had clearly and firmly stated 'the case' at breakfast the previous day she didn't reply. After a pause David informed her, "When you were upstairs I spoke to Dad about Felicity's behaviour and accusations."

"I expect he was relieved that I haven't accepted your proposal."

"Don't be ridiculous! Sorry, wrong reaction! I can assure you,

you weren't the subject of his conjecture. He wants me to write to Felicity informing her should any rumours be circulated about you or another incident like last night reported, a civil injunction will be issued against her."

"Dear me, that's rather harsh!"

"Is it? Last night I had a fleetingly opportunity to warn her I wouldn't tolerate her upsetting you. Her response was she was trying to protect me! I was so livid, I'm afraid I hissed, "You! Protect me! I need protection from you." Her reaction was 'Anyone would think you hated me'. I confess I looked down my nose as if she were a nasty smell and cautioned, 'You have given me every reason to do so.' At that I turned on my heel and walked off."

Rosie knew all too well how David had the ability to make a person see the error of their ways, so ludicrously she began to feel sorry for Felicity, "I wish, as Jane did for me, I could introduce her to Jesus. We'll just have to pray someone who lives in her world will do so." David reached over to pat her knee. Warmth rose up within her at his approval. As the car drew up outside the garage at 'The Grange', she considered the scales were tipping in David's favour.

Before they were out of the car Bertie and Declan appeared arm in arm, eager to demonstrate the little cart Jack had helped them create, which had four wheels with a piece of rope attached to a cross plank at the front that steered the wheels. Jack explained, "Bertie and Declan have been practising and I've told them if the twins want to ride in it, they have to stay within the confines of the courtyard and kitchen garden." It was obvious the twins were enthralled at the idea of being pushed down the narrow paths in the kitchen garden. Once installed and calling the paths the 'twain twack', they set off with shrieks of excitement and seeing David and Jack engrossed in discussing the Bentley she headed to the kitchen.

Cathy, closing the oven door, turned as she entered. Her face seemed etched with worry, and her first words were, "Oh Rosie, I'm so glad to see you. Jack says all this talk of the property and estate being sold is just pie in the sky, but those men returned yesterday saying their inspection had brought up questions that needed answers."

Rosie having reassured her that further interest wasn't a guarantee of a sale, reiterated the positive options for their future. Tears filled Cathy's eyes, "It's hard to believe you are your father's daughter, you are constantly using what you have to benefit others."

"I said much the same to Rosie only yesterday" David boomed as he entered the room and strode over to put his arm around Rosie's waist. Rosie quashed her initial reaction to move away and saw the admiration in Cathy's eyes as she took in the tall, well built, grim faced and raven-haired man by her side as he said, "Believe me no one is going to pay the asking price for this place, despite the amount of land involved."

Rosie's brow creased as she turned to look at him, "How do you know what the asking price is?"

"I thought to visit the Estate Agent in town while I was waiting for Jack's windscreen to be fixed. He said he had given up hope of seeing this place sold. Too big for a family home, too small for a hotel, and dubbed as English heritage the house couldn't be pulled down so any purchaser would have to do extensive renovation work. Any offer would have to take into account the cost to make it habitable."

Cathy sighed heavily and folded her arms, "It appears the prospective buyers are doing that." And with an edge of despair added, "Why now? We've just given a home to Helen and Declan! They are helping Bertie extend his horizons, giving him confidence, and now Helen is weaned off her drug habit, we don't want her getting in with the wrong crowd again."

Rosie moved to peel the vegetables, "She wasn't on drugs when I shared the flat with her and Jill. I'm sure she only used them to obliterate the pain of all she had lost." David sitting in the armchair stretched his legs with a distant look in his eyes. Cathy turned on the mixer to whip egg whites for a meringue, and Rosie chopping the carrots decided she must get her cottage valued.

"Dinner will be in half an hour." declared Cathy closing the oven door. David, you're quiet. A penny for your thoughts?"

He chuckled, "I'd like to think they were worth more." Cathy giggled, "Tell us and we'll be the judge of that." Rosie wiped her hands and gave him an expectant look.

"I was thinking of possibilities. You are both hardworking and honest. Cathy you know how to run a household and are a splendid cook, and Jack introduced himself to me as 'a man of all trades'."

Jack entering the room chortled, "I did! But remember I also said 'I was the master of none'."

"But Jack the new owners would need people like you. Would

259

you be interested in staying on?"

Cathy replied, "We have Bertie to consider."

"Maybe they would renovate the cottage and you could live there."

Not wanting to give the Hawkins false hope Rosie argued, "They would be more likely to pull it down. It has only one room up and one down, a rotting conservatory, scullery with only a sink and cold tap, no bathroom and revolting chemical toilet in a shed at the back."

"But remove the nearest trees that make it dark, clear behind it and it could easily be extended in the 'V' in which it stands. It could have much bigger rooms and it is possible to make a useful size garden at the back. With the trees cleared between that and the lake, its possible you could have a view on it from there."

"A good thought, worth more than my penny."

"Cathy, as idyllic as that... " A loud scream cut across Rosie's words, followed by the sound of a child howling. Cathy rushed to the window, David leapt up and Rosie cried, "Rebecca," as she opened the French door and ran across the courtyard. Once through the door into the kitchen garden, she could see Bertie trying to comfort a hysterical Rebecca. White faced Declan was lifting the wooden cart off Joshua laying beneath it. Behind her David boomed, "What happened?" Rosie headed to Rebecca who had landed in the thick strawberry patch, and despite the splattered blood spots across her tear streaked face, she didn't appear hurt.

David on his knees beside Joshua was asking if he could hear him. Cathy panting from the exertion arrived to demand, "Let me see?" After a quick examination she proclaimed, "He's more shocked that injured." And as if to prove that Joshua began screaming. Cathy indicated to David to pick him up but warned, "If he keeps falling asleep or is sick, get him looked at."

Upset, Bertie's explanation sounded gibberish as they returned to the house. Rosie seeing Rebecca rubbing her face and licking her fingers realised she wasn't bleeding but spotted by juice from squashed strawberries! Joshua however had sustained what Cathy called 'strawberry' grazes to his arm and leg, due to being dragged by the go-cart along the gravel path. Chocolate buttons eased the trauma, wounds were cleaned and plastered and Joshua's crying became a tearful sniff. Not long after Cathy declared it was dinner time. It was obvious Joshua's injuries hadn't impaired his appetite, but Declan's empty chair gave reason to believe it had his. Worried he might run away Jack went to find him. When he reappeared with Declan, he twisted his shirt in agitation as if fearful of reprisal.

David pushed back his chair declaring, "Declan don't be upset, accidents happen" but he cowered behind Jack as David approached. They watched when smiling reassuringly David crouched several feet away, opened is arms and coaxed, "You aren't in trouble, I'm not going to hurt you. You've had a nasty shock. You need a hug." Declan looked up at Jack, saw his nod and tentatively moved forward. David waited until he was in the circle of his arms before gently hugging him. At that the little lad began to sob as if his heart would break, bringing David to draw him closer. And with an expression of sadness and consternation, he lifted him and took him to sit with him in the chair by the fire.

Bertie, upset for his friend, wanted to go to him but Cathy held him back. Taking Declan and David's plates she put them in the oven, and as Declan wept they ate their meal in silence. Gradually Declan quietened and lifted up his arm to rub his wet eyes and snotty nose. Before he could do so David had flicked out his handkerchief and given it to him. "Here use this. You can keep it." The surprise and delight on Declan's face was such that David could have given him the crown jewels. And having used it, he let David lead him to the table where he shovelled his dinner into his mouth as if expecting at any minute it would be taken from him. The adults at the table looked at each other and Rosie realised what she had suffered at the hands of her father was nothing compared to this young boy's experience.

It was just gone two o'clock before Rosie, Bertie, Declan and Cathy left for the hospital. In the car Cathy confessed, "I thought it best to wait to tell you that yesterday I popped in to see Johnny."

"You did! How is he? Can he speak? Sit up? Did he ask after me? Oh, I can barely wait to see him."

"It's amazing Rosie! Two days after opening his eyes he can do most things."

"Oh, thank you Lord for answering my prayers!" She ignored Cathy raising her eyebrows to ask, "What did he say?"

"I only had a minute because the nurse said he needed rest. He nodded when I asked if he remembered me, but not the accident. I told him you'd been visiting each week. He smiled and pointed to the tape recorder." Cathy paused, "But although understanding all I said, I'm afraid he is unable to speak."

"Oh, no!" Rosie wailed.

"I also saw the Brigadier. He said Johnny has been diagnosed with a temporal lobe problem which can happen after a hard bang on the head. Apparently, that's the part of the brain that affects speech, memory and understanding."

Worried she asked, "But he will get better, won't he? Speaking, preaching, is his job."

"The Brigadier said the prognosis is good and they believe that with speech therapy he will be fully restored, but it may take time. The nurse who ushered me out said it was thought the music on the tapes had played a major part in stimulating his brain back to consciousness."

"Oh, that's wonderful. I can't wait to see him."

Cathy lowered her voice not wanting Bertie and Declan to hear. "Is David happy about your need to visit Johnny?"

"He understands Johnny is an old school friend, and I'm concerned about him."

"To me it's obvious you are very fond of Johnny."

Rosie waited until they were in the car park, and Bertie and Declan were heading off together before saying, "David is offering me so much more than Johnny could, but what of love? To give David his due he's trying not to run my life or control my actions, but I often feel he is. I'm not employed, so feel I should speak my mind, but it can be a battle of wills. For example ,I see the twins as individuals and within reason I let them choose what to wear, but even that has led to tension. David wants to make it work and his parents are keen we should marry". They entered the hospital, "Last night David's ex-fiancé Felicity was at the Ball and she accosted me and said some spiteful things. David insisted he should show his interest in me, and I confess I enjoyed acting out our fairy tale of love."

"Oh Rosie, perhaps if you did that more often you'd find it to be the truth."

"David mentioned Felicity had told you about your father's gambling. Our idea was to shield you and Bertie from the little we knew about your father's antics. Bad enough you seeing your mother's anxieties and depression develop."

They arrived at Johnny's room where eyes closed he was resting against a mound of pillows. Now the bandage was off, the deep gash was obvious across the top of his forehead, and looked worse by the area above it being shaved. He had lost weight and his face had thinned bringing him to look more like the gaunt, wiry boy she had known. Each time she saw him, something akin to love stirred within her. Cathy said quietly, "I can see how special he is to you. Go on, I'll visit Helen."

As Rosie entered the room Johnny's eyes opened, but she was unprepared to see the pleasure that brightened those eyes and the warmth of the welcoming smile that greeted her. Her heart thudded in the way it had each morning they had met at school, and it was hard not to be that child again and run to hug him.

He lifted his hand and as she sat beside the bed, she took it in hers. Feeling emotional, tears filled her eyes. He squeezed her hand and tried to speak, but nothing intelligible came forth. "It's okay, I'll do the talking." To that he grinned, pointed to her and made a talking sign with his hand! Rosie laughed knowing in their childhood friendship she had done most of the talking. The words were obviously in his head. He tried to communicate with signs, she spoke out her interpretations, and he used his thumb to indicate up for 'yes' and down for 'no'. "Cathy says it's early days, your speech will come back. Bertie has that problem, he uses a typewriter for his questions, You could write yours down."

Johnny touched the back of his ear, pointed at her and then moved his hand to indicate talking. "Are you saying you heard me on my previous visits?" He gave a wiggled thumb's up. "If so Reverend Hall, you've heard the confessions of a very mixed up woman!" His smile was warm and his eyes twinkled, an expression she had always found enchanting. He crossed his hands over his heart and pointed to her which she interpreted saying, "You always accepted me". His thumb pointed down. He made the gesture again, she laughed, "Oh alright, you've always loved me, and I you. I should feel embarrassed that I told you my deepest secrets but at an early age, I knew I could trust you." In trying to communicate frustration filled his eyes. "Think of it as playing charades. For years Bertie and I have had our own private sign language." She giggled, "We could talk without the adults understanding. Bertie would tap his nose to indicate it was our secret."

Johnny fervently tapped his nose. "Whatever you heard I knew you would keep it a secret." His thumb went up, he crossed his hands over his chest and then picked up her left hand and pointed to the third finger. To which she answered, "Love and marriage haven't been something that I have considered but the day before I met you, David asked me to marry him." In seeing Johnny's eyes sadden she rushed on, "Do you remember David? He arrived at the accident. He does tend to take over but does have a gentler side. I had just agreed to a six-month courtship so in fairness I need to keep my word." Johnny gave a sad nod and she explained, "Jane, David's first wife, died just after having twins. She introduced me to Jesus saying it wasn't a religion and Jesus wanted to be my friend. I just had to ask Him in, He would forgive my sins and start me on a new life. As I had so thoroughly mucked mine up, I thought to give Him a try and can scarcely believe what has happened since." Seeing he was drifting into sleep she added, "And what about you being the Brigadier's son?" He grinned at her, "You need to rest, we'll talk again." She stood to leave when his hand, unexpectedly strong, caught her wrist. His eyes questioned, almost pleaded with her. Intuitively she said, "I'll try and come next weekend." With a wide-eyed expression he pulled her toward him, she kissed his cheek and said, "Dear Johnny, you'll always have a special place in my heart. Work hard at the speech therapy and then you can tell me how you came to be a curate." By the time she reached the door he was asleep.

CHAPTER 18

True to her word, she was there the following Saturday, but it had been a difficult week which she considered while travelling on the train to Petersfield.

Rebecca in cutting a tooth had been grumpy. David was equally on edge, probably due to lack of sleep. Tuesday evening she had helped with the twins bathing, cleared up as David read the story and when he hadn't called her to say 'goodnight' to the twins, she found they were all asleep on his bed. Carefully she extracted Joshua and then Rebecca. Neither awoke as she put them in their cots. Taking an eiderdown from one of the single beds in their room, she gently placed it over David who didn't stir. To see him asleep on his bed felt strange, but it brought her to realise that he too was a vulnerable human being with a need to be loved. Yet all she felt for him was compassion.

Mrs Smith was cleaning David's flat when she returned from visiting Joyce on Wednesday. Uneasy she had asked bluntly, "What are you doing up here? Where's Mrs P?"

Before answering Mrs Smith looked her up and down, "Mrs P weren't able to come today." Before Rosie could question further, she added with an underlying sneer in expression and voice, "Yer never know who, or what, might turn up! And, 'ere you are, acting like a 'igh class dame. I'd bet 'e, 'the master' as Mrs P calls 'im, don't know nuffing about the nasty mess I was left to clean up."

Not liking her attitude or wishing to discuss Jill's inability to keep her flat clean and tidy or Rachel's vomiting ability, she had intended to walk away. But Mrs Smith went on, "The extra pay came in 'andy, very 'andy indeed." With a wide-eyed 'knowing' look she had stared at her before remarking, "Extra cash will keep me from saying nowt to no-one." Rosie frowned for she'd not asked her to clean. It was then Mrs Smith pointed to the family photo of David, Jane and the twins on the sideboard, "That's 'im then, the one Mrs P calls the Master?" At her nod, Mrs Smith remarked, "'e's a 'andsome devil, ain't 'e, in a rugged sort of way." As she turned to walk away Mrs Smith had given a wily chuckle before remarking, "Dead wives are always best, they can't turn up unexpectedly." Taken aback at such a coincidental cruel jibe, Rosie swung around and caught the sly grin on Mrs Smith's face before nodding at the twins in their play pen, "Clever! Look after 'is kids, get 'im to marry you, gives you 'is money and a bonus of a ready-made family. Yer not want to spoil that by being stingy."

The twins squabbling over a toy rabbit took her attention. Mrs Smith said to her, "I'll collect me money next week" and when she turned the woman had left.

Disturbed, she relayed the strange conversation to David over their meal. Preoccupied again with urgent work to complete, he acknowledged it sounded odd, brushed off anything being personal, and said she'd done them a favour but expected to be paid. Conversation was then rather stilted and she'd left early. The following evening she asked about his expansion plans for IT. His reply was so succinct she didn't enquire further and when David didn't protest when told she was going home, she was irritated by his still treating her as the twins' nanny.

On Friday night they had agreed to baby sit for Paul and Jill, but any thought of a relaxed evening was thwarted by Rachel's screaming and refusing to drink Jill's milk from a bottle. Fretful cries heard through the basement speakers caused David to go up and down several times to settled the twins. They were both exhausted when Rachel finally slept and the twins were settled. Their evening had consisted of snippets of conversation which included David apologising for being preoccupied during the week and his lack of sleep. His father considering a business venture to combine with semi-retirement - which he didn't elaborate on - and his parents worry about Jill. How they were arriving tomorrow to stay for the weekend, his mother hoping to discover what ailed her. They suggested they should all have a day out.

She agreed it would be a good idea for him and his family, adding it would give her an opportunity to have a quiet weekend with her family and visit Johnny.

Taken aback David declared, "Now he's conscious and recovering I thought you would be staying here. Will you be wanting to do that every weekend?"

At his querulous tone she had responded, "David, I've not accepted the role of mother or wife. My life has barely changed from being the twins' nanny... except I don't get any days off." Paul and Jill returning cut short further discussion but she had the last word. "Courtship is meant to be a time to get to know one another but it is rather difficult when we are constantly distracted by others." He had stared at her as if trying to fathom out her thinking.

And as the train clattered over the tracks, Rosie considered how after a month she had gauged that the role of wife and mother was over-rated, and felt pity for Jill thrust in at the deep end with no means of escape.

Cathy was waiting to greet her at the station. Walking towards the car she asked in her usual direct manner, "So David isn't coming and you're staying overnight. What's happening?"

To that she snapped, "He's got a lot on his mind and it's not me!"

Cathy glanced in her direction, "Perhaps he's concerned about your need to visit Johnny when you are supposed to be courting him."

Rosie made a face, "Believe me, there has not been any courting going on. His parents are coming this weekend and he expected me to be there. David seems easily preoccupied and I see little benefit in being a wife. I'm an acting mother but beyond loving the twins I don't see any perks in that. Even a nanny gets days off. I enjoy Johnny's friendship. He can't speak but he makes light of it. We can laugh and I've time and freedom to be me."

"Does David know how you feel?"

Rosie shrugged, "If he does and cares, he would surely try harder to woo me!"

"Aren't you being a bit hard on the man? The twins awake him in the night and he has to rise early to give them breakfast. He does a day's work and has family and business responsibilities that concern him. This isn't a 'normal' romance with the first flurries of love, enjoying life without any ties and a gradual build up toward marriage, but that surely doesn't make it untenable. If you desire to make and see the best in David, you will find encouragement, satisfaction and fulfilment, which will turn into a much deeper caring and rooted relationship."

Crossly Rosie retorted, "Oh, and since when have you become such a wise old owl?"

Cathy laughed, "Not sure! Perhaps listening to and watching others! And that brings me to ask if you've considered that Johnny the man may be very different to the boy you once knew. From things I've heard, a vicar's wife can feel that the parishioners' needs are greater than hers, especially when her man has to instantly respond when called out to minister to the sick and needy. A knock at the door means one of his flock expects his immediate attention."

"Okay Cathy, you've made your point. You believe David loves me, I believe he just needs me. I know Johnny loves me, and I him. Doesn't that make the difference?"

"As a child, a friend yes, but adult relationships are far more complex."

"All I know is I don't want to end up like Doug and his wife in a loveless and unhappy marriage."

Sharply Cathy informed her, "David's not a man to have affairs."

"True, but also I'm not Jane. I expected companionship, friendship and our faith to bind us together, but again this week he has barely talked to me."

Cathy looked thoughtful and observed, "When here he is communicative and engaged with all that is going on. Did Jane ever feel ignored?"

Rosie grimaced, "She did and got cross about it. Described him as having an overly tidy mind, his life filed into different boxes, but she would giggle saying she knew how to mess with that!"

Although Cathy was driving, she grinned across at her. Knowing Cathy thought David was deep, dark, sexy and attractive she stated, "Don't go there. I'm certainly not drawn to him in the way Jane was."

After a thoughtful hum Cathy added, "It's early days." Rosie let out a loud humph! A minute later Cathy asked, "Would you say you were drawn to Johnny in that way?"

"Honestly Cathy, what sort of question is that?"

"A viable one! You almost skipped into school because he made you happy, but as an adult do you feel a sexual attraction to him."

Rosie stated, "Love shouldn't be based on sexual feelings and as you said about David, 'it's early days'."

Cathy sent her a wry smile, "Imagine your father's reaction if you should marry Johnny! He slammed the door in his face when he wanted to see you. Mind you, he did the same to the Brigadier for trying to help Bertie."

"My father's judgement will not affect mine."

"Good! Which reminds me the Brigadier has invited Bertie to join in Johnny's speech therapy. Their problems are different but the Brigadier thought Bertie would - if nothing else - enjoy trying the exercises."

"How kind! Like father, like son."

Cathy smiled, "Bertie joined in yesterday, was excited, enthralled and tried some of them on Helen, and went back to see

Johnny while I collected Declan from school. When I returned, he and Johnny tapped their noses with their forefingers. They grinned at each other, just as you and Bertie used to do." Bringing the car to a halt outside the garage, Cathy declared, "In these last few weeks I've felt I'm doing something useful with my life."

Rosie contested, "Your whole life has been doing something useful."

"I mean beyond the day to day. I cared for you and Bertie, but with Helen and Declan here I've gained a new purpose."

Jack appeared, bringing Rosie to leap out of the car to greet 'the best man in all the world' with a hug and a kiss.

It wasn't until after they had eaten lunch that she said, "I've been thinking about David's idea of renovating and extending the gatekeeper's cottage. I thought to ask my father to either give or sell it cheaply with the view to you and Bertie living in it."

Jack snorted! "Your father sees no responsibility toward us or Bertie. David said loyalty works both ways, and we need to be looking out for our interests, not his."

Cathy raised her eyebrows at Jack before asking, "Do you still write to your mother?"

"Occasionally. I told her of Jane's death, her leaving twin babies and how I enjoyed helping to look after them. Mum replied months later saying my father said Jane's death was surely a God send, and I should consider stepping into her shoes. Cathy gasped. "I was so incensed, I wrote back immediately saying from what I had witnessed of their marriage it seemed wiser to forego that institution!"

Shocked Cathy exclaimed, "Oh Rosie you didn't?" Jack chuckled.

"I did and not heard from them since. And after a month of being a pseudo mother and wife I see no benefit in marriage." Jack and Cathy exchanged a look. With relish she added, "Although I was considering writing to my parents - not to encourage their thoughts about David - but how their friend Freddy Greenhaigh has a 'love child', who turns out to be my old school friend Johnny. A friendship they discouraged and I am now restoring."

Although shaking her head, Cathy was smiling as she stood to clear their plates but Jack cautioned, "I would leave that news until after you've broached the subject of buying the gatehouse. But whatever happens, I feel this offer for the Grange is a catalyst for change. I suggest you ask the Estate Agent to value that triangular piece of land and derelict cottage!"

"I did that for my cottage and believe it will be more than enough to restore, enlarge the cottage, and secure a future for Bertie to enjoy the land that rightfully should be his."

Bertie, his head on one side, awkwardly crossed his arms on his chest, and pointed to Jack and Cathy. Cathy smiled, "Yes, Bertie, we love you too, we see you as the son we never had."

Jack agreed, "Spot on Cathy. You've a life ahead of you Bertie, and we will stay with you as long as you need us." Rosie noticed Declan head bowed, tracing the pattern on the cloth with his finger. She nodded to Jack who immediately confirmed, "Declan, we're here for you too." Declan's head jerked up, he stared at Jack in disbelief. "Come here son, and have a hug."

When Declan emerged from Jack's embrace, his emotion had given him a runny nose, his instinct was to rub his face on his jumper, then he remembered his handkerchief embroidered with a 'D' and proudly took it from his pocket.

At the hospital Bertie, keen to communicate with Johnny, insisted on accompanying her for the half hour she had been allotted to visit on both Saturday and Sunday. They taught Johnny their sign language bringing laughter into his eyes, and she saw if married to Johnny he would be happy for Bertie to live with them.

On Sunday she told Johnny about buying the gatehouse. He looked puzzled and wrote 'money?' on the notepad she bought him. When she answered she would sell her London cottage, he seemed even more puzzled, bringing her to realise he hadn't heard all of her past confessions! Suggesting to Bertie to go, buy and deliver to Helen her favourite sweets from the WVS shop, she was able to speak freely.

His hand reached out and took hers. Sadness and sympathy filled his eyes. He nodded as if remembering some of it, as she explained why she was given the cottage. Johnny's mind wasn't impaired, for at the end his eyes widened and, despite his lips always having a permanent smile, she suddenly feared his contempt at her accepting it. She finished, "Cathy and Jack felt I should. Doug's career was taking him to greater heights, while mine was in ruins. They thought it was a small price to pay for him to pay for the physical and mental agony I had suffered. It was a place to live and would help me to start a new life." Johnny patted her hand. "Months later, the Brigadier, your father" she grinned, "helped me get a job in London. I lived in the mews cottage for three years but the last four I rented it out as Jane,

270

David's wife, wanted me to share the basement flat in their house with his sister Jill. Selling it now will provide for those I love."

Johnny smiled broadly and held up his thumb. "The Brigadier has been good to me and instrumental in both our lives."

From the doorway a deep voice said jovially, "Bless you my dear." Rosie's face heated with embarrassment. How long had the Brigadier been standing there?

Shyly she smiled up at him as he took the chair opposite her, "It's true you have given us both a hope and a future. Johnny is only a few weeks older than me, but at school he listened and cared about me. God had him in training at an early age to be a priest. For reassurance she looked at Johnny, he squeezed her hand and they smiled happily at each other.

The kind of jovial comment she associated with the Brigadier wasn't forthcoming. When she looked at him, he appeared thoughtful, and then as if realising he needed to respond he boomed, "True, true, my dear! And by the number of 'get well' cards he has received in these past weeks, it appears many appreciate his compassion and ability to bring comfort. I confess to be surprised at seeing you here now Johnny is recovering. It's good of David to bring you each weekend."

"Oh he's busy with his family this weekend, so I came to be with mine."

"I understand your need to visit Johnny, but rest assured the accident wasn't your fault, nor do we blame you for his arriving unaccompanied. The use of your tape recorder and music was inspirational and believed to have drawn him out of his coma."

"That's kind of you to say. I expect talking of childhood memories helped."

"True, true. But a childhood love should never be mistaken for an adult one." Feeling awkward she glanced at Johnny who was giving his father a hard stare as he continued, "The moment Jennifer and I set eyes on David, we knew he was the man God had chosen for you. He has the ability to restore all that life stole from you."

The Brigadier's observations made her feel uncomfortable and she slipped her hand from Johnny's. Was he deliberately diverting them from any romantic illusion? She glanced at her watch and was truthfully able to declare, "Oh dear, I hadn't realised the time. Bertie and Declan will be waiting for me in the car park."

Johnny responded with unintelligible words. Rosie sent him a small rueful smile, but his eyes seemed to lock on hers in what appeared loving desperation. About to assure him she would be back next week the Brigadier stepped in to interpret, "I think Johnny wants to express his thanks, coming all this way each weekend to see him. Physically he is recovering and we're expecting him home by next weekend. The speech therapist is going to visit and Bertie is welcome to join us. It will encourage Johnny's progress."

Unsure how to respond, she thanked the Brigadier for his kindness to Bertie, and wanting to convey her affection for Johnny she bent and kissed his cheek. His hand grabbed hers, his eyes seemed to plead with her as she slowly backed from the bed. To reassure him she stated, "I'll be down again in a couple of weeks. I'm making a dress for Diana as she told me the skirt I made sold quickly. I'll see you there. When you feel able, Cathy suggested you might like to visit the Grange."

Johnny's eyes held hers, his hand didn't let go until both their arms were at full stretch. The Brigadier watched them, before jumping up to head with her towards the door. In his usual jovial tone he said, "Please thank Cathy, Johnny will probably enjoy a change of scenery. It will be good for him to meet David and the twins. Johnny loves children and has always said when he marries he wants at least half a dozen!"

Rosie turned quickly to look at Johnny who was frowning and moving his head from side to side to indicate she should ignore that remark, but it was like a knife opening up an old wound. She pasted on her enigmatic smile, blew Johnny a kiss, and before her happiness completely deflated, she hurried away.

Bertie was letting Declan play 'hide and seek' around the cars causing her to snap, "Bertie that's dangerous, you should know better. Get in the car, both of you!" And saw the grimace that passed between them.

Declan piped up, "Helen's hoping to be out of hospital this week."

"Is she? So is Johnny. You and Bertie can help look after her." And she thought - somewhat unkindly - Declan would be a distraction to any romantic inclinations Bertie and Helen might have. Back at the Grange, being told by Cathy that David had rung, she was still feeling disgruntled enough to demand, "What did he want?"

Cathy frowned, "To know which train you would be on so he could meet you. He thought to save you the trek across London."

At Rosie's derisive grunt she observed, "He misses you."

"Misses me looking after the twins, I dare say!"

"Oh dear, you are in a strop! What brought that on? I thought you would be pleased David was thinking about you."

"Brigadier Greenhaigh upset me." At Cathy's questioning look she continued, "He said Johnny might be home next weekend and will stay with them. When I spoke about Johnny visiting us, he made it clear he felt David was the man for me and added, Johnny loves children and wants six of his own!'"

Cathy observed, "Surely you're being over sensitive."

"Am I? There were other asides, and I had the distinct impression I was being thanked and dismissed. Not by Johnny, he looked upset and appeared to negate his wanting six children." Cathy hummed thoughtfully as Rosie stated, "Bertie though is invited to Johnny's speech therapy sessions."

"Yes, he's excited about that! He really likes Johnny." Rosie bit back the response of 'so do I' as Cathy was saying, "Just as he will be when he hears that David and the rest of his family are coming on Bank Holiday Monday…"

Rosie's voice raised a decibel, "They are doing what? I know nothing about this? The rest of his family! Who does he mean? Jill has been pushing to come, keen to see the rundown mansion…"

Cathy interrupted, "If you'll let me speak!" Rosie glared at her. "Apparently, his parents are going to stay with him on the Bank Holiday weekend, and he thought on the Monday it would be good to meet up with Paula's family here and have a picnic."

"Good grief Cathy, that really is too much!"

"No, it's fine. We'll enjoy it. David said I didn't have to do any catering, they would bring the food with them."

"I don't care! It's… too soon. I'm not ready to merge the families. I can't believe he even suggested it without consulting me. That makes me so mad!"

"Rosie he was just asking my opinion."

And then seeing Cathy's disappointment she added, "I'll see how I feel about doing that on the August Bank Holiday. Maybe by then David will have learnt to ask me, before suggesting and deciding things without me. I had enough of that with my father! I still can't believe you kept it from me that my father had gambled my mother's money away in India, and coming here continued to do that with Mum's late uncle's estate."

"Would it have made you think better of him?" Rosie shook

273

her head. "Then best not said." Cathy shrugged, went to fill the kettle and leaving it to boil said, "When your father didn't arrive or write from India, we thought he had abandoned Dee-Dee. Then one day he turned up without warning. It wasn't long before we saw he was a charmer on the outside and a manipulator full of spite on the inside. We felt sorry for you and your mother. It's at her request that we stayed. We loved you, and later Bertie. Our aim was to make a better life for you both. And I see your father as a sad man who doesn't know how to love or be loved. And your Mum was almost demented when you were blamed for Bertie's deformities and sent away. Leo, or His Lordship to his face, dismissed her upsets by calling them 'ravings' and if we hadn't been here, I reckon he would have had her committed to an asylum."

"I wondered about that in the same way I concluded years ago that boarding school had been arranged weeks if not months before."

Cathy looked sad, "He only told me the week before and I didn't expect it so soon. It's not unusual for English children in India to be sent to boarding school at eight, but the way it was done and the timing, that was cruel."

"Did you know about the Lord Dawes' Educational Trust? Mrs Whelan at School mentioned I'd been funded by it. I recently looked into Trust Funds and found his was set up for the sole purpose of education and the expenses incurred. I suspect my father siphoned off the expenses claiming for new uniforms, hockey sticks etc, when I only received second hand goods." Cathy's wide-eyed look said it all. "The positive side was that I was away from him and had the benefit of an excellent education in expensive and exclusive schools. I wonder if he found a way to siphon off the money for the non-existent son's non-education?"

"David could probably find out, he seems very resourceful. He told me he trained as a barrister. He used that skill to find you."

Flinging her arms around Cathy's small dumpy figure she said, "Oh Cathy I so love you and Jack, what would I have done without you both? I'm going to make it up to you, I promise!"

A big grin appeared on Cathy's face, "Now, now Rosie, there's no need, life hasn't been that bad. We've had a roof over our heads, food in our mouths, and the pleasure of seeing you and Bertie grow up." The telephone rang. "That'll be David."

The negativity in which she had been talking reflected in her voice as she answered the phone. "Oh Rosie, I wish I could have been with you. We've all missed you." Unkindly she thought 'looking after the twins' but instead she gave a non-committal hum. "When I spoke to Cathy earlier I sounded her out about the family coming down on Bank Holiday Monday."

"Yes, she told me."

"It's up to you, it's your home, I've not mentioned it to the family."

"Then that's something to be thankful for."

There was a pause as David took that in and then verified, "Cathy seemed keen on the idea."

"She is but I'm not."

"Oh Rosie, you are cross with me, I'm sorry. Dad and I had useful discussions and Jill talked to Mum so it's been a useful weekend. Paul and Jill have offered to listen out for the twins tonight, so I thought to collect you…"

"Oh, don't put them out on my account. I'm quite able to use the underground. I've done it for years."

"That maybe so Rosie, but it's important we talk and review this first month of our courtship." She heard the tightness in his voice and guessed he was determined not to become ruffled. Cathy's advice to be kind came to mind as he confessed, "You may not have had my undivided attention last week but I did hear you, and in sharing your worry about Mrs Smith, I visited Mrs P."

Surprised she queried, "Really?" and then remembered David saw her as a treasure.

David's voice warmed as he spoke of Mrs P being pleased to see him, "Apparently Mrs Smith called for her on Wednesday, but finding her not feeling well, she offered to tell us and do her work."

Still irritated she snapped, "Really! Well I felt it was an excuse to spy on us, and she made me feel very uncomfortable with her weird conversation and asking extra money in cash."

"I'd like to talk further to you about that. If I collect you from the station we can either go for a drink or to your cottage now Wilhelm and Grace have left."

"What's there to talk about? I find her rude. I don't like her. And if I had any say I wouldn't want her around."

David's tone hardened, "Is that so? Mrs P made a few comments that I need to clarify with you before Mrs Smith comes on Wednesday. And as it is Joyce's turn to visit us, you will be home when she comes."

Feelings of guilt arose in her. What had Mrs Smith said to

Mrs P? Stirred by mixed emotions she protested, "Can't we talk tomorrow evening? The train won't get into Waterloo much before 9.00 pm."

"Rosie, I recognise I've upset you and am sorry. I thought you would be pleased to talk away from distractions." David's conciliatory tone continued, "Cathy says Johnny is recovering, so that's good news and less for you to worry about."

Aggravated by his assumption she snapped, "Is that what you think? How can I not be worried for my friend who can't speak? Communication in his job is paramount. His recovery will take weeks if not months before he can preach, teach or pastor again the people in the church."

"But Rosie you weren't responsible for his accident, nor are you for his recovery."

"Have you been talking to the Brigadier?"

As if not wanting further argument he added, "Rosie, I'll collect you from the train. We'll talk later."

The line going dead ruffled her, but then she had been very negative and certainly not communicative.

CHAPTER 19

Three hours later as she alighted from the train, Rosie groaned. David was at the ticket barrier with a large bouquet of flowers that was drawing attention from the ticket collector and the alighting passengers. Behind her a woman's voice commented, "Who is the lucky woman who has that dark, rugged and sexy man waiting for her?" Rosie moved between several people so David wouldn't see her. The owner of the voice passed her by while saying to her friend, "Let's give him a smile, hang about and if she doesn't turn up maybe one of us will be in with a chance."

Rosie knew Jane would have enjoyed the occasion, but she slowed her pace and hid behind people in the hope of being last and having as few witnesses as possible. But David had spotted her and her name was boomed down the platform, and the ticket collector was letting him through! People turned wanting to know who was Rosie. Highly embarrassed she pasted on her enigmatic smile as he approached. The annoyance in her voice was lost on David as she received the over large bouquet, saying, "David you shouldn't have" before he kissed her in what she considered longer than necessary. An elderly voice remarked 'how romantic'. David's arm snaked possessively around her waist as he led her to the car, but that didn't stop him sending a broad smile to the two young women, ogling them. Although peeved by the attention he had drawn, she wondered if she should be grateful - if not proud - to be seen as his girlfriend.

As the car pulled out of the station yard David suggested, "I would prefer to go to the cottage than a pub or hotel." As if he sensed her hesitation he teased, "Of course if you've left the place in a terrible mess..."

She pursed her lips and countered, "The only thing on offer is coffee and cake."

"That's more than I expected!" He sent her a wide smile as a sudden squall of rain hit the windscreen. The car lights in front blurred. She cringed and held tightly to the safety belt. David glanced toward her and reassured her by patting her knee. The windscreen wipers restored her view bringing with it an unexpected urge to share her thoughts with David, "This may sound silly, but like the heavy rain I feel under a continual barrage of emotions. I need Jesus like the wipers to clear my vision so I can move forward without fear of doing the wrong thing."

"That's not silly. When at Easter you left us, I felt called by my continuing dream to invade your territory. And since I did that your privacy has been bombarded by events, past and present."

Without thought she said fervently, "Tell me about it!" David raised an eyebrow in her direction and accelerated away from the lights, "Rosie, we are all on a journey, if we view it as an adventure it's up to us whether we endure or enjoy it. If we believe the Lord loves us, does everything for our good and has plans and purposes for our lives, we can find peace and rest."

To that she blurted out, "I've decided to sell my cottage."

David's 'Why?' was directed at the windscreen.

"I'm going to ask my father to sell me the gatekeeper's cottage and the land behind so Bertie can then remain living on the land that by right is his."

"I'm not sure that's the best…"

Interrupting, she retorted, "You suggested it."

"Buying the gatehouse yes, but I suspect if the estate is purchased, you'll get a better deal from the buyers than your father. My advice would be to keep him out of it. You could ask the estate agent dealing with the sale to contact the buyers with your proposition. I would suggest asking for the acre or so of land behind it that goes down to the lake. It will give room for expansion, and Cathy could have a good size kitchen garden." David sent her a brief and sad but wise grimace. They drove on in silence as she considered that, and within a short time were drawing up outside the two-storey converted stable in a pretty cobbled mews.

Once inside David reiterated his comment from his last visit, "This is such a cosy place. Although the kitchen extension with bathroom above takes up half the back yard, it's still a sun trap. This has been an ideal base in London for Wilhelm and Grace. If they knew you wanted to sell they would have bought it."

Rosie carrying the flowers into the kitchen turned to agree, "I know! I wish I had thought of it. I spoke to an estate agent in Kensington High Street last week. He's eager to see it, saying from the location and description - and if the conversion has been done to a good standard - it could fetch enough money to purchase a new four bedroom house outside of London."

"That's true." David followed her into the narrow but functional kitchen and rested his back against the curved archway, "But I'm not sure of the wisdom of selling it right now. London housing prices are set to rise far beyond anywhere else in the country. And no offer has been made for The Grange." He looked thoughtful and took himself off to settle in the armchair by the fireplace. The kettle on, she delved into the cupboard for the tin containing the Victoria sponge she had made the previous week. Missing the constant companionship of sharing the flat with Jill, Paul and their children, she found she was replacing the sound of voices with a need for comfort food.

David stretched out his legs as she put the tray on the coffee table and smiled broadly, "What more could a man ask for? A beautiful woman who shares his faith, loves his children and is a very good cook." Flattery brought reminders of Doug but she didn't respond, instead went to find a large vase, arranged the flowers and placed them in the empty fireplace. As she moved to pour the tea David asked, "Rosie, should I be encouraged that in deciding to sell the only home you have, you intend to marry me?" David munched on a mouthful of sponge with a hum of enjoyment.

Immediately she spun around to contradict his conclusion, "Not at all. If, and when needed, I would have a home with the Hawkins. They have been beholden to my father long enough and would leave if they had somewhere else to live."

David having finished his mouthful queried, "But if you haven't this place to live in, decide not to marry me, and having bought the gatekeeper's cottage, or a four bedroom house in the suburbs, how could you look after the twins?"

"Just now I'm more anxious to give the Hawkins the comfort of knowing they can have their own home. But provided you still would be willing when Jill and Paul leave, I could move back into your basement flat, and share the rent with two others."

"And Johnny... from my understanding he too is a contender for your hand?"

"To be honest David, like the rain and the wipers, one moment I seem on one road, the rain comes down, and I find myself on another. I keep asking which way is the diversion and which way is my destiny?"

There was silence as they ate, drank and inwardly considered the options.

Putting his cup back on the tray David asked, "What would you say to my buying this place from you at the market price?"

Now it was Rosie's turn to query, "Why?"

"Well first it would be a good investment. Second, however the future pans out I could rent it out to you at an affordable rent. That way you would still have a home you could call your own. When you were living in my basement, you gave so much of yourself to us you morphed into being 'family'. At the time you didn't feel 'used', but that expression has come up several times lately." He put up his hand seeing her about to protest, "I know you expected more from me and I apologise for my tardiness, but believe me I do have your interests at heart." David cautioned, "Living in the basement and being easily accessible to the twins would make you susceptible to feeling 'used'. Not only could your privacy be invaded, but your flatmates are unlikely to want them around. Let's say you decide to marry Johnny and you continue to look after the twins. If he finds a parish in London, I'm sure he would prefer to live here than in the basement of my house."

"You would still want me around even if I were to marry Johnny?"

"Why not?" David shrugged, "I've already said if you only want to be a nanny or favourite aunt to the twins then so be it. My consideration is for the twins in the same way you desire the best for the Hawkins.

"David, that's 'big hearted' of you."

With a small smile he acknowledged, "I'd say the same about you." David's eyes surveyed the room before he observed, "And I also endeavour to be wise. Mews cottages like this, in years to come, are going to be highly sought after." He chuckled, "Call it my pension fund!"

With a wry expression she remarked, "Not something you'll ever need to consider." After a pause she admitted, "Johnny's communication is limited, but there is a bond between us. He has indicated he loves me." She paused to see if David declared he loved her, when he didn't she said, "It's as you described. I've let my drawbridge down and the unexpected has crossed it. I don't know if 'young love' with Johnny will develop in adulthood, but as with you it's a 'getting to know' process."

David gave a derogatory grunt and running his hands through his hair concluded, "So it is possible Rosie that you may choose a penniless vicar over me. The Greenhaighs think highly of you and I'm sure would support and love you for that."

"That's odd." Finishing off his cake, David questioned her with his eyes. "Only this afternoon the Brigadier was extolling your virtues to Johnny and how marrying you I would have a ready-made family."

David's brow creased as he responded, "Is that so?" "My family also hope you will accept my offer of a home, money, and having seen you blossom in the twins' love a desire to see you fully fulfilled in motherhood. But should you choose Johnny, I would not keep the twins from you."

If his 'offer' had included a declaration of love and companionship it would have endeared her to him. He liked a challenge so with a rival for her affections she had hoped he might try harder to win her heart.

David stood to say tiredly, "If you can stay on tomorrow evening we'll talk then." Taken aback by what appeared a defeatist attitude, empathy and irritation vied within her, "David, you knew crossing the drawbridge into my life would bring hurdles." She stood to challenge, "Are you going to fall at the first one?" His hand on the door latch stilled. He turned, but unable to detect his reaction from the set of his harsh features, she needled him further, "You've got competition, a battle you didn't expect. The David Reinhardt I thought I knew wouldn't surrender but fight to win." She paused to let that sink in, "From my perspective you crossed the drawbridge, found the castle in need of far more restoration than originally thought, and Johnny's entry, like Felicity returning her engagement ring, is the excuse you needed because you have had second thoughts about marrying me."

Immediately came his boomed objection, "That's ridiculous!"

"Is it? For a man in his prime I don't see that my idea of a 'marriage of convenience' would be particularly inviting. David was about to speak as she remarked, "I wouldn't blame you. So far our courtship has been a round of misunderstandings and clashes of wills."

He strode towards her saying, "Add to that jumping to wrong conclusions."

Cross, Rosie contested, "Have you considered the need to adapt, combine and perhaps change your preconceived opinions and ideas on marriage and parenthood? If I remain the twins' nanny, you may listen to my opinions, but your children will remain primarily under your care. Should I become their mother, they will be my children too. Are you willing to share them, the parental responsibilities, to discuss and agree on all decisions regarding them? I don't think you are."

Anger, frustration and fear seemed to pass through his eyes before he took hold of the clenched hands by her side and said quietly, "Rosie, we are all a work in progress and sometimes the hardest part is the initial shaping, after that it's easier to envision the details. Being married to Johnny, I am sure, would be far more peaceful than to me, but Rosie there are still five months - or longer if needed - to make your decision. I can't guarantee that clashes, misunderstandings and you feeling 'used' won't happen, but everything will have the twins and your best interests at heart."

"And David, my interests and responsibility to the children's best interests will only be served if we are both fully informed, can discuss, and if not agree, come to some kind of resolution."

"I know I need to do that. But you will have to trust me. And there are times, like the Jane Austin Ball, where they can be surprises you really enjoy. I wanted you by my side, and feared you would refuse, but the choice was left to you. Please accept I don't intent to upset you. I appreciate and want to thank and bless you." The broad, renowned heart-stopping smile appeared briefly. At her conciliatory nod he said solemnly, "And you know it's a rare occasion that I don't think something through. You are what I and the twins need. The difficulties we face are the squalls of rain hitting the windscreen blurring our vision. Let's see them as opportunities to wipe away the past, clean up present, and I truly believe we will see ahead and gain the same vision. We've worked together, lived in close proximity, and in times of camaraderie I've seen the ingredients of a very fulfilling marriage." At her sceptical expression, the amusement in his eyes was borne out by his mouth twitching into a wry smile, "A man might know how to work a bow across the strings of a violin, but only the knowledgeable and practiced are capable of making a beautiful sound."

Grimly, she pulled her hands from his, stepped back and stated, "That sounds like Doug talk! He thought he had flair, but it was only good to his ear. What makes you think you're different?"

David stepped forward, caught her hands again and drawing them close to his chest answered, "A woman's body is similar to an instrument. To enjoy the fullness of its creation you have to learn how to play it. Banging out a simple tune isn't what it was made for." Rosie grimaced. David smiled and continued, "Our bodies are made with different erogenous zones which like musical notes have to be learnt and then combined to make the chords of pleasure." Blushing at the intimacy of the conversation, Rosie's eyes concentrated on their joined hands as David added, "Practice and timing builds that to a crescendo so the climax touches mind, soul and spirit. It's the fine tuning by an expert player that brings the keys to make a melody from the heart."

Rosie immediately quashed the stir of desire David's words had engendered by glaring at him and contending, "And you think you are such an expert. That is man's talk to persuade a woman into his bed."

David chuckled, "Not man's but Jane's description of sexual harmony." Astonished Rosie stared at him. He explained, "Jane loved music. There were times when playing the piano, the Lord touched the depths of her being." Tears formed in David's eyes.

Rosie's eyes returned to look at her hands in his. Her mind contemplating the rumours and talk of him at ITP before he had married Jane. Frightened by his kiss that Christmas four years ago, she had reacted out of survival, according to her instinct to ensure he kept his distance. However, the interim years had proved she could trust him, and she had lowered her 'don't touch me' defence in agreeing to their camaraderie against Felicity. But in realising his growing interest in her and worried history would repeat itself, she had needed an excuse to run away. For months after that 'office' kiss, she had feared his reprisal for rejecting him, but worse was the memory of his mouth on hers. Something deep, primeval, had that day risen up in her, producing a fierce anger because that pain of hunger was for something which she didn't believe existed. Yet the thought of sexual activity sickened her.

David's hand uplifted her chin and he looked into her eyes, "Rosie, I didn't think I would have a contender for your affections, and if you choose Johnny so be it. But please, allow me these months to help both your mental and physical wounds to heal. Jane's identifying physical union with music is how it should be. I would like the opportunity to coax that melody forth."

Flustered, she pulled her hands from his, and moved away to stack the crockery on the tea tray. Behind her David said quietly, "Rosie, I'm only asking that your response to physical contact be at an elementary level, and you set the pace."

She lifted the tray, and turned towards him. The sincerity in his voice was mirrored in his eyes as he reasoned, "Don't let past fears colour the present. I want to help you make a decision that will bring you the most fulfilment."

'I want to help you' had been Doug's ploy to ensure she did what was right for him. Memories of that surfaced and in a panic she burst out, "I can't... I don't... oh, please don't ask me" and she rushed toward the kitchen, the crockery rattling on the tray.

Upset, the tray skewed across the work surface causing the cups to fall over. Rosie was aware of David following her. He stopped in the doorway and there was a hesitant tone in his voice as he said, "Rosie, I'm trying not to feel jealous of your obvious affection for Johnny. Please, all I ask is give me a fair trial."

Astonished at his confession and plea she turned to stare at him. "However, if you choose him over me, I would like to think I'm mature enough to deal with it."

In a desire to affirm him she burst out, "Oh David, you've already proved what a good and mature man you are. I know Jane spoke of hidden treasure, but I may not be the treasure she spoke of. Granted you found a note in Jane's Bible saying, 'Remember Rosemary' but you've no obligation to do so."

"Believe me, I am not acting out of obligation. To me you are a treasure, and one I wish to keep and discover more about. I confess to wanting that same fondness that enters your eyes when speaking of Johnny to happen when you see me." His eyes filled with sadness, "If that isn't possible I would like to believe that our time together would be God's catalyst to free you from the past, and give you a clearer view of the future."

"Oh…David" she stammered, "I… it… everything is happening so fast." His hand reached out toward her. Underneath those stern features she knew there was a generous heart. Why couldn't she just accept and love this man? What was wrong with her? He deserved to know how she felt, "I don't know what I feel for Johnny beyond fondness for the friendship and kinship of our formative years. But I want to be there for him as he was once for me." Her voice quavered, "He showed me love when I most needed it." With a sad smile David stepped forward to lift her hand to his mouth, kissed it and looked into her eyes. She felt compelled to admit, "I see Johnny's eyes lighting up when I visit, I want to bring him comfort and so I hold his hand." Tentatively, she suggested, "But I would be happy to visit him together."

David's response was immediate, "Thank you, but that's not to mean you can't visit him alone. All I want to know is for now I have your allegiance."

Surprised she frowned, "I agreed to six months courtship. In that, my loyalty to you won't be divided."

Quietly he added, "Then please, allow me to come closer." Before she could agree, his mouth moved towards hers. This time as his lips nuzzled hers she felt she shouldn't stop or resist him. The kiss deepened, his hand slid around her neck, his flexing fingers causing her mind and body to relax. But as that deep seated ache for fulfilment stirred, frightened she pulled her head from his to gasp, "Let me go." Startled, the desire in his eyes was quickly replaced by concern. "Rosie, what is it? What's the matter?"

Even she could hear the panic in her voice as she apologised.

"I'm sorry, I can't, I can't do this."

In a bid to escape she went to move past him, frightened she squealed as he blocked her way, his hand rested briefly on her arm, "Rosie I'm not going to hurt you. I might have a reputation for causing women to feel light-headed or weak-kneed, but I don't take advantage of that!" Laughter boomed from him, causing her to wince.

Not amused, she retorted as it died away, "I certainly wasn't weak-kneed, more sickened to my stomach." With pursed lips she stared at him, despite her inner voice telling her that was uncalled for and unkind.

David eyed her carefully, nodded thoughtfully and then commented, "I think Rosie, when we have discussed more fully Doug's treatment of you, we'll understand what causes you to feel that way. What I would like to do now is change the subject and talk about the problem Mrs P highlighted."

What had Mrs P reported? That she restricted the sweets Mrs P bought the twins? Her insistence they ate the food on their plate before anything else? Did she dislike her way of disciplining them?

"Don't look so worried. Mrs P is your avid supporter. Please can we sit down and talk this through?" Rosie waved her hand to indicate her agreement while wishing he would leave.

As if reading her mind David said ruefully, "I'm sorry to bring this up now, but Mrs P is anxious about the way Mrs Smith speaks to you, and about you. She hints she knows things, and you are not what you seem. But when Mrs P asks, she just gives a knowing smile."

Puzzled Rosie observed, "She's certainly said a few strange things. Could she be mistaking me for someone else?"

"That would have been my conclusion except Mrs Smith knows your double barrel surname and told Mrs P you worked for an MP in Parliament."

Frowning Rosie asked, "How would she know that?" David shrugged. "I don't know if your name or scandal was in the newspaper, but maybe she read about it." Rosie said, "It was odd how she picked up your family photo and said, 'dead wives couldn't turn up unexpectedly'. I took it as a nasty jibe for she couldn't know Doug's wife did that." Seeing David's eyebrows rising she added, "One evening I came home from work to find Doug's wife waiting for me. Bitterly she declared, 'I thought as much. He's shacked up again with another Parliamentary whore.

Well your time is up, pack your bags and leave.'"

"Aghast at such a description, I contested that, and told her I was expecting Doug's baby. With a patronising look she said, 'Really! And what does Doug think about that?' I told her he didn't yet know, but once used to the idea, he would love our child. To which she replied, 'I wouldn't bet on it' and with that she upped and left."

"My thoughts had been of wonder at the life growing within me. But I suppose inwardly I knew Doug wouldn't be pleased, so I delayed telling him, believing if it were too late he would look after me and his 'love' child. I never anticipated his wife arriving to turn me out. Naively I thought in knowing I was expecting his baby, and Doug wanting to marry me, it would make a difference. I had seen Doug get angry when drunk, but his wrath that evening had me cowering in the corner of the settee to protect my eighteen week old baby."

Rosie heard, but ignored David's sharp intake of breath. "Doug ranted 'what the hell did I think I was doing? Why hadn't I taken precautions?' As you can imagine I asked him, 'why hadn't he? I repeated over and over how I thought he loved me, and hadn't deliberately become pregnant. He raved on about his Parliamentary career. I told him I had thought it through, and decided to leave my job so as not to become an embarrassment for him, and would do temporary work for as long as was possible.'"

"What did he say to that?"

"He calmed down and I foolishly thought he was offering to support me and his 'love' child when he said, 'I'll help you, but you can't stay here. You must go before the weekend. I've brought the money you'll need'. And then he looked me up and down and concluded, 'It's fortunate you aren't so far gone that you can't be rid of it'. Angry I shouted, 'I'll be happy to be rid of you, but not our child, I love it, even if you don't!' At that he stalked out slamming the door behind him." The emotion brought tears to her eyes, "I had been duped into believing he cared for me, and realised then I was what he called 'his beautiful sex toy'!" David had sat forward, his fists clenched. Now he gave a stifled but derisive growl.

"Even when I felt used and abused, he would cuddle me afterwards and say how much he loved me, I made him happy. I was foolish and should have left him before I became pregnant. Next day, I went to work, handed in my notice, and was grateful Doug was working his constituency. Each evening, I packed up my things with the intention that weekend of telling the Hawkins my plight."

There was an underlying contempt in David's voice as he boomed, "And then you used the money to have an abortion. How could you? Surely you knew Jack and Cathy would be there for you and the child?"

David's assumption made her cringe. Tears fell from her eyes, for the very word 'abortion' conjured up the pain and horror she had been subjected to, causing her to whisper, "It wasn't as simple as that."

David gave a heavy sigh, "So you often tell me." His frustration was evident by the running of his hand through his thick hair. Wiping her eyes and blowing her nose she hesitantly admitted, "It happened before I had the chance to tell Jack and Cathy." At his wide-eyed questioning look, she quietly asked, "David, do you remember I told you I had been attacked getting into my car and had something precious stolen from me?" She waited for him to nod and added, "I was talking of my unborn child."

Before she could say more David sat forward to repeat loudly, "Your unborn child... was stolen, I don't understand?"

"I fought the two men who grabbed me. They put something over my mouth and I passed out. Abortion was against the law, a botched one brought no sympathy from anyone, no-one believed it was done against my will. Visitors were 'family only' and the hospital staff thought Jack and Cathy were my parents. To outsiders the assumption was that I had an appendix operation. My colleagues sent flowers with a card. I had no close friends. After a week, still unwell, I was transferred to Portsmouth Hospital. They realised I had septicaemia and pumped me with antibiotics. My mental and physical recovery took months. My resignation had been accepted so at the end of the first month, the Department wrote saying they were sorry to lose me and wished me the best for the future. After my transfer to Portsmouth and subsequent illness, by the second month, with exception of one London police officer who visited twice, no further questions were asked. It appeared 'filed' away and the 'hush up' complete. It was a surprise in the third month to receive a carefully worded letter from the Bradfords' solicitor."

David's attention heightened. "It was along the lines that Mr and Mrs Bradford denied all knowledge, claims and accusations of their involvement in my carrying Mr Bradford's child, and the child's subsequent abortion. In order to save them and myself further embarrassment and investigation, it would be appreciated if I would sign and return the enclosed documents. Included was a statement rescinding my allegations, and came with a guarantee that in signing, the police would drop their charge of criminal action in aborting an unwanted child."

David's face was grim so she added, "With those documents was another, not mentioned in the letter, which was a transfer of ownership of the mews cottage to me, two copies already completed, signed and witnessed for me to complete my copy and return."

"Blackmail to silence what perhaps was an ongoing investigation of the scandal of all scandals."

Rosie sighed, "Maybe. I wanted justice, would have liked retribution for destroying the life of my child, but after all I had been through I had no fight left in me."

"I guess you signed it and thus colluded with them,"

Sadly Rosie nodded, "Jack and Cathy had witnessed the nurses' attitude toward me and had pushed for my transfer to Portsmouth. They were anxious that if my full report to the police found its way to the newspapers, I would become as notorious as Christine Keiller."

"I see, and all is forgotten until Mrs Smith arrives and makes comments like 'That girl knows how to fall on her feet' and calls you 'a high class dame'. She wants you to know she knows something and has insinuated to Mrs P that you've deliberately inveigled yourself into our family. Mrs P refuted that in telling her you were Jane's friend and knew her before we were engaged, and was a bridesmaid at our wedding. And added, you had given up a good job when Jane died to help with the twins."

Rosie smiled, "Oh bless her. Can't we tell Mrs Smith that Jill and her family are moving sooner than expected, and we no longer need her help?"

Grimly David declared, "Oh, no Rosie. If she has blackmail on her mind, telling her to leave won't stop it. I intend to get to the bottom of it."

Rosie's eyebrows rose at David's fervent decree, and she protested, "It could just be something and nothing. In asking for cash and saying 'I'll say nowt to no-one' maybe she just wants to avoid paying tax."

"Are there other things in your past you would wish to remain hidden?"

"Do you believe me about the abortion?"

"Rosie, to believe you would do such a thing goes against everything I know about you. I gathered Gerald knows something about it, but does he know it all?

Rosie blew her nose. "From me, the bare details. Did he tell you I was giving a statement regarding Jill's debacle, and the doctor being questioned about Lord Mallory's identity heard my voice, and also confessed to botching my abortion." David nodded. "He went on to tell Gerald he followed me home and rung the ambulance. As a detective Gerald, I am sure, would have looked into the case, and in discovering I now owned Doug's cottage he realised I'd been paid off, decided to let that rest and has never talked to me about it."

David frowned, "Gerald told me the police hadn't investigated your claims." Rosie sighed, "They interviewed me several times while I was in hospital in London. I gave them a very full report, whose child it was, what had been said, every detail I could remember. My guess is Gerald couldn't find anything, because what was said was deliberately buried or lost, from my perspective the police lost interest."

"Gerald did tell me that my Dad helped that doctor to disappear in the same way as he had Ben. I was so mad about that, but Gerald said he'd done what he could to save your life and so Dad had felt to save his."

"Your Dad knows about that?"

"Only that like Ben his career had been shattered by a mistake. He'd been forced to do an abortion, but had saved the woman's life."

"It's true. One day I maybe able to tell you the details."

David grimaced, "The details Gerald repeated from the doctor were horrific enough. If I've found hearing about this harrowing, to talk of it must be far worse. Let's talk again tomorrow."

Conflicting thoughts reeled through Rosie's head as she followed David to the front door. On reaching it he turned, gave her a gentle smile and stroked her cheek with the knuckle of his forefinger. After brushing his lips against hers he said quietly, "I appreciate your honesty. Whatever has happened, or will happen, rest assured I'm on your side." Turning on his heel he was out of the door and striding down the cobblestone street to his car.

CHAPTER 20

Vivid flashes, like lightening across a night sky, brought recurring scenes from the abortion, awakening her in terror in the early hours. Finally, she called on Jesus. He knew she had loved and wanted her baby and would, like the windscreen wipers, clear her mind and bring her peace. Jesus' life had been taken from Him, and He had asked the Father to forgive those who had done that. She spoke into the darkness, "Jesus, I forgive those involved in my abortion. They didn't know you are the only one who should give and take away life." Next time she opened her eyes, it was to daylight and the deep-seated pain of her memories had ceased. It was as if the Lord had lanced them, but she sensed the pus of guilt and shame still had to be released. Wondering what the day would bring she asked the Lord to give her strength.

The twins were washed, dressed and fed when she arrived and they ran to greet her. Over their heads, David sent her a concerned smile and as he left, placed a gentle kiss on her lips with the promise 'we'll talk this evening'. Joshua and Rebecca seemed to sense she needed reassurance of their love. They told her that umpteen times during the day, and played happily together that she felt it was either an answer to prayer or David had primed them!

However, that evening despite the children having been good, Rosie knew she had the beginning of a migraine causing David to insist she went home, they could have time together the following day.

The following evening she prepared David's favourite dinner which he insisted should be accompanied by a bottle of wine. He talked and they discussed ITP's continuing expansion programme beyond trade exhibitions to advising, assisting and making global trade agreements.

The apricot crumble had almost been forgotten when David observed, "I continue to be indebted to you." At Rosie's puzzled expression he added, "Not only have you been part of the twins lives since birth, but chose to be their nanny over that incredible job offer Wilhelm tailored for you. Tonight, your questions, suggestions and ideas brought me food for thought." Rosie reminded of the crumble jumped up to retrieve it. "You would have been an incredible asset to the Overseas Department with your wisdom, knowledge and languages." Embarrassed Rosie gave a shy smile as David went on, "We think we've now found someone suitable to liaise the trade links across countries but after

Robert's debacle, Wilhelm has gone to great lengths to check their background, academic qualifications and references."

Rosie handed him a bowl, "A prime case of learning by our mistakes."

David acknowledged that with a wry smile, "I enjoyed visiting the different countries. My heart is to develop it further."

"I work where my heart is! But I'm still interested in ITP and the developing business world."

"This reminds me of evenings with Jane, coming home to a delicious meal, talking of work and the people involved." His eyes saddened and he confessed, "At Jane's funeral, I realised how little interest I showed in her activities, and how selfish I'd been." Rosie sent him her enigmatic smile. "I get enthused by my work! But please tell me if you feel I'm not listening to you."

"David, my activities beyond the twins aren't diverse or riveting. Although, I would be concerned if you are thinking of travelling again. We've barely glimpsed the challenges the twins will bring and - married or not - I wouldn't want that responsibility on my own."

"It's early days for the Overseas Department. I don't know how that might pan out and in three years the twins will be at school. Let's have our coffee in the lounge." Once settled David said, "While talking to the Lord this morning… " he swallowed hard, the pitch of his voice deepened, "I can't bring back Jane and you can't restore your lost baby but I was reminded that God is a loving Father who tells us nothing can, or will, separate us from Him, not even death. This may sound foolish but it came to me that you are in a place to love and nurture Jane's children, just as Jane is in the place to nurture yours."

Tears leapt into her eyes. She placed her hands as if in prayer around her nose and mouth. Was that possible? Jane had clearly shown David there was life after death but could her baby be alive in heavenly places, "Oh David, that is such a comfort. On Sunday night my nightmares returned. I spoke aloud forgiving those concerned and called Jesus to wipe away my fear. When I awoke I felt Jesus had lanced those boils of terror but now I have to let Him draw out the pus of guilt and shame."

David added, "He loves, listens and desires to make us whole. The Lord speaks to me in dreams, to you it's in analogies. Can I work with you to bring that healing?" Rosie nodded. David sat beside her saying, "Just relax against me." Slowly and gently his hands moved up and down her back. Instead of a sexual connotation she sensed God's hands, the labour of His love delivering her from the past to bring comfort during the birth of His child. She felt an incredible peace and when David stopped she moved her head, saw a wet patch on his shirt and looked up at him to see her sadness reflected in his eyes. On a gentle smile he dangled his handkerchief between them saying, "It might be a little late for this."

After a quiet 'thank you' she wiped her eyes, blew her nose and in an emotional voice explained, "I thought about your words and my baby in heaven. I feel I've just birthed a greater understanding of how God so loved the world, He gave His only Son, Jesus, to die so our sins can be forgiven."

"When we let God into our lives it's extraordinary what He can do in us, for us and through us. Even Jane's death is being used for good. Mrs Smith doesn't know it but she's being used to help you release your past. That's not to say we don't need to know what she knows! As an ex-barrister to deal effectively with any situation, it is necessary to know all the facts." Rosie cringed. "I believe the Lord has brought you to relax and trust in Him. And when you feel it is right to speak of your ordeal, I believe it will aid the healing process."

Was she ready to do that? David's expression gave her to believe he was praying, something she guessed he had been doing earlier.

Within she cried, 'help me Lord'. "David I... I want to tell you, but... " she took a deep breath and with a catch in her voice admitted "... I tried to stop them, but they had been paid to kill my baby." He gave a sharp intake of breath as she remember for months awakening in night screaming. Without Jack and Cathy's love and support she would have gone mad. Now, sitting on the settee she pulled up her knees, with her arms around them she began rocking back and forth. David quietly suggested as he had to Helen, "Breath slowly in 1, 2, 3 and out 1, 2, 3. There's no hurry, take your time."

After a minute or so, the slow breathing technique calmed her. She spoke hesitantly, "It was a Friday evening. I'd packed up my things at the cottage and put them in the car. The car wouldn't start. I got out to ring the AA. A man offered his help. He lifted the bonnet. We both peered in. I remember a hand across my mouth and a cloth pressed against my nose. I tried to pull the hand away, struggled, kicked and hit the person behind me, but I felt myself fading."

As David boomed, "Good grief!" Rosie put her fingers to her lips and with a finger pointed upward, afraid David would awake the twins. With less vehemence David said, "Two men abducted you off the street and no-one saw anything?"

Rosie rocked back and forth, "Later I found myself lying on a hard bed with hands pressing my bare stomach. I heard voices but not what they were saying. Disorientated, I tried to focus on the man wearing a medical mask and heard him declare 'she is too far gone'." Rosie closed her eyes and continued rocking. "I... I thought I was dying. Mentally, I assessed my body. I felt no pain. I managed to whisper 'What happened?' He turned toward me. He was young with sad brown eyes. My mind went to the baby. I asked 'My baby, is it alright?' I saw his sadness turn to anguish before he turned and walked away. Frightened, I struggled to get up. A woman dressed in blue - I presumed a nurse - put the weight of her hand on my shoulder indicating not to do so. I asked 'What's wrong with me?' She answered 'Don't worry dearie, rest easy, it'll soon be over.' I struggled to process the situation. The doctor was arguing with someone just outside the room. The nurse looked peeved and closed the door. With a thin smile she said 'No point in hanging about, let's get you ready'. When I realised her intention was to remove my underwear, I questioned then protested. Her hand restrained me and her voice was harsh as she declared 'Now don't start.' I looked into her cold and determined eyes. She tossed her head toward the angry voices outside the door 'It's bad enough he's causing a fuss. One way or another we've been paid to rid you of your little problem, and we shall do it'."

Caught up in the past Rosie rocked harder, her voice became shrill, "It came to me. They were going to kill my baby." She let out a scream and feeling an arm restraining her, her eyes flashed open. She realised David had stopped her careering head first from the settee.

In a quiet voice, he gently drew her towards him, "Relax, relax. Come, rest back against me." Trembling Rosie did as he bid and took comfort from his warmth. His arm came around, his hands splayed in protection over a baby that no longer existed.

She closed her eyes and described the scene, "Another woman entered and told the nurse 'The doctor was told it was a simple evacuation. He's not prepared to do anything more.' To that she retorted 'Then someone better tell him what his choices are'." Rosie shuddered. She could feel David's hands tightening over her stomach. She drew comfort from them, "I shouted several times 'I want my baby. I don't want an abortion.' The nurse commented 'These high class plumy voiced tarts often make the most fuss.' Incensed I tried to sit up but the women held me down. I shouted 'I'm not a tart, I want my baby, leave me alone' and did everything I could, squirm, jerk, and kick out to get off that examination couch. Over my tirade the doctor appeared and yelled 'Where's that chloroform?' I saw a small dark bottle upside down being waved above my head. Angry the doctor said the obvious 'It's empty!' and then questioned 'How am I meant to do this with her kicking and screaming'?"

Despite wanting the security of David's arms around her, Rosie pushed away from him. He moved to keep his arms around her. She brushed away the tears rolling down her face and sobbed, "Do you know... do you know what they said?" She didn't wait for a reply but burst out, "Oh stuff her knickers in her mouth that'll keep her quiet". From behind her David growled his fury. "There were more lewd suggestions that amused them but the doctor's eyes reflected his disgust. I saw him draw aside, take money from his wallet and order a man in the outer room to go to the off-licence and buy a bottle of whisky. I heard them haranguing him, believing as I did, he needed a stiff drink before taking on the task. But they were wrong. He poured the whisky into a tumbler, ordered that I be sat up, heavy hands rested on my shoulders while he commanded I keep drinking until I passed out. I refused, I begged, I pleaded with him not to kill my baby. I saw him clamp down on his distress to inform me if I didn't drink voluntarily, he would get the two men to pour it down my throat. Sobbing, crying and begging they let me go, I was barely able to swallow and my throat was burning. Finally he said impatiently 'Drink it down now or face the alternative'."

David hugged her closer, his voice faltering, "Surely, Doug... Oh God... Oh Rosie, surely he hadn't condoned that. Despite abortion being illegal, there were surely more decent places... but to pay such people... "

Fresh, silent tears rolled down her cheeks, "Either he, or his wife organised it, no-one else knew I was pregnant. Obviously later he learned of the outcome, although not the horrific details. You really don't want to know."

She tried to move away as he said, "Rosie as awful as it was, you have to release it. I've got you, you are safe."

In knowing he was right, she closed her eyes and continued, "The drink made me feel woozy. I was pushed down I guessed on a massage couch, the two men holding down my shoulders and arms as the nurses positioned and held my legs. I felt the doctor beginning. My words became disjointed. I don't know how long I was unconscious, but excruciating pain over-rode it. I heard screaming, it was me! I thought I was going to die. If not from the pain, from choking on the whisky poured down my throat the moment my eyes opened. Each time, the doctor yelled words like 'Stop her screaming. Hold her down. It's impossible to work in these conditions. I told you to do this would need proper analgesics. If she goes into shock... if she dies... I won't be held responsible'."

"Doug should have been." David said with deep disgust.

"It wasn't until Gerald talked to the doctor that I found out he was in the midst of removing the foetus when I vomited. In order I didn't swallow it, they had to move me and when my body started to go into shock he knew something was badly wrong. He patched me up, said 'job done' and legged it."

"Oh God, Rosie... I've seen child birth and the pain endured but this, this... "

Determined to finished Rosie reported, "Apparently the doctor watched from his car, saw what appeared to be three drunken revellers emerge, hail a taxi which they pushed me into, and he followed it. The taxi driver, thinking I was drunk, pulled me out of his cab at the cottage, dragged me to the wall, took money from my purse for the fare, and left me to slide down the wall. I have no recollection of any of that, due to either the alcohol or blood loss. I was told an ambulance had been called and they found me in the doorway of the cottage."

David's voice was cracked with emotion, "Dear God... Oh Rosie, why weren't you believed. The taxi taking you to Doug's cottage surely was proof of his involvement."

"When I regained consciousness I was beside myself with grief. The police were rude and disgusted at what they perceived I had done. I told them all I could remember. A policewoman horrified by my story wrote it down. When I repeated it a third time in Portsmouth Hospital, it seemed no-one believed me. But that detective did come twice. The second time to ask questions about my involvement with Doug. He upset me by trying to refute everything I said. When it appeared I wouldn't say where the abortion had taken place he shook his head and left. Within two days I was too ill to tell anyone anything."

David drew her close, his warmth at her back, "Oh Rosie,

Rosie."

"I spent two weeks in Portsmouth hospital. One in intensive care with septicaemia, and if it hadn't been for Jack and Cathy I would have lost the will to live."

Puzzled David commented, "Gerald said beyond the initial report the police weren't involved!"

"I know he looked into the information given by the doctor. It would seem that the massage parlour was demolished due to the construction of the Westway flyover."

"Oh God! Rosie when I hear about incidents in your life, I feel quite desperate for retribution, but God always reminds me that vengeance should always be His. I wonder if Gerald guessed there had been a 'cover up' when, despite you having given statements, he couldn't find any evidence of the police being involved. Whether lost or destroyed, I would guess the paper you signed to collude with the Bradfords is in safe keeping somewhere. And the fact Felicity knew about your relationship with Doug, and you confronting his wife, but didn't taunt you about the baby and abortion does mean that information was kept closely under wraps. Dear me Rosie, I need a stiff drink."

He gently released her and headed toward the sideboard, "I've a very good malt whisky. Do you want one?"

Rosie slid from the settee, "No thanks. I hate the stuff."

"Oh Rosie! Sorry. Can I get you a glass of wine or maybe a cup of coffee?"

"I need to go. I feel very tired."

"That's understandable. Before you leave I have two suggestions. Keep out of Mrs Smith's way by going out tomorrow with Joyce and the children. And as Gerald knows what happened, think about our consulting him on what to do about Mrs Smith's insinuations?"

"Both seem good to me."

"That's my girl!" He hugged her and taking her hand decreed, "We'll believe the pus is released, and this wound can begin to heal." At the car his kiss was brief, and as she drove home she wondered when the stirring up of the quiet still pond of her life would end.

The next day she, Joyce and the children spent the day in Richmond by the river and in the park. They were barely home before David. Jill met her at the front door to tell her Mrs Smith had initially been pleased to receive an envelope containing money to cover her cleaning, but Mrs P had reported that Mrs Smith had grumbled that in the circumstances it had been a mean amount. Rosie assured Jill it was the 'usual' rate.

Two evenings later, Gerald - with his endearing 'rabbit features' pocket cheeks and slightly buck teeth - played with the twins. Afterwards, as David battled with getting two excited children to bed, Rosie told him Declan's progress and the Hawkins wish to officially foster him.

The coffee made, Gerald was enticed to have a brandy and settled in the lounge. Rosie broached the subject of Mrs Smith's odd and worrying snippets of conversation. Gerald took out his notebook, thumbed to a page and wrote as she spoke. David added information gathered from Mrs P. After a quick glanced at his notes he concluded, "She is a cleaner not afraid of mess and called you a 'high class dame'. Legalisation has killed the abortion trade. I'd guess she recognised you as the woman brought in to get rid of a problem!" Rosie cringed and bent forward to pour the coffee. "What is odd is her ending up here as a cleaner, but stranger things have happened. She may know more, and in concluding you have inveigled your way into David's life, you'd pay her to keep her mouth shut." Gerald looked across at them to ask, "The question is what action do you want to take?"

Puzzled, Rosie handed Gerald his coffee, "That's what we're asking you?"

"The bottom line is if I get officially involved it could mean charging her, a court case, and... " he gave Rosie a wide-eyed look, "... a 'can of worms' being opened, which might be best left shut."

Rosie sighed, "Being a good detective you must have guessed I accepted the cottage to keep silent." Gerald gave a sad grimace. "But if she doesn't keep silent that could have ramifications on David's family." David's face remained in its usual stern repose, his steepled fingers tapped against his mouth.

"It might be wise to just ignore her. David already knows, so who else can she tell?"

Rosie suggested, "The newspapers?"

David sat up to take his coffee and declared, "Not if she doesn't want to be charged for being involved in the illegal abortion trade and blackmail."

"The latter she could deny." Rosie worriedly chewed on her lip.

"I would say find out what is on her mind. Play her along. Let her tell you what she knows." Gerald grinned, "You could set her up."

"How do you propose we do that?" David asked somewhat tetchily.

"Using the babysitting microphone. If Rosie talks to her in the twins' room you could listen in either your lounge or basement?"

David didn't look convinced. "The basement would be best." Rosie had a thought and added, "You could record the conversation."

"Unless you have a signed statement, recorded conversations are rarely admissible in a court of law." Rosie frowned, unsure if David's scowl and gruff voice was due to the possibility of her being blackmailed, or because she and Gerald had the idea.

"Why all this cloak and dagger behaviour?" Gerald's eyebrows rose at the evident exasperation in David's voice, "The best action is to just confront the wretched woman?"

"Not in my experience! I find out more by appearing bemused and friendly. And, if nothing else, a recording could act as a deterrent to blackmail. David you wouldn't have to rely on memory, but listen to it again and again, and use your legal expertise to decide how best to proceed. To that David looked thoughtful. Amused Gerald added, "I have it on good authority you can be extremely intimidating to those who would seek to thwart you! You've the ability to extract an apology and bring such contrition that the person not only sees the error of their ways, but determines never to do it again!" Behind her hand, Rosie hid her smile seeing David's creased brow as he puzzled who the 'good authority' would be to give him such an accreditation. Gerald chuckled, "David, no-one could fault your questioning technique. I fell victim to it when you wanted to find Rosie. I realised all too late I'd given away confidential information and am pleased Rosie that you have forgiven me."

David turned towards her with a piercing look, before he gave a non-committal hum as Gerald pointed out, "When Mrs P is around, there is no reason why Mrs Smith should seek entry. This flat has a door. I've never seen it shut, but suggest it is, if nothing else to stop the children falling down the stairs."

As David's gaze returned to her, Rosie knew he too was thinking about the traumatic incident only three months earlier as he confirmed, "Yes, we need to do that."

"My advice would be to wait and see if anything more develops. If it does, record it, and only intervene if you feel it necessary David." Gerald returned his cup to the tray, took a look at David's disgruntled expression and announced, "I think it's time I left." As he rose to his feet so did David. "Thank you again Rosie for a most delicious dinner. And I'm always happy to help in any way I can."

That night her mind wouldn't rest. But finally she slept and came into semi-consciousness as sunlight dappled through a crack in the curtains, and joy filled her from a fading dream. She didn't move in a desire to recall how she had been walking in a sunny garden framed with flowerbeds full of riotous colours. She had been on a narrow path, nearly hidden by large bushes in glorious bloom and bordered by trees bearing unrecognisable but delicious looking fruits. Clinging to the dream, the sunlight dappling through her window was much the same as that which had come through tall, forest like trees beyond which water was shimmering. Drawn to that, she stood on the bank of a wide stream where water cascaded from tall rocks, about fifty feet away, and rushed along the river bed. There was a strain of music in the air. Full, leafy trees lined the narrow grassy bank, and curious, she began to walk from the waterfall to what appeared a deep gully where the water cascaded over, causing a water mist. Within it she could hear the voices of children. When nearer, she walked along the grassy rim around the top of the chasm until she could see the water thirty feet below. It had formed into a natural pool where children were swimming.

Opposite, in the basin and rising out of the water, was an outcrop of rock from which children were diving and jumping in. A boy about to do that glanced up and seeing her waved. Such joy filled her she waved back. A little girl's voice echoed from the chasm, "Johnny, catch me when I jump." The boy looked down to where the voice came from and answered, "Wait until I call you." Again he looked in her direction, his body language seemed to say 'watch me' so she waved again. He waved back before executing a perfect dive that cut through the water.

Her attention was then taken by a little red-haired girl about four years old, climbing up the rock steps to the outcrop. She awaited her turn at the edge and then called 'Johnny'. He reappeared swimming towards her. He stopped, outstretched his arms before calling up to her 'Ready Jenny Wren'. Even though it seemed a long way down, without hesitation she jumped into the water straight into his waiting arms, and she didn't even get her hair wet.

The picture and that place were so beautiful that in her semiconscious state she wanted to stay and watch, but the dream began to fade. Both children looked up and waved as children do when saying 'goodbye'. The bright sunlight coming through the crack in her curtains finally blocked out her view. She turned over reliving it again, and tears rolled silently down her cheeks onto the pillow, for Johnny looked the age her baby would have been if he had lived. Johnny of course was on her mind, but if she had a boy maybe she would have chosen his name. And like his namesake, he seemed such a kind boy. Had the Lord given her the chance to glimpse her child alive, well and growing in heavenly places? And in having that glimpse, she found she could re-run it over and over in her mind and take encouragement from it. The only person who - without doubt - would believe her was David!

She took her Bible from the bedside table and read aloud the verse in Romans 8 where Paul writes that he was convinced that 'neither death, nor life, would separate us from the love of God'. Joy swept through her along tears of gratitude and happiness. She closed her eyes to bring again the scene to memory and felt a wad of pages from her open Bible flop over. Her eyes flashed open, she looked down and read, "Before I was born you called me, from my birth He has made mention of my name." Jane had shown her those verses to comfort her. Jane was convinced that life was created from the moment of conception and neither life nor death can separate man from God, and across the page her eyes read 'I will contend with those who contend with you and your children, I will save… ' The Lord had saved her child. She could barely wait to tell David!

In the weeks that followed, her perception of God changed. His heart was for her, as was His love, His goodness, and now when David was distracted, made decisions on her behalf, or the twins were challenging, it didn't disturb her peace or inner happiness. Those who knew her commented on how she seemed more alive, responsive and open. It wasn't until she saw Johnny in the middle of June, the first time since his leaving hospital and recuperating at the Brigadier's sister's home in Cornwall, that she felt prompted to tell others of her dream.

David's parents were staying for a few days to celebrate Jill and Paul's wedding anniversary and William's fourth birthday the following week. So she took time out. It was strange to be free of children but good to lunch out with Diana. They discussed making clothes for her shop. And the bonus was Johnny returning that evening and the two of them accepting an invitation to tea the following day.

Her heart leapt at the sight of Johnny. His hair had grown back, the scar on his forehead was fading, his eyes were bright and appraising, his permanent smile bringing a desire to hug him, just as she had each morning at school. Even if his speech wasn't always clear, his feelings were. Her courtship with David was halfway through, and she was determined to be faithful to it. So beyond sending a card wishing him well she had not communicated with him further, leaving Diana to keep her informed of his recovery.

As it was a beautiful Sunday afternoon, Cathy suggested tea by the lake. Jack, preferring to be active, took Declan and Bertie with him to see what repairs were needed at the boathouse. The sunlight dappling on the water reminded her of her dream and as she shared it, the others were quickly absorbed. Helen asked, "Do you think the boy waving knew you?"

"I felt I knew him. A little girl shouted his name." She smiled at Johnny, "It was yours! I sensed he wanted me to watch him execute a perfect dive and then my attention was drawn to a little girl with bright red hair about four. She climbed up the big rocky steps to wait to jump into his arms. Johnny called from the water, 'Ready Jenny Wren?'"

"Oh, my God!" They all looked at Helen. Wide-eyed she exclaimed, "Ben would put his hands on my stomach and say 'Hello Jenny Wren'. She would be four now."

"Tears flowed down both their cheeks and in an emotional voice Rosie observed, "Johnny looked about nine. I lost my baby nine years ago, and if a boy may well have chosen that name." Helen looked dazed, not just by her confession, but in considering her child was alive. Rosie told them about the highlighted scriptures and finished. "It stands to reason when life is created, it never dies." There was silence at the enormity of that revelation.

Cathy, wiping her tears, swallowed hard to ask, "Do you think my lost children were there?"

"From my dream, I would concluded that those not born on earth are born into heaven and grow much the same as on earth. Your lost babies would now be late twenties, early thirties. I'd hope every conceived child - however they died - would become part of our heavenly Father's family."

"Oh Rosie, there is such comfort in that."

She knew the dream had affected her, but had had no

comprehension on how it might affect others. Johnny was shaking his head before saying carefully, "I believe you but have never heard anything like that before."

Diana queried, "You lost a child nine years ago what happened?"

Cathy intervened by confessing, "I'm beginning to understand God loves us. He created us to have a relationship with Him."

"If David hadn't had some interesting experiences with the Lord, I would have thought it was my imagination. Just before that dream or vision, David had said that as I was looking after Jane's children, maybe she was looking after mine."

Helen chipped in, "And you wouldn't have heard Ben call our baby 'Jenny Wren' because he only said it when… that's spooky."

"Not spooky!" said Johnny, "It's wonderful. It's an incredible revelation of God's love."

In seeing Jack and the boys approaching, nothing more was said, but the observant Jack gave Cathy a questioning stare, at which she gave him her 'not now Jack' look and began serving their picnic tea.

Later, Diana and Johnny took her to the station. As he kissed her cheek he asked "Please come again, soon."

She nodded, "I'll try" and thought how easy he was to love.

CHAPTER 21

On the journey back to London, she felt filled with joy and was the first to alight from the train. She smiled broadly when spotting David at the barrier and waved. With a wifely kiss and slipping her arm through his she asked, "How did you know which train I was on?" And before he could answer she added teasing, "Last time you met me you came with flowers."

She expected him to laugh but his expression remained stern and his answer brief, "I rang Jack. He told me." Her heart sank. What else had Jack told him? Was he upset that she'd invited Johnny for tea?

Once in the car he turned towards her, "Rosie, there's no easy way to tell you this. Mrs P had a heart attack." Dismayed, Rosie immediately asked questions but he cut her short to explain, "Mrs Smith rang. Paul has gone to the hospital to find out more. We'll talk about the ramifications of that later. Mum and Dad are staying on until Wednesday. They're babysitting and said not to hurry back. We've all missed you. William's party with three boys from play school was extremely trying. They rampaged around the garden, and I fear it's now rather worse for wear! Shall we go for a drink? I know a riverside pub and we can sit outside." Rosie nodded, "They also hope you'll join their proposed boat trip on the Thames on Tuesday.

"The last boat trip I went on didn't end too well."

"Surely you weren't sick?" David gave her a wry smile.

Rosie cringed. "I felt sickened by two very undesirable deck hands who thought I was fair game!"

"I remember Jill saying about that after the annual ITP Party." He chortled, "This time you'll have me as superman!" Rosie hummed remembering Ben's arrival on that scene.

Twenty minutes later, with drinks in hand, they left the crowded pub in Chiswick to stroll along the tow path to a small park overlooking the river. As they lent on a railing looking across the river she said excitedly, "David, you'll never guess what happened this afternoon when I shared my dream."

He gave a wry smile, "In that case you'd better tell me." When she finished he exclaimed, "That's incredible" before teasing, "And I thought it was me, that you were happy to see me."

"It's certainly a pleasant end to the day."

"Good." He drew her closer, "Mum and Dad were pleased you'd convinced Jill to join our visit to the seaside to celebrate the twins' birthday. They'd like you to persuade her to come on Tuesday."

"I'll try. You realise the children will need close supervision, William in particular."

"It will be fine. Now about Mrs Smith." Rosie groaned. "She insisted while speaking to Paul that Mrs P wouldn't want to let us down so she'll come on Tuesdays to clean our flat."

Aghast, she stepped back to exclaim, "What! Oh no!"

"Paul not knowing what to say left it at 'thank you'."

Alarmed Rosie's response was vehement, "That can't happen. I'm not going to be exposed again to her 'funny business'."

To which David reasoned, "She's not tried it again. And should she do so we'll deal with it as Gerald suggested. I'll ask Jill to take Wednesday, saying it's more convenient for cleaning when you are often out with Joyce." He gave a rueful smile, "Will that help?" Rosie nodded but wasn't convinced. "Let's return these glasses. Time to take you home."

When Jill heard Rosie was going on the boat trip she agreed to go. Despite five children under four and the warm weather, it was remarkably relaxed and enjoyable.

Paul's report on Mrs P was that it was doubtful she'd work again. Rosie seeing her in hospital was saddened at the way she had aged overnight. The worry it caused her was eclipsed days later by David's grief over Jane and his wedding anniversary. A week later, at the twins' birthday party at the seaside it was obvious his heart wasn't in it. Throughout, she fought with hurt that he either wanted to be alone or talked with Paul who had experience the death of his first wife. And within days it would be the anniversary of Jane's death.

Rosie felt it unfair to confide in Joyce and although David's mother Margaret rang regularly, his answer had become an abrupt 'fine' and little more. When Margaret rang while David was at work, she was surprised to be asked her opinion of how David was coping. In a need to be honest she replied, "He's tired, grouchy and generally uncommunicative" and becoming unexpectedly tearful she confessed, "I'm trying hard not to let it upset me and the children."

An hour later Margaret rang again, "Rosie, would you consider coming tomorrow and spending the week here? It will give you both a break, a change of scenery and hopefully time to relax together. Jenny says she can help and we'd enjoy time with our grandchildren."

At her fervent 'yes please' Margaret chuckled, "He'll agree if you ask him."

"You have more confidence in my influence on him than I do." But later she approached the subject with trepidation. Instead of refusal or anger at her discussing him with his mother, with a resigned expression he merely nodded, while she hid her relief, delight and two Wednesdays without seeing Mrs Smith.

A week of blue skies and warm weather had proved a wonderful rest. The first day David disappeared wanting to be alone. Margaret and Franz took the twins to Bristol Zoo and she read a book enjoying the novelty of peace and quiet. As David began to unwind and they talked and laughed about Jane, it was obvious he wasn't ready to replace her and Rosie felt fine about that. She just appreciated being in good company. Without the twins, they had the opportunity to have leisurely lunches in delightful pubs and visit nearby places of interest.

Back home while nurturing the children she took daily pressures in her stride... with the exception of Mrs Smith! Whereas Mrs P would clean upstairs in the morning and downstairs in the afternoon, Mrs Smith seemed everywhere they were. Despite that, she was quicker and more thorough than Mrs P.

The first Wednesday after their holiday, Joyce had a toothache. Halfway through the morning Mrs Smith requested, "Make us a cuppa dearie" politely Rosie suggested she help herself. Next and without invitation she sat to eat her lunch with them, demanded a drink and talked of things of no interest to her. When she mentioned Mrs P ironed David's shirts Mrs Smith rudely replied, "You want to be his wife. That's your job dearie, not mine."

The next week Joyce had her tooth out. On several occasions Mrs Smith called her 'my girl' in such a derogatory fashion that Rosie suggested, "Call me Rosie."

"In that case Rosie, when yer make me tea, I'd like biscuits with it." Obediently she opened a packet of digestives which had Mrs Smith remark, "Is that all yer got? I likes more fancy ones." Then it was Rosie this, and Rosie that, at which she tried not to cringe or retort. Then she declared, "Rosie when you make a sandwich, make me one, I ain't got none today." She obliged but pointedly commented, "Mrs P had three weeks in a convalescent home, I'm looking forward to her return."

Whereupon Rebecca happily informed Mrs Smith, "Mrs P give us sweets."

Rosie inwardly groaned but smiled and commented, "Yes bless

her, but I'd rather she didn't."

The next week, Mrs Smith seeing she and Joyce were taking a picnic to the park, said with a sneer, "Now Rosie don't yer forget to make me sandwiches, but no need to worry about me tea and biscuits, I'll 'elp meself." Joyce later confessed she found her intrusion difficult, didn't like her personal questions and congratulated Rosie's skill of succinct non-informative answers. At the end of the day while giving Mrs Smith her pay Rosie decided to advise, "I'm happy to provide you with drinks but please don't expect more. Also I'd rather you didn't try and engage my guests in conversation." Mrs Smith's immediate response was a tirade which included, "Rosie, yer a mean woman. I's just being friendly, and yer'll find it works best that way." Dumbfounded Rosie stared at the flat door as she banged it behind her.

Jill agreed she was rude, but a small price to pay for such good cleaning. David said to ignore her, but with Joyce and Ted on holiday the following week and David working late, she decided she wasn't going to be inveigled into talking or making sandwiches. She quickly left to take the twins swimming. They ate in a Wimpy Bar, and as it was raining visited the cinema to see Willy Wonker and The Chocolate Factory where the twins promptly fell asleep. On their returned Mrs Smith greeted them, arms folded and foot tapping, "What do yer mean by not being 'ere?"

On a deep breath Rosie straightened and looked her in the eyes, "You have been here several weeks and don't need my guidance on how to clean."

"Now, look 'ere my girl, not so much of the ''oity toity'. You've come up from nothing like the rest of us. Fancy begrudging me biscuits and a sandwich. Well I 'elped meself and to more than yer stingily provide."

Annoyed, Rosie stated, "Have you indeed? In that case I'd prefer you to stick to cleaning the basement flat."

"That's the way of it, is it? Yer want to do me out of a well-paid job. Yer treat me well, and I'll keep me gob shut about well… yer know what?"

A pull on her skirt brought Rosie to look down at two upturned anxious little faces. At Mrs Smith's contemptuous expression Rosie nodded towards the twins saying, "Not now Mrs Smith." With that she drew the twins into the lounge, pulled out their bricks and engaged them in building while praying, "Lord help me."

Behind her Mrs Smith scolded, "Don't yer turn yer back on me."

Outwardly calm, inwardly nervous, she stood and faced her. In her late fifties Mrs Smith still had suppleness and energy, carried an air of youth and dressed accordingly. Today, in annoyance, her grey hair in a pony tail bobbed up. Oddly, Rosie had a glimpse of hurt and rejection in the eyes of the once pretty woman behind the painted, prematurely lined face. Quietly she replied, "You are upsetting the children."

"Them's will be upset if yer don't see me right. Treat me well dearie, and we can be friends."

Rosie thought that as unlikely as David letting Mrs Smith leave without knowing what she knew. "Look, clean next Wednesday and after the twins' nap I'll arrange for Jane's mother to take the twins out. I'll be in their bedroom clearing out unwanted toys and clothes and you can tell me then to what you are referring."

"Don't give me that my girl, yer know to what I am referring. Yer not yer mother so stop acting as if yer the lady of the manor."

Needled, she drew Mrs Smith from the lounge to the dining room, "What do you know about my mother?"

"Yer mother, Lady Doughty-Dawes has been cheated in every way. The man you know as yer father is a gambler who finds a money source, milks it, and moves on."

Rosie winced, her mind raced as she asked, "How do you know that? Does he owe you money?"

"Scared, yer mother clings to him. He's so in debt them's bin forced to flee the country and upped sticks to India. And from what I know, and it stands to reason like father, like daughter, so a little gift now and then won't hurt yer to keep me quiet."

Your judgement is mistaken" she retorted and realised she sounded like David!

Grimly Mrs Smith declared, "Yer life is built on lies."

Rosie countered, "I beg your pardon?" And remembered saying just that to Hawkins after David marriage proposal. Since then truth kept surfacing, but she had discovered if she faced and embraced it, its negative influence dissipated.

A thumping on the flat door had Rosie rushing to open it. Breathless, Jill with Rachel in her arms cried "Rosie...help... she's...been...so sick...over carpet, stairs. Paul's out... with boys... "

Mrs Smith pushed past and headed downstairs as Rosie

offered, "Let me take Rachel." Worried by the silent, cold baby she ordered, "I'll take her downstairs and run a hot bath. By the time Jill arrived in her bedroom, the bath was filling, the baby stripped and wrapped in a warm towel while Rosie holding her close walked back and forth rubbing in warmth and speaking in life. Once Jill was in her undies, Rosie laid the child on the bed, grabbed the dirty washing, shoved it in the machine and rushed upstairs where the twins were happily playing. Later she was to question if what she'd seen as the Lord's divine interruption into her situation had been used as His intervention in another.

Mrs Smith was over an hour cleaning up and returned to snatch her pay packet and declare, "Kids! Yer better not 'ave deducted me pay over today's interruptions." With a knowing stare she stated, "I'll be back to clean next week, and we'll have that little chat."

By the following Wednesday, Paul had Rachel admitted into hospital with chronic dehydration and finally diagnosed with phyloric stenosis. An operation was performed on the muscle, tightening and narrowing Rachel's stomach opening, so food could now pass into her small intestine rather than out of her mouth! And with all the basement occupants elsewhere, it brought Rosie to hope today's operation with Mrs Smith would go equally smoothly as she waved off Joyce and the twins. The basement flat was set for David to get a clear recording.

Upstairs, in a pretty box on the bedside table near the door was the babysitting microphone which had been tested for sound. A suitcase was open on the far bed to ensure Mrs Smith would sit on the one near the microphone. Mrs Smith having cleaned the bathroom remarked, "Ah there yer are, Rosie, yer got them biscuits?" Seeing them she looked pleased and plonked herself on the bed in the prime position for her voice to be picked up, "I'll give it yer, yer good at being what yer ain't, with that plumy voice, smart clothes and posh behaviour.

"I am who I am Mrs Smith. I make no pretence."

"Rosemary Doughty-Dawes. Doughty, there's plenty to 'doubt about thee'." She gave a cackle of laughter.

Puzzled Rosie asked, "Why should you doubt me?"

Mrs Smith rosed to the challenge, "How about yer trying to murder yer baby brother leaving 'im disabled?"

Astounded Rosie strove not to react, "Who would say such a thing?"

"Come on, it wouldn't do 'im inheriting what yer consider yers."

Mrs Smith's lip curled, "Yer were sent in disgrace to boarding school to stop yer trying it again. Clever though, yer made friends with a girl who already ill, developed pneumonia and died."

Shocked, Rosie shook her head but asked calmly, "And your point?"

"Yer milked being broken 'earted, became 'ead teacher's pet and she treated yer to all sorts." Flabbergasted at the lies within truth, Rosie could only shake her head and wonder at Mrs Smith source. "How about that then?" She gave a nasty laugh. "Then there's yer money making scheme?" Rosie refocused with a questioning look. "Yer buy expensive clothes, copy 'em, return the copies to the shop and get a refund."

Irritated Rosie stated, "I return the originals to the shop for a refund!"

"So yer say! But it's still stealin' 'em designs." Mrs Smith gave a derisive laugh, "Still not as bad as stealin' someone's 'usband. Ah ha, now that surprised yer! He were rich and powerful, bit like this 'master' fellah Mrs P talks about. Did yer find a way to bump his Jane off?"

"Now you are bordering on the ridiculous!"

"Yer fought wiv Doug Bradford's baby yer'd be set up for life. Didn't bank on his wife knowing 'e liked 'igh class prostitutes and warn yer off." She chortled, "Fancy telling 'er 'e'd marry yer 'cause you were 'aving 'is kid!" I 'eard she told 'im to be rid of yer and 'it' before 'is marriage and career was ruined. Doug Bradford paid others to do what 'e couldn't."

That news was like a stab in the stomach. Rosie sat heavily by the suitcase. Even when the Bradfords had given her the cottage, she hadn't wanted to believe Doug had instigated the abortion of his child. At her obvious dismay, Mrs Smith's eyes sparkled with satisfaction, "All the doc' expected to do that day were' little more than take' out a soft lump of flesh, but he soon discovered differently and 'ad to crush the 'ead of your boy to…"

Her mind only heard, "Boy' it was a boy! Tears filled her eyes, her mind refocused on the supernatural scene, ecstatically she cried out, "I've seen him. His name is Johnny. He's not dead, he's alive."

At her declaration Mrs Smith's eyes widened, she stood and back towards the open door. Rosie moved around the bed to explain, "When I gave my life to Jesus, He not only saved me, but my baby boy. I saw him, he's now eight."

"Yer mad. Religion's gone to yer 'ead. Don't give me that,

Jesus may have been raised from the dead, but yer baby....." Mrs Smith gave a cynical chortle and with a curved lip snarled, "If that were true, many women will, one day, meet the babies they thought they'd got rid of." She gave a sharp laugh, "I kept mine. I struggled bringing her up, they called her a bastard. She's..." Mrs Smith hesitated, shrugged and continued, "You lost yer child but yer gamble paid off. Yer got a cottage in Kensington! Not a bad outcome for a bit of suffering!"

Incensed Rosie burst out, "That's terrible thing to say. I didn't want an abortion. I fought against it. I wanted my child, not a cottage. Tell me who gave you such twisted and warped information?"

Mrs Smith gave a self-satisfied grin, "See, I knows people. 'em coppers 'ad evidence to bring cases against several men for their activities. We was paid good money to keep our mouths shut. I 'eard Bradford 'ad to give yer 'is mews cottage to ensure yer kept quiet. "Yer must 'ave known yer story would stir up a nest of the 'orny men in Parliamentary circles!

"Now you are verging on fantasy."

Sitting again Mrs Smith grinned, "No dearie. Fantasy is what yer create with a posh voice, lady like manners and expensive education, so as not to appear a common tart, but one just the same. I've seen and 'eard fings I dare not repeat. Believe me Parliament dangles men like puppets on strings. And some of 'em, well... if folk knew what they were up to, they'd be disgusted. Still one day the truth will come out, it always does. They closed ranks around Bradford. Police enquiries were thwarted with people dropping their charges, or changing their minds when they realised thy'd be caught up in the publicity. If exposed, Bradford would be in prison today, but it seems yer God decided to take 'im out."

"I had no indication the police believed me. And I was too ill physically and mentally to pursue it. I took advice from those I trusted, and the cottage in London gave me the impetus to get well and start a new life."

"Didn't yer fink it was rather an extravagant gesture?"

"No. Doug wasn't poor. I thought it was his way of expressing his sorrow. From what you have told me I was wrong. But why are you telling me?"

"For such an educated woman, yer a 'slow thinker'. Yer father owes me. Yer my insurance policy for me future."

Mrs Smith had just revealed she knew her father, proving one source, but what of the rest? If coaxed, or coerced, what more would she reveal?"

"Like 'im you are good at being what yer not! And it looks to me as if this time the gamble for rich 'usband, 'ome and family is going to pay off. By looking after 'is children's needs this man Mrs P calls 'the Master' is drawn to you, and by keeping 'im from your bed, 'e 'as now proposed."

Grappling with all she'd heard she felt to ask, "And your point?"

"Point, point!" Frustration brought Mrs Smith to almost screech through closed teeth, "Yer want to marry 'im don't you. 'e don't know yer use your charms to make men part with money. Yer don't speak of yer background or past, 'e sees the 'ouse and estate and thinks yer family 'as fallen on 'ard times. Do yer want 'im to know the truth?" Mystified, Rosie's brow furrowed. "My guess is in acting coy about marriage, yer've plans to get money from 'im before shying away from any commitment."

Although astounded at the way Mrs Smith perceived her, years of discipline at keeping silent allowed Rosie to give an enigmatic smile, which encouraged her to continue. With a straightening of her back, Mrs Smith looked pleased as she declared, "I was right, I knew it!" Her mouth curved into a supercilious smile, "If the 'Master' and 'is father with a MBE were to find out the truth…" She let that hang in the air before adding, "Now yer wouldn't want that to 'appen, would yer?"

Rosie gave a heavy sigh before contradicting her assumptions, "Mrs Smith, the 'Master' is aware of all you have told me, and he and his family accept me. Now, unless you have something more to say, it would be wise to forget this conversation and the inference behind it."

As a way of dismissal, Rosie began packing the suitcase and hoped Mrs Smith wouldn't see her hands shaking. But by the disparaging look on her face she had more to say.

"If 'is family believe yer, they are fools, all of them." Carefully placing clothes into the suitcase, Rosie considered if she should deign that with a reply as Mrs Smith proclaimed, "More fool 'im to be taken in by a beautiful face."

"The Reinhardts aren't fools, and I see no purpose in you telling me or them anything."

Mrs Smith's eyes narrowed before she spat out, "There's purpose! I'm not getting any younger. I need a regular income beyond me working life. Married to 'the Master' you'd barely miss a few pounds a week."

"Let me get this clear. You won't tell anyone what you know about me, as long as I pay you a regular sum for the rest of your life?"

Mrs Smith pointed her finger and with a patronising expression said, "Now dearie, at last, yer got it."

Rosie could feel anger rising but said with relative calm, "Despite being 'a slow thinker' I recognise those twisted truths have come from my father. And those who know him - and know me - often question if I am my father's daughter."

Mrs Smith gave a cynical laugh. "With 'im dearie, well, but let's say yer 'a chip off the old block' alright. Like 'im yer lie, cheat and find ways to condone yer actions. He's living it up in tea plantation of 'is, no thought for me in me old age. Surely yer see it's a small price to pay to ensure yer future and the family yer desire."

"As you are convinced gambling is in my blood you won't be surprised if I take my chances, and let you tell the Reinhardts whatever you like."

Mrs Smith frowned, "Not a good idea dearie. Newspapers love gossip about rich folk. The juicer the story, the more it is believed. When 'the Master' was in the papers, people talked as if 'e 'ad committed murder. Florrie, Mrs P lives in my block of flats, kept telling people she knew 'the Master' and 'e ain't done no murder. It's funny 'ow things come together. I recognised yer face in the background of one of 'em newspaper photos. I showed interest, befriended 'er, and discovered yer were the twins' nanny…the rest is 'istory."

"Mrs P will have told you I was Jane's friend, a bridesmaid at their wedding and my living here was at her invitation, and no-one could have predicted her death."

"Gambler's luck if not 'im, one of 'is rich friends. Yer family background looks good, but ain't what it seems."

"Enlight me."

With pursed lips, Mrs Smith body shook with annoyance. "For a start yer father ain't no Lord."

Rosie gave a wry smile, "That Mrs Smith I've known for years! Lord Dawes' title could only pass through his sons, all of whom are dead. My father is married to his niece. I also know you can buy titles. But my father didn't even do that, he just took it, and it seems no-one has questioned it."

"Well yer won't know this. As a boy Lenny was always ducking and diving with tricks and scams. 'is father was a 'rag and bone' man with a 'orse and cart, 'is mother a skivvy in some seedy joint. 'e left school at fourteen only good at counting cards and money. From twelve 'e did well out of the misery of others in the tenement blocks in the East End. The landlord paid 'im to collect rents and 'e added another charge on top. If any part wasn't paid 'e'd send in the 'bother' boys to extract it. There was always plenty of cash in 'is pocket, but it was gambling that did 'im in."

Could this be true, that her father known as Leo was to Mrs Smith Lenny? Rosie nodded encouragingly and she continued, "Lenny's debts piled up. The 'bother boys' went looking for 'im, and when no-one could find 'im, it was thought they'd done 'im in. There weren't a body though to prove it."

Rosie's interest was sparked, enthusiastically she asked, "Tell me more?"

To her surprise Mrs Smith voice became chatty, "We lived in the same terrace of 'ouses in the East End of London. 'e were two years older than me, we went to the same school. My we 'ad a few romps, 'e was a 'andsome devil, but me Ma said there's no future in a man who ain't got a steady job." She paused and then refocused. "In 'is mid-twenties 'e told me 'e was moving up market and would keep in touch. 'e didn't say when or where, and then 'e was gone. When I tried to find 'im, I found I wasn't the only one looking. 'e owed money to some dangerous people so I finally 'ad to accept 'e were dead."

"Yer could 'ave knocked me down with a feather when I bumped into 'im in 1948. Even with that ridiculous moustache I recognised 'im. I says, 'Good grief, it's you Lenny, I thought yer been dead and buried these twenty years.' 'e caught my arm, said it was best it stayed that way, and then turned on the old charm. When I asked what 'appened to 'is business venture, 'e gave me a grim look. The kind that 'as you shiver, but after a few seconds 'e said quite cheerily that 'e'd gone to India, married into money and life had been good to 'im. With a run of luck, 'e 'ad won a tea plantation in a card game. Then 'is wife 'ad unexpectedly inherited a mansion in England so as 'e'd spent most of 'er money, 'e'd sent 'er packing to live in it."

Rosie informed her, "Along with me, his daughter, born in India in 1941 and the Hawkins, a couple he paid to accompany us."

Mrs Smith hummed, "'e didn't mention that. 'e 'ad no intention of returning to Blighty, but troubled times in India left 'im no choice and it 'ad turned out the inherited mansion was crumbling, cold, dark and dank. No-one 'ad money to buy it, there was little money to maintain it, and 'e 'oped in London to make 'connections'. I saw 'im several times. In 1950 'e turned up uninvited to me Elsie's wedding, looking very well to do, 'is gambling paying off."

Rosie grunted, "Money he'd made selling off the 'home farm' and upsetting the farming community. The idea was to refurbish the house, but only in part. He used the money to further his ambitions."

"Lenny said drink befuddled the mind, but on an occasion 'e talked of 'is pathetic wife, Dee-Dee, who'd unfortunately conceived a stuck up little brat. In jealously yer'd deliberately dropped 'is son, and tried to push 'im under the stair balustrade to the floor below."

Rosie gasped, "It was him. He wanted to kill Bertie."

Mrs Smith brow furrowed but she continued, "In trying to stop yer the boy 'ad bin left disabled. I tried to ask questions but 'e was too upset to say more."

"I bet he was!" Rosie exclaimed. Taking a deep breath she determined to ask calmly, "Have you heard of cerebral palsy?"

"Of course, dearie, as a 'ospital cleaner you 'ear about all kinds of fings."

"My brother Bertie, was born with a withered arm and gnarled hand and within days of his birth was diagnosed with that. When he started to walk he couldn't use his deformed foot, but has learnt to use a stick."

"Is that why you tried to kill 'im?"

"I didn't. I'll tell you exactly what happened which can be verified by the Hawkins who still care for him."

As Rosie enlightened Mrs Smith she began to look uncomfortable and finally said, "Oh! There 'ave been times... I've wondered... " Rosie waited, but she reverted to her original aggressive tone, "Yer father said yer were a nosey, jealous and spiteful kid, good at telling tales. When 'e found out about an educational trust set up by Lord Dawes, 'e'd not only sent you into boarding school, but ripped it off to pay bills for things 'e needed and you 'adn't 'ad. I fink around that time 'e was moving in circles that accepted 'im as Lord Doughty-Dawes, pleased to accept 'is invitations to 'is 'ouse. Lenny said, them were easily parted from their money."

"And did he tell you that we, his children, were banished to live like servants, eating leftovers and wearing hand me down clothes."

"Ducking and diving 'as always been a part of Lenny's life."

"As has been his aim over the years to spend my mother's money, undermine her confidence and health and neglect his children! We lived off the goodwill of others." Her voice faltered, she swallowed hard, but it still sounded strained as she added, "The Hawkins who accompanied us from India stayed and throughout the years have loved and helped us." She spoke of her father's treatment of the Hawkins, his desire for Bertie to be abandoned in a mental institution and how he seemed to condone his dislike of her by twisting the facts to put her in a bad light.

With a hum Mrs Smith said, "Whenever 'e visited me, 'e'd have some tale to tell. In 1963 'e came to say life had got difficult, 'e was returning to India. 'e told me yer'd shacked up with an MP, got pregnant and 'ad a botched back street abortion. I didn't let on I cleaned at a 'no questions asked' massage parlour and guessed it must 'ave bin yer I saw."

Horrified Rosie stated in an unsteady voice, "You! You were there."

"I told yer I's knew. I went to clean, was told a 'oity toity woman with a double-barrel surname 'ad been brought in and they'd been paid good money to get rid of 'er baby. 'She'd been screaming she wanted 'er baby, the doc had refused to abort it saying she was too far gone, but neither 'ad any choice. I's drinking a cuppa when the door was flung open and a young man, 'is shirt soaked in blood charged past shouting 'I've done what yer asked, if you don't want 'er dying 'ere, get 'er to hospital'.

From the amount of blood, vomit and the place stinking of alcohol, it was obvious fings 'ad gone badly wrong. I was called to 'elp. Yer were like a rag doll when we dragged you from the massage couch. Between us we bundled you into a taxi, but the address given wasn't a 'ospital. There was then an urgency to clean up and get rid of all the evidence in case the police turned up."

Even though Rosie had no recollection of that she felt physically sick hearing about it.

"Dear me, dearie, yer've gone quite pale. Put yer 'ead between your knees. Nasty business, best kept between ourselves. That alone is surely worth a couple of extra pounds a week in me pay packet. We'll talk about the future later."

Rosie forced herself to stand, "Thank you for telling me about my father. His past has always been a mystery. I can arrange for you to meet the Hawkins. They know everything. After the abortion they cared for me. They still look after Bertie. Despite his disabilities he's an intelligent man. Should you not prefer to know the truth, it will be untenable for you to continue cleaning here."

"You fire me and yer man will be told what I know about yer father."

"I'd hoped… " Rosie paused seeing David in the doorway.

As he boomed, "Mrs Smith" her eyes widened, she jumped up, turned around, to face David looking very much 'the Master' of his house. With cold challenging eyes, his mouth a grim line he looked down his nose to state, "I am Rosie's man. I know all I need to know, and have nothing but admiration for her. If you have more to tell we are both keen to hear it." David waved a cassette tape. "All you have said has been recorded. I put it to you that we are in a better position to blackmail you, than you us."

In an instant, Mrs Smith had snatched the cassette from his hand and ripped the tape from its case. With a grin she declared, "You ain't got noffing on me now."

David gave a cynical smile, "All you have done is destroyed a brand new tape, and the recording of our conversation still continues."

Rosie expected a tirade of anger, but from confident aggression Mrs Smith withered into pitiful grovelling, "Oh Sir, I didn't mean nought by it. I ain't got much. I didn't fink it could 'urt to ask. This is a good job. I ain't done noffink like it before. It just seemed, well… a God-given opportunity to get an extra bit of cash."

In his cultured voice and tone of a barrister, David spoke slowly and clearly, "The only 'God-given' opportunity for you to receive extra cash in this household will be in working extra hours. You are an excellent cleaner, but from what I have heard today, and your obvious disrespect of Rosie, I have…"

Mrs Smith interrupted him to say ingratiatingly, "I like yer family and kids. Mrs P says she's treated like family," she finished in a derogatory tone, "but I ain't found that with 'er."

David's eyes and voice hardened, "Mrs P has earnt that privilege through her years of commitment, loyalty, and a willingness to go the extra mile to protect, serve and support those who live under my roof."

"Yer got a lovely 'ome 'ere. It's a pleasure to clean. It's the best job I've ever 'ad." Having heard about Mrs Smith's previous cleaning experiences that didn't surprise Rosie. "I's let me self and

Mrs P down. I's sorry Sir," she turned towards her, "and you Miss for believing all Lenny said." She moved towards the door and became agitated as David blocked her path, "I won't say noffing to no-one 'bout what I knows. If you let me by, I'll get me fings and go."

"Not so fast Mrs Smith."

Anxious to be gone she whined, "I ain't taken nothfing, 'cept a bit of food, a sandwich and biscuits."

"I believe you, but you need to know the truth, the whole truth and nothing but the truth." David sent Rosie a wry smile, "If you were willing to do that it is possible you too could become as committed and loyal as Mrs P has been to us, our family and friends. And in due course we may be able to give you extra hours." David looked across at her, as Mrs Smith said sadly, "I didn't always believe Lenny. Please, I'd like to know the truth."

"Rosie, how would you suggest we organise that?"

"The meeting of the Hawkins and my brother Bertie?"

David nodded, "We were considering a family picnic on August Bank Holiday at Rosie's family home. If that goes ahead shall we invited Mrs Smith to come along and judge from what she sees and hears as where her loyalty lays."

If Rosie was surprised at David's invitation, Mrs Smith was astonished, and looked at Rosie, "Yer'd invite me to yer 'ouse?" In knowing David had the ability in confrontation of appearing to side with people, believe them, then use it, Rosie gave a small smile and nod.

"Mrs P is right, yer're good people. And I know yer Dad tells lies. I's sorry I believed him. But I can't come, I'd not fit in, with the likes of you. But fanks for asking."

David gave her his winning smile, "If Mrs P was invited would you come then? Rosie sent him a questioning look, then shrugged, for the delight was evident on Mrs Smith's face as she answered, "Oh yeh, she's me friend."

"Then, as she's our friend too, let's hope she'll feel well enough to come."

CHAPTER 22

Outside her bedroom window the twins were shrieking, "Can't get me!" When she looked out, Paul's twenty-one-year-old daughter Maria was chasing them around the large basin of the disused fountain. Maria had accompanied David earlier that morning as he drove from London to join her and the rest of his family, arriving around noon. Rosie sighed and prayed that having finally succumbed to their visiting on the Bank Holiday Monday, all would go according to plan. With a few scudding clouds in a blue sky, the warmth of the sun and the beautiful display of the countryside around, The Grange was impressive even if the interior wasn't! Her clock showed her it was time to replace her scruffy work clothes with 'Johnny's' skirt' and a plain silk green sleeveless blouse.

Originally, this was to be a Reinhardt family picnic, but it had evolved into a buffet lunch with other invited guests. Fortunately, Cathy had no qualms about catering for the escalating number. Her motto was 'the more the merrier' and her simple answer was to use the ballroom with the choice of eating inside or out. And now Cathy was eagerly waiting to meet the Reinhardt family which she'd heard more about in the last five months than in the five years since she'd met Jane.

It was two months since she had seen Johnny, but Diana kept her informed and at a recent day with her in London she reported his speech was improving. She'd invited them both with a desire to balance the Reinhardts with other guests like the Brigadier and Jennifer, having seen them in church the day before. Joining the party was also Gerald who had happily agreed to bring not only Joyce and Ted but also Mrs Smith and Mrs P.

The Hawkins' care of Helen and their desire to officially foster Declan had made Helen more responsive and responsible. She'd help clean and with lessons from Cathy made dozens of choux buns, now filled with cream and piled up ready for the chocolate sauce to be poured over them. In a huge antique bowl, she put together a sherry trifle which alone could feed the thirty guests. Declan's devotion and Jack's response to him was a delight to behold. Bertie was benefitting in so many ways from their constant desire to include him in what they were doing.

David - adamant in his desire to contribute - had sent a generous cheque to pay for whatever was needed. It enabled Cathy to buy the food but also several much needed items of clothing for

Declan, albeit from a charity shop.

On two Saturdays in August the women had a cleaning spree with the help of little Rebecca. Meanwhile David and Joshua had pottered about with Bertie, Jack and Declan, repairing the boathouse, mending deckchairs, and making improvements to the larger, safer, go-cart. With David decreeing the drive dangerous, they placed a large tree trunk across it just beyond the gatekeeper's cottage. Since Jack had nailed a notice instructing callers to use the Tradesman's Entrance, and if not known the number to ring.

Today, despite its faded grandeur the entrance hall looked impressive with its black iron balustrade and stone staircase. On the highly polished circular antique table stood a cut glass vase filled with four dozen long stemmed white roses - a gift to her from David. In the East Wing, overlooking the front courtyard, the ballroom with its long ornate mirrors and the adjacent lounge were also revived by flowers. Declan and Jack had removed and re-erected the long dining room table along one side of the ballroom. A pristine white cloth now awaited the platters of sliced ham, turkey and beef, cheese flans and a dozen large bowls containing a variety of salad items. Earlier, having put thirty-five jacket potatoes in the oven, Rosie had checked several times it was switched on.

By the front door below her window she recognized Richard's deepening voice, "Hello Uncle David, it seems we're a tad early." If David replied it was drowned out by the twins shouting in unison Richard's name and his laughter and exclamation, "My, you've both grown!" A quick peer over the window sill revealed Richard had also grown, not as broad or tall as his uncle, but strong enough to whisk the twins off their feet and run with them shrieking with delight.

Phillip's voice floated up, "I did say Uncle David that Rosemary was right for you. Just look at this place!" Rosie grimaced remembering that remark during a family meal not long after Jane died. "You said to pray about it. Mum says you've asked her to marry you, but she'd not yet said 'yes'." He sounded puzzled, "Surely inviting us all here is a good sign that God will answer our prayers."

There was mirth in David's succinct and fervent 'I hope so'. Encouraged, Phillip remarked, "Well you managed to persuade her to return to look after the twins!" David's guffaw turned into an ill-disguised cough. Phillip didn't seem to notice as he thoughtfully added, "Maybe she would marry you if you agreed to live here. Couldn't you commute to London?" Rosie guessed David appeared to be considering that because Phillip, warming to his pitch, began pointing out the investment prospects of house and estate, ending with how the twins would benefit by living in the country and saying, "They'd love it here."

The fact David commented, "You've certainly made some good points" gave Rosie to believe he was impressed at Phillip's interest.

Enthused Phillip added, "If you lived here, we could come and stay."

David's serious tone had an underlying amusement, "We must continue to seek God's wisdom." Rosie imagined Phillip nodding, his face serious, as David added, "It is up to Him to…"

Paula's strident voice cut across David's as she demanded, "Phillip, stop foisting your views on Uncle David."

Jane had called Paula fun, fat and forty. Today, waddling slowly across the courtyard only two years past that age, she appeared to be weighty and waspish."

David walked into Rosie's view as his voiced boomed, "You have two fine boys. And believe me Phillip for his age is very wise."

Rosie moved away from the window to slip on a pair of pretty but comfortable flat shoes and left the bedroom. Down the corridor Bertie was heading towards her dragging his twisted leg behind him. Dressed in cream trousers and shirt with a jumper tied around his shoulders, he looked like a cricketer. It was sad that he would never be one.

Sliding her arm through Bertie's damaged one, they slowly descended the staircase into the hall. Below them accepting a glass of sherry from Cathy were Paula and her tall, skinny and very staid Jim. Cathy smiled up at them, they both turned and their smiles froze. Jim with his forefinger pushed the centre of his glasses back on his nose, Paula frowned and both appeared to recoil at Bertie's disabilities. In the seconds before they joined them, their apparent discomfort grew. Bertie, unable to lift his head, had to look sideways at them, his mouth moving oddly to say indistinctly, "Hello and welcome."

Jim outstretched hand was quickly withdrawn as he saw Bertie resting one hand to balance on his stick and the other gnarled into a fist. Paula with a stiff smile muttered, "Pleased to meet you."

To cover their awkwardness, Rosie redirected their attention, "You've met Cathy. Jack, her husband, is organizing the car parking. They have been like parents to us. You are welcome to wander, sit on a deckchair, admire the view or Cathy will take you through the ballroom to the lounge."

Paula's relief to follow Cathy was evident as was her belief Bertie was deaf! Paula's comment was clearly heard, "We didn't know Rosie's brother was a spastic. I thought they were kept in mental hospitals." Rosie glared at their backs, but guessed Cathy's expression brought Paula to realise she had said the wrong thing for she quickly added, "It's very good of you to look after him."

Cathy's reply was distinct and succinct, "Bertie is physically impaired, but mentally more intelligent than most of us. Excuse me..." With that Cathy hurried away through the baize door, leaving them halfway to the ballroom, seemingly bemused.

Rosie squeezed Bertie's arm, "Take no notice." He shrugged, his attention fixed on Mrs Smith clinging to Mrs P's arm. She certainly wasn't dressed as a woman in her late fifties. Her motley grey hair was in a French pleat, with a back combed 'bee hive' on top. Her skinny body clothed as Twiggy, a tight top, short skirt and stiletto heels. Black eyeliner and mascara framed her eyes in a face thick with foundation, her lips a slash of red.

Since their confrontation Mrs Smith had been behaving 'ever so 'umble', conversation limited, but polite. Now she rushed forward greeting her as a long lost friend, "Oh Rosie, it's lovely to be 'ere, and 'ow lovely yer look." With a fast blinking of her eyelashes, as though to stop tears, she said, "And yer, Bertie," before nearly unbalancing him in a hug. Rosie steadied Bertie, received a kiss on her cheek before she was told, "Now yer both must call me Ida." Rosie tried not to cringe at the alcohol smell on her breath as, in raptures of delight, she told Bertie about their lovely journey with Gerald, her surprise at the size of the house and estate, and how she had known their father for many years.

Beside her, Mrs Perkins dressed very appropriately appeared embarrassed. Rosie gave her a big smile and a gentle hug, "I'm so pleased you felt well enough to come. We've missed you. Wait until the twins see you!"

Mrs P drew her aside, "Ida's been drinking. I don't like her pushy ways. I wish I 'adn't suggested she come to clean. What are the likes of us doing 'ere?"

"You are here because I like you." Rosie gave her a reassuring smile, "And even if you don't return to work, we would like you to visit us."

"Thanks luv. But 'er? Fancy dressing like that. Does she

really know yer father?"

"It seems possible. As they say Mrs P, life can be full of surprises."

Mrs P gave a shy smile and offered, "Me name's Florrie, short for Florence, you can call me that if yer'd like." In seeing Cathy returning through the baize door with a tray of drinks, she introduced her as Florrie, the wonderful Mrs P, bringing her to retort with a chortle, 'oh get on wiv yer!" Ida broke off from Bertie to listen as Rosie spoke of Jack and Cathy's role in her life. At Ida's interest, Rosie suggested she talk to Cathy later and they wandered around the West Wing, having seen the horrified look on Paula and Jim faces at seeing David's house cleaners.

Gerald entered - he had been outside surveying the estate - his mouth with his buck teeth formed what Rosie nicknamed his 'happy bunny' smile. He first kissed her cheek and then Cathy's before remarking, "Thanks to you Cathy, Declan is already a different child. When he saw me, he ran over, hugged me and thanked me for bringing him here." 'Here' Rosie has been a well-kept secret, and I feel honoured to know Lord Dawes' 'great' niece. He was a good man who played a vital role in the security of this nation."

Rosie smiled, "And I feel equally honoured to have your friendship." Gerald grinned, saluted Bertie who gave his hee haw laugh and reciprocated with his gnarled hand. "My mother didn't know Lord Dawes. My parents never showed an interest in him beyond any financial gain. I'm pleased he was a good man, I wish the same could be said for my father! How sad his inheritance has been allowed to rot, no-one wants to buy it. In April there was fresh interest, but brief probably due to the restoration costs!"

Gerald nodded, "Mrs Smith has been drinking. She said she's a friend of your father, doesn't know I'm a cop, and became quite informative. Poor Mrs P looked horrified, Ted and Joyce amused, rest assured nothing was said about you, otherwise I would have intervened.

"Thank you. I can only hope that in talking to the Hawkins, she'll recognize the truth that I'm not like my father."

"I did listen to the tape, and have made discreet enquiries. There is no 'missing person' record, or any offences recorded for a man named 'Doughty'. He applied for a National Insurance number in 1948, but there's no trace of his being employed. Either he lived on funds from India, this estate or his gambling habit. The sale of the Home Farm and the land fetched a good price, enough to refurbish this place, but looking around I guess he didn't do that. Ida Smith said she knew your father up until 1928, and thought he was born around 1904. I've looked around those years for a record of his birth at Somerset House. It's possible he was illegitimate and his birth not registered. I did discover that Ellermans - the main shipping line to India - has a record of a 'Doughty' paying cash in 1936, two days before the ship sailed. He would have needed a birth certificate to get a passport in that name. I've yet to access the Passport Office…"

"Hello Rosie, is Gerald telling you about our interesting journey." Joyce sent him a wry smile, "This place is bigger than I expected. David was just telling us his first thought on arrival was to compare it to Munster Manor." She giggled like Jane, "David would make a good Herman!"

Rosie smiled at Gerald, "We'll talk later."

As she accompanied Joyce and Ted to meet Bertie, Ida and Florrie reappeared with Florrie anxiously saying, "Is 'elen stil ''ere? I fought she were living at yer cottage. Gerald told us yer saw her just after Christmas living rough, taking drugs and brought 'er 'ere? We've just met Declan, 'er brother. Rosie you've such a generous heart."

Rosie responded, "If the place sells the Hawkins hope to keep Declan with them."

As Ida drew Florrie away Ted observed, "I guess Florrie wanted to balance Ida's revelations on the way down. I've always thought the Reinhardts are a class act, but life isn't always as it seems, and this certainly has all the elements of being a very eventful day!" He glanced at their retreating figures and added, "Rosie, whatever the truth about your background, we believe you'll be an excellent mother to the twins."

"Thank you Ted, I appreciate that."

Ted grinned, "Get Franz to buy and renovate this place, he could afford it. And he's far more suited to the role of Herman than David."

Rosie chuckled, and then looking beyond him said loudly, "Franz, Margaret, welcome to…"

"Munster Manor!" Franz's voice boomed just like David's. Rosie didn't dare look at Ted as Franz added, "David would make a good Herman." Ted gave a snort of laughter, Franz glanced at him and proclaimed, "I suspect certain people would cast me in that role!"

Joyce, with her hand over her mouth, giggled while Margaret

looked skyward before declaring, "Sorry about that. He's trying to be more sociable."

Franz frowned, Ted and Joyce looked surprised, and Rosie without thinking tucked her hand through Franz' arm and teased, "I'm sure you are trying!"

Ted and Joyce sniggered, Margaret grinned and surprisingly Franz' harsh features were transformed by a smile. Despite his voice being on a lower decibel, the hall amplified his words of pleasure at seeing her again, causing her to wonder if he had a tipple before arriving. But as he kissed her cheek there was no tell-tale odour, and he certainly wasn't fazed at seeing Bertie, "Pleased to meet you, my boy. David tells me there is a great deal more to you than meets the eye. We're very fond of your sister and look forward to getting to know you too."

Bertie looked delighted, and seeing him desperate to speak she acted as translator. "Pleased to meet you. David good, kind man. Helps me. Gave us colour TV, typewriter for my questions. Brings twins, I love them."

Franz patted his shoulder, "So do I." He addressed them both, "This house is bigger than I anticipated, wonderful views, and much potential."

Bertie nodded, Rosie agreed and added, "A potential limited by money. Jack's doing a tour of the grounds after lunch, there is a lake beyond the West Wing. And David wants to show you the vintage Bentley in the garage."

"I've seen it. Excellent condition, worth a great deal! Sell it. Use the money to renovate the house."

With a wry smile she stated, "Unfortunately not my house, not my car." She challenged, "But if you want to buy either I'm sure my parents are open to offers" and added quietly by his ear, "You are one of the few who could afford this place."

Franz' scowl wasn't unlike David's when he considered something inappropriate had been said. But surprisingly, he added in a conversational tone, "Those two flats of David's are only suitable for childless people. When Jane left us it was marvelous the way you all pulled together. I know you try to help Jill, what do you think is wrong with her?"

Uncomfortable at being asked, Rosie answered succinctly, "Overwhelmed by having three children in a short space of time" and changed the subject, "If you would like to see beyond the first floor, ask Jack to take you. I've not been up there for years. With damp, dry rot, rats etc. Jack considers no-one should venture up there alone."

Puzzled he stated "Is that so? I understood the roof was in good order."

"Dad!" David boomed and apologized, "Ignore him! Jack is parking the last car and everyone is accounted for. Franz gave a distinct nod, did a very German side step as David drew him away to speak to him, only interrupted by Cathy offering them a glass of sherry.

Again, Franz' boom was easily heard by all, "Good to meet you, a wonderful woman by all accounts. You and your husband's loyalty to Rosie's parents and your input into Rosie and Bertie's lives is of great credit to you." Cathy went bright red.

On seeing Jill waddling across the hall, Rosie realized just how much weight she had gained, and although Paula was eleven years older than her, they looked more like twins. At least Jill was clean, tidy, with a new outfit and sporting a haircut that suited her. Since Rachel's operation Paul had determined to wean Rachel from her mother, and today six month old Rachel was smiling and taking an interest in her surroundings, while Luke clasping Jill's hand peered shyly around her voluminous skirt. William's bright blue eyes sparkled with mischief, and had no compunction about running into her asking the whereabouts of his cousins. Cathy told him they were playing with Maria in the kitchen garden. Anxious to be with them, he zoomed nosily around the hall bringing David to suggest he should take William and Luke with him.

Paul rubbed his full beard between his forefinger and thumb, his kind brown eyes reflecting his usual appreciation of Rosie, while Jill wide-eyed was commenting, "Good heavens Rosie, you're a dark horse. This place may be run down but it's huge. Why all the years of secrecy?"

Rosie shrugged, "Life taught me to be a private person." She gave a wry smile, "Unlike the Reinhardts who are known for saying it as it is!" At Jill's puzzled scowl she added, "It's an observation, not a criticism." Amused, Paul looked up as Ida and Florrie came down the stairs. In her haste to get to the group at the bottom, Ida nearly tripped into Paul as she prattled, "Dr Paul, Jill, how lovely to see you." Florrie looking uncomfortable hung back, but that quickly changed to embarrassment as Franz made a beeline for her with an outstretched hand to boom, "Mrs P it's good to see you. On the way to a full recovery I hope?" And as she tentatively took Franz' outstretched hand, Ida promptly joined her. "Without your help Rosie could have been lost forever, and we would not be here today. Mind, I had hoped today to celebrate an engagement!" Florrie not knowing how to respond looked flustered, but Franz had already turned to say, "Mrs Smith isn't it? I gather you have now taken on Mrs P's job."

Ida stuck out her hand, "You can call me Ida. I know Rosie's father."

Rosie cringed, Franz didn't appear perturbed but just boomed, "Is that so!" Ida appeared to bob a slight curtsey, causing Rosie to consider if he too had the ability to make women go weak at the knees?

Rosie's attention was diverted by Helen slowly coming down the stairs, wearing brightly patterned cotton trousers and matching top. She looked very much the girl with whom she had shared the basement flat, and confidently called over the balustrade "Mrs P, do you remember me?"

Florrie looked up, "Of course, dear. When I saw your brother's shock of red hair, I was reminded of you, and hear you both live here now."

Bertie nudged her. Rosie looked up to see the Brigadier, Jennifer, Diana and Johnny entering. Smiling, Rosie headed towards the Brigadier, hand outstretched and declared, "I'm here to make your welcome a great deal warmer than the last time you visited!"

"Thank you my dear, I appreciate that." After kissing her cheek he made a beeline for Bertie. Jennifer, in handing her a sheaf of flowers commented, "Freddy gets such a kick out of using Bertie's sign language - such a help to Johnny."

Rosie while greeting Diana could almost feel Johnny's eyes drinking her in. When she turned and their eyes met he said slowly, "Not quite alone at last," he grinned, "hey sis why don't you push off." Diana raised her eyebrows, Rosie frowned, but immediately their eyes locked transmitting to her something far deeper than words. Understandably he had lost weight, his face was thinner, but that just accentuated his perpetual smile. Behind her the Brigadier gave a gentle cough. She whipped around, caught Jennifer's thoughtful expression before apologizing and pointed them to Cathy with her tray of drinks. David, with hand outstretched, cut across their path.

Diana observed, "Rosie, that's one generous, gorgeous sexy man! If you don't want him I'll have him." Johnny clicked his tongue, Diana grinned and remarked, "Love your skirt. Johnny has good taste" and with a giggle she hurried to join the Greenhaighs.

Johnny slid his hand under the sheath of flowers and with his eyes gazing into hers he stretched across to kiss her cheek and carefully pronounced, "You are beautiful." From his pocket he pulled out a flat packet and placed it on the flowers saying, "Music! My words."

Her eyes widened, "Oh Johnny, a record! Let's slip away after lunch and play it." Johnny squeezed her hand twice for 'yes'! Amused Rosie warned, "Your father is learning our secret language. Your speech has improved since June, but you were rude to Diana."

Johnny grinned, waved at Bertie, and said, "Telling people to 'push off' was in our early years part of my charm." Rosie's mouth twisted into a wry smile, and wondered at David's reaction if in shaking Johnny's hand he had received such a response! However as Diana vivaciously joined the Greenhaighs, if David ever had such thoughts seeing her acting like Felicity, she guessed that could spark his wish that she should push off.

"Rosie everyone is here." Cathy turned to Johnny, "Could you take Bertie into dinner? Helen's going to sit with him during the meal, but I need her to help bring out the food."

"I'd better put these flowers in water. Can you ask David to deal with the wine?" As she headed towards the baize door Florrie with Ida in tow called, "Rosie, we'd like to help." She stopped as David murmured beside her, 'Thanks for rescuing me.'

Cathy bustled up to them to say "Yes please, follow me." As they headed into the large old-fashioned kitchen, Rosie went into the family kitchen and filling a vase with water quickly read the card attached to Johnny's gift.

Rosemary means 'remember' and I have in so many ways. Your dark, long, straight curtain of hair to either hide behind, or peer out from, in your shy and endearing way. Your expressive eyes, often dulled by trepidation, that lit up on seeing me. Your rosebud lips would pout when upset, but in thanks and happiness formed the sweetest smile. Your loneliness met mine. Our friendship was so precious. Rich girl meets poor boy, and gives him her trust, and friendship.

Then you were gone. But the memories of those few short years remain in my mind, my heart and my life. This record says what I cannot. It's what my heart feels, wherever my Rosemary goes, young love still flows, and grows. Johnny xx

Tears ran down her cheeks and she wiped them with the back of her hand as she arranged the flowers. Johnny was the opposite of

David. He was easy going and fun. His bright eyes - even when ill - reflected inner joy. He had a permanent smile, a gentle voice and with his adoration, her confidence was boosted.

Cathy interrupted her thoughts declaring, "Let's use those flowers as a centre piece for the table. We're ready to go! Only the trifle and profiteroles are left in the kitchen and we'll make the chocolate sauce between courses."

David was waiting for her at the ballroom door, his arm snaked possessively around her waist and a kiss was planted on her mouth. Was that for Diana or Johnny's benefit? Jack drew everyone's attention by tapping a spoon against a glass. He introduced himself, welcomed everyone, gave important directions to the two functioning bathrooms and explained the dangers of visiting the upper floors of the house, walking on the pot-holed drive, and stepping into the weedy lake, "To my knowledge no drownings or murders have happened here, nor have there been ghostly sightings, but it came to my attention that some people have renamed this house Munster Manor!" He grinned and added, "Should those who know the TV programme cast votes today for the role of Herman, David assures me he would be the winner."

Over the laughter, clapping and comments Franz boomed, "And Rosie, as such a nurturing mother, would make a delightful Lily." Rosie blushed as everyone looked at them, David squeezed her waist. Jack tapped the glass again for attention, "This afternoon, for those who wish it, I'll take an escorted walk around the lake, but now and without further ado, I declare 'lunch is served'." He stood back indicating the long table laden with food. As David instigated the clapping, Jack bowed and began handing out plates while Cathy hovered to help.

Rosie circulated around her guests and sidling up to Johnny said quietly, "Volunteer to wash up".

Picking up a plate David joined her to observe, "The family picnic seems to have extended way beyond its original parameters."

Unsure to which parameters he was referring Rosie stated, "With few to call family, I thought I would invite those who have played a valuable part in my life. We may also have over catered."

An hour later, even Jill and Paula had been persuaded - with the promise of a deck chair - to go as far as the boat house, but the other guests opted to walk the mile around the lake. Their start was slightly delayed by admiring the cart Declan and Jack had been upgrading with bits from a scrap yard. It now sported chains and pedals, operated from what they called a 'jump seat' and even the wheels had a rudimentary braking system rather than having to use your feet. Phillip and Richard were as keen and enthusiastic as the children to ride in it down to the lake. David was cautious about the safety aspect, but he and Rosie were quite surprised when Franz offered to police the direction and speed of the contraption.

Margaret teased, "Are you making up for your lost childhood?" Franz scowled, and quickly informed them that as a child in Germany, he and his Uncle had made a similar cart for him and his cousin. "Hans went on to design cars for Mercedes Benz." Margaret remarked, "And did very well for himself!" Franz grunted. Margaret smiled. "Hans, like you, followed in his father's footsteps. The difference being your pharmaceutical background enabled you to bring medical breakthroughs, market important drug treatments and build your own company." Franz scowling, now from embarrassment, began helping his four grandchildren under four, into the cart.

To Phillip's delight, his grandfather suggested that with his new-found friend Declan they should ride 'shotgun'. They started slowly, but once they began going downhill the children inside the cart started shrieking with delight. Rosie watched, but her view was quickly blocked by the men walking alongside and the women strolling slowly behind.

David hadn't objected to her staying behind to wash up and give Cathy a rest. Before Florrie and Ida could volunteer, Helen, Bertie and Johnny slipped away to the family kitchen. With the plates already stacked in the sink soaking and the cutlery placed in a washing up bowl of hot soapy water, it wasn't going to take long.

Within minutes of Helen turning off the mixer whipping the cream for the scones, Cathy was asleep on the settee. Johnny and Bertie dried up and with Helen putting away they were soon finished. However, she did feel rather clandestine to lead Johnny upstairs. She admitted it and on entering added, "I've never entertained a man in my bedroom."

"Not even David?"

"He's been in here but not like this. She told him the story of the rats, but left out the bit about Jack catching her naked on the bed with David, "This could have been a happy home if my parents had been different. I could have stayed at the local school, and as you were my best friend been invited for tea. We could have done our homework together, and not had to wait twenty-three years to come up here and play records. The words in your card were lovely."

Slowly he said, "We are here now". And, looking out of the window he commented, "When you marry David, the Reinhardts being obviously rich, I think they would be keen to refurbish this place."

"It's unlikely for Franz believes children should forge their own careers and live within their means. I'd happily live within David's means. My hesitation in marrying him is knowing he is not an easy man to live with, and... well, I'm not physically attracted to him."

Johnny's eyes filled with cheeky amusement, "Diana's very taken with him."

"Most women are! You know what happened, David sees marriage as an opportunity to become a mother to his twins. It's about friendship, companionship and trust. This six month courtship was my idea to see if we have enough interests to make a marriage." She took the record from its sleeve and placed it on the turntable, then indicated he sit in the easy chair, "I've only heard this song once. The words in your card brought back memories of our school days. She placed the needle on the edge of the record, and stood to listen and watch his face.

"She ain't got no money, Her clothes are kinda funny, her hair is kinda wild and free. Oh, but love grows where my Rosemary goes. And nobody knows like me. She talks kinda lazy, And people say she's crazy and her life's a mystery. Oh, but love grows where my Rosemary goes. And nobody knows like me. There's something about her hand holding mine. It's a feeling that's fine and I just gotta say she's really got a magical spell and it's working so well that I can't get away."

Rosie gave him an amused smile, which caused him to stretched across, take her hand and fix his eyes on hers.

"I'm a lucky fella and I've just got to tell her that I love her endlessly because love grows where my Rosemary goes. And nobody knows like me. It keeps growing every place she's been and nobody knows like me. If you've met her, you'll never forget her. And nobody knows like me. La la la, believe it when you've seen it. Nobody knows like me."

As the record finished, their interlocked gaze didn't, for her deep memories of his protection and comfort were surfacing. The

330

needle bobbed up and down on the record. She didn't want to break the magical spell. Johnny indicated she put it on again. Hand in hand they stood looking out the window. She drank in the words and sighed as it came to an end, "Oh Johnny if it wasn't for David, I would eagerly sung,

"You ain't got no money, being a Vicar is kinda funny, and your eyes are cheeky and bright, Oh, but love grows where Johnny goes, And he knows what nobody else knows, about me. There is something about holding his hand, it's a feeling that's so fine, there's magical spell, it's just working oh so well and I've just gotta say, there's a love between us, which is never going to fade away."

Johnny drew her to him and she admitted, "Cathy says I light up when I see you. Were we made for each other?"

Slowly he spoke, "I'd like to think so, but David has staked his claim."

Fervently she declared, "But he doesn't love me! I do love his twins and they me! Is that enough to marry a man I like, but don't love? And the commitment is as a mother 24 hours a day, 7 days a week, and on call day and night. Courting has been difficult with David's work and the children. His heart is still with Jane and mine still feels with you. David is a man of integrity and assured me if I chose you over him, I could remain the twins' nanny and their favourite auntie."

Johnny put his hands on her shoulders, "Which proves he cares for you."

"But Jane was the love of his life. You tell me I'm the love of yours." Johnny stared into her eyes, and a magical spell of reciprocal love flowed through her. For a few minutes they were held in that thrall and then Johnny indicated his need to write. With pen and paper, he sat at the table and standing behind him with her arms around his neck, she read as he wrote, 'In hospital, the more I heard of your life and past, the more I loved you and your honesty. My life hasn't been eventful. I've no ambition beyond being a vicar. I have no money, no real prospects, except my job provides a home. We could foster and maybe adopt children, but unlike David I've not travelled, nor do I have business interests. My world consists of God and His flock. With me, I fear you would soon be bored. If you choose David, I hope I could be a friend, like a brother, to both of you."

Johnny pushed back the chair, saw the tears in her eyes and hugged her as she whispered, "But you love me and I love you." When he stepped back, instead of seeing his eyes filled with love, his brow was furrowed and his eyes focused beyond her and out of the window. Puzzled, she twirled around. At the far end of the drive, she could just make out what seemed to be an army lorry, its rear covered in green tarpaulin and heading up towards the house.

"Good grief! Didn't they read the sign about visitors and deliveries using the tradesmen entrance? They must have removed that large tree trunk blocking the drive." The lorry began to ascend the incline. "David feels those gutters on each side, permanently filled with water, are undermining the drive, and the potholes in the tarmac are an accident waiting to happen. A lorry of that weight and size..." She rushed to a big drawer, rooted in it while asking, "Could it be army manoeuvers and they have taken a wrong turn?" Grabbing a bright red jumper she suggested, "I'll try to stop them coming further." With that she dashed out the bedroom door as Helen called out, "Someone is coming up the..."

"I know. I'm going to try to stop them."

Johnny shot out of the door behind her as Helen said, "Jack put up a..."

Rosie looking up from the stair landing said, "Yes he did!"

Helen wailed, "Oh Rosie, I don't like the look of it. I remember..."

"I know. I'll shut the front door behind me. Bolt it, and ensure the other doors are locked. If I feel in danger I'll come back in via the kitchen garden. Tell Bertie to watch from his room."

The red jumper was snatched from her hand as Johnny bounded down past her, and was out of the open front door before she started down the final length of staircase into the hall.

CHAPTER 23

From the front door she could just hear the heavy lorry pressing forward. Surely the potholes were enough to reveal the drive was dangerous!   Johnny had already run beyond the courtyard to the flat grass and was now waving her red jumper. She saw him jump the two foot ha-ha before slowly negotiating the downward incline, his red flag fluttering from him. Through the sparse leaves of the tall trees on each side of the drive, surely both the passenger and driver in their army truck could see him! Whatever their purpose they must be able to see it was foolhardy to press on, unless… unless those within the truck were coming with ill intent.

Worried, she ran past the end of the West Wing, across the top of the drive, and stood where she could see around the whole lake. The men were congregated on the far side, near where Jack was probably explaining how the sluice gates in the river worked to fill the lake. Not as far around as that, Declan with Phillip and the young children were running around the go-cart parked on the grass. The women were either strolling away from the house or sitting in deck chairs at intervals around the lake. It would take her five minutes to run to the first group by the boathouse, and still need to attract the men's attention.

Unsure of the best course of action, she walked back and looked down the drive where in the distance she could see two figures in front of the vehicle. The potholes in the drive would make it dangerous to run down there. She returned to the courtyard to see that the lorry was making slow progress as it lurched from side to side while reversing back and forth.   The air was filled with the sounds of gear grating, engine revving and a rumbling not dissimilar to that of an oncoming train. To her consternation two men in army fatigues began to run up towards Johnny and as they came near he raised his hands in defence.

Anxious for his safety Rosie yelled, "Oh God, help!" and was astonished when, within yards of Johnny, all three men fell to their knees as the rumbling sound grew louder. The moment it passed by they were all back on their feet, the men running to the lorry, while Johnny swiftly headed diagonally up and away from the drive.

The two men were wildly gesturing to the driver who - ignoring them - continued his attempts to get traction and move further forward. Throughout, the spinning tyres were biting deeper into the tarmac and stirring up a dust storm. The spindly branches of the trees shook with the wind pressure around them.

That same deep rumbling grumbling rolled again up the hill towards her and as the four trees on each side of the vehicle fell like matchsticks, her hand flew to her mouth in fear they would hit the two men. Obviously spooked, one appeared to call to the passenger before he joined the other man running away down the hill. The revving ceased, the engine was turned off, and without that sound the rumbling was more obvious.

Rosie ran towards Johnny as he jumped the ha-ha and saw from his expression that something was very wrong. He grabbed her hand and kept running across the lawn towards the house. Anxiously she shouted, "What are we running from?" But it wasn't until they reached the courtyard that Johnny let go of her hand. As he bent over to catch his breath she felt a vibration similar to that of an underground train passing beneath their feet. Grabbing on to Johnny she cried, "What's happening?" His response was a grimace, a shake of his head, and his arm encompassing her. It stopped seconds later and turning, they saw the dust around the lorry settling. Rosie stared at it and then asked, "Johnny is it my imagination or are the front wheels of the lorry slightly raised from the ground?" Her hand was squeezed for 'yes' causing her to conclude, "The back wheels must have made a large pothole and they are stuck in it." A few seconds later she exclaimed, "The front wheels are rising!" Horrified Rosie gasped, "The drive behind them has collapsed." Transfixed they watched - as if in slow motion - the underbelly of the cab was revealed, bringing Rosie to question, "If the drive behind them has collapsed, surely they should now be slipping backwards, not tipping upwards." The cab door opened, the passenger jumped to the ground and Rosie guessed the driver was doing the same on the other side. The passenger straightened and stood looking up at the open cab door. Within those few seconds the vehicle became fully vertical and began wobbling precariously as if balancing on a precipice. All along, it was accompanied by a deep growling reminding her of a lion awaiting to devour his prey. The lorry appeared to jolt, but to their astonishment it didn't topple backwards. Instead the earth appeared to gradually swallow it up. The sound grew louder as the back wheels and the long tarpaulin cover disappeared, and the vibrations beneath their feet were again noticeable. They both jumped at the loud bang as the open cab doors hit the ground and broke off. The growling became louder as the vehicle's bonnet and front wheels disappeared into what had to be a very large hole.

Astonished they didn't move. In the surreal silence Rosie saw movement and nudged Johnny. An hysterical giggle broke from her as - like people standing upright on an escalator - the thin tall trees were moving downward to collapse on those fallen by the lorry. The sound reminding her of the bible verse 'the trees of the field will clap their hands' but this wasn't a time for celebration. It was the scene of a disaster movie and she clung to Johnny for comfort until reality broke through. "We need to help" and with that they ran hand in hand towards the West Wing to alert those by the lake.

They passed under Bertie's window on the first floor, and with such a good view of all that had happened, she knew either Helen or Cathy would have rung the emergency services. About to call up to Bertie's open window, a strange cracking noise drew their attention and cautiously they moved towards its source. The grey tarmac of the drive was breaking like a biscuit into pieces, each piece rising and nudging the next causing it to edge forward. It had slowly started, but the momentum was building and after the tarmac, small stones then larger ones were cascading and tumbling down, until all that was left of the drive's foundations was thick wet mud. In those minutes the hole in which the lorry had fallen was filled in, a mound was built over it with a wall of large stones in front of it. In a numbing inertia they watched as if it was an outdoor cinema screen.

In the uncanny stillness that followed, broken only by an occasional rock or stone dropping, they remained still until Rosie gasped when the wet mud began to move like a volcano's black lava, taking anything left in its path where fortunately the newly built stone wall caused it to spread across the ground rather than build up.

Helen calling her name pulled them from their reverie and they turned to see her leaning out of Bertie's window. Amused she said, "Wow Rosie. You scream out 'God help' and the earth literally moved! But I ask, did He have to make such a mess of the drive?" Johnny stifled a nervous chortle. Helen looked towards him, "I suspect you were party to that. Your God certainly spooked those two men. It's a pity He let them get away. Cathy thinks she saw someone in the lorry cab before it disappeared. Hold on…" She paused, "Sorry got to go. I'll unlock the front door. See you in a minute."

Rosie shivered, looked at the devastation and lamented, "I hope Cathy is wrong. It doesn't bear thinking about that someone could be buried in that hole. When those men jumped out, did they get clear before the cab doors broke off?" Johnny frowned and shrugged. "To think, only a few months ago I drove my father's Bentley along that drive. David used it three times and declared never again! Let's pray that the emergency services won't take too long."

They returned to look over the lake where the men were now in groups. Even from a distance, she recognized the Brigadier's marching walk and guessed his companions were David and Jack. It was possible to see the top of the trees that had lined the drive from the far side of the lake, had Jack spotted their movement and was it their reason for heading back? Or perhaps hearing the noise they thought a thunder storm was approaching? Although there was no sign of urgency in anyone returning. In the distance she guessed it was Franz lifting the children into the go-cart ready for their return journey.

Helen joining them certainly wasn't fazed by the drama, for she chirped happily, "It was like a film. The earth swallowed up a lorry, the trees in perfect line move down the hill by themselves, and finally the drive folded up and rolled down after them! And I thought it was dull living here." Smiling at Johnny she placed a hand on his arm, "Isn't there a story in the Bible about God opening up the earth and destroying a whole tribe?" Johnny nodded and moved so her hand fell away. Not seeming to notice she added, "I thought as much, but seeing God in action does make Him seem real."

Rosie concluded, "He is real, but we need to pray no-one was hurt or buried alive."

Helen raised her eyebrows, "I've heard Jane say 'God works all things together for good of those who love Him'." Rosie's brow furrowed. Helen gave a derisive laugh, pointed to the devastation and remarked, "Well, no-one will want to buy this place now and the house could be next!"

Crossly Rosie retorted, "That's ridiculous!" And realizing she sounded like David added, "The house has stood for several hundred years, the foundations are as solid as a rock. It would take a very powerful earthquake to damage it, and this country isn't susceptible to those."

Undeterred Helen asked, "Well, whatever caused the vibrations, it was enough for several books to fall off Bertie's shelves. I bet the less heavy tomes in the library have too, although Cathy hasn't reported any damaged… well so far." With a winsome smile, Helen turned to again place her hand on Johnny's arm, "You need speech exercises so do tell me about this God of yours?"

"For heaven's sake Helen, not now!" At Helen's scowl Rosie asked, "Did the emergency services say how long they might be?"

"They aren't coming."

In agitation Rosie screeched, "What do you mean they aren't coming!" Johnny laid a calming hand on her arm.

"Cathy went to the phone to call the police when Johnny warded off those two men, but the line was dead." At Rosie's dismayed exclamation Helen stated, "That spooked her too! She was going to drive to the phone box, but the parked cars were blocking her in. We ensured all doors and windows were locked. I tried calling you from your window and then Bertie's, but you couldn't hear me."

With Helen and Johnny in tow, Rosie hurried back to the lake to check on David, the Brigadier and Jack's progress. They obviously weren't in a hurry, as they were talking towards those around the boathouse. It caused her to murmur, "Maybe I should run down and hurry them up."

Helen shrugged, "What can they do? Surely you don't expect them to rescue those men! It was obvious their intentions weren't good…"

Johnny touched Rosie's arm to slowly state, "Not sure… intentions."

Helen gave a cynical laugh, "Well, God didn't like it! Neither did Cathy. She returned to Bertie's room with the gun Jack uses to shoot rabbits. She said she knew how to fire it, but I bet she never …"

"Drat!" Rosie cut across her, "David and the Brigadier are heading off to the cottage!" Jack couldn't have heard her but he looked up towards the house, giving Johnny the opportunity to wave the red jumper. Elated Rosie put her arms above her head and waved frantically hoping to indicate a problem. It worked, for across the lake all the men were suddenly galvanized into action. On the far side, one group set off on a run across the grassy hill seeing it as the shortest route to the house, obviously not knowing it was also the steepest and the most slippery. Two others took stock and saw the safest way of return was the path and began a steady jog.

Rosie breathed a sigh of relief, which quickly dissipated as Helen informed them, "Cathy's thinks those two men who jumped out were caught under the cab doors. Like you she seems to think it's our duty to help those 'poor' men! When I left her she'd retrieved that first aid kit you bought for the car, was gathering 'useful' items that might be needed, and assigned Bertie to the garage to gather equipment the men could use for a rescue mission. I'm to be in charge of tea and refreshments. I better get back." She chortled, "Cathy may need me to tear up an old sheet into strips for bandages... Oh, hi Gerald, you've made it in record time!"

Despite sweating profusely, Gerald wasn't out of breath. His grass-stained shirt evidence he had scrambled and climbed the steep slope more than run up it. He was quick to notice and ask, "What happened to the drive?"

Helen chortled, "The 'happening' was the earth moved because Rosie called on God!"

Gerald's eyebrows lifted and he said, "I see" but Rosie wasn't sure if that was surprise at Helen's news or in seeing Johnny's hand in hers? Slipping her arm through Gerald's, Rosie headed him to take a closer look at the black scar on the landscape while explaining the events and possibility of injuries. In the midst of which he frowned to ask, "Does the telephone line often go dead?" Rosie relayed their suspicion of foul play and their inability to reach the phone box. The loud bantering of Richard, Phillip and Declan was heard as Declan declared he was first, and seconds later appeared in front of them. He called, "Jack told us to run up here to see if we can help." He grinned at Gerald, "Wow! So it was you heading up here as if your life depended on it."

Gerald's exertion had given him a red-face but it went a shade darker and to cover his embarrassment he declared, "You boys all seem pretty fit too." On seeing the devastation all three boys' mouths fell open. "There's a lorry buried under that, and we need you to run to the nearest telephone box."

Declan advised, "It'll take about ten minute to run from here."

Phillip seeing Paul arrive shouted to him, "A lorry is buried under that mud slide."

Paul's first question was, "Is everyone alright?" Rosie had just expressed their fears and the lack of a telephone when Jack arrived.

Breathless and seeing the devastation, he looked so distraught that Paul put out a hand to steady him as he said shakily, "Tree notice... drive unstable. Saw ... treetops moving. David's investigating... never imagined..." He trailed off, stared at the scene and rubbed the sweat from his forehead with his arm as Rosie filled him in. Recovering he questioned emphatically, "Who are they and why did they ignore the warning?"

"We don't know. Johnny waving my red jumper tried..."

Declan interrupted, "Shouldn't we go to the phone box?"

Gerald exchanged a look with Paul and Jack before saying to Declan's upturned eager face, "In the circumstances, it would be better to find David and take him to the phone box. As an adult he's more likely to be believed."

Declan nodded, "Will Uncle David believe me?

"He will if I come with you." Said Phillip with confidence.

Rosie smiled and suggested, "Then all three of you go."

Jim panting from exertion caught the end of her words, "No boys, you aren't going anywhere with that red-haired ruffian."

As his boys protested, Rosie saw tears form in Declan's eyes. Jack was about to speak, as was she, but Paul intervened by lightly placing his arm across Declan's shoulders. Surprised, Declan looked up at him as he admonished Jim, "That remark is totally uncalled for. We have an incident here, Declan knows where the phone box is and we need to alert the emergency services. Your boys need to go with him. And boys, on your return please help your grandfather push the young ones back up in the go-cart." Paul turned his back on Jim while suggesting they head to the house and the boys left without a second bidding. Gerald pointed out it would be at least half an hour before any help arrived. Paul asked if he would go down to co-ordinate the rescue party. By the fountain Bertie and Helen had assembled a collection of spades, shovels and rakes. Rosie watched as Gerald and Johnny began cautiously descending the long grassy slope, each holding a shovel and a spade. Ted arrived, apologizing for being at the far side of the lake, admitted he was unfit, but didn't hesitate in joining the rescue operation. Jack reappeared with Cathy, and having downed a strong cup of tea, he set off with Ted and a knapsack packed with 'useful' items. With coils of rope around his shoulders he insisted he should also take a spade, saying it would help his balance going downhill.

Helen and Rosie could barely stifle their mirth when the long-faced serious Jim emerged from the front door. His expensive suit trousers were covered by one of Cathy's voluminous gardening overalls and his handmade leather shoes exchanged for Wellington boots he could barely walk in. Around his waist and tied with string were four plastic buckets containing further 'useful items', including a coal shovel and a hard hand brush. She suspected Paul had conscripted him, aided by Cathy and abetted by Helen. Jack, at least ten years older than him, had to stop and help him across the ha-ha, and obviously fearful of slipping on the grassy descent, Jack handed him the spade to aid his balance.

Paul emerging from the house spotted Maria, the first woman to return, and with no further explanation called, "Maria you're with me. There's been an incident, casualties expected." Was the spring in Maria's step due to working with her father, or like him relishing the challenge of accidents and emergencies?

Rosie strolled back to look across the lake. The way the women were meandering back showed they were oblivious to the situation. Franz, sitting on the jump seat of the cart, was at the bottom of the path up to the house. Despite peddling hard, he was barely gaining ground and she could just hear the shrill voices of his grandchildren, but his booming laugh resounded as the cart accelerated forward due to Richard pushing. Florrie and Ida slowly climbing the path moved to the side as Franz beeped his horn so the cart could pass. Diana and Joyce deep in conversation were approaching the incline and not far behind were Jennifer and Margaret. It appeared that Paula and Jill were still snoozing in their deck chairs.

Rosie headed back to the courtyard where Bertie waved the binoculars at her. From there, she had a reasonable side view behind the rubble wall and she saw the Brigadier had arrived. With Ted they examined the stability of that wall while Johnny appeared to be trying to locate the position of the cab door. She spotted Gerald just as he disappeared behind the mound and guessed his mission was to locate the other cab door. When Jack and Jim joined the rescue party, Johnny relieved Jim of his buckets, indicating the smaller rubble that needed shoveling and putting into them. And Jack handed the Brigadier his rucksack before heading with the rope towards the woodland area, while Ted began hoisting out the larger stones on the edge of the mound. Bertie wanted to see, but without the binoculars she was still able to see Jack had found a sturdy tree and was tying one end of rope to it.

In his own inimitable way Bertie reported, "Ger'd mund." She looked towards the mound where Gerald - on the top of it - was beckoning to Paul and Maria still descending the hill. She guessed he'd found the driver.

In the midst of the unfolding events, it seemed incongruous to hear loud and deep booming laughter coming over the hill, especially from the usually stern and often abrupt Franz!

Bertie handed her the binoculars. Johnny and Ted were still removing larger rocks which indicated their belief that the cab door was buried there. She reported to Bertie, "Jack must feel the ground is unstable, he's tied one end of his rope to that tree and the other around the waists of Johnny, Ted and Jim. They look like a chain gang." He took closer look, while she - with a bird's eye view - looked for Gerald, Paul or Maria. Anxiously, she looked around while inwardly, she questioned the wisdom of trying to clear such a dangerous area when they didn't know if anyone was trapped. Had David made the phone call? How much longer would the emergency services be?

Her musings were interrupted by the children singing, "The wheels on the bus go round and round…" as Franz appeared to do the finishing stretch past the West Wing. Bertie nudged her. She looked to where he was pointing. The Brigadier and Gerald were acting as crutches to a beefy man and she guessed they were taking him to the gatekeeper's cottage. A close up view showed the man's trousers were torn to the top of his tattooed and bloodstained leg, above his knee was a wide bandage.

Rosie glanced round as Franz passed by. He gave a questioning look before he steered the cart around the fountain bowl to halt at the front door. Richard and Phillip lifted the children out, Franz peeled himself from the jump seat and Cathy chivvied the children inside. Franz joined her watching the rescue operation and asked to be briefed on the situation. Before long they were joined by Margaret, Jennifer, Diana and Joyce wanting to use the binoculars and asking the inevitable questions. It was a relief when Cathy drew them inside for tea and scones, at which Bertie promptly joined them and she could again clearly view the site. David reappeared on the flat part of the drive that ran parallel to the trees and the road. Looking up at the house he waved, which surely meant help was now on its way. And in finding the driver injured, it was obvious they were hurrying to locate his passenger. Paul and Maria weren't tied to the chain gang, but were helping to speed up the clearance by emptying buckets of stones into new piles beyond the site.

At the screech of horror in Ida's voice, she saw her leaning heavily on Florrie's arm viewing the mud slide. She hurried over to help Florrie who sent her a wide-eyed look. Rosie acknowledged that by stating brightly, "We had unexpected visitors who didn't heed Jack's warning and subsequently destroyed the drive."

Ida looked around her asking in a wavering tone, "Where are they?"

"Hopefully not in the army lorry now buried under that mound of rubble."

"Oh my God!" Ida seemed to wilt against her.

Grimly Rosie supporting her declared, "We need to get you inside and give you a strong cup of coffee." Drawing her towards the house she added, "Our men rescued the driver he appears to have a nasty leg wound above his tattoo…" Ida swayed heavily against her. "When the fire brigade arrives they'll find the passenger and see if there's anyone else in the lorry".

Ida's hand flew to her mouth, in her throat was a cry of anguish. Cross at her inebriated state, Rosie said sharply, "There's no reason for you to upset yourself!"

Ida muttered, "…shouldn't have come. Lenny will be furious. The army may sue and…!"

Exasperated Rosie cut across her to remark, "Fortunately Ida, it's not my fault, not my mess, and should anyone consider suing, not my worry. But it happened on a good day."

Startled, Ida straightened and sobered enough to ask, "Why?"

"We have six strong men who have volunteered to dig them out and one is a doctor trained in emergencies."

Cathy at the front door saw them and rushed to help as Ida murmured, "Yer 'elp people, them's likes you… " Over her head Rosie mouthed 'drunk'. Cathy nodded, and having taken Ida

342

away to sober her up, Rosie returned to viewing the scene while briefly considering 'Lenny's' reaction to the news!

Rosie focused on Johnny and Ted as they carefully removed stones and put them in the buckets. She caught a glimpse of a ridge of metal, it had to be the edge of a cab door. Jack replaced the buckets, and either David or Paul emptied them away from the site. Jim was left to sweeping up the smaller debris. It appeared gloves had been one of Cathy's 'useful items' from thick yellow rubber ones to gardening and knitted ones. The latter, worn by Ted, wouldn't be fit for purpose again! When the men stopped working, she had another brief but clear view of the partially excavated cab door, and underneath spotted the sole of a shoe at the end of an ankle.

Once the larger stones were removed and the smaller debris swept off, Johnny and Ted carefully negotiated their way around the door, their backs to the mound of rubble under which the lorry lay. David and Jack moved into position opposite them and together they slowly lifted the door. With Jim near the man's foot to give it extra leverage, they tipped it, removing the residual rubble and then lifted it high enough for Paul to crawl beneath. Rosie held her breath feeling it was risky, but within seconds Paul put out his hand with a raised thumb. As David and Jack lifted it higher, Jim guided it while Johnny and Ted moved aside so it could be slowly lowered against the mound. She saw that as a clever move as it would protect them all against falling debris from an unstable mound. Now she could see a man lying face down, not moving. Maria came forward with Paul's medical bag.

Rosie was focusing on them when suddenly they both looked up, their mouths opened and their eyes widened. Paul leapt to his feet. She kept the binoculars on him as he ran to Ted and was astonished when he wrestled him to the ground.

A quick overview of the site showed Jack running in the opposite direction and David now weighing into Ted. The binoculars revealed that to be true, although partially hidden by the wall of debris it seemed Jim also decided to join in the fray. None of it made sense. Another overview revealed Jack running back with several loops of rope. In his haste, he stumbled over the legs of the unconscious man. She frowned as it was so unlike Jack. But what had caused 'steady Teddy' as Joyce called him, to cause such mayhem? With Jack winding rope around the cab door against the mound, Rosie trained the binoculars on him bringing her to question if it was at a slightly different angle than before. The only think she could see of Jim was his Wellington boots as he lay across the top of the pile of men. Jack bent to speak to them, and then Jim and the others slowly peeled off Ted's prone figure. But as Paul rolled off, he stayed - she guessed to minister to him - and when he moved back Ted was sitting up and David took his place completely blocking her view. But she had had a briefly glimpse of Ted, his clothes in shreds and his face and arms bloodied.

In the hope to understand, she put down the binoculars. Paul was taking Maria's place attending to the lorry's passenger and the other men were clearing bits of rubble or walking about in a listless way. David reappeared, they gathered together, and then he walked off the site. As he left he stopped and looked up at the house. She waved and trained the binoculars on him. His face was grim, his fingers ran through his thick dark hair so it was obvious he was upset or worried. Then he placed his hands together indicating the need to pray, before turning on his heel and walking briskly down the hill towards the cottage.

Despite hearing Franz' frustrated voice booming "Keep going, a bit of exercise won't kill you" from the top of the path by the lake, Rosie kept her eyes fixed on David until he went out of sight. Whatever the problem, she prayed the Lord would give him peace and wisdom. Franz pushing Rachel in her pushchair was noticeably irritated by Paula and Jill struggling to keep up. Sweaty and equally annoyed on arrival, Jill aired her frustration at Paul for having more concern for the sick and injured than her and their children. Paula complained that Jim had insisted on wearing his best suit and shouldn't have joined the rescue party to dig rubble and bathe in mud. Franz' grim expression and the steely glint in his eyes were very reminiscent of his son when thwarted by what he couldn't change. Rosie was glad she wasn't the subject of his ire. It seemed the dire event had completely bypassed the two women. It was hard to disguise her own exasperation as she chivvied Jill inside, "Be proud of Paul he's down there saving a man's life. And your Jim, Paula, was kitted out by Cathy so as not to spoil his clothes."

Cathy inviting them in to tea and scones was quick to assure her, "Paula, your man made a fine sight, and I'm sure is being most helpful. Rosie time you came in."

"I'll do that when the emergency services arrive." And, as if on cue, distant sirens and bells could be heard. Cathy grinned, "I'm pouring your tea right now."

But the spectacle of two fire engines, an ambulance and a police car arriving to fill what remained of the bottom of the drive, brought everyone out to the courtyard to watch. David returned with the Brigadier, and together with Jack were talking to a fireman. Others prepared their equipment and appliances. The police cordoned off the area and two ambulance men, one with a stretcher, the other with various bits of kit, headed towards the injured man.

Everyone wanted to use the binoculars and it was suggested they take it in turns and report what they saw. Even though the police were chivvying the men, Rosie knew that whatever had happened they were reluctant to leave.

Margaret was the first to report, "David and the Brigadier are leading four of the firemen towards the mound of rubble with the lorry door against it. The men are standing around Ted. Oh my, he looks in a sorry state."

Joyce pushed forward, "My Ted… let me see?" Margaret handed her the binoculars and directed her view. With a sob in her voice she stated, "He looks as though he's been in a fight."

Rosie frowned as Joyce bursting into tears, shoved the binoculars into Jennifer's hands and almost fell into Cathy arms who said reassuringly, "I'm sure he looks worse than he actually is. Come inside." Joyce shook her head, promptly sat on the grass and put her head between her knees.

Jennifer ordered, "Joyce look up. Your husband is the centre of the firemen's activity, and from the pats to his shoulder I would say he's being commended. Ah, there's my Freddy! Dear me, by his excessive gesturing he seems distraught, he likes to be the one in charge."

Franz response was blunt, "That's not likely to happen."

Ignoring him Jennifer continued, "Now that Paul isn't in the way, the injured man looks pretty lifeless."

Ida, despite mugs of black coffee, still appeared unstable. Franz standing by her said, "You'd be best inside." In Ida's anxiety and not wanting to leave, she realised the men's refusal to leave the cordoned zone might be for the same reason. What had they seen or found? Or what did they know?

Margaret assured them, "If that man were dead the ambulance men wouldn't be taking the time to lift him so carefully."

Jennifer held out the binoculars to Cathy, "What do you think?" Ida grabbed them. Those around her exchanged a worried look as she tried to see through them.

"Ida, what do you see?" Rosie asked.

"Can't see! The stretcher is on the ground. Paul's in the way." Her East End accent became more prominent, "Oh, me God! I see 'im now, 'is face is battered and bloodied, 'e looks bad."

Cathy stated, "But he's still alive."

"But 'is face is so mashed up, 'is mother and wife wouldn't recognize 'im. Oh, I'd never 'ave thought…" She broke off, pushed the binoculars into Cathy's hands, "If anyone gets queasy best not to look" and with no further ado she sat on the grass beside Joyce.

Jill put out her hand, "I'd like to see what that husband of mine is doing." But as Jill focused on the scene, the children shot out from the house shrieking, screaming and chasing each other around the fountain. Jill ignored them, Paula glared and Franz barked, "Stop that!" Rosie caught Joshua, bringing Rebecca and Luke to a standstill, and Franz whipped William off his feet.

Several heads from below looked up in their direction. Richard red faced apologized. "Sorry granddad, William wanted to go to the toilet, then he ran outside and the others followed."

Franz patted his shoulder, "Not your fault. Good of you and Phillip to look after them." He scowled at Jill's back.

From the doorway Helen called, "Who wants to find where the Smarties grow? Come with me and you can pick them, but not eat them until we know who has found the most." Franz, his hand in William's, walked towards Helen. They spoke briefly and disappeared inside as Mrs P sidled up to whisper, "Rosie I's sorry about Ida, she don't usually drink, said she needed 'dutch courage' to come today. It was lovely that you invited us." She lowered her voice, "Yer'll do the 'Master' proud! And 'im and 'is Dad could make somefing of this place."

Their attention was drawn to Jill complaining, "Paul had better not be going in the ambulance with that man."

Paula asked, "Let me see?" Seeing through the binoculars she gasped, "But you can't begrudge him going with Ted? Even with David's help the poor man can barely walk, his clothes are in shreds and he's covered in cuts and grazes."

Joyce leapt up, snatched the binoculars and wailed, "Oh my poor Ted? He looks in agony." She thrust the binoculars on

Rosie, "I have to go to him. I have to be with him. I've lost a husband and daughter, I can't lose him too." Rosie's reassurances that Ted was unlikely to die from his injuries were interrupted as Paula pointed out that Paul had jumped down from the back of the ambulance to join David and together they were valiantly trying to stop Ted collapsing on the ground. Now desperate, tears running down her cheeks, Joyce looked around and pleaded, "Please, please, someone help me? I have to be with him."

Rosie quickly pointed out there was no easy or quick way down, and with a ten minute walk to the cottage, no chance of her reaching Ted before the ambulance left. Cathy pointed out, "Unfortunately, the Brigadier's car is parked so close to the back gate that no-one can leave until he moves it."

"Oh Cathy, I'm sorry! I didn't realise our car was a problem. I've got a set of keys. I'll drive Joyce to the hospital." Jennifer moved towards Joyce, "Come on dear. On my way back, I'll pick up Freddy and anyone else who wants a lift back up that hill. Now the emergency services are here, there's no point in them staying down there."

Jill wailed, "Paul's going off in the ambulance." Angrily she stated, "Why does he always desert me and his children in favour of others?"

Franz scowled and boomed, "Unfair and untrue! He's dedicated to you and the children. You married a doctor and have to accept there are times when saving a life is more important than you!" Jill burst into tears and pushed past Joyce and Jennifer heading inside.

Margaret frowned at her husband before suggesting, "Franz, it would be helpful if you were to suggest to Jennifer to find and bring Paul back with her."

His response was to take a deep breath, stare at her, and then in a grim voice state, "I'll help Jennifer get her car out" before heading around the house towards the Tradesman's Entrance.

CHAPTER 24

They watched the ambulance moving off and once it had disappeared into the trees towards the main entrance, Florrie drew the inebriated and ridiculously distraught Ida inside, followed by Margaret and Paula. Those left were as fascinated as Richard and Phillip at the activities of the firemen. One fire engine having backed up to the mound had a large folded ladder and what appeared to be two cart wheels hanging off the end and seemed the centre of the action. Phillip asked, "Are they going to use that ladder to climb down into the hole?"

"Problem is, bro, they are going to have to move all that rubble before digging a hole big enough for it to go down. They need to make it safe, for they can't risk a collapse taking their men with it." Phillip hummed thoughtfully.

Diana, her eyes glued to the binoculars commented, "I thought Maria would want to stay around those hunky firemen, but she's going somewhere with David. Is she attracted to him?"

Irritated Rosie snapped, "Doubt it! He's the same age as Paul, her father. She's a nurse going to check on the cab driver who they took to the gatekeeper's cottage."

Diana turned, her surprise was evident, "Paul is her father? I thought she was his children's nanny."

Rosie took the binoculars saying, "His first wife died in childbirth" and putting them to her eyes she reported, "Jack seems determined to stay within the cordon. The others are gathering just below it but I can't see Johnny"

At a tap on her arm she saw Richard, "Please, may I and Phillip take a look?"

She handed over the binoculars and at Diana's questioning expression apologized, "Sorry Diana, it isn't my story to tell. Ask Jill." Diana nodded and she wandered across the courtyard to see if she could get a better view. But on not seeing Johnny, she concluded he must have gone to give spiritual solace to the cab driver. Returning, she stood by Phillip and Richard taking turns using the binoculars. Phillip observed, "I thought that thick rope tied to the tree was attached to the cab door, but on a closer look it doesn't seem to be."

Richard took a look, "I see what you mean."

Rosie informed them, "Jack tied the rope to the tree and around the men as a safety measure. He used another rope to tie down the door."

"Two ropes? I can see one around the cab door. There is another. Its end is… going into a small hole."

Rosie frowned and asked, "Are you sure?" while trying to remember when she'd last seen Johnny. Despite the rising fear, Rosie stared at the firemen counter balancing the ladder as it was extended and lowered into a more horizontal position alongside the unstable mound. "Richard, let me see."

"Uncle David wouldn't be happy to know you were eyeing up the hunky firemen."

"Believe me Phillip, that isn't my intention." Richard grinned and with a close up of the scene, she focused on where the door had landed. Had it fallen awkwardly after they lifted it? And finally pinpointed what the boys had seen. Why had Paul and Maria looked up and been so aghast? As panic opened up like a black hole she handed the binoculars back to the boys and fought to remain calm and process the events. Johnny had been tied to that rope, and Ted next. Within seconds of lowering the door everyone was jumping on Ted. Johnny hadn't had time to leave the scene. If… and it was an if… wasn't it? If the door had fallen and created a hole in the unstable ground Johnny could have… Oh God, it didn't bear thinking about. But she had to. It would explain why all the men fell on top of Ted… he was next on the rope… he was dragged towards that same hole. It would account for Ted's injuries, and that scuffle on unstable ground probably refilled the hole so it now looked smaller. It would account for the men seeming distraught and reluctant to leave the scene. David indicated the need to pray. Was the Brigadier's pacing back and forth an indication of his distress? She couldn't just stand here imagining this and that. She had to know if Johnny was buried under that rubble. A silent scream twisted and tore up from within her, unable to deny what now seemed clear. Joyce's words about having loved and lost echoed in her mind. Inwardly she prayed 'Lord, I've loved and lost my unborn baby, my friends Sylvia and Jane, please Lord don't take Johnny, I know he's my soul mate.' The same overwhelming urge when Joyce had to be with Ted flowed through her. She was wearing flat shoes. As she had done many times before, she could run down and be there for him. Best not to upset anyone with her imaginings. Without further ado she ran, jumped the ha-ha and carefully paced her speed down the hill.

Behind her, Richard and Phillip shouted her name. Half way down Franz voice boomed through the air, "Good heavens! What's she doing?" Inwardly Rosie groaned, now everyone at the house would be out to see just what she was doing!

Further down the well-trained firemen had been alerted of her descent for they briefly turned their heads before resuming their tasks. Declan was running towards David and the Brigadier on the flat area between the hill and trees. They looked up and saw her. David then headed into the trees. She guessed to circumvent the police cordon and meet her. Declan ran up to the police cordon, ducked the tape and continued up the incline towards Jack, the only one left within it. On a level with the mound, he had remained as if guarding the tree and the rope attached to it. Seeing her approach his hand rose but not in a welcome wave, to her a confirmation of who was on the other end of the rope. In those last hundred yards a deep aching cavity opened up within her. She stumbled, but knowing to fall would only add to their troubles, she trained her mind to arrive safely. Before reaching Jack, Declan with his ruddy face smeared with tears ran up towards her. As they met his arms closed around her waist, and head bent he snuggled against her. She drew him close and together they made the final yards to Jack whose expression said it all. Her fears founded she queried breathlessly, "It's Johnny isn't it?"

Jack nodded. Sick with fear anguish gripped her and she would have collapsed if Declan hadn't been holding on to her. Declan looked up at her, she responded with a weak smile, but was unable to stop the sob rising as she cried out, "Oh God, why Johnny?"

Jack drew Declan gently aside and took her in his arms. "Oh my little love, I was hoping we wouldn't have to tell you. Declan wanted to but we felt it best to wait in the hope of a positive outcome." Tears rolled down her face. "Oh Rosie, don't take on so. Draw on your faith."

To that she wailed, "Jack, you don't understand. Johnny is my soul mate. All these years we've been parted, I've only just found him again. First it was the car accident, and now this! Am I not allowed to love and be loved?" She choked on her sobs, and buried her face into his shoulder. Although his hand comfortingly patted her back, Jack declared, "You're upset, but try not to be irrational."

Taken aback she pulled away to argue, "I'm not Jack, I am not. Each time Johnny and I meet we realise we love each other and then something contrives to separate us." Jack gave a heavy sigh, his eyes fixed beyond her. Rosie spun around and came face to face with David.

How much had he heard? Shocked she stared at him, but he

merely raised an eyebrow and reassured her, "The firemen know what they are doing. They have equipment, experience and thanks to Jack's rope they are confident they will be ready to haul Johnny out within the next half an hour." With a small sad smile at Jack, he placed his hand under her elbow and suggested, "Come, you'll get a better understanding of the rescue nearer the scene, but to avoid the police cordon we need to walk through the trees."

Rational thought left her as it had the day she had come home to find her best friend Jane dead in David's arms. She was aware that neither man had assured her Johnny was alive. Staring ahead she allowed David to guide her through the woods. They came out to the grassy slope at the bottom of the drive. One fire engine was across from them, the other as close to the mound as the firemen thought safe. The extended ladder and a chain of firemen with large buckets were now quickly and carefully dismantling the mound.

From the house she had an overall picture, but this perspective revealed the enormity of the affected area, and the greater reality that the earth had swallowed up a whole truck. She glanced up to where Jack was again testing the taut rope and the knots tying it around the tree. He obviously felt he was Johnny's life line!

David commanded quietly, "Stay here." As he strode out towards the fire engines a small hand slipped into hers. Her response to Declan's upturned, dirty and anxious face was to squeeze his hand, draw him closer. Then together they walked up to meet Jack heading down to the bottom edge of the cordon tape. Now she could see beyond the second fire engine and a police car was parked outside the cottage. As Johnny's father, she could understand why the Brigadier had and was pacing up and down around the fire engines.

As Jack gave his perspective of what she had seen from above their eyes were fixed on the firemen's activity, "Johnny stepped back, the cab door slid sideways hit the mound, disturbed the debris which fell inwards taking..." His voice cracked, she slipped her arm over the paper tape and through Jack's. He cleared his throat, "The firemen have removed the door. They are quickly removing the rubble and that long ladder is being gradually lowered. My guess is they will anchor it horizontally across the hole to become a bridge from which the rescue will take place."

"Is... is Johnny..." she couldn't voice her fears, but instinctively Jack answered, "We don't know." Rosie looked up towards the house where those gathered outside were barely distinguishable and were surely debating why she'd left in such a hurry. If the boys told them what they had seen it wouldn't take long for someone to reach the same conclusions as she.

An approaching fireman drew Rosie's attention, "Hello, I'm Paul Harding, Commander in Chief, otherwise known as 'Hardy'." He gave a reassuring smile, "I understand this is your parents' house and estate. By the way you ran down that hill, it is obvious you've done it many times." His head indicated towards the rope, "I gather you've concluded Johnny is on the end of that." Biting her lip Rosie nodded. "When we told Johnny a young woman was on her way down, he laughed and said, "Rosie."

"Johnny's alive! He's able to speak!" Rosie looked at Jack, his relief appeared to have robbed him of speech, but not Declan who jumping up and down hit the air with his fist and shouted, "Yes! Yes!"

Rosie felt almost too fearful to ask Hardy, "Is he injured?"

"He tells us not and I quote 'When the earth gave way I didn't fall, but floated down like a feather.' Johnny's speech is rather slow, due I gather not from today's incident, but an accident a couple of months ago." Rosie nodded and murmured fervently, "Thank you Lord."

"Amen to that" agreed Hardy before looking at Jack, "He said that rope was the life saver in his descent between what appears a cave wall and the lorry. He swung himself on to the lorry's upturned windscreen which was inches deep in a mixture of stones, tarmac and dust.   He has reported that although there's little light the rear of the lorry appears to be resting on a cavern floor at an angle, its underside protecting the cab from the larger rubble. We are being careful not to disturb the lorry and what is on top of it. Johnny has the impression the cavern is wider at the bottom than the top and can hear a stream trickling through it. We're making the area safe and carefully enlarging the hole to get him out."

Anxiously she asked, "How long will it take?"

"We need to ascertain what we are dealing with. I'm told you saw the whole incident. It would be helpful to know what you saw." As she spoke and answered Hardy's questions, her confidence grew that Johnny would survive this ordeal. Now and then, she glanced towards the site where a fireman was laying along a horizontal ladder and appearing to communicate to the earth. When she finished, Hardy nodded and said wisely, "Sounds as if the lorry's movements opened up a sink hole." At their puzzled expressions Hardy explained, "Over hundreds of years, acidic rain or groundwater erodes away the rock until one day the ground over it collapses. It would seem the weight and difficulty of the lorry's progress was the final straw to that underground instability. I gather the drive had already been deemed unsafe due to potholes and often waterlogged. I don't foresee a problem in Johnny coming out in the same way he went…" Hardy turned his head in response to his name. A fireman on the large ladder beckoned him. He gave him a thumbs up before saying, "You'll have to excuse me" before jogging over to join his men.

Despite Hardy's calm confidence her stomach tightened in fear. Had the lorry moved? Had the heavy rubble become dislodged? Was Johnny now injured? Jack, she and Declan drew back together to watch Hardy's actions as the Brigadier and David headed up towards them.

On his arrival the Brigadier gave her a long thoughtful look. Was he upset by her being there, or did he now know of Johnny's interest in her? To put him at ease she smiled and explained, "I thought as Johnny and I saw what happened, it might be helpful for me to be here." The Brigadier gave a cynical grunt, but it was drowned by the bells of an ambulance on the main road, which a minute later was coming up the drive towards them. When it stopped, one man jumped out and carrying a medical bag swiftly walked to join the firemen. The ambulance turned around on the grass ready to make a speedy exit.

Hardy, obviously guessing they would be anxious, gave them a reassuring wave and sent one of his men to speak to them. "The Chief said to tell you Johnny is fine, but he isn't a man who sits and waits to be rescued. He's been clearing the rubble from the windscreen and believes there is someone inside the cab. As a precaution we've called an ambulance. In situations like this, it's always wise for those rescued to be checked out at the hospital. Johnny has suggested that to enable him to assess the situation, we ease him a little more rope to allow him to maneuver around the windscreen into the cab." Jack looked anxiously at the coil of rope around the tree. "But we aren't happy to put those we are rescuing in any unnecessary danger, so Hardy has to make that decision."

Gruffly the Brigadier pointed out, "If Johnny is in the cab, he won't be in danger of heavy falling rubble. Surely that will speed up operations."

The fireman nodded, "True! Rest assured every avenue will be considered in order to bring him out safely." With that he hurried back to the men who under Hardy's direction were making preparations around the bridge of ladders.

Frustrated by the little she could see Rosie announced, "No-one is monitoring this cordon, and it's up to you, but I'm going up the hill for a better view." Jack grabbed her while pointing to the site where Hardy had thrown up his hands as if in despair. With a sob in her voice Rosie asked, "Oh! Now what?" But her anxiety was quelled as Hardy turned to give them a thumbs up before leaving his men to join them.

Once in earshot he confirmed, "Johnny's fine. But he didn't consider the danger or heed my advice to stay put. On hearing a pained cry he undid the rope around him and slid into the lorry's cab."

Wide-eyed, Rosie put her hand to her mouth as the Brigadier boomed, "That's my boy!"

Hardy laughed, "Communication will be more difficult with Johnny having to lean out of the cab, but he assures us he's not in any danger. Now we've been able to give him more light, he reports the water below him is across the cavern floor and looks about two foot deep and would have broken his fall. In the cab there was a teenager who had been too frightened to jump out, and was knocked unconscious when the cab door broke off and any movement brings pain. Our priority is to get the teenager out, but Johnny will shortly follow. I'll be involved in that, but one of my men will keep you informed." David boomed their thanks as Hardy was already running back to his men.

Encouraged the Brigadier stated brightly, "When a man in danger thinks of others, he's a man to be proud of. I'll wander back down. I want to be there to greet that boy of mine."

Jack looking thoughtful suggested, "I'll walk with you. I want to take a look at the lay of the land."

Without asking, Declan accompanied them, leaving her and David alone. With the need to say something she turned to face him. He gave her a questioning look causing her to say hesitantly, "David… I'm sorry. It's only today… I knew… I love Johnny and he loves me."

"Rosie, a catastrophe brings many emotions to the surface."

"Yes, but… Johnny…we'd been talking and in my anxiety that I might lose him… I'm so sorry you had to hear it like that." David's expression didn't change, but his eyes reflected sadness. She rushed on, "David, you are a true friend. I have so much to thank you for. I care about you, as you care for me, but it isn't love is it?"

354

She didn't know if he felt hurt or disappointment as he murmured, "I had hoped it would be" before he boomed in his usual fashion, "We'll talk later, work something out. Let's watch and pray for a quick safe rescue operation."

They turned to watch the firemen. The silence between them lengthened. Reminded of how the binoculars could focus on them, and not wanting people to worry, Rosie smiled and waved towards the house and received a waving response. As she considered if they were questioning the arrival of another ambulance, Jim divested of his overalls was walking in his Wellington boots with Gerald towards them. Gerald's first words were, "The police have taken the lorry driver off to the hospital. Jim wandered into the cottage, he told us about Johnny and…"

Jim interjected while pushing his glasses on his nose with his finger, "You made quite a spectacle coming down that hill, leaping like a sure-footed deer with your skirt billowing around you it brought to mind the opening of the Sound of Music."

Rosie detected a derisory undercurrent, and saw Gerald and David exchange a glance before Gerald reassured her, "I can understand your need to be here. I thought you'd like to know the name of the lorry driver. Does George Kent mean anything to you?" She shook her head. "The door hit and trapped him. He has a deep nasty cut on his upper leg. Paul didn't think he was concussed, but obviously traumatized by his continual repeating 'My mother is a God-fearing woman' and giving his name, rank and army number. I suspect a crime was to be committed but there's no evidence to back that up. He mumbled a name during the police interview. When asked again, he seemed bewildered and said, "I'd a grand-daughter."

"Did he mean he has a grand-daughter and she is in the lorry?"

"I asked and he repeated it. Maybe he lost a grand-daughter?"

Rosie frowned. "This may sound ridiculous, but perhaps he was saying, "Ida's grand-daughter."

Gerald's eyes widened, his eyebrows rose and combined with his pouch-like cheeks, he looked even more like a surprised and endearing rabbit. Rosie stifled a ridiculous urge to giggle. "Whatever this is about, I find I am agreeing with Helen about God's intervention. George too seems obsessed with God. Maybe there are benefits of inviting Jesus into my life." Rosie smiled, David said to do so was the best decision he would ever make while Jim's face reflected a thinly disguised sneer before he muttered, "I'll wait in the cottage until this is over."

Jack slightly breathless joined them, "I climbed the hill overlooking the drive and lake. The mound on that side is still about five foot high, but the firemen have cleared and extended the hole to about a six food diameter. And from the ladder anchored across it are preparing to lower Hardy into it. The best vantage point will be from the top end of this cordoned area. Five minutes into the firemen being in place David exclaimed, "Good heavens! There's Declan. What has he been up to?"

They all looked towards Declan talking to a fireman before running up towards the cordoned area. That fireman went to consult with another, and then seemed to be checking on something. Immediately Rosie felt guilty at not missing him and her hand went to her mouth in realising he wasn't just dirty, but covered from head to foot in thick mud. Nearing the tape line Declan shouted but they only heard the word, "…disappearing."

David bellowed, "Where have you been? What have you been doing?"

Declan's approach slowed, as the Brigadier many yards behind him answered, "He was going to the house. I told him to stay down here."

Apprehension appeared on Declan's face. He stopped near enough to be heard, but not near enough to get a cuff around his head. He wailed, "Please don't be cross. I'm sorry about my clothes."

Rosie quickly reassured him, "You aren't in trouble. Your clothes will wash."

"I wouldn't have said nothing, honest. I just wanted to be with Richard and Phillip."

Rosie smiled, "You aren't in trouble. I'm pleased you made friends…"

Impatient and frowning David interrupted to boom, "Yes, yes, that's all well and good, but a lorry and Johnny have disappeared down a hole and you, Declan, look as if you've fallen in one. For goodness sake, what happened to you? And what is disappearing?"

David's forbidding expression and stern voice brought fear into Declan's eyes causing Rosie to declare, "David, you are frightening him."

Jack opened his arms, "Declan, come here." Declan looked cautiously at David as if expecting him to block his path to Jack.

In a gentle and quiet voice David apologized, "Sorry Declan, I didn't mean to frighten you. I'm just anxious to know what is disappearing!"

"It's the lake!" He looked up at Jack. "The water don't look right." Declan turned to her, "Rosie, halfway up the path to the house I saw at the top a muddy bank, it weren't there before. And in the middle weeds are sticking out of the water." Rosie looked at Jack as Declan concluded, "I reckon it's draining out."

Jack groaned, "Oh God, that's all we…"

David running his hand through his hair interrupted, "Johnny reported he heard a stream, you can't hear water if its deep enough to break his fall. It's no longer a stream." They were taking that in when Declan added, "I ran around to take a look." He gave a rueful grimace, "The water is dragging the weeds, I slipped in the mud, grabbed at them and felt the water's pull."

Jack frowned, "I considered the possibility of the lake somehow undermining the drive. I looked, but didn't see anything amiss."

"From this end it looks normal."

Jack's voice became urgent, "In which case the water is leaking out somewhere."

Declan pointed to the damaged drive, "From what Johnny says I reckon under that hill and into that cavern." All eyes followed his finger.

Jack said thoughtfully, "The river water fills a bowl in the land, the path goes around the edge. I would estimate the bottom of the lake is in line with what Hardy called, 'a sink hole' in which case…"

The Brigadier boomed out, "Is that my son?" All eyes went to the stretcher being carefully eased out of the hole by several firemen on the ladder. One gestured it wasn't. The Brigadier's voice had a sob in it as he warned, "They better hurry and get my boy out of there. I wasn't there when he was a child, but I'll be there when he comes out of this." With that he hurried down the slope towards the site bellowing, "Get Johnny out. The lake's filling up that hole." A fireman gave a thumbs up and pointed to a hose that ran down the hill, bringing them to hear the low background noise of a pump. Had that been a precaution, or had they known about the danger, or had Declan alerted them?

David exclaimed, "Well done Declan." He put his hand on Jack's arm and ordered, "You stay here. I'll tell them about the sluice gates, it would help if they closed the river inlet."

Grimly Jack replied, "I fear it won't be soon enough, if that dank and dirty water is already filling up that cavity."

David set off at a good pace while Gerald assured them, "That

357

pump should help to stop the rising water. They've got the injured teenager out, so Johnny shouldn't be far behind."

"The police haven't returned, so I'll pop down and find out if it's a boy or a girl!" Gerald grinned and quickly outpaced the Brigadier and was at the ambulance well before they put the teenager inside.

They all walked up the incline to get a clearer view and realized the activity around the site heightened giving the impression of greater urgency. Rosie and Jack's attention was drawn to the creaking tension on the rope tied to the tree. "Do you think Johnny is being retied to that rope?" Oh Jack, who would have imagined this?" But seeing Jack's distraught expression she added, "None of it is your fault. You did all you could to ensure everyone's…" she broke off to ask, "Did you feel that? Was it an earth tremor?" The Brigadier, resting on a tree trunk behind the fire engines, jumped up and stared at it before brushing his rear. Amused she commented, "Did that vibration made him think he had 'ants in his pants'?" But her smile disappeared as a low deep, growling sound coming from beyond the incident site seemed to roll over it and towards them. The firemen jumped from their ladders and the motor of the pump went off. Gerald and the ambulance men paused, and then all three ran towards their vehicle. She grabbed Jack as the sound reached them causing the earth beneath their feet to tremble, and when gone left an eerie silence. The firemen resumed their position. The stretcher had just been placed in the ambulance when the sound came again. It was louder, stronger. It reminded her of standing on the platform when an express train passes through. Firemen staggered, some fell to their knees. Gerald jumped into the ambulance with the men, who closed the door before an unseen force seemed to shake it from side to side.

Was another sink hole about to open up to draw others into its inky depths? The Brigadier, having hugged the tree stump he had previously sat on, ran to a nearby oak tree and promptly sat down under it. Following his example Jack grabbed Rosie's hand, and they sheltered and held on to the tree with the rope as the ground beneath them shook. The branches moved, the leaves rustled and fell on them. Wildly, she looked around for Declan. The shaking stopped, the noise abated. Shocked they didn't move. Jack, looking fit to cry, finally asked, "Oh Rosie, when will this nightmare end?"

"Soon I hope." Rosie gazed up at the house where people were still congregated together in the courtyard. Had they heard the noise, felt the tremors? There wasn't any sign of panic. And then she spotted Declan in his muddied condition on the hill, scrambling up halfway between them and the house. She pointed him out to Jack saying, "This will certainly be..." the faint rumbling noise appeared to grow louder without coming closer. She raised her voice to finish her sentence, "...a day none of us will forget."

It grew to a roar that in itself seemed to shake the very air. The firemen trying to rescue Hardy and Johnny didn't leave the ladder, but the others either lay, sat or fell to the ground as Jack shouted to her, "Sit between the tree roots with your back to the trunk. It will protect us against falling branches." Within seconds, the earth undulated beneath them and above them the branches creaked and swayed. They clung together, the tree roots acted like cot rails, stopping them being tossed from side to side as a ship in a storm. It was only a few seconds but it felt like minutes, bringing her to realise she didn't fear death but the horror of being buried alive.

Could they pull the men out before what sounded like a trapped monster venting his fury in his desperation to escape? Being slightly higher than the site, even sitting under the tree, they could see firemen clinging to the ladders lashed to the main one across the sink hole. To her surprise they all scurried off the ladders and indicated to others to move back from the site on to the grass. Before she could consider why, came a deafening roar. The men collapsed on the grass, and a fierce jolt came from the earth and up through the tree. Their cry, more in surprise than pain, was drowned by the ever deepening and greater intensity of a sound like a lion roaring in pain. And then they gasped as two geysers of water shot out of the sink hole and probably rose about twenty feet before raining down water and debris on the site.

Jack gasped, "Water from the lake!" It stood to reason. If the lake had been leaking into the hill maybe for decades, it wouldn't just have undermined the drive, but would have gradually eroded the rock to make a water course for itself. And aggravated by today's incident, the stream Johnny first saw at the bottom of the sink hole had been growing. And now it seemed the force and sheer power of the water had broken through into the sink hole in such intensity that it had siphoned up around the army lorry, which under pressure had caused the geysers to burst forth.

The breeze carried the water spray like rain through the tree leaves to meld with the tears rolling down her face, for it was unlikely that Hardy and Johnny had survived. In Jack's arms she cried, "Oh God" and buried her face in his chest, for if ever there was a time to call on God this was it.

Jack moved and coaxed her not to give up hope. Rosie reminded the Lord that when the disciples called upon Him, He calmed the sea and delivered them. So she murmured, "Please Lord, do it again."

Rosie, come on, get up!" Obediently she opened her eyes, took Jack's outstretched hand and stood. With his arm around her, they looked across to where the firemen were silently standing ankle deep in water, blocking their view of the sink hole which must now be filled with water. Although the height and pressure of the water had diminished to a light fountain which they could just see above the firemen's heads, the overflow of water was streaming down the hill, across the flat part of the drive and into the trees beyond. She'd no doubt they were waiting for two dead bodies to be washed up.

Grief like a geyser rose up in Rosie causing her to bend with an internal wrench of pain. To her unspoken belief Jack stated, "Don't assume the worst." As the remainder of the firemen joined their colleagues, some stood aside to let them through, revealing others kneeling and pulling several things from the water. And then, to her astonishment chuckles of laughter reached them and they began patting each other on the back. One of them cheered and as the rest applauded, they stood back to reveal the newly formed pond with two bubbling fountains in its centre. Incredulous, Rosie rubbed her eyes for in the midst of the firemen stood two men. "Jack, Jack! Oh my God. It is, it is…" and then doubting her sight and remembering how Jane, after death, had appeared to David, she added, "Isn't it?"

Jack squeezed her toward him, "Oh my little love, it is! It's a miracle. Johnny and Hardy are alive and well." Both men were dripping wet, but appeared unharmed if not exhilarated by their experience, in the way they were patting each other's backs. And then came a surreal moment when Hardy and Johnny shook hands as if they had been in nothing more than a diving competition.

A long, loud whistle took everyone's attention. It had to be Declan! He might be small but his whistle was amazing. She spotted him in the crowd above them. Johnny waved at them, they appeared to clap. They must have seen him in the water, and now Declan could tell them of Johnny's misfortune. Jack nudged her, Hardy was pointing to her. Johnny blew her a kiss and crossed his hands over his heart. Relieved she kept repeating "Thank you God" as the firemen in their helmets had come through the falling debris relatively unscathed. The Brigadier brushing off forest fragments from his clothes was paddling in the wet grass as he began walking up the incline towards Johnny. At Jack's bemused expression, Rosie slipped her arm through his and suggested they head across the cordoned area to the site. They arrival was simultaneous with the wet-footed and heavily perspiring Brigadier. As he wiped his brow with his handkerchief Jack declared, "Rosie can't stop praising God for the miracle of your boy being safe." The Brigadier only acknowledge that with a hum, but she didn't dwell on it as her attention was drawn to Gerald who, with a very smug expression, was coming up beside the fire-engine from the ambulance. Rosie concluded he'd obtained interesting information from the traumatized teenager in the ambulance. Whatever the intentions of their unexpected visitors, God had heard and answered her prayers. Johnny was alive, loved her and David seemed resigned to that.

Johnny and Hardy reappeared as the Brigadier exclaimed, "Good grief, that's my car coming down the road." Rosie didn't hesitate, she rushed toward Johnny declaring, "I was so frightened for you but thank God you're safe!" Their eyes met, love overflowed between them. He bent to whisper, "love you" and might have kissed her if the Brigadier hadn't boomed behind her "Oh my boy, safe at last!" She stepped back and noticed Jennifer heading up towards them her voice brusque as she called, "Freddy! I'm here to collect you." Seeing Johnny wrapped in a blanket she frowned and exclaimed, "Have you been swimming in that lake, you were warned not to." Johnny grinned and Freddy declared, "My son is a hero."

Jennifer grimaced and raised her eyes heavenward before riveting her gaze on Rosie and asking, "How did you get here?"

Gerald chuckled, "She ran down that hill to be with Johnny." Rosie scowled at him.

Jennifer brow furrowed further as Paul having joined the group stroked his beard and confessed, "At the hospital there was no point in worrying you unnecessarily. Johnny slipped and fell into the sink hole with the lorry.

After her shocked exclamation, Johnny slowly declared, "It was a God incident to save a life before the water swept me up and out." Exasperated Jennifer retorted, "Oh really, not a very likely tale."

Rosie confirmed, "It's true."

Jennifer glared at her, and then turning she admonished

Johnny, "Your heart to rescue people is commendable, but warnings are to be heeded, getting involved isn't always right." Despite her scowl at Freddy, Rosie felt she was included in that warning.

Freddy mumbled wearily, "Not now love, let's go home."

Paul sent him a sympathetic look probably because he'd soon be facing his own wife's ire. Rosie looked around and asked, "Where's Maria?"

"With Joyce. Ted's wounds appear superficial but painful, best checked with an x-ray. I was dropped off at the hospital and stitched up George's leg while he waited for his X-ray. Dennis was taken to Southampton with suspected internal injuries. Jennifer arrived with Joyce with an edict from Franz to return to my wife. As her car is blocking the ambulance I've taken the opportunity for a brief acquaintance with Debbie and assessed her injuries."

Rosie questioned sharply, "Debbie?"

Gerald grinned as Paul replied, "The teenager in the ambulance. She's badly bruised and has a broken arm and leg."

Hardy reappeared carrying one bright pink and two khaki knapsacks dripping with water. "The people who own these are fortunate there were so many fit men to dig them out, and I'm given to believe Doc you saved the passenger's life."

Gerald winked at Rosie as he prompted, "Uncle Dennis' life!"

Rosie's eyes widened, Gerald nodded as Hardy continued. "Jack, if you hadn't tied Johnny to that rope this would have been a different story. Johnny is unharmed, he found the injured girl and was a great help in her rescue. He indicated the bag, "I've no doubt this is hers. Jennifer's face went as pink as the bag! I'm sure when this gets out Johnny is going to be the local hero." Hardy smiled at Freddy and Jennifer, "Because Debbie asked your son, he risked his life to climb into the back of the lorry and retrieve this bag. He also brought out these believing their owners would like them. Now excuse me I must help my men packing up."

As Hardy walked away there came a chorus of 'thank you's'. He acknowledge those with a wave as Gerald concluded, "I think a young girl with a pink knapsack indicates your visitors wanted to be friends, not foes." Jack looked as perplexed as Rosie felt.

Slowly Johnny said, "Not threatening. I raised my hands in case they were."

Rosie claimed, "It looked as if they were going to attack you."

"Tried to tell… so much… so fast."

Rosie blew out a heavy breath, "But the dead phone line…

them using the drive. Who were they? What did they want?"

Gerald, with an amused glint in his eyes, answered, "I can shed some light on that. I'll take those knapsacks, but I doubt there is any incriminating evidence in them." He waved his hand, "This was an accident waiting to happen. The police's only concern was the use and loss of an army lorry, but saw no reason to charge George or Dennis.

Paul interrupted, "Johnny, despite coming out unscathed having been in that dank water you should go in the ambulance to be checked out. Johnny shook his head, "Should you feel unwell in the next few days please seek medical advice."

"It'll be pneumonia if he stays much longer in that wet blanket. Now I need to move my car so come with us."

"Sorry, see Debbie first." Johnny ran to the ambulance. As they began strolling down the incline Franz' Jaguar drew up behind the Brigadier's car. Diana leapt out and cut across Johnny's path to hug him. Jennifer called, "He's coming home with us, and you." She turned to Paul, "Now Franz is here he'll take you to your wife." The Brigadier marched ahead, past his car to talk to Franz standing beside his. After their boomed greeting, Freddy lowered his voice, they glanced in her direction and Franz looked thoughtful at her before he sat back in his car and reversed it down the drive and around the cottage. Jennifer tooted the horn, Johnny ran from the ambulance to the car but not before he blew her a kiss and with his hand indicated he would ring her.

The ambulance followed and it was only minutes that the two fire engines did the same with tooting horns. Assured the ground was safe, they begun collecting up the equipment used and Franz brought up his car. As Rosie placed a bucket of the 'useful' items in the boot of the car, the incident, the scene and the silence suddenly overwhelmed her. Tears streamed down her face and she was taken by surprise by Franz putting an arm around her shoulders. "It's OK Rosie. Tears relieve the tension. It's been a difficult day."

"I... I'm being ridiculous. This was to be a lovely day for my friends and then ..." Words failed her.

"My dear girl, in all this you have been absolutely splendid." He chuckled, "And we've had a day none of us will forget!" Then in a quieter voice he added, "I gather you are rather taken with Johnny, but that doesn't alter the fact that Margaret and I are very fond of you, as is David. We would like you as our daughter-in-law but whoever you choose, it will not alter our appreciation of the commitment, faithfulness and love you show the twins. We feel you are part of our family. David has ideas. He needs to share them with you."

Rosie sniffed, wiped her tears on Franz' proffered handkerchief and said with a sigh, "David always has ideas."

"That's because he's a man who makes contingency plans. And his heart is for the twins to know you as their mother."

"I know! And believe me I love the twins. I enjoy being part of your family, but marriage is for life, not just for children."

Franz hummed and opened the rear car door, and with a rare smile decreed, "Well my dear, dry those tears, enjoy life, and give yourself time to consider carefully your options. Jack, Gerald and Paul are heading this way, and as they too think the world of you, I don't want them to believe I've upset you." He chuckled, his smile so like that of his son.

As she slipped into the car, she said fervently, "Thank you. All you have said means a great deal to me."

"Good! Draw strength from that." He shut the door and boomed, "So gentlemen have you retrieved all you came with?" Jack slid in beside her and patted her knee. She squeezed his hand. As he drove Franz reported with steel in his tone, "Jim told Diana that Johnny had fallen into the abyss and they didn't know how they were going to get him out. Fortunately, Declan looking like a waif and stray appeared, he assured us Johnny wasn't hurt. I was about to drive a distraught Diana down here when the geysers went up. That was a tense moment as all we could make out were the firemen bending over the water. Cathy had the binoculars and shouted, 'It's Johnny." When he waved we were assured he was alive and well. Then David arrived to tell us he and a fireman had closed the river sluice gate fearing the lake was leaking water. He was on the path up to the house when the earth shook, and a sudden jolt nearly knocked him off his feet. Behind him came a loud gurgling sound and he turned to see the lake disappearing in a swirl sucked into what had to be a large hole. We concluded that the build-up of that pressure had broken into the sink hole and caused the geysers."

Franz drove into the Tradesman's Entrance and informed them, "I had a quick look at the lake. I'm afraid Jack it is now a huge muddy bowl with a few feet of water in the centre." He parked and turned to Rosie, "I believe your father is trying to sell the estate at some extortionate sum. I rather think today, not only has the bottom fallen out of the lake, but so have his market prospects!"

CHAPTER 25

It seemed Bertie had watched their clearing up and departure and was waiting for Franz' Jaguar. He led them around the house where the remainder of the party was waiting to cheer the heroes of the hour. They were bombarded with questions as Cathy chivvyed them towards the ballroom where afternoon tea was laid out. Not wanting to talk of her love for Johnny, Rosie excused her abrupt departure by a need to be involved in all that was going on.

But it was the welcome from two little people that brought her tears. The instant they saw her, they pulled from their father's hands calling 'Oosie, Oosie'. David lifted his hands as if in defeat while sending her a wry smile, before striding over to support her as they ran to hug her legs. She smiled up at him and mouthed 'Thank you' but as they began demanding, 'Cake, cake' she wondered if this was the attraction and not her!

The men were able to make considerable inroads in the food while telling their individual tales but all she could stomach was a cup of tea. While she prepared the twins a scone she asked, "And what have you two been up to?" Their enthusiasm was obvious by their expressions, hand movements, and the way they added to each other's comments, "Grandad drove cart. Rick and Flip pushed us. We played hiding seek. Flip helped us count 1, 2, 3… "Heln took us on tresser hunt. Smarties in garden!"

Rebecca's eyes glinted in challenge as she reported, "We ate them all."

"Then Rebecca it has been a special day." Paul touched her shoulder. His gentle brown eyes indicated his wish to speak to her so she responded, "Thank you for all you did today."

He smiled. "It was good to be here and despite the empty lake and sink hole, this is still a beautiful place to live. Jack and Cathy are gems." He drew her away and nervously stroked his beard, "Forgive me if I'm speaking out of turn, but Bertie's disabilities hide the fact that he has a sharp brain. If his mental capabilities were assessed, advice would be given on how to harness it. There is also an operation which would shorten his leg and turn his foot to help him walk normally. It would entail a few weeks in hospital, and my thinking is that now Rachel is settled we'll soon be leaving David's flat. Jack and Cathy could stay there with Bertie and Declan. And you would be close at hand to lend support."

"It sounds good to me. Now Bertie is registered and has an NHS number we can encourage him to see what treatment is available. I'll talk to him and the Hawkins."

Paul patted her shoulder, "When our lives are in God's hands, He always shows us when it is the 'right' time."

Coming up behind her Gerald chuckled, "Just as I was there at the 'right' time to help David lug your heavily pregnant wife downstairs, giving you only seconds to deliver your child. And after today I'd agree God works in mysterious ways. I'm not sure about His wonders to perform, but as you say time and truth will tell."

"Believe me Gerald it was a miracle! We were here so any other time it would have been an entirely different scenario."

Jill joined them as Gerald confided, "Believe me it's not just a sink hole that has opened up. I've another tale to tell which Rosie should be the first to hear."

"I expect Rosie you will tell us, but for now we need to get the children home. Paul, the children are in the car and Mum and Dad are waiting to say 'goodbye'.

"I've thanked Jack for the sterling job he did today. What a resourceful man."

"And I thanked Cathy. We had a lovely chat. She is so understanding. Jill turned to her, "Rosie thank you for inviting us. I'm sorry I've been so tetchy. Today has been a breath of fresh air after being cooped up in that flat with two young children and Rachel's constant crying. Rosie hugged her as David arrived. "This house maybe dowdy, but with the grounds and despite today's devastation, it has a lot of potential."

At which David promptly asserted, "Which would take a vast amount of money to put to rights Jill."

"As your father said, 'the bottom has fallen out of the lake as will any market interest'!"

Jill pulled on Paul's arm saying, "Ted thinks our family is 'a class act' so after today one wonders what the next episode will be in the Reinhardt saga. Now we must be on our way."

Gerald said "Paul, before you go, I'm sure you'd like to know Ted's x-ray were fine, but with the extent of the lacerations and a chance they could be or get infected, they are keeping him in along with George wanting to monitor his confusion. Also a local orthopedic surgeon has been called in to set Debbie's broken arm and leg."

"How do you know that?" David boomed.

"While you were talking and eating, I investigated the telephone line. I traced its entrance into the house from the overhead cable and found the telephone originates in the Butler's Pantry."

"I could have told you that."

"I'm sure Rosie you could. It was also understandable in the circumstances that you assumed the worst. But after an incident a couple of months ago I'm surprised it didn't occur to you that this could be the work of a rat?" Horrified Jill mouthed 'rats'! Rosie's hand covered her mouth. David grunted, Paul frowned and they all looked to Gerald who explained, "I pulled out the desk. The wire had been chewed, along with a half-eaten profiterole."

"Oh no!" Rosie admitted, "I was carrying the profiteroles from the pantry when the phone rang. I put them on the desk. One must have fallen off."

"And that's not all! Gerald chortled, "I was on my way to forage in the garage in order to make a repair when I met Declan. He confessed that a week ago, Bertie had been cuddling his pet rat when it wriggled out of his hand. Rosie's hand flew to her mouth and Gerald obviously enjoying the story added, "Despite their searching Pixie hasn't been seen since." Looking around he stated, "And believe me folks, that's only the start of today's unfolding tale."

Wide-eyed Rosie observed, "I'm not sure I can cope with it. I am appalled how easily it is to draw the wrong conclusions."

"Many years of detective work have brought me to realise that like the old adage, 'you can't tell a book by its cover!' Now I have to go too to pick up Maria and Joyce from the hospital. With information from Debbie, I'll visit George and see if it jogs his memory."

Paul backed out David's Rover, they waved them off, and Gerald followed him out the gate. Declan grabbed her hand as Jack suggested they take a closer look at the devastated lake. At his despondent expression Rosie stopped to give him her attention. "I'm sorry about Pixie. I thought we'd find her without anyone knowing. Don't take them away?"

"Just promise me you'll only take them out in the kitchen garden."

Declan nodded then frowned, "Aren't you cross that Pixie stopped the telephone working? Uncle David's Dad had a real go at Richard and Phillip's Dad for upsetting Diana. He shouted back that he'd been humiliated by the Reinhardts one time too many and never wanted to set eyes on them again. He was then angry because his boys didn't want to go. I liked them, but don't suppose I'll see them again."

"You will. And you aren't in trouble. Now come on." She smiled down at him, gave his hand a comforting squeeze and swinging his arm back they set out to join the others.

"Are you going to marry Johnny?"

Rosie put her finger across her mouth, "Maybe, but for now it's a secret."

"Phillip says it's a secret between him and Uncle David that they are praying you will marry him.

"Rosie stifled her laughter and said, "Really! One thing you can be assured of is the Reinhardts will always be my friends."

His face brightened, "Cor…that's good then, I really like the twins." Barely pausing for breath he continued, "Uncle Gerald is clever. He showed me how to mend the telephone wire, and quickly caught Pixie in his trap." Rosie grimaced bringing Declan to reassure her, "It didn't hurt and she's back now with her family."

"Good! One problem dealt with and let's hope the remaining ones will be quickly solved."

Declan gave her an anxious look, but was diverted by the twins running towards him and Joshua demanding, "Declie play with us? Build tower, we knock down."

And as he took their hands Rebecca jumped up and down, "Me do it first!"

Rosie grinned as Joshua muttered, "Is that so?" At two, he had already his father's words and expression, bringing her to wish she had had a father with something she desired to copy. She joined the group taking a closer look at the empty dark scar on the landscape as David advised, "A geologist will be able to tell if there is any further instability in the land."

"I can't see my father bothering with the expense of that, or the cost of filling in a sink hole."

Franz boomed, "The army will want its lorry back. They might help."

They considered that before Jack returned to report, "I can't see where the water drained out, the silt has covered - if not filled - the hole. My understanding is that the river was originally diverted to fill a natural basin and collected water from the hills around." He scratched his head, "I can't imagine what will happen now. There's no insurance as His Lordship always said he couldn't afford the kind of money this place attracted."

Margaret looked worried, "But he could be sued for damages

or injuries?"

David answered, "Fortunately Mum, Jack put up a sign and blocked the drive with a huge tree trunk, so they would have no case to answer."

Rosie was tempted to say, 'Is that so!' but instead asked, "Have you got it? Gerald said he and others didn't see it. However he knows something and is keeping us in suspense."

"That's the detective always drawing on lines of enquiry to get the full picture."

"I agree Dad." David looked at his watch, "And I'd like to stay and know what he has discovered. Rosie could the twins sleep in your bedroom until then?"

"Of course! And Cathy, with Ted in hospital overnight we'd better prepare a room for Joyce."

"Consider it done! Ida wants to make amends for being intoxicated and Florrie is a dear soul always on hand to help. They have been such a boon in clearing and cleaning, both preferring to be behind the scenes."

Franz commented, "Although I am curious about today's events, I think Margaret we should leave these good people to rest and take stock. We'll come with you David and say 'goodbye' to the twins."

Cathy drew her aside so they could stroll back together, "When Ida was in the toilet being sick, Florrie told me she'd met her only weeks after Jane's death. And she wished she hadn't introduced her to clean 'the master's' house because Ida was continually hinting you weren't all you seem. Apparently, in the car Ida told everyone she knew your father and asked me if that was true? My response was 'nothing about that man would surprise me'. Poor Florrie looked so bewildered. I told her I'd practically brought you up! She told me she knew little about Ida and was horrified this morning that Ida had been taking a 'tipple or two for Dutch' courage'."

Rosie shrugged, "The tipple certainly tipped her over the edge with all that distress and unintelligible muttering. She's certainly seen worse than that."

"When she felt better Ida told me, wait for it, your father was her childhood sweetheart! And she's been in touch with him most of her life. I confess I replied in a derogatory tone 'then you'll know exactly the kind of man he is' but I didn't say more." Cathy sent Rosie a questioning look, "I guess you had a reason to invite her?"

"And you would be right!" Rosie put her arm through Cathy's, "Gerald knows about it, and unbeknown to her is on her case. I'll tell you about it later."

"Fair enough. And regardless of events I've really enjoyed today, meeting all those people you have talked about." They stopped outside the front door, "When Jane came into your life, she did more than introduce you to religion, sorry... a relationship with Jesus. She birthed children for you to love and left a man who wants you as his wife and their mother. His family respect you for stepping into the breach, and his parents are keen to welcome you as a daughter-in-law. It's all I could want for you."

From the bedroom window above the door David's voice boomed out, "Well said Cathy, you tell her. I'm not giving up hope!"

Stepping back, Cathy looking amused called up to him, "And they say eavesdroppers never hear well about themselves" to which David smiled, saluted and closed the window.

As they stepped into the small vestibule Cathy added quietly, "Except Rosie, I realised today how much you love Johnny. It was him you rushed down to, not Jack or David. He was, and still is, your childhood sweetheart. What greater proof could anyone need to show you aren't like your father. You aren't after money, home and ready-made family, but to the love you have in your heart."

Rosie smiled, "Today we acknowledged we love each other."

Cathy's eyes overflowed with love for her, "I understand. Johnny's a kind man with a sunny personality."

"Oh Cathy, David overheard me telling Jack I loved him. I felt awful. A brief conversation later confirmed that David doesn't love me any more than I him, and is happy to remain friends and that I continue to care for his children."

"Then you have the best of both worlds."

Ida and Florrie sitting at the kitchen table looked up as they entered. Jack appearing in the opposite doorway informed them, "I've emptied Franz' car boot of our equipment, but not sure what to do with these wet bags."

As Ida yelled "Oh God no!" they stared as she leapt from the table and knocked over a chair heading towards them. Florrie put her head in her hands while Bertie, Helen and Declan playing Ludo looked startled as she screamed, "That bag. That pink bag. Where did you get it?"

Wide-eyed, Jack dropped the bags on the floor, raised his hands in defense and answered, "Gerald put them in Franz' car."

Distraught Ida stared at him. Jack added, "Johnny took it from the lorry."

Irritated Rosie declared, "Ida calm down. That pink bag belongs to the girl who was trapped in the lorry."

"Oh God…" Seeing Ida's legs buckling Jack stepped forward. Declan picked up the fallen chair and together they lowered her on to it.

Cathy said quietly, "Ida, when Johnny fell into the hole, he found there was a girl left in the lorry. Ida's eyes widened with fear. "He helped rescue her…"

"And as we speak, she is being operated on for a broken arm and leg." At Ida's deep moan, Rosie assured her, "She'll be fine, but there's no reason for you…"

David's loud, cultured voice cut across Rosie words, "The twins are waiting for… What's going on here?"

Wearily Jack confessed, "I bought these wet bags in and …"

Rosie with sudden clarity cut across Jack, "Ida do you have a grand-daughter named Debbie."

Ida blanched and nodded. A gasp went up bringing Rosie to conclude, "Gerald told us that the lorry driver kept muttering 'I'd a grand-daughter'. My fatuous comment on how that sounds seems to be correct."

In a whisper Ida confirmed, "Debbie is my Elsie's child."

Furious Rosie stood over Ida to state, "Then it stands to reason that you also know George and Dennis Kent?"

Ida cried, "Why! Why did they come?" She put her head in her hands and wept.

David stepped forward, put a restraining hand on Rosie's shoulder, and crouched down before Ida, "As soon as we know Debbie is settled on the ward, I'll take you to visit her."

Ida looked up, black streaks from her mascara were running down her thin face, but Rosie didn't feel sympathetic. But Ida, surprised at David's offer looked up to say unsteadily, "Yer, yer'd do that for me?"

David drew up a chair beside Ida, "Is there any reason why I shouldn't?"

"I caused this mess."

"I'm puzzled as to why you should think that, and would appreciate hearing how you draw that conclusion." Ida frowned, and as he stood to call upon Cathy to give Ida a strong cup of coffee, Rosie guessed Ida was finding David's words confusing! When David was heard to suggest she stay the night, Cathy gave

Rosie a questioning look, at which she nodded.

David looked towards her, "Rosie we need to say 'goodnight' to the twins."

Ida having bent to rummage in the wet pink wet bag at her feet, cried out as they turned to leave, "Debbie takes this everywhere". In her hand was a soggy teddy bear.

Cathy suggested, "Ida, if you go and wash your face and the bear, I'll get my hairdryer and hopefully we can dry it, and you can take it to her." Ida looked around seemingly stunned by their kindness. David drew Rosie into the corridor as Helen could be heard suggesting to Declan and Bertie they should play their board game in the ballroom.

The twins, exhausted from their exciting day, were laying together in the centre of Rosie's bed with thumbs in mouths and already asleep. Love for them overwhelmed her as, like parents, they looked down at their cute innocence.

David accompanying her downstairs suggested, "Give Ida an opportunity to talk before you judge her." Rosie pursed her lips, but felt too tired to argue. On the table, the contents of Debbie's bag were spread out to dry and Jack dozing on the settee informed them that Ida, Florrie and Cathy were preparing Ida's room. Rosie in need of tea put on the kettle. David rang the hospital and returned to report that Debbie was out of surgery and the Chaplain had visited her, but 'no visitors until tomorrow'. In repeating that to Ida, she looked relieved and prompted by Cathy, began to tell them what she knew.

"Years ago my Elsie told Debbie about her grandfather. When I told Elsie I was coming 'ere, Debbie wanted to come. I told 'er she weren't invited. Four year ago I took Debbie to meet 'er new uncles. She was very taken with 'em and their boys." Rosie and David shared a questioning look at which Ida explained, "Rosie, your Dad's real name is Leonard McCreedy." Jack's astonishment had him wide awake, but Cathy's expression was filled with contempt.

"'E collected rents and was known as 'Lenny the Greedy'. In 1928, it was fought when 'e disappeared, the 'bother boys' caught up wiv 'im and done 'im in. When I saw 'im again 'in 1948 'e'd changed his name to Doughty, like that 'e 'ated anyone to 'doubt 'im'. Ida cackled, "But cor blimey, they'd reason to. Told me 'e'd left Blighty in 1936. 'E'd get angry if I asked 'im where 'e'd been in those 'missing eight years' since Wapping." Ida's gaze rested on Rosie, "Just lately I've 'ad even more reason 'to doubt 'im', 'specially after 'e upped and left for India. When 'e' left me in 1928, I fought my heart would break 'cause I'd just realized I was up the duff."

David glanced at Rosie before clarifying, "You had Leo's, Lenny's child in 1928?"

If that were true Rosie realized Ida's child was her step-sister, which Ida confirmed, "See we're family." Rosie gave an enigmatic smile. "Unlike Rosie, I'd connections but no money for an abortion." Florrie's dismay at that news was evident in the way she looked at David who mouthed with a smile 'It's okay'. "Cor, I wer' mad when I saw Lenny after all 'em years. I told 'im I'd tell the 'bother boys' he wer' still alive. He told me to keep me mouth shut or else." Ida cackled, "I told 'im, there wouldn't be any 'else' if they got to 'im first. That made 'im laugh, and the spark between us was still there. And after... well, 'e knew I'd keep silent, but still 'e'd always leave a fiver or more on the side."

Sharply Rosie stated, "So you continued your affair with my father?"

Ida's eyes narrowed, "Like you, with a married man!" Rosie saw Florrie's worried look at David, and his mouthed response 'I know'.

"Unlike yer, we didn't live together or meet often. When I told 'im I 'ad 'is daughter 'e looked shocked. I told 'im 'er name was Elsie. 'e laughed saying, 'a case of believe me, or Else!' After that 'e pestered me, wanted to see 'er, and when 'e did 'e delightedly reported, 'she's a chip off the ole block'. But I thought 'e'd hit me when I's told 'im, 'unlike 'im she'd not a devious bone in 'er body'. Elsie disliked 'im on sight. 'E weren't invited, but 'e turned up at 'er wedding the following year looking very well to do. Gave 'er a hundred quid. She wer' barely polite, took the money, told me 'e' owed it 'aving deserted 'er as a child. She and Archie used it as a down payment on a 'ouse, and I've never given 'im 'er address. If 'e 'ad money we'd 'ave a good time. I like to fink, wiv me expecting Elsie, we would 'ave married life turn out differently."

David sighed, "Ida as interesting as that is, I fail to make the connection with George and Dennis Kent."

"Yer see the 'bother boys' failed to find Lenny in 1928, but in 1968 'is boys found me."

"His boys! David demanded, "Are you saying George and Dennis...?"

Ida interrupted, "It wer' a shock to me. 'Is youngest one wer' severely disabled, died at ten from same complaint as Bertie. At least Bertie weren't born a dribbling wreck. The other two are more brawn than brains. I've no idea why Lenny chose Kent 'cept Joseph Vine, Mary's father owned several green grocery shops in Kent." She cackled "Maybe he fought he was like Superman! Lenny ain't be around these four years to ask. Mary, like your mother, was the unmarried daughter of an elderly man. Gambling is Lenny's downfall, but 'e can charm the birds off a tree if 'e sees a way to part people from their money."

Rosie processing Ida's information didn't respond. "Joseph Vine 'ad no idea until Lenny disappeared in 1936, that 'e'd been milking the profits of 'is six shops and he died within weeks from a 'eart attack. Mary struggled to keep one shop and the flat over it, and 'ad just enough to bring up 'er three boys. Seven years later Kent - like McCreedy - was presumed dead."

Cathy shook her head in disbelief, Jack looked stunned, Florrie captivated and David's expression was thoughtful and forbiddingly stern. Rosie with furrowed brow queried, "These men are using the name Kent, so did my father marry their mother?"

"Mary's a kind soul, nuffing to look at, so understandable she wer' taken in by Lenny's charms. She told me about 'im and showed me 'er marriage certificate."

"So she's still alive?" Ida nodded. "In which case that brings me to conclude that we can add bigamist to fraud and embezzlement on the list of his crimes against my mother. But how do we tell her that?"

David ran his hand through his hair, "At present we don't." Rosie sent him an enquiring look. "Think about it. There's much to consider. We need to establish the facts, speak to Mary Kent, find marriage records. How did McCreedy change his name, not once but twice? He would need two forged birth certificates, one to marry as Kent, the second as Doughty to obtain a Passport? Those crimes could land him in jail for life."

Rosie stated churlishly, "Good! Best place for him. Can he be extradited from India?"

David raised his eyebrows, "It's possible, but should he get wind we are on to him, he could just disappear again, and have to be declared dead again before justice can be done."

"If we can prove Leo Kent is still married, his name is as phony as is his marriage to my mother, as must be his name on the deeds of this house and estate. After all, she inherited it in her maiden name, and if her marriage isn't legal then he has no rights to it."

"I wouldn't be so sure for I well know the law can sometimes be an ass."

"David, he sold 'home farm' and profited from the proceeds. We can't get it back, but we must stop him selling this house. Mum, not being married to him, probably wouldn't have a claim on his tea plantation, but Mary Kent could benefit."

"Agreed, but this needs due consideration if we are to find the best course of action." There was silence as each were immersed in their own thoughts.

The despondency in Rosie's voice was clear, "First we have the drive, then the lake disappears. There's no money or insurance to cover that. Even if we knew the prospective buyer was still interested, they would not want to hang around for whatever action we decide to take. And my father isn't likely to return voluntarily to face the consequences of his actions."

Ida piped up, "But yer now got a family, one sister, and two brothers, along with one niece and four nephews!" Rosie acknowledged that with a weak smile.

David promptly boomed, "And one thing we can be sure about is none of them have any rights or claims to this house and estate."

Ida gave David a peeved look, "I weren't saying it for that. George and Dennis are good boys. They'll want to put things right, and could help you fill in that big 'ole."

David stated, "If nothing else we need to sort this legal mess out. I'll consult with others, and look into similar cases that have been brought to justice." As Rosie murmured 'Thank you', voices heralded the arrival of Joyce, Maria and Gerald.

Jack admitted, "We have always known that Rosie's father is a cheat, a gambler and robbed Dee-Dee of her money, but this…" The door opened to the little group with Joyce looking pale and tearful. Rosie stood to greet her, but Cathy moved forward to put an arm around her and reassure her, "Oh my dear, we're here for you. We've prepared a room so you can stay." Tears slid down Joyce's cheek. "Come on, I'll take you upstairs and you can tell me all about it."

Gerald looked around the room. Jack looked stunned, Ida appeared sheepish and Florrie uncomfortable. David invited him to sit, and Rosie made the inevitable tea! Maria obviously gauging the atmosphere said sensitively, "I'll make myself scarce." At which Rosie plied Maria with food and drink and suggested she joins the others in the ballroom until Gerald was ready to take her home. Florrie overhearing suggested, "When Joyce comes back down, Ida and I can sit with her in the music room. She told me after Jane died, she found comfort playing the piano, she might like to do that now."

Rosie was quick to respond, "Florrie that's a brilliant idea, thank you."

By the time the group resettled around the table, Gerald had been informed of the latest developments and began to relay his, "I'd say George and Dennis are probably resourceful. George is a long distance lorry driver and Dennis a bricklayer. Despite George telling me he had a God-fearing mother, his words are peppered with expletives. In my brief time in the ambulance with Debbie she told me she had come to visit Ida, her grandmother, but appeared far more interested and concerned about Johnny than her uncles." Rosie felt a stab of jealousy and realized she needed to get over that reaction if she were to marry Johnny, as it could lead to a very slippery dark path.

Gerald continued, "I've investigated cases of bigamy, fraud and embezzlement. Occasionally someone has committed all three, but to have taken on three personas and got away with it three times, the last using a landed gentry title, is extraordinary. He's either a very clever man, or an extremely lucky one."

While running his hands through his hair David announced, "We have a big problem!" Everyone looked at him. "The press would have a field day with this story. A gambler who reinvented himself twice, married and embezzled his wife's business, became a bigamist, took over a woman's estate and a title which wasn't his to own. In that time he fathered two daughters, four sons, two of which were disabled and he abandoned. His younger daughter lived with a married Cabinet Minister…" As Rosie buried her face in her hands, David apologized, "I'm sorry Rosie, I won't go on, but you see the reality!"

Gerald looked worried, "We have to keep this under wraps and find a way to get justice without involving the police. I told the police this was a family and friends party, assume those in the lorry were coming to join you, but as only one of many friends, I didn't know them. The tree trunk pushed to the side of the drive wasn't spotted, and thankfully the sign had gone."

"It was in Debbie's bag." Rosie sighed, "To think all this started when Ida came to clean and thought she could blackmail me."

Cathy's eyes widened, Jack repeated in a horrified tone, "Blackmail! Rosie you didn't tell us. Why on earth did you invite her?"

"My father had filled her with twisted information." Rosie looked at David, "We felt it an opportunity for her to hear the truth."

"And now if she decided to go to the press, she may not only ruin David's career and reputation, but you marrying Johnny could ruin his." Worry etched Jack's brow.

Crossly, Rosie countered, "If it did, it wouldn't be following the Christian teaching of Jesus accepting the fallen woman!"

Gerald grinned, "I think it was a good strategy. Ida felt welcomed, she could see you are good people. I don't think she'd deliberately expose anyone, but we have to face the fact that if she meets a shrewd reporter offering money, she might give away enough information for them to investigate and find out for themselves."

"In which case we must ensure that doesn't happen."

"And how, David, would you propose to do that?"

"Gerald, I've been studying her. She's lonely, feels hard done by and needs money. A subtle way to buy silence is with love and acceptance. Cathy befriending her made her eager to help. When shocked into telling us about the occupants of the lorry, we didn't accuse or abandon her. We witnessed her astonishment at my offering to take her to the hospital and she was overwhelmed when we suggested she stays."

"David is right. Jane extended that kind of friendship to me. Jesus told us to love our enemies, in the belief it would bring out the best in them."

"Do you think Ida values friendship enough to be loyal? The inside story of Lord Leonard Doughty-Dawes life would bring in a tidy sum." The ensuing silence revealed none of them had the answer to that. Gerald continued, "Even knowing he lied, Ida resumed her affair with Lenny in 1948 and, in an odd way, was supported by him. That brings me to how Ida and the Kent boys found each other forty years after Lenny's first disappearance. Debbie's name sparked George's long term memory."

Gerald pulled out his pocket book and thumbed through it, "Five years ago, the Evening Standard ran a story about alien abduction. Ida wrote to the newspaper and they published the letters alongside a subsequent article." Gerald absently mindedly sucked on his pencil, "I'll get the original article, but bones of it were, Ida wrote that her boyfriend went missing in London in March 1928. He was presumed dead, although no body was found.

In 1948 she saw him in a pub in the West End. He said he'd been given a ticket to India in 1936, but seemed unable to recall those missing years. Could he have been abducted and his memory wiped?"

"Surely she didn't believe that?"

"David, I'll leave you to be the judge of that. Gerald's amusement was obvious, "Maybe she suspected he'd been in prison, but my guess is she knew he was deliberately hiding something. He had returned to India for good so she had nothing to lose. For years people have reported seeing UFOs. Ida told George that Lenny also enjoyed sci-fi stuff, so maybe Lenny had hinted at abduction to detract her questions. And if her letter was published, there was a chance someone might come forward with information. And that's exactly what happened."

Rosie and David exclaimed in unison, "No!" Jack and Cathy shook their heads in unbelief and Gerald looked delighted. He pocketed his book and explained, "George and Dennis are interested in all things 'alien'. They read the articles, talked to their mother and bingo! Her curiosity was aroused and she wrote to Ida via the newspaper. Ida replied with Lenny's age, a few salient details, but the fact that clinched it for Mary was Ida's comment, 'with a moustache he looks like Lord Kitchener'."

"Good grief!" exclaimed Rosie, "His taking on Kitchener's persona, strutting about, giving his orders to Jack and Cathy turned out to be his undoing. I hated the way he would twist the ends of that handlebar moustache. I'd fantasized about cutting them off while he was asleep."

David roared with laughter, Gerald grinned and Cathy looked astonished at such a confession, but Jack preoccupied with the story questioned, "Did George tell you why he was driving an army lorry? It's not the usual mode of transport, or clothes to wear if going to a family party."

"George can't recall recent events. I was dismissed in his need to rest. I also had Joyce and Maria waiting for me."

Jack addressed Rosie, "Do you think Ida felt she might need 'Dutch courage' in case they decided to gatecrash the party?"

"I can throw some light on that." The loose pockets of Gerald's cheeks wobbled in his delight of successful detective work, "When I asked after Debbie, I was told the Chaplain had talked with her, and held her hand as she went down to the operating theatre. Johnny is well liked and I was directed to the Chaplain's Room where he was awaiting her return." Rosie banked down on another stab of jealousy. "He was writing down Debbie's version of events. I suggested I visit George and come back to collect it." From his pocket Gerald produced several pages of foolscap lined paper folded in four. "I briefly read these, they provide answers, but I'd prefer to be the messenger, not the informer or the police officer." And with that he handed them to David. As David read Johnny's words, Gerald discreetly passed her a folded sheet from another pocket.

She smiled and instantly opened it.

Dearest Rosie, I apologise for Jennifer's abrupt behaviour. I don't know what is wrong with her and Freddy. She wasn't pleased, but did take us back to Diana's flat rather than their house. I promised Debbie I would go to the hospital and stay with her, but still had to remind Jennifer as the hospital chaplain it was my job! Rosie sighed, that was a truth she needed to embrace!

Rosie looked up as David boomed, "Gerald don't look so worried, I know the battle for Rosie's heart has for now been won by Johnny, but I'm not giving up on her until the wedding bells ring!" Gerald looked embarrassed, Rosie frowned and David chuckled, "It will only be then that I shall leave behind the castle of her heart." Rosie sent David a cynical look, noted Cathy's appreciative nod, but Jack's anxious expression remained. As David scanned the pages, Rosie read her letter. *'Inadvertently, I heightened the tension in the car by telling Jennifer and Freddy that I loved you, and nothing would separate us again. I think she thought I was intending to abscond to a pre-planned assignation and insisted on waiting until I'd bathed and changed, in order to take me to the hospital. I know they like you, and have prayed for you for years so it can't be you, but their behaviour is odd.'* Odd was right! The Greenhaighs' withdrawal seemed to be linked to her friendship to Johnny, yet they had no hesitation in encouraging her relationship with David. Did they think she was either too good, or not good enough for him?

Rosie tuned back to Gerald saying, "… he's a good listener and has done a brilliant job getting information from Debbie."

Rosie added, "Johnny says here, *'Please thank those involved in my rescue. I look forward to telling them about my extraordinary experience of not falling, but floating in what felt a bubble of peace and love, and sensing I was part of a bigger plan'.*"

David putting Johnny's notes on the table commented, "We'll look forward to that. Now with the time factor I'll skim over these notes and hope not to repeat what we already know. Dennis and George live in Bromley. Since finding her uncles, Debbie's parents sometimes let her stay at weekends. Neither family owns a car, but her uncles are in the Territorial Army and are lent a lorry when cadets need picking up, and she sometimes goes along for the ride. On Friday, her uncles were going near Petersfield so she suggested they visit despite Ida telling her to stay away. But curious Debbie nagged her uncles to make the diversion and have a peek at their father's place. She needled their interest and said they had a right to be there and suggested they ring from a phone box nearby. She pretended to dial a number and talk to someone and told her uncles they were welcome. At the tree trunk she tore off the sign, said the warning was for cars, but their solid army truck used to rough terrain wouldn't find it a problem. At this point Debbie burst into tears, said it was all her fault and what would her parents say?"

Rosie grunted, "Debbie doesn't know her grandfather, but seems to have inherited his persuasive ways!"

David looked up, "All of us have said and done things in our life that we later regret. Let's not judge before we meet her. Johnny says the police aren't interested in her. It would seem Gerald they bought your story of family which now has truth in it. Johnny writes, 'In knowing George's name, rank and army number, the police have probably traced and notified his wife, and either she or the police would notify Dennis' family. I told Debbie I'd ring her parents, but there's no reply. I hope I'll get to them first."

As if on cue their phone rang and as Jack went to answer it, Gerald suggested the need to explain to the Kent families it was in everyone's interest to keep to the story of a family party."

Cathy stated, "Ida will have their telephone numbers, perhaps Rosie you should make those calls. Leo Doughty-Dawes is without doubt a bad egg, but we can bring unity by telling them they are welcome here, and that Mary and Dee-Dee suffered the same fate at his hands.

"I wonder why my father didn't up and disappear again when Bertie was born."

"I think Rosie, he might have done, but having packed you off to boarding school, he felt the place was big enough to hide Bertie, giving him freedom to continue entertaining and living off his gambling proceeds, along with whatever he could find to sell. Those yearly parties were awful, I was grateful you weren't here."

David refolded the sheets of Johnny's large, bold handwriting and handed them to Rosie. "As I said earlier let's not do anything hasty, carry on as normal, get our evidence, and decide how to go from there. We certainly don't want your father to get wind of what we now know."

"There is bound to be some press coverage about George and Dennis' army lorry disappearing into a sink hole on this estate."

"True Gerald, but let's make the truth as simple as possible, so it's only a one day wonder. The Hawkins were hosting a party. Debbie's uncles were giving her a lift to visit her Gran who is staying here. If we can keep the press attention on the sink hole and the lorry falling in, the story will then focus on Johnny, the fire brigade, and the rescue of Debbie without mention of any other names."

Jack re-entered the room saying, "That was the police to tell us they've found the two young boys dressed in army fatigues and are taking them home. They've also informed George and Dennis' wives of their accident along with the TA who will contact us regarding the retrieval of their lorry."

Cathy having listened intently suggested, "I'll go and talk to Ida. We need to talk to their wives. Debbie said that neither family had a car, so we could offer to collect them from the station, take them to the hospital and them bring then back here and get them on side. And if Ida was to stay here while Debbie is in hospital, that would ensure she's away from any press intrusion."

Rosie sent Cathy a questioning look as Gerald commented, "That would certainly add credence to our story."

"I agree!" David boomed before adding, "Ida will then be seen with Debbie at visiting times. Johnny can prime Debbie to keep to family connections with the Hawkins and not speak of her grandfather." With a devastating smile David looked at Cathy, "That is good of you for it will place more of a burden on you."

"Believe me, Ida won't be a burden. She's a good cleaner, hard worker, and a great help if, in the next few weeks, we have people coming to stay. And it won't be long before there is fruit to harvest, jam to make, vegetables to bottle, and as they say many hands make light work. I'll go and talk to her. Good job it's summer, for the bedrooms in this house are perishing cold in winter."

"If we can get through the press coverage without uncovering the past, I think there is a way to solve all this in a simple, legal and not expensive way." David glanced at his watch, "Now we need to get home. I've no doubt tomorrow the press will be on the doorstep wanting the story. Appear friendly and open, but keep names and personal information to a minimum." David stood, "Right Rosie, let's make a move."

Rosie's eyes widened, she pursued her lips, "David, I know I am meant to return with you, but I can't leave Jack and Cathy to shoulder extra responsibilities alone."

David ran his fingers through his hair, "Surely you see the sense in you not being here? It can then be assumed the party was for the Hawkins' friends."

"I do, but I prefer to be consulted, not commanded."

Cathy gave David a wry smile before addressing Rosie, "I went to India because I didn't want a dull life. I ended back here, where except for your father's frolics, these last years have been quite dull. I've enjoyed the challenges of Helen. Jack and I love having Declan here. The way I see it as long as we live in this crumbling mansion, why not share it with whoever comes?" Jack nodded. Cathy finished, "David and the twins need you, and you need time away to process all you have heard today."

CHAPTER 26

Cathy and David had been right about her needing time to process the events and revelations of August Bank Holiday. For nearly two months after hearing about her father's life, she felt she'd become mentally and spiritually unstable. David used the term, 'an emotional crisis' to describe her difficulty in coming to terms with the truth. Almost immediately after that day it seemed the twins were constantly testing and pushing their boundaries in acts of defiance and rudeness. Her response would bring bouts of anger and unnecessary shouting while the twins would look on in wide-eyed innocence which pushed her further. It came to a head the day the threatening wooden spoon was put to use on Joshua's backside. The shock - more than the pain - had both children crying, and later subdued and wary of her. She knew from experience that to accuse or speak negative words had far more potential to cause damage than physical discipline from a loving parent, but had been annoyed at David pointing out that if anger was to be considered righteous, it must come from a calm and positive spirit. And then he added, if possible, any discipline should come from him.

Feeling undermined, she'd given way to a rant before bursting into tears and admitting, "I can't cope with them."

She'd allowed herself to be drawn into his arms, and been taken aback, when he confessed, "I've years of training to act cool and calm when angry, but with those close to you it's far harder. Let's take up an ABC in disciplining: authority, boundaries and correction, and together decide how to act so the twins will recognise we don't reject them, just condone their actions." She wiped her eyes and nodded before he grunted, "I fear that like all children they will learn to quickly say 'I'm sorry' to get out of punishment, but we haven't reached that stage... yet."

Johnny lovingly described her as being like a dormant volcano, which a spark could easily re-ignite. His cheery disposition drew her out to talk about her anger and its link with thinking she'd forgiven her father, but the latest revelations had proved her inability to do so. Johnny always found a positive slant if not a solution, but on one occasion he'd quoted scripture, and in sheer frustration she'd snatched the Bible from him and thrown it against the wall. He'd looked at her, his Bible and back at her, and asked with a sad, but loving smile, "Did that help?" Shocked at her reaction she'd shaken her head and burst into tears. He'd waited for her to pick it up and apologise before drawing her into his arms and telling her how much he loved her.

Daily she called upon the Lord to 'forgive her, and those who had trespassed against her' and gradually her hatred dissipated, as did her fits of unrestrained anger. And without the pressure of contemplating David as a husband, she found it easier to appreciate his friendship and advice. He suggested that when Dennis would have recovered from the accident, she should invite the three families together and discuss how to bring their father to justice.

Near the end of October, Jack and Cathy came to London with Bertie for an appointment with one of Paul's colleagues to discuss the straightening of Bertie's leg. As it was mid-week Johnny came with them and they all lunched with David in his flat. The first thing he did was to show them the newly decorated basement flat and repeat his offer, that whether or not Bertie decided to go ahead with the operation, the Hawkins were welcome to spend the winter there. Cathy was wide-eyed at the luxury she was being offered.

That evening - at David's suggestion - Mandy, Dennis' wife, organised the adults of the three families to come together in a local pub, with David billed as legal adviser. Once drinks were distributed, David ended the small talk and asked Jack to give an update on events, "I haven't received a reply to my letter informing your father of the sink hole, and the danger of a large open hole on the grounds. But thanks to our unity, beyond the reporting of the sink hole, Johnny's heroic rescue of Debbie, and the photos of the huge army's crane retrieving the lorry, there's been no further press interest. Jack grinned at George, "Your boys really enjoyed watching that."

George lifted his beer glass, "I drink to a great day out and only a small dent in the lorry. It's usually a b… to get started so when it fired first time, I cheered the loudest. I should smack its rear into a hole more often." When the laughter died down he added, "Fortunately, being old, the TA wasn't bothered about the dent, but I was demoted due to using it for private purposes and told I'll have to foot the bill for the crane."

Francis said bitterly, "Heaven knows where we're going to get that kind of money with our two boys to support."

Dennis, who'd been the beneficiary of a collection by his builder mates, admitted, "We shouldn't have listened to Debbie and ignored the notice." To George and Francis he offered, "We're in this together, so we'll help out." And to Jack and Cathy, "I know we have apologized for the trouble we caused, but we are so grateful for all you did for Mandy and I especially over those weekends I was in hospital. Harry and Declan became great pals, he and Charlie would love to visit again."

Ida chuckled, "I didn't fink I'd like the country, but I enjoyed meself. I didn't want to 'ome after them six weeks."

Cathy smiled and replied, "I enjoyed your company and help. Bertie loved having so many people around."

Bertie made excited movements of his hands as Rosie addressed Dennis. "Now the water has drained through, Jack tells me you could organize truckloads of hardcore to be delivered to fill the hole and offered the use of a concrete mixer."

"It's only a start. With cities and towns being regenerated, there's always plenty of hardcore available, but neither of us have the money to pay for the enormous amount of sand and cement needed to make the concrete to fill a hole of that size."

Immediately David boomed, "I appreciate that kind of spirit, obviously influenced by your mother, not your father!" He smiled at them, "You get all the hardcore delivered. Dennis knowing about such things could find out the cost of hiring a commercial mixer which will make and pour the concrete in. It seems a good idea for you both to visit and talk to Freddy Greenhaigh who told me that in the war his army colleagues built both a dam and a bridge. With his help we could repair the breach in the lake at the same time."

"Our boys would love to help out, what about yours George?"

He nodded enthusiastically and suggested, "It's half term next week. We could come down, gets some ideas, see what we could do now, and at least put a temporary fence around the sink hole so stray animals won't fall in."

Cathy smiled, "If you look after yourselves you could all stay the week."

"I could help with the cooking, and bring Debbie."

"Ida that's a wonderful offer, but the boys might find Debbie a distraction!"

Mandy laughed, "If you'd like Francis and I to paint more

rooms, Debbie could help with that."

Cathy smiled at Jack who asked, "I believe George you are quite a handy man. I'd appreciate advice on repairing our dodgy electrics."

"Good heavens!" Rosie proclaimed, "This is going to be quite a work party."

David looked at George and Dennis, "Jack has probably told you the house and land have no insurance, so you can understand any help you can give would be appreciated. If you can make a dam and fill in that sink hole, I'll put up the money to hire a concrete mixer." Rosie's brown furrowed and deepened as he added, "When that's done, I will also pay your debt for the crane hire."

George exclaimed, "You... you'd pay for the crane? Why, why would you do that? It's a great deal of money, and I don't mean to be rude, but it's not your house or land."

Rosie pursed her lips and gave David a hard stare. His response of a questioning eyebrow caused her to challenge, "David, George has a point. If I were marrying you that offer would make more sense, but I'm not. It isn't my land or mess, but I don't want you to finance the repair and crane for then I will feel obligated to you."

"Rosie, that's unkind and unfair."

Although Johnny had whispered his words she turned on him to rant, "There's a great deal in life that's unfair..." David interrupted by booming down the table, "That Rosie goes without saying, but let's not follow your father's example." At Rosie's scowl he added. "I know you desire to find a way forward, and I have a desire to see justice. And contrary to your emotional outburst I assure you, you will never be obligated to me in any way. I suggest you appreciate and accepted all the offers of help for they will be more beneficial to you than to your father". David stood, "I've had a busy day. I'll leave you to discuss the arrangements between yourselves. Rosie, I understand Johnny is returning with the Hawkins and Bertie tonight. I'll be in the car waiting for you, please don't be long."

Just inside the pub doorway Rosie tried to get Johnny on side, but his expression remained tight and his voice firm, "I'm not going to agree with you. David's intentions are good. Stop judging him and trust him! Don't let your anger at your father colour your thinking and understanding, this man has your interests at heart." With that he kissed her, put his arm around her, and headed her to David and his car.

It was so unusual for Johnny to disagree with her point of view. She first sulked and then knowing she had been unreasonable apologised to David adding, "You are a man who thinks things through. But it seems foolish to invest money in repairing a property you don't own, and not likely to. I have the money you gave me in March, but see no reason to line my father's pockets. It would be helpful if you were to enlighten me on why you are intending to do that without any guarantee of its return."

David ran his hand through his hair, "I would have preferred to have completed the deal and report the outcome before countering your ire."

Rosie gave a heavy sigh, "Right! That sounds to me you are making decisions - deals even - that concern me without involving or consulting me."

David gave a resigned nod, "Not because I didn't want to involve or consult you, but because as you said my plan needed much deliberation if it was to work. I will tell you, but not while I'm driving. Can we discuss this at your cottage?"

She could hardly say 'no', but once inside she indicated a seat and sat opposite waiting for him to speak, "Look Rosie, it's difficult, and Jack did feel I should tell you…"

"Jack! Jack knows something I don't…"

"Now don't be upset with him. I was investigating the idea when I was the only man in the running for your hand in marriage. When I discussed it with Dad…"

With a pained look Rosie interrupted, "Your Dad also knows."

"I only told him of my interest with the variables and possibilities."

"'Only investigating, only man in the running, only interested, what else is 'only'?"

With a wry smile he bantered, "I will only accept Johnny is your husband when the wedding bells ring."

Rosie pursed her lips, gave him a hard stare and countered, "That's not funny."

Undaunted, David remarked with his high wattage smile, "Then I best tell you the other 'onlys' involved."

Irritably she declared, "Oh for goodness sake David, get on

with it! We haven't got all night."

"There's the pity!" Rosie took a sharp intake of breath as he continued, "Jill commented…"

"Oh great, Jill knows too! What are you doing, collecting people to agree with you?"

"Oh Rosie, I love this banter, I'm reminded of the fun I had with Jane." She glared at him as she'd no intention of contemplating a night free to enjoy the fun he had with Jane.

"It's alright Rosie, only Jack and my father know about this. Well, I would expect Jack told Cathy. After the surveyor, architect, plumber and electricians had been in the house, I wanted Jack to know that whoever bought the place, I'd ensure they - along with Bertie, Helen and Declan - wouldn't be out of a home. When he knew you intended to marry Johnny and not me, I assured him I would honour my promise."

Rosie shrugged, "What's that got to do with financing concrete and crane?"

David appeared not to hear but gave a broad smile, "In my dream, I am still in your castle. Dad hearing about Johnny said I shouldn't give up hope. He pointed out that Jane had taken months to fall in love with me. He also said in order not to lose you, he will happily include Johnny in our family."

"That's kind of your father. And, if Johnny hadn't come back into my life igniting that old flame of first love, maybe I would have accepted your proposal. Jane had your heart, just as Johnny has mine. I appreciate our friendship, especially lately when I've been an emotional wreck. You've been patient, kind and desired to help me in the quagmire my father's life had created. And I have noticed you listen and desire to honour me as if I were the twins' mother and your wife."

"I'm pleased to hear that." David lips twitched with amusement, "As far as I am concerned you are their mother and I shall continue to treat you as such. I'm grateful that even though you have chosen Johnny, my children and myself will still benefit from all you bring into our lives. If it were the other way around, I sense Johnny would say much the same."

Rosie nodded, "Marriage to Johnny, and the unconditional friendship you offer me, are something I value and will decree, 'let no man cast asunder'."

David's laughter boomed out, "Remind me of that next time we argue. But joking aside, let me explain what you will see as my 'plotting' without consulting you. You know Jill is feeling lonely without our company, and William and Luke miss the twins. Several times since visiting The Grange, she's suggested that between us we jointly buy a large property and bring up our children together. And Phillip - bless him - believing we were going to marry, suggested many good reasons for living in a big house and grounds."

Rosie grinned, "Hmm, I heard him telling you."

David, revisiting that conversation, observed, "He's a good lad with a great heart and brain. Dad is setting about finding ways to encourage that."

"And your father's prediction was correct, the 'interested party' hearing about the sink hole pulled out. Oh no! Surely he's not considering buying The Grange?"

"You know his view on 'handouts'!"

Rosie nodded, "It's odd how things come together. There was little interest in the estate until you proposed to me. The charitable organization appeared keen and we guessed had been deliberating when the sink hole put them off."

"A tactical move."

"Really? What makes you think that?" At David's amused expression she queried, "What's so funny?" His smile and the way he shook his head caused her to think back over what had just been said. When she realised she cried out, "Oh my God!" before her hand came up to cover her mouth. David chortled as she reasoned, "It wasn't odd at all, was it? Jack said he'd find out the name of the charity, and when later asked he said it was someone's name but couldn't remember it. It's the Jane MacKenzie Trust isn't it? Why didn't I consider that, or more importantly why didn't you tell me?"

David shrugged, "At first I was only interested in the selling price. The Agents - keen to get a sale - assured me if I were to have an estimate of the cost to renovate the property, your father would drop the price. He did, by a few thousand pounds. It wasn't enough for us to be interested, but we left it open to further negotiation."

"And then came the sink hole."

"Dad nearly clapped his hands in glee, realizing the market value would drop to rock bottom. It was God's perfect timing. We waited for the publicity and then felt it wise, albeit briefly, to withdraw our interest. The Estate Agent hoping for sale asked to keep us informed. Your father hasn't replied to Jack's letter, but he did instruct the Agent to obtain quotes to fill in the hole, and replace the lake. The quotes from several from major contractors were extortionate! It was no surprise he informed the Agent that he didn't have that kind of money available. The Agent advised with planning permission refused on several occasions, no insurance cover and an urgent need to secure a large hole on his land, maybe he should take whatever price we offered. I think in desperation he finally agreed to a price the Trust considered fair, and the deposit is now paid, guaranteeing the sale."

"I can barely believe it, Jane's Trust will own The Grange. I'm sure it couldn't be in better hands, but it will need a massive injection of money to bring the house up to a reasonable standard. My only 'ire' is that you didn't tell me what you were doing."

"The Trust didn't pay the deposit until Thursday, so up to then there wasn't anything to tell. Apart from the initial visits to the Estate Agent, I've kept out of it. The negotiations and legalities have been done between Dad's solicitors and your father's. But my plan is to your father's detriment not his gain."

Rosie, although quick brained, struggled to comprehend that, "But you've paid my father a deposit, and you are paying Dennis and friends to fill in the sink hole and build the dam."

David gave a broad smile, "Why not help out your father's family, especially as it will cost half the price quoted to your father."

"So how is that to my father's detriment?"

"The estate belongs to your mother and he obtained it under false pretenses. He has now illegally signed a purchase agreement, and his solicitors have received a deposit. I've been gathering evidence of your father's identity fraud and now we have a current issue of your father intention to cheat your unsuspecting mother out of what is truly hers. Dad's lawyer, as you know, is one of the best. A solicitor in England has to keep within the law, but your father's man is known to bend it to suit his clients and his pocket. We have drawn-up a watertight agreement which states that due to the danger to people and wildlife of a huge sink hole on the land, the repairs to that and the lake are deemed urgent, and the purchaser (the Trust) will bear the cost of such. The quoted amounts will be deducted from the deposit guaranteeing the sale. Should Lord Doughty-Dawes, for any reason, withdraw the sale of the Estate, the full deposit including the cost of repairs and legal fees incurred, will be refunded to the Trust within seven days."

Rosie said, "Let me see if I've got this right. If my father's crimes are exposed, the sale of the house in those circumstances has to be withdrawn."

"Correct. Leaving your father in debt to his solicitor, who I suspect has connections to, as Ida calls them, 'the bother boys'. Your father will then have to pay for the damage to the land, which he has claimed for years to be his."

"There's justice in that, but is only a fraction of what he got from selling the home farm. Does this come from a devious or astute mind?"

David sent her a wry smile before stating, "I would hope for the mind of Christ, for He gives wisdom and loves justice. However, there is more before we can bring this to a satisfactory conclusion. We aren't going to inform your father's solicitor that his client isn't who he says he is. We will also delay the completion of the sale, as the Trust needs time to draw together the necessary funds."

"I assumed as part of the Trust your father was backing this?"

"He is. Just another tactical move. Our intention isn't to buy the Estate from your father, but you and Bertie."

Confused Rosie shook her head, "You've lost me, but go on."

"The next stage is for somebody to inform and produce evidence to show your mother that she isn't married to your father, and his passport and birth certificate in the name of Doughty are forgeries as have been previous documents. Gerald's obtained copies of the police 'missing' files under 'McCreedy' and 'Kent" which have photos. He has talked to Mary, and now has a copy of her marriage certificate and unexpectedly his forged 'Kent' birth certificate. Ida, who is entirely on our side, has agreed to sign an affidavit that McCreedy, Kent and Doughty-Dawes are the same man, and would be willing to testify to that in court."

Rosie smiled, "Offering friendship has paid off. And as Ida would say 'that will really stitch him up' and answers my question. Whichever way this goes either the Trust or we, will benefit from the work George, Dennis and his mates do. The only flaw I see is my father lives in India, and once he knows he's been rumbled, he'll disappear again leaving his debts behind."

"Should that happen, despite changing his name, he is legally married to Mary and she'll have a claim against his tea plantation. Basically, the object of this exercise is to return to the Dawes family what is truly theirs in the simplest manner. Our idea is to present your father with strong reasons to see it is in his interest to reassign The Grange and its estate to his children. Your mother may not want to leave him, and under his control I've no doubt he would find a way to borrow more money against her property, persuade her to it and take the money.

"That's true. When faced with my father's bullying tactics, Mum can only stammer, cringe and comply with his every whim, making as the Brigadier said when he last saw her 'a mere shadow of the lovely, vivacious woman he had known in India." Scenarios that resulted in her mother having a migraine lasting for days, flashed through her mind. "Believe me, my father when challenged is very unpleasant. He shouts, argues and will bluster his way out of any problem."

David looking grim, hummed thoughtfully as Rosie continued, "I'm sure all the legal papers will be watertight, but I would advise if he and Mum are persuaded to sign anything, it must be done there and then, before his scheming mind finds a way out. Whoever you send, they will need clear jurisdiction, supporting evidence and an intimidating manner to over-ride and refute every claim and lie my father makes. And need to be able to threaten imminent arrest. Could a document be prepared that calls upon the Indian authorities for his extradition?"

"We're working on that one." David grinned at her, "There's a possibility a British Embassy official will provide us with a letter saying that on receipt of the person's name and documentation clarifying our claims, an arrest would be immediate."

"Good! Have you someone in mind to send?" questioned Rosie.

"Gerald and I are keen to meet with your father." David's eyes were steely, his stern features at their most forbidding.

Rosie's eyes widened in surprise, "You!" He'd certainly meet his match in you. Shrewd business deals, demolishing arguments, cutting through lies, drawing people to see the error of their ways… you have quite a reputation for bringing truth and justice."

"Thank you, but I hope you would remember that when mercy is needed, I am able to be fair and kind."

Rosie's mind reverted to her devastation at losing her job before Jane stepped in and said candidly, "And who would have believed how far your mercy would extend." David's smile was wry as she continued, "I don't know about sleezy solicitors and 'bother boys', but I do know it's not a pleasant experience to be on the wrong side of David Reinhardt."

"To be honest Rosie, I'm rather looking forward to 'demolishing' your father's arguments, and that brings me to the next stage of the plan."

"You mean there is more?"

"I would really like to visit the countries in which ITP has set up trading opportunities, one of which is, as you know, India. If Bertie has his leg straightened, the Hawkins will take up my offer of the basement flat. It seems an ideal time for me to be away and combine that with a visit to your parents."

Eagerly Rosie agreed, "The sooner the better, but the Hawkins got the impression the operation wouldn't be until January. Cathy is keen to live in your flat, says it would feel like an extended holiday."

"And one they so deserve."

"How long do you think you would be away?"

David flinched, "Two months." and added quickly, "With the Hawkins around you wouldn't be alone. Do you think you could cope that long?"

"The Hawkins would love it. The twins would miss you, but no longer tied to your working week, I would be free to take days off mid-week, spend time with Johnny, and together we could look after the twins. With Johnny back at work taking Saturday weddings and Sunday services and I with only weekends free, we don't get to see much of each other.

David smiled, "It sounds as if it could work for both of us. Once Bertie has made his decision, I'll leave you to talk to the Hawkins, and then we can start putting plans together. January will give plenty of time for Daniel, Dad's lawyer, to put the paperwork together, and the Trust can easily stall the final exchange date until after that. This is a gamble your father will not win. He will be furious, with no house to sell, no property to finance his debts and a bill for the shortfall from the return of our deposit, the solicitor's legal fees. My thinking is to give your mother the opportunity to leave, saying the Hawkins would welcome her, and she could return to England with Gerald.

"So that's your mercy and kindness taken care of, but I doubt she'll agree, better the devil you know…!"

"I can't imagine why any woman would want to stay with a man who has deceived, robbed and treated her children so appallingly. In case you have mentioned my name to your parents, I thought to shorten my name as Jill did at ITP. I'll be Mr Hart when I represent the Trust as their lawyer. Gerald will unofficially represent the arm of British law should it become necessary. And needless to say, the Trust will be waiting in the wings to purchase the house from you and Bertie."

"Should we wish to do so!"

David didn't appear to hear the irony in her voice for he added, "The money will be enough to purchase outright two large central London houses. The remainder if well invested would be enough to keep you, Bertie, your mother and the Hawkins in retirement comfort."

And then, as if catching she might not be thinking of selling, David conceded, "That of course would be up to you and Bertie. With the skills of your newly acquired family, and your ability to find ways to make money, you could remain owners and gradually restore the place. It would be quite a responsibility and an expense to upkeep. Gone are the days when people could afford living-in servants."

"How did you and your father envisioned using the place?"

David sat back and put his hands into a steeple, "First, as you pointed out we would need to spend a considerable amount of money to restore the property. It would cut a good size hole in Dad's fortune, but it would be done quickly. As long as it is a family home, we don't need planning permission and with two wings and the shape of the house, it would be easy to make separate accommodations, each containing one, two or three bedrooms with bathrooms, living area and kitchen. The ground floor would remain communal areas where we could eat together or not, as we chose. The children would be together. We would be able to help each other out with babysitting and enjoy the company of others, but be alone if desired."

David chortled, "Mum loved the idea, Dad growled 'I

suppose if we had a two-bedroom flat in the attic at the back of the West Wing overlooking the lake, we might get some peace and quiet.' He then added 'Better put in a lift - we're not getting any younger'."

"With everyone living together, I would then be free to travel again, as the twins would have you and others looking out for them." David smiled at her, and then as if noticing her somewhat stony expression he added, "I hope you and Johnny would be part of that, and you'd wish to continue as mother to the twins."

Tight lipped Rosie commented, "You appear to have put much thought into this." David missed the sarcasm while Rosie's irritation grew at his being free to travel and leave others to take care of his children.

"We've had to consider if the Trust could or should purchase the estate, and how we could make it a viable investment. The Hawkins would keep their caretaking role and enjoy the fruit of the land." Rosie took a deep intake of breath causing David to say, "Wait Rosie, hear me out. They would live rent free, and be guaranteed their home for the remainder of their lives. And for as long as they wanted to work, would receive a percentage of the maintenance fees included in the rents the rest of us would pay. Should they wish to continue to care for Bertie and pour out their love on people like Helen and Declan, the Trust would also encourage and finance that."

"That's very generous, but are you imagining we could live as one big happy family? It may have been like that when we all pulled together after Jane died, but it wasn't without its tensions and arguments." Rosie gave him a wide-eyed questioning look.

"This living together would be more separate. With everything there are problems that can rock congeniality, but surely we can endeavor to be family and remain friends."

"Easier said than done! Your father wanting to live in the attic to have peace and quiet, indicates he doesn't want to live in bedlam. Once Bertie and I own the property, we'll discuss and make our decisions about its future." Rosie emphasized the 'we' and 'our' to make her point, bringing David to agree fervently that was the case. "As confident as I am David in your abilities, what will you do if my father isn't intimidated by you and the consequences of his crimes?"

"When he knows what we know, believe me he will be! To sign back a house to his children and no further action being taken, is nothing compared to the alternatives he faces."

Shrugging her shoulders she proclaimed, "So be it."

A week or so later when considering that conversation, Rosie realised she had not written to her mother since April. She had told her she met Johnny, her childhood sweetheart, who was now the curate of the local church. Her mother hadn't replied, but maybe she ought to write a friendly letter giving her an edited version of both the friends for lunch and the events around the sink hole. She also included the newspaper cuttings relating Johnny rescuing a young girl. And mentioned Jack had written to her father about the sink hole and the need to deal with the hole in his land. In telling her mother she was still living in London and enjoying looking after Jane's twins, she didn't mention the Hawkins' recent decision to move into David's flat in the middle of November, or Bertie's scheduled operation in January. But did say she was going out with Johnny, and Helen was living with her at the cottage, having recently filled a vacancy on the ITP switchboard.

In December David had interviewed Graham Turner, a home tutor, who immediately realised Bertie's physical appearance had no bearing on his mental capabilities. Bertie's eagerness to learn meant Graham spent hours with him in hospital. Once home, their friendship expanded into helping Bertie in other areas and in taking him out and about, he did far more than his paid hours.

A few days before Christmas, a card arrived from India with a note from her mother informing her they had accepted an offer from the J.M. Trust. The deposit was paid, and completion for 'The Grange' should be around March. She asked 'Please tell the Hawkins to find somewhere else to live. And regrettable as it is, with no home or income, the Hawkins won't be able to look after Bertie so could you please make alternative arrangements for him. Your father feels he has provided for him long enough, and it's time he was put into an institution'. Furious she had screwed up the letter and thrown it in the bin, but later retrieved it to first show Johnny and then David, both of whom were lost for words.

Christmas to New Year, she declared was the best ever! Johnny preached on Christmas Day and drove up in the Hawkins' car in time for dinner at 4.00 pm and stayed for the week, sleeping on the studio couch in David's study. David's parents opted to stay at the Royal Garden Hotel. Johnny collected Joyce and Ted on Christmas morning and Helen and

Declan were included in all the celebrations. They ate and socialize in David's flat, but the whole house was filled with delicious smells along with fun and laughter. On New Year's Eve, she and Johnny were invited along with all the Reinhardts to gather at Jill and Paul's house in Kent. After a light buffet lunch, they set off to the country house hotel where Franz had organized they stay the night and hired a private dining room for the adults to have a sumptuous evening meal and see in the New Year together. The late afternoon they walked in the gardens, and swum in the indoor poor. Tired out, all the children were fast asleep by eight o'clock. Franz, cheery with alcohol, put his arm around her to joke, "Rosie, we'll get that house of yours sorted and refurbished so next year we can gather there." Her response was an enigmatic smile, and hope that 1973 wouldn't be as traumatic as this year had been.

David left for India in the second week of January, the same day that Bertie went in for his operation. Bertie did remarkably well, as did the twins despite only brief times to talk to their father on the telephone. And the irony was that in David's absence she slept in his bed.

The weeks flew by. Rosie was staying two nights a week in Petersfield and Johnny two nights mid-week in London. Since September, they'd had the fun they'd missed in their youth, and as winter came they took days out around London, meals at country pubs, trips to the theatre or pictures. If the twins were with them, people mistook them for a family. Despite the terrible two's, with others to call upon, she was learning to remain calm throughout their tantrums and pushing of boundaries.

Gerald left on 4th March for Delhi. David joined him and they flew to Guwahati for their surprise visit the following morning. She prayed, but was on tenterhooks for several days until David called from Bombay, his last stop before his return home. From there he reported Gerald was flying home alone, their mission accomplished and gave a brief account.

"It's truly a beautiful place to live. Your father nervously tweaked his moustache when hearing we represented the Trust and our 'searches' had produced several anomalies that a personal visit could clear up. We insisted your mother be present and he denied then blustered about the 'anomalies' pertaining to their marriage. She didn't speak but Gerald's evidence was the trump card. Poor woman she looked shell-shocked.

"I explained our interest was in the Estate not his personal life, but we'd opened a can of worms and advised he didn't returned to the UK. That would mean he'd be unable to benefit from the sale. He argued about that. Gerald informed him large money transfers abroad could alert a money laundering investigation, not a problem if you've nothing to hide. We let that sink in.

"Next came bravado sprinkled with expletives. His tea plantation was his gold mine. He hated the UK. 'The Grange' was a millstone around his neck. It could rot. Gerald said probably not wise for eventually the authorities would chase up the Estate's unpaid debts and expose his false identity triggering an extradition order. He looked shaken. I said we'd come as not wanting the Trust involved in a possible scandal. I smiled saying we'd come with a solution. He brightened and then swore when I suggest he should reassign the property to his children. He said you wouldn't sell to us. I said it was a risk we'd take, but had prepared transfer documents as a solution to his predicament. In bad grace he suddenly capitulated, barely read all the documents, Gerald checked his signature and we, Raj and your mother witnessed it."

David chortled, "We'd only revealed what was necessary. He gambled on us not telling the authorities. I guess even now we don't know it all. I said we'd lodged the paperwork with his solicitor and fortunately his plantation was a gold mine for he would need to fully refund our deposit and due to the reassignment, pay off the significant loans and unpaid taxes against the Estate.

Rosie laughed, "Properly stitched up!"

"I gave you mother my 'high wattage smile' and told her despite Mr Doughty's offences her children would welcome her home. It was then he realized. He became very unpleasant, raised his fists and shouted no end of abuse. Your mother stared as if unable to comprehend and he turned on her, 'If you think you can leave me, think again, for thanks to me you have nothing!' With that he stalked out, slamming the door behind him. Bewildered she looked around and I asked if she'd like to come with us, we'd pay her airfare, but shaking she asked we call Raj who I'd suggest had heard it all. He obviously cared about her and said he'd look after her. I gave her a card of a colleague in

Delhi to contact should she decide to return home. Raj hurried us out, saying "Go, go, before his Lordship returns."

"Gerald will deliver the paperwork to Daniel. And as you have both officially registered your surname as Dawes, the Deeds will be re-registered in that name. Now, as this call costs a pound a minute, get the twins and I'll ring again to chat to them." Her 'thanks' were cut off as he put the phone down.

Bertie whose existence had been denied by his parents received on the 21st March - his 24th birthday - the paperwork informing him that he and his sister were the owners of The Grange.

She wrote, Bertie typed, their surprise and thanks. Rosie added they didn't know if they would keep or sell the estate, but reiterated her mother would be welcome. Bertie told them about his tutor Gray's amazement at the ease with which he did difficult mathematical equations. He added that a leg operation in January had enabled him to walk with only a slight limp, and he enjoyed going to the pub for a drink with his new friends.

David's arrival home at the end of March coincided with a letter from Martin Foster, her father's solicitor, which read 'We are of the understanding that Lord Doughty-Dawes has gifted you with 'The Grange' and its estate. Urgent repairs were undertaken by the J.M. Trust in good faith of a sale, and there are outstanding charges against the estate. Should you instruct us to reinstate the sale, either with the Trust or another purchaser, this can be recouped at no cost to yourselves. However, should you not take up our offer, as the current owners it is your liability and payment should be sent to us within thirty days.'

Upset, she had arrived at David's house while a bleary eyed and jet lagged David was eating his breakfast with the twins rampaging around him. Waving it at him, her voice full of panic, she told him the contents as David nonchalantly chewed on his cornflakes. When she finished, he calmly responded, "We expected that. My friend will deal with it. You aren't liable for your father's debts, they may well be his undoing, but not for you to worry about. However, should you wish to sell in the future, the Trust will be happy to reinstate their offer, but would advise you not to instruct your father's solicitors. The Trust will continue to finance your charitable acts and one that is long overdue is to send the Hawkins, who have worked tirelessly and without reward for years, on a holiday of their choice."

CHAPTER 27

Jack and Cathy were dispatched on their holiday of a lifetime in April. They did not need to return to the Grange as everything they needed was at the flat. And although Bertie's operation and his recuperation had occupied them, they felt as if they already had been on an extended holiday.

In the winter months, Dennis had taken charge of the outside work. His mates came each weekend, stayed in the servant bedrooms, and shoveled tons of hardcore with concrete into the two sink holes. With the Brigadier's expertise, they constructed a concrete dam to ensure water wouldn't erode again into the hill and it would be hidden when the lake was refilled. The grass growing in the mud left no evidence of a drive and similarly, once the sink hole was filled with concrete and earth spread over it, the grass disguised its position.

George decreed the whole house needed rewiring, and made temporary repairs until the future was decided. As a priority, he restored the Aga to provide a large warm kitchen and hot water to two other bathrooms in the West Wing. Rosie felt overwhelmed by their help. Ida cleaned and cooked for the 'workers' canteen, but a skeptical David had encouraged Gerald to take her down each weekend to keep an eye on progress and report back. Both pleased to have a role to play.

When the weather got warmer, the two families started congregating there at weekends. George with Dennis helped lifted floor boards to extend the temporary electrical repairs to all the servant rooms and installed a downstairs toilet. When that was done Mandy and Frances decorated them, along with larger bedrooms for the two Kent families to stay in at weekends.

Assured by Gerald that the electrics were safe in the West Wing, David agreed he and the twins would stay for the May Bank Holiday week and were allocated the bedroom above the breakfast room overlooking the lake. Ida and Gerald had already commandeered two of Frances' newly decorated bedrooms in the servants' quarters. Helen, Declan and Debbie would be in those they'd previously used. Bertie had invited Gray wanting him to see what he now owned and they were going to drive down with Declan and Helen. The two Kent families arrived by train, with little luggage as they'd slowly established themselves in the two double bedrooms next to the Hawkins', overlooking the inner courtyard. And their four boys, not noticing the cold, were always delighted to share the large bedroom over the Music Room.

Rosie found her and Bertie's rooms spotless and felt the house had never looked so dust free. After a light lunch where everyone was gathered, they ventured forth to see all that had been accomplished. Despite the size of the original kitchen, Ida's canteen felt very crowded when they ate together. The weather was deliciously warm, and with the lake freed of weeds the refurbished sluice gates were opened. They watched it begin to fill, the next day paddled, the following day used inflatables and finally swam on Tuesday afternoon when David returned with a light rowing boat for both children and adults to enjoy, bringing Johnny to comment, "This feels like the holiday camp my parents used to take us to each year."

The happy atmosphere brought her to consider David's idea of the estate being owned by the Trust and turned into separate flats. It was a place to enjoy. The Hawkins would love being part of a community without the worry of bills and maintenance. They would have the freedom to do what they wished and, like Declan, others would blossom and flourish in their love and care.

Gerald's regular visits had assured the Hawkins that all was going well. On Saturday, they would have been away six weeks visiting places they never expected to see, and she doubted they would expect a welcome party for their arrival home.

David collected them from Heathrow. Johnny, Diana, the Brigadier and Jennifer arrived together and Declan waited by the gate to alerted them. They all gathered outside the front door while Bertie escorted them around the side of his house. Jack and Cathy were laughing and then looked overwhelmed to see so many familiar faces and later at seeing all that had been accomplished since November. With everyone gathered for lunch in the ballroom Bertie nudged her, "Say something." Rosie smiled at him, "Before we eat, Bertie and I wish to thank you all for your hard work over these past months, and are pleased that this week you had the opportunity to enjoy the fruit of your labours. Bertie and I can scarcely believe that in eight months we've gained family members and become the owners of this house and estate, on top of seeing how much you all have accomplished." She picked up her glass, "Here's to family, friends and many more occasions like this."

As everyone cheered Johnny approached her. To her astonishment he dropped to one knee, took hold of her left hand and declared, "Rosie Dawes, you have always been the love of my life, but now you are a woman of substance, I need to ask again will you accept my hand in marriage?"

Rosie's face reddened, tears pricked behind her eyes, embarrassment and love flowed together, and unromantically she replied, "Oh Johnny, do get up. Nothing has changed. I've wanted to marry you since we were eight years old." Everyone laughed but Johnny remained on one knee, fished in his pocket and pulled out a three emerald and diamond ring which he placed on her finger. At the clapping he stood, twirled her around and kissed her, and then proclaimed to their audience, "I've booked the church for August Bank Holiday. Rosie and I have waited long enough. You are all invited to witness and celebrate our marriage."

Once back in London, Rosie realised she had much to do and organise. Decisions would have to be made about The Grange, but for now the Hawkins, Declan and Bertie would continue to live there. Already, the utility bills from people staying at The Grange had dwindled her savings, and she didn't want to take the Hawkins only income from the rented fields, but selling the Bentley would raise money. They agreed they would live at her cottage mid-week and Petersfield at weekends. David offered Helen his basement flat on the condition he had a say in who she shared it with!

Martin Foster was apparently still demanding money, but despite that she felt she should invite her mother to the wedding. A fortnight later an envelope arrived from India. The letter read '*Your mother tells me you are marrying Johnny, that down at the heel, grubby, cheeky boy I turned away who was quite unfit to be your friend. I gather he's risen above his station and become a priest, probably did that in the same way he thinks it will further his career to marry a woman of property. I guess you haven't told him about your checkered past and inability to have children due to a botched abortion.*'

'*If you wrote to us expecting a wedding gift, tough - you've had it. And your mother won't be coming to your wedding. I am incensed that having given you and Bertie the house, you've instructed a solicitor to tell mine, that as you neither owned the estate at the time, nor sanctioned the urgent repair of the sink hole, any previous debts attached to the estate aren't your responsibility. To add further insult to injury, the garage I instructed to collect my Bentley tells me that Jack refused to let them have it and told them Miss Dawes is the registered owner and already has a potential buyer. Martin informs me it was in one of the legal documents I signed. There are words for people like you. Have you any idea how much that Bentley is worth? It is a rare model of which there are only seven in existence.'*

Rosie smiled. Franz knew it and had insisted he purchase the car at current 'book' price which went some way to compensate the selling of the home farm thirty years earlier. *'I never want to set eyes on you again. I'm also told you aren't selling to the J.M. Trust. I urge you to change your mind before your stupidity puts us into grave debt. If you don't, it will become a millstone around your neck as it has mine!'*

That evening Rosie handed Mr Hart, aka David, the letter to which he commented, "Justice has been done, you and Bertie now own what was rightly your mother's. Don't take it to heart, remember should she wish, your mother knows you would welcome her."

Rosie agreed, but felt sad that her Mum was probably the brunt of her father's ire. Two weeks before the wedding, she wrote again telling her she wished she could come, explaining her plans for the wedding: how she'd made her dress, a marquee would be on the lawn, Johnny's parishioners providing the food, and the twins involvement. She promised to send photos and added Johnny was aware of her past and his father wasn't the man his mother had married. Johnny might have been poor, but his class is as good as her as Brigadier Dawes had returned to India without knowing his mother was pregnant.

She awaked on her wedding day with the sun shining. It was highlighting the hanging cream silk wedding gown with its heart shaped neckline and the tiny hand-made deep pink rosebuds which accentuated the 'V' boned corset at the front. At the back, the full skirt lengthened into a short train and twenty small loops and exquisite rosebud buttons ran down the back. She'd been grateful to Mandy Kent's expertise in making them and putting the dress together. A similar dress, the first attempt, in pale blue was for her chief bridesmaid and it was hanging in Helen's bedroom.

A knock on her door and it opened to reveal Cathy. Behind her Helen announced, "Breakfast for the bride, needs eating while hot. It'll be at least 2.00 pm before you get to eat again." The crockery rattled as Helen dumped the tray on the table under Rosie's window. "I still can't believe Johnny asked David to be his best man! Jack said even last night he was still declaring he is not Johnny's best man but yours, and not giving up on you until the wedding bells ring. What I do know is the best man will not be getting off with the chief bridesmaid!"

Rosie laughed as she headed to the table, "Oh come on now,

he's not that bad he's letting you live in his house. She lifted the metal dome from the plate and gasped, "It must be a very special day!" seeing the full English breakfast."

Cathy challenged Helen, "David's been good to us all. Bertie is not only walking but having introduced Gray into his life who - in telling him he could be the Einstein of the 20th century - has given him such confidence to meet people and speak to them. Cathy shrugged, "I like him and Johnny and don't mind which one you marry. But Johnny is such a kind, loving and gentle soul."

"Bertie is still not sure about his wanting to give you away, but is excited to walk up the aisle with you." Helen grinned. "I assured him he wasn't losing his sister but gaining Johnny as a brother, he liked that idea. And there's no doubt Johnny is very popular! I suppose it's because he is not your stereotype priest, he's always happy and makes people laugh. With the number of people downstairs, I'd say the whole congregation of his church is involved in making today special."

"Bertie, unlike Jack doesn't have to make a speech. And he is nervous about that and acting as 'father of the bride' barely touched his breakfast. He says David's will be witty, his boring."

Rosie finishing her cornflakes said, "Cathy, tell Jack from me that he has - in truth - been like a father to me and to just be himself." Spearing her fork in the bacon she added, "The same goes for you Cathy in stepping into the role as 'mother of the bride.' I'm so proud of you both."

"I'm sorry about your Mum and guess that right now she is probably smoking and drinking to drown out her feelings. I'd hoped she would send a card or at least had replied to your letter."

"I'll send her photos when Johnny and I get back from the Isle of Wight."

Helen headed to the door, "As your chief bridesmaid, I'll be back at 11.00 am to help you dress."

"And I'll make sure when David arrives with the twins that they don't come rushing in to see you. I'll help him dress them and take them downstairs."

"Thanks Cathy." As the door closed Rosie felt she would burst with happiness. Through the open window, she could hear the string quartet tuning up in the marquee on the lawn and see people she didn't know putting finishing touches to the tables and chairs, and bringing more flowers. Crates of bottles and glasses chinked together, carried by men in black trousers and white shirts, but gradually the voices and flurry of activity lessened as Paul, driving

Franz' Jaguar arrived to take Cathy, the twins and Helen down to the church. The photographer having taken poses in her bedroom now took more as she headed down the staircase decorated in cream ribbon and pink roses, and on her way to the front door.

Bertie, handsome in his suit, was waiting for her. Arm in arm, they posed outside the door and by the fully restored fountain and basin. Beyond that stood a tall, broad chested, impeccably dressed white haired gentleman beside the open door of the Bentley. His usual forbidding features transformed by a broad smile as he raised a chauffeur cap at her in salute. To that she laughed, before smiling at the small group of helpers standing around to admire her dress, wish her well and take their photos. As Franz helped her into the car she declared, "I'm nervous and excited at the same time."

"Is that so! That makes two of us! My dear you are beautiful, you look stunning, that dress looks a million dollars. It truly is my privilege to drive you in this rare, vintage car to the church. Bertie slowly walked around the car. As Rosie lowered herself into the seat, Franz leant in to help arrange her dress and said in a surprisingly quiet voice, "My only regret today is that you aren't marrying my son."

Lightheartedly Rosie exclaimed, "Oh Franz, I might have done if years ago Johnny hadn't stolen my heart." And then felt embarrassed to see tears forming in his eyes. Franz shut the door and walked swiftly around to see Bertie safely in beside her. Soft music played in the car. She thought of the twins and how a few weeks earlier, a shop keeper had said, 'Can you hold this for your Mummy' and Rebecca had replied, 'We don't have a Mummy, we have a Rosie'. Maybe if Johnny hadn't reappeared, she would have married David.

As the car drew up outside the church, Helen stepped forward to help her out while Franz assisted Bertie. A few yards away, Rebecca with her hand in Jill's was impatiently jumping up and down in her silver shoes, her Alice band sparkling in the sun. The moment Jill released her hand, Rebecca in her pale blue dress with its cream rosebuds rushed forward. Rosie bent to tell her, "You look like a little princess." Joshua in his smart pageboy suit reacted to Rebecca as did his father, a raised eyebrow and shake of his head. Together they stood smiling proudly for the photos. She knew she loved them as if they were her own. She bent again to question, "Do you two know what to do?"

They both nodded fervently. Joshua volunteered, "Becca and I hold hands and walk behind Auntie Helen, and Auntie Jill will follow us. Then I'll sit with Auntie Helen and Becca with Auntie Jill."

Rosie grinned at Jill, "You've drilled them well."

"They've been so excited. I don't think David got much sleep last night."

The car and bride attracted the shoppers and a crowd grew as photos were taken. Arm in arm, she and Bertie walked from the gate to the porch and stopped to pose again. Seeing Jennifer Greenhaigh pacing up and down just inside the door drew Rosie to enquire, "Is everything alright?"

"Oh God, Rosie I don't know. Freddy since…well…he just hasn't been himself. I think he's being ridiculous, I've tried to reason with him and even got cross. At eight o'clock this morning the phone rang. I was in the bath. Ten minutes later, dressed for the wedding, he said an old friend needed him, he would be as quick as he could, and not to let the wedding start without him. I asked him and now you, 'How am I meant to do that?' With that he grunted and rushed out. And despite you being five minutes late, Freddy still isn't here! I don't know what to do. I should be sitting at the front with Diana and Johnny's mother."

"If you sit at the far end of that pew, he can slip in down the side aisle without causing any disturbance."

"Sorry Rosie, I'm holding you up." With a warm smile Jennifer stood back to admire her, "Johnny is a very lucky man. From November he did all the commuting and since the Bank Holiday Freddy hasn't seemed him, so apologies for not seeing much of you." Oh dear, Peter is tapping his watch, I better slip in before you."

Rosie gave Peter, the Vicar, a wry smile as Jennifer slipped through those standing at the back. Not wanting further delays Peter beckoned her forward, and moved to the centre aisle to announce, "Please stand for the bride." With the organ playing Wagner's "Wedding March" she and Bertie moved slowly forward. At the top of the aisle she stopped, released the train of her dress from the band around her wrist, and as Helen bent forward to straighten it, she realized every seat was filled. Johnny had a small family, and like hers, their fathers' sins meant they had gained step brothers and sisters. She was amused to hear one of his theological college friends comment, "No wonder his childhood sweetheart stopped his interest in others." Another voice commented, "God brought them back together."

On Bertie's arm she progressed down the aisle, her eyes fixed on the two men waiting for her. One over six foot tall, broad shouldered, immaculately dressed, ran his hand through his hair, his normally grim features transformed by his admiring eyes and welcoming smile. The other man, five foot ten, of medium build, smartly dressed, brushed his light brown hair away from his eyes, his pleasant features and perpetual smile lit up by the adoration in his eyes. Johnny with a wry smile winked at David, knowing he was about to get his girl.

As she drew next to Johnny, their eyes met and a wave of love flowed between them. She turned to give Helen her bouquet and caught David's downcast which brought her such sadness that she blinked back tears. David was the rock on which her daily life was built. Johnny was her loving and light-hearted friend. Helen gave her a questioning look. She turned back to face the altar. When David knew of her love for Johnny he had made friends with him. In the brief scuffling as the congregation and her entourage sat down, she turned so Johnny could lift back her veil. He produced his handkerchief and smiled. Rosie dabbed her eyes, hoped her mascara hadn't run and thought of David's continual support and his insistence that she remained a mother to his children. Was that an example of unspoken love? It hadn't penetrated or altered the bond of love she and Johnny shared from childhood, or her desire to spend the rest of her life with him. Peter drew her attention saying, "Dearly beloved, we are gathered here today…" In her head she prayed, 'Oh Lord, bless David. Bring him a woman who will truly love him and be worthy of the good man he is'.

"First, it was ordained for the procreation of children…" Johnny gave her hand a comforting squeeze, she thought of her love for the twins, and then turned her attention back to Peter. "Thirdly, it was ordained…" at a titter of stage whispers he slightly raised his head and then his voice, "…for the mutual society, help and comfort, that the one ought to have of the other, both in prosperity and adversity." The disturbance grew. Peter looked up, frowned down the aisle and spoke louder, "Into which holy estate these two persons present come now to be joined." And then called " Please, those at the back be quiet." They turned but couldn't see the problem, his words having had an immediate effect. They faced Peter again and he continued, "Therefore, if any man can show any just cause, why they may not lawfully be joined together, let him…"

"Let me go!" screamed a woman who then shouted, "There's just cause."

Rosie whirled around to murmur, 'Mum' as a distraught wisp of a woman broke through the crowd at the back of the church. Her clothes looked as if she had slept in them. Her long thin greying hair trailed down her back. And in an obviously inebriated state her mother headed haphazardly down the central aisle towards them. Rosie moaned, "Oh no!" Johnny squeezed her hand as her mother declared to what was now an enrapt audience, "I came as quickly as I could." There was a gasp as she stumbled against the side of a pew and righted herself. Breathlessly she called, "Freddy said we would be here in plenty of time."

Rosie gave Johnny a questioning look, and his brow creased as Jennifer Greenhaigh could be heard whispering, "Excuse me, excuse me." before she walked swiftly down the side aisle towards the back of the church.

"He can't find anywhere to park" shouted Dee-Dee towards Jennifer as she hurried away. When she turned back Jack had stepped into the central aisle. Dee-Dee frowned and veered across the aisle as though to avoid him. In seeing Cathy in front of her, she smiled and Cathy responded by slipping her arm through Dee-Dee's saying loudly, "We're so pleased you've come" before assuring her "You aren't too late, you haven't missed the important part. Come and sit with me."

Dee-Dee pulled forwards, her voice shrill, "I have to tell Rosemary…"

Cathy responded in authoritative voice, "Yes love, you can talk to her later."

Under her breath Rosie muttered to Johnny, "How many 'gin and its' has she drunk? Normally she wouldn't say 'boo' to a goose!"

"You'd better go to her."

What was meant to be the most beautiful and significant moment in Rosie's life was fast becoming a nightmare. With a deep breath, she picked up her train and joined the little group in the aisle. Even speaking quietly, Rosie knew the church acoustics would magnify her every word, which every ear would strain to hear. "Mum! I'm so glad you made it." She beckoned Johnny over, "Let me introduce you to Johnny. You'll love him as I do."

Her mother stared at him as he walked towards her and then shrieked hysterically, "You can't marry him!"

Rosie now near to tears, swallowed hard aware of the tense silence and their audience of several hundred people. Cross, her response was sharp, "Mum, you've had a long journey, you're are overwrought. Dismayed by her intervention Rosie said abruptly, "Mum, just sit down with Jack and Cathy."

Dee-Dee looked wildly around her, "Freddy said he would be here." Her hand went to her throat as Bertie moved towards her, "Oh there's my Bertie, walking without a stick!" Her mother's eyes focused on the man beside him, "Good heavens Mr Hart, is that you?" Rosie groaned. Her mother pushing back her straggling hair pasted on a sweet smile, stretched out her hand and said unsteadily, "Thank you. Your colleague paid my airfare." The slight rise in David's eyebrows told Rosie he knew nothing about it. As David shook her hand, her mother's words were clear to all in the congregation, "You've met Leo, you know what he's like. When I read Rosie's last letter I had to tell him and Rosie the truth." Do you know what Leo said?" David put his hand under her elbow in a vain attempt to draw her towards the vestry but she announced, "He told me he wasn't a fool. He'd known for years that Rosie wasn't his daughter, but I'd been a useful cash cow, and if I left not to return."

There was more than a titter across the congregation, causing Rosie to say quietly but frantically, "Mum, not here, not now!"

Peter, seemingly recovered from the shock of having a response to 'speak now or forever hold your peace' stepped in, "Mrs Doughty-Dawes…"

"It's Dawes. I should have 'doubted' Leo when he asked to marry me. He's a bigamist, isn't he Mr Hart?" The church acoustics were proved excellent by the very audible gasp from the congregation.

David looked down at Dee-Dee, gave her his 'weak at the knees' smile and with an arm around her waist almost lifted her off her feet as he said, "We'll continue this conversation in the vestry." He gave Peter a questioning look. He nodded and led the way. Dee-Dee said loudly, "Leo said he'd hoped to be rid of us when the Hawkins brought us to England."

Beside herself Rosie burst out, "Mum this is my wedding day. It really doesn't matter if Leo isn't my father?"

"It matters greatly" came the Brigadier's deep booming voice from the back of the church. Red-faced he appeared to announce, "I am your father which makes Johnny your brother."

In the shocked silence, Rebecca's childish voice was heard to say, "I've got a brother and I love him."

Dear Reader,

I am sorry that this fourth book has taken much longer than anticipated. And hope having read it you felt it worth the wait. I knew the end, but throughout had no idea where the story was going and who would join the characters from the previous novels. It is the same with each book and when I re-read them I ask myself, 'Did I write this?' I truly believe that in every aspect I receive divine help.

This book was more complicated as it had to tie in with past books and the known facts about the characters who are becoming more alive with birthdays and anniversaries. In fact several readers have commented they have begun to think of the characters as family members. Due to the growing Reinhardt family I needed to prepare a family tree to help me, and included it to help you coming back into their lives after a rather long break.

Without doubt I had supernatural provision in the writing. I'd just begun researching India when a friend of forty years - out of the blue - mentioned her mother had lived there, and in the right time span!

Stuck in the plot for months I tried various alternatives, prayed about it, and awoke one morning with idea of a traumatic scenario and when I looked into it I realised the way had been paved in the previous novel and developed in this one without me realising it. As I wrote the storyline dovetailed in and enlarged, bringing me to feel tense in getting right characters in the right place at the right time! When needed knowledge of how to resolve the issue I mentioned it to the friend who lives with us who told me, "I've just emailed a fireman who worked in the seventies"!

And, perhaps not oddly, there were things I wrote as fiction which I later discovered to be truth! I had to edit scenes out due to size, but already I see they will merge easily into the unfolding story of 'Janice'.

I hope as this tale unfolded you, like me, saw the scenes and had times of laughter, were caught up in horror, the air of mystery, the supernatural intervention, felt the tension, and relished the unexpected twists and turns so gripped until the very end.

I would love to hear from you, and keep you informed on the progress of 'Janice' so please email me at:

Ruth.Johnson@emanuel-publishing.com.

ADDENDUM

Rosie, like me was in her twenties before experiencing Jesus' love. And as the story, I shared an office with Jane who befriended me and told me of her love of the Lord. In this series my character Jane does just that despite Rosie's spitefulness towards her. You could be a Jane and find someone to befriend in a similar way.

Or maybe your life has been similar to Rosie's where you have been the victim of your parents anger and frustration. And this has left you struggling with fear, feeling worthless or unworthy of love. but Jesus doesn't see you that way.

For others it could be you experienced loneliness, misunderstanding and mistrust which has made you live behind a mask. Jesus sees beneath that and wants to see you blossom and grow into all He has created you to be.

Life is fraught with problems and situations and you don't know what is right and which is wrong? To Jesus every life is precious as He breathes His life into us, from conception and if we ask and listen to Him, He helps us overcome, all our guilt, fear and shame.

Man's words can maim, steal and destroy our understanding of how precious we are. Jesus promises are true, He is always good, always loves us, and He will never leave or forsake us if we trust in Him and His Word.

Although the story and characters are fictional, the relationship with the Lord that Rosie and David experience is written from my journey which is full of faith inspiring adventures.

To forgive and be forgiven is fundamental to the Christian faith and the ability to do that doesn't come overnight, but through a daily relationship with the Lord. When you talk to Him about your hurts and fears He will listen, you just have to believe that He is and can help you. It could be through a Christian, a song, the Bible, a picture, creation and the more you exercise your faith the more your ability to hear Him will grow. Ask him daily into your life, talk to Him as a friend about matters concerning you. And through that you will have peace, joy and an ability to walk in His plan and purpose for your life even in the most difficult of times.

It's nearly fifty years since I asked the Lord to come into my life. He changes our ideas and perceptions, brings us into the truth of who He is and who we are in Him. I keep in touch with Him throughout the day, and He has been there for me through the good and bad times and I know His love has never failed to take me beyond myself and my circumstances.

You've nothing to lose, but much to gain and here are three reasons to make that choice.

1. You can't go back, but Jesus can.
The Bible says, 'Jesus Christ is the same yesterday, and today, and for ever.' (Hebrews 13:8) He can walk into those places of sin and failure, wipe the slate clean and give you a new beginning.

2. Jesus knows the worst, but believes in the best in you. He sees you not as you are, but as you were meant to be, and will be when you allow Him into your life. When you stick with Him, you will get to know Him as He knows you. (John 15)

3. Who else is there that you can fully trust?
In His hands you are safe and secure – today, tomorrow, and for eternity. His Word says, "For I know the plans I have for you… plans for good and not for evil, to give you a future and a hope. In those days when you pray I will listen' (Jeremiah 29:11-13)

Action:
Speak to the Lord as you would a friend, and if you aren't sure ask Him to help you. (John 15)

And when you are ready to put your trust in Him say this simple prayer and give Jesus time to speak to you, and your life will change.

Dear Jesus,

I understand that your Father God so loved the world that He gave you, His only Son to die on a cross to save me from being a sinner in your sight. (John 3:16)

I am sorry for everything I have done that has separated me from you. I ask you to forgive my sin and help me to get to know you as you know me. Please come into my life, seal and fill me with your Holy Spirit that I may know I am fully adopted into your family. (Ephesians.1)

And that I may seal this prayer by telling others of my belief in you. Romans (10:10) Thank you Lord for new life.

TO HELP YOU FURTHER

Find a church:
 Try different types of church in your area until you find the one you enjoy being in, and then get to know the people and join in their mid-week activities.

Need help:
Contact for Christ, https://deo-gloria.co.uk/contact.php who will put you in touch with a local Christian of similar sex and age.

FOR MORE INFORMATION:

United Christian Broadcasters have a website:
www.lookingforgod.com

Tune into UCB Digital Radio 1 or 2
You can also use an app. Via UCB.co.uk/player

Need prayer: call UCB's Prayerline for prayer   01782 36 3000
It's manned from 9.00 am – 10.30 pm, Monday to Friday

Sign up for the FREE quarterly UCB Word for Today
UCB.co.uk/my copy or Tel: 01782 911 000
Stories of ordinary folk touched by an extraordinary God.
A schedule of UCB programmes
A daily Bible reading plan to read the whole Bible in a year.

THE HEARTS DESIRE SERIES
Www.heartsdesireseries.com

Book 1 JANE   (Year 1966)

Jane's sheltered existence is disturbed by the caresses of a stranger in a darkened room. Haunted by the incident she determines to experience life. Her encounters and challenges bring fun and fear as she searches for the reality of love. But love is gently hovering awaiting release and its unexpected arrival encompasses all her heart's desires...

Book 2 JILL   (Year 1968)

Jill, despite failed relationships, is looking for Mr Right. A chance encounter sets off a chain of events which threatens her, her friends and family. In this, Jill discovers there are many faces of love, but there is only one who will bring her the fulfillment of her heart's desires...

Book 3 DAVID   (Year 1970)

David likens his marriage to riding a rollercoaster blindfold, their shared love the track that holds, keeps and guides them. It's in going from the greatest exhilaration to the darkest despair that he draws on love's strength and finds it casts out fear, brings restoration and expands his vision to re-evaluate his heart's desires....

Book 5 JANICE   (Year 1974)

Janice, battered and homeless finds an unexpected refuge. Her arrival causes shock and dismay, her attitudes and behaviour lock those involved into a battle to hold onto love. Even as she holds them to ransom, she experiences an unforeseen love growing within her, making her rethink her heart's desires....

Book 6 MATT   (Year 1976)

Matt's past haunts him across continents, in spite of unexpected friendship, love, provision and fulfillment in his chosen career. His caring heart brings a chance encounter and brings rewards he hadn't envisaged, unveiling that love that has no bounds as he is set free to know his heart's desires....